W9-DEM-227

The Black Queen

Ron Stiles

PublishAmerica

Baltimore

© 2004 by Ron Stiles.
All rights reserved. No part of this book may be reproduced, stored in a retrieval system or transmitted in any form or by any means without the prior written permission of the publishers, except by a reviewer who may quote brief passages in a review to be printed in a newspaper, magazine or journal.

First printing

ISBN: 1-4137-1464-1
PUBLISHED BY PUBLISHAMERICA, LLLP
www.publishamerica.com
Baltimore

Printed in the United States of America

Acknowledgements

Every successful writer has someone who believes in him and in the story that they are telling. My wife Maria steadfastly encourages me and I want to thank her for believing in me. My good friend Bren Jacobson spent countless hours talking to publishers and mailing hefty copies of *The Black Queen* to them because he felt I had a good story. I thank both of them for their support and acknowledge their role in this book coming to press.

There are others to thank, such as my friend who escaped with his life from Iran during the revolution. He helped me with aspects of the story as it pertains to Iran and characters from that country. I don't mention his name, for his safety's sake. Finally, there is Chi McIntyre who willingly coached me to make me a better writer. To all, thanks!

Chapter One
November 12, 1979
Tehran, Iran

Roger heard the young girl's whimper as he put the lid on the last of the shipping crates. The wooden crate muffled her sobs, but not enough. He really wished that she would stop. She had to stop or they all would perish. Not nicely, either. He had been watching the crowd, rather mob, out in the streets. Only yesterday, he had stopped to look out the window, his attention drawn by the unusual cadence of chants.

Roger would never be able to purge that scene from his memory. Members of the angry crowd had taken a man by his legs, several men to a leg. Others had his arms. Literally, they had pulled him apart. The man's screams had been audible even above the fanatic chants and vengeful cries of the frenzied masses of the Persian mob.

This whole damn mess was too unnerving. Roger was known for his nerves of steel. Nevertheless, he was coming unraveled. His thumb throbbed, bloody from smacking it twice with the hammer. It came from being in too much of a hurry, constantly looking over his shoulder, checking to see if someone might be coming through the door. Even from the fourth floor of the Bradford Oil Building, he heard the angry shouts in the street below, every bit as intense as they had been yesterday.

"Death to America, Death to the Shah."

He knew enough Farsi to be able to understand the chants of the angry Persians. This had once been the choice of assignments for Americans working in the oil industry. Its people could be the most hospitable in the world, or, they could, as they now were, the most hostile and dangerous. Over the last two years, it had become increasingly volatile. It was an internal matter really, one of a government failing to understand its people. The Shah had sought to modernize his nation, thinking that he did so for his people's sake. However, the Shah's own greed, his bowing to the powers of the West,

5

proved to be his and the nation's undoing. Iran was an ancient nation, its way of life developed over centuries of conquering, being conquered. One element, however, had always remained unswerving, Islam.

Attempting radical change in the spell of a few decades, change that seemed to spit upon fundamental beliefs concerning the Great Prophet, offended the people and united old enemies against the Shah. Greed of government officials, military leaders, all of it angered and provided fuel for an inevitable explosion. Finally, a burning ember came into contact with that fuel, a burning ember known as the Ayatollah Khomeini; the result was an unquenchable inferno.

The whine of the freight elevator caught his ear. Roger drew a feeble, frightened breath, held it for a moment, and then slowly let it tremble out. He glanced at his watch. It was past time for the crew of Afghan laborers to arrive. Better late than never; besides, he was just finishing up. In a moment now, they would be walking into what had once been the Iranian based Bradford Oil Accounts Office. What would the laborers do if the girl once again whimpered loud enough to be heard from within the crate? Turn him in? Likely not, but they would, no doubt, run away, making it impossible for him to fulfill his promise to his good friend, Abdul. Then, what would Abdul do? In the sands of the Middle East, nothing was more venomous than a close friend betrayed.

All three of the Senior VP's and their staff had left immediately after the American Embassy had been stormed and seized. They had left Roger to pack up shop amidst the terror, the killings, and the rioting. He was the low man on the company's executive totem pole. Quite expendable, he realized. Of course, they promised him a substantial reward for his risk. It had hardly seemed even worth it when offered. They would give him a mere $50,000 to brave this political upheaval. Roger would have simply said, "hell no," but for the fact that Abdul had sweetened the pot in a manner that at the time seemed well worth any amount of risk. Two million dollars, American currency, safely tucked away in a Swiss account, never to be taxed. Abdul had paid in advance, surety, in case something happened to him. All Roger had to do was leave the Bradford property behind, and, instead, smuggle Abdul's family out of the country. The flight was going to Paris. Roger would simply off-load his human cargo there. The French willingly provided asylum to all Iranians fleeing persecution and death in this maddened land. There would be no problem once in France.

Roger would then simply destroy the manifest and tell Bradford that the

Iranians had impounded the company's property at the last minute. If they did not like his story, they could come to Tehran to prove him wrong. Besides, he already had the two million dollars in a Swiss account; he could not care less how Bradford Oil reacted to his failure to return without their precious records.

All around Tehran, Persians merely suspected of once being affiliated with the former government, were being picked up. In most cases, their incarceration was short, ending with a bullet to the back of the head after a brief bout of interrogation and torture. Some, however, were fortunate enough to be released, strongly urged to find a new home in France or the U.S.

The sound of boots in the hallway reached his ears. The Afghans? Roger took a deep breath and shuddered. Goose bumps ran up and down his spine. The Afghans would be in sandaled feet. The sound of boots could only mean one thing.

"Mr. Cowling," said a familiar, but chilling voice, "I am surprised to find that you still remain." It was Abdul's dreaded rival, Sahed, not the Afghan laborers. Sahed's gaze was penetrating, full of accusation. Though heavily accented, he spoke good English. "The fervor of the crowds is beyond which we can control. It's dangerous for you to still be here."

"I stayed behind to pack up my company's equipment and files," said Roger, trying to control the shaking in his legs, listening to the self-damning crack of his own voice. He had been expecting the Afghans. Instead, it was Sahed, self-proclaimed religious enforcer, responsible for creating a frothing, angry sea of chanting fanatics in Tehran's once peaceful streets. Abdul had once warned Roger that Sahed's veins flowed with the venom of asps. "It was okayed by your government."

"Which government?" sneered Sahed. The three men with Sahed laughed. "At the moment we seem to have three of them. Long live the Ayatollah. He is our legitimate government. I doubt that he would care about your company's property. It is ill-gotten gain from the people of Iran."

"Where are the Afghans?" asked Roger, trying to muster some strength behind his words. Suddenly, the chances of him ever spending the money from the Swiss account seemed dim. There were strong rumors that Sahed was responsible for various kidnappings and murders of foreigners. Roger was both an American and Abdul's good friend. The animosity that existed between Sahed and Abdul was well known. Roger imagined himself a tempting target for Sahed. Two days ago, he had felt up to this risk. Not so now.

"Unless they have met with the wrong people in the street, they are driving out of the country just as fast as they can," said Sahed, laughing. "As you should be doing. I am very concerned for your well being."

"I have a plane sitting at the airport," said Roger. Would the girl whimper again? Or what if the old man sneezed, as he had earlier? As though reading Roger's mind, Sahed glanced at the crate in which Abdul's father hid. "All that I need to do," said Roger, stuttering, "is get these crates on a truck, put them on the plane and then I'm gone. Gone with much regret, I might add."

Roger did everything in his power to keep his voice steady. Nevertheless, he could hear his fear reverberate through the room. An excellent poker player, a merciless mastermind in undermining any competitor, he was good at holding a losing hand and still winning. Without question, he was engaged in his most challenging hand ever; and blowing it. The lives in the crates were the ante; his life was the jackpot. Despite the stakes, he was unable to put on his best poker face.

"Regret?" asked Sahed, his voice carrying the exaggerated kindness of an interrogator wishing to explore some new avenue.

"Very much so," said Roger. He knew Sahed was toying with him. However, he was thankful for anything that would draw Sahed's attention from the crates. "You have one of the most beautiful lands upon God's earth, and the most wonderful people. Our president should never have insulted Iran by allowing the Shah to seek refuge in our country. Someday, I hope to return. Let me present a humble gift to your government, a show of gratitude, let's say. Long live the Ayatollah." In a room to his left were the word processors and desktop calculators of the clerical staff. It was not much, but perhaps enough of an appeasement to get him through this.

Roger felt a cold chill go down his spine as Sahed, not commenting, simply ignored him. Instead, he began to walk along the line of wooden crates. At each one he stopped, standing stalk still, as though listening for any telltale sign of Roger and Abdul's conspiracy. It was almost as if he already knew what the crates contained.

Roger's heart thumped so hard that it felt as though it would pound right out of his chest. The slightest sound emanating from one of those crates would be his death sentence. On the end crate was the shipping manifest. He breathed a sigh of relief as Sahed picked it up, examined it thoroughly, and then tossed it back down onto the box as though satisfied. Were they aware, within the crates, of the extreme danger of the moment? Did the young girl's mother have her hand clutched tightly across the girl's mouth? Roger certainly hoped so.

"Many who were loyal to that bastard the Shah are trying to flee the country," said Sahed, once again looking towards the boxes and then sharply at Roger. Sahed gazed inquisitively into Roger's face, and then he spoke as though trying to impart understanding to a pupil. "Your good friend, Abdul, for instance. Though he is a true brother and a mighty believer among Shiites, his father collected taxes for that devil the Shah. His mother and his sister refused the veil and encouraged other women to do the same. All such things are abominable to Allah. Abdul's family, they are no where to be found, you know?" Sahed then looked towards the door to the other office area. "Anything left in there?" There was accusation in his eyes.

Roger's heart began to beat very fast, his palms sweating so that he feared puddles would form on the floor. He knew that the door was locked, but would that stop Sahed and his men from kicking it in? In that room were all of the equipment and file cabinets listed on the manifest. These had been the ones belonging to the firm's accountants. Suddenly, the prospect of never leaving Iran alive seemed to loom large. "No," he said. "It's all here in these crates."

"This is it then?" asked Sahed. "All that needs to get to the airport?"

"This is all that goes," said Roger. Perhaps there was just a glimmer of hope. "All I need is a crew and a truck to help me get it there."

Sahed looked once again at the boxes, then he glanced one more time towards the locked door. "Abdul has spoken well of you. Says that you understand the Persian, that you respect who we are. It's not the way of Islam to despise others for their false beliefs. We are a people provoked to violence because your government has supported that bastard the Shah in all the evil that he has done. But, for that, Mr. Cowling, you should not be held personally accountable. We will be back in a little while with a truck. We will see to it that you and your cargo get to where you belong. Ahu akbar." The smile that Sahed wore chilled Roger to the bone. What exactly did he infer by *"where you belong?"*

Sahed, his eyes fixed on the locked door, rocked the wooden crate nearest him. "Heavy," he said.

"File cabinets full of paper," Roger quickly answered. "Probably should have left the file cabinets and just packed up the records." Would the devil Sahed now suggest that the crate be opened, and the records removed from the heavy metal file cabinets?

"Oh yes, I think I know what you mean," replied Sahed coldly. "I'm sure that you have orders to keep your records locked away from scrutiny. Otherwise, those that serve Allah would see how the sons of dogs, the American oil companies, rob the people of Iran." He studied Roger intently, as though searching for any conspiratorial sign. Finally, he turned to his men and simply nodded towards the exit. They left in silence, Sahed not once looking back.

Roger's legs went to jelly as they left. Collapsing into a heap on the floor, he attempted to gather his wits. Perhaps Sahed would hide in the building, waiting to catch him in the act of smuggling fugitives out of the country. He forced himself to his feet and went to the window. From there he was able to watch as Sahed and his three men crossed the street, the crowd parting like the Red Sea before the noted Revolutionary leader. He took a long breath, and with trembling hands, took a cigarette from a solid gold case. He had bought it here, in Tehran, where gold was cheap.

Sahed was not going to hide in the building and wait for him. Instead, he would shortly return with the truck as he promised. The airport, however, would not likely be their destination. Both Roger and Abdul's family would be driven straight to the makeshift court and prison where hundreds were being processed as enemies of Allah and the Ayatollah.

Just as he touched the flame from a matching gold encased cigarette lighter to the tobacco, another whimper came from the crates. He dropped the cigarette and quickly jammed the lighter deep into his trouser pocket. Perhaps the noise had simply been his imagination. Regardless, this was a no win situation. "Sorry, Abdul," he muttered. Across the hall was an employee lounge, now devoid of life. An open window led to a rusting, squeaking fire escape that hugged the back of the building. He took it at a run, aware that his escape was far from being silent as the rusted metal squealed beneath his weight.

Roger descended into the narrow alley behind the Bradford Oil Building. Now outside, the chants of the mob in the street out front, grew ever louder. Parked below him was his VW Rabbit. He would have followed the truck to the airport in it. It was much more practical than a BMW or a Mercedes in a country where one might become blocked in on all sides by goats or carts. There were enough dings and dents in it so that it blended well into a driving culture where the only traffic laws were to simply get to where you are going as fast as you can get there. His feet touching the ground, he paused a few seconds. With a sense of foreboding, he examined the long, cylindrical package, wrapped in thick plastic sheeting that protruded all the way from the folded down front passenger seat to a couple of feet out the back of the car. He really should get rid of the rug. More over, he should return upstairs and at least free Abdul's family. That would provide them at least some chance of escape. However, it was really too late. Even at this very moment, Sahed could be returning, satisfied that Roger's nerves were sufficiently frayed.

Ali Akbar Hazdiz, Abdul's father, had given him the rug. It was a gift of appreciation for agreeing to help his family flee Iran. However, there was no time to unload it. Roger clawed his pocket for his car keys; horrified that they might have still been in the building. He found them. Keeping the rug would not cause Abdul to hate him any less. As for the money that he had already confirmed to be in the Swiss account? Well, it was not as if he could call Abdul up and say sorry, I did not live up to my contractual obligation and I'm returning the money. No, Abdul would not care about the rug or the money. If Abdul survived the dark abyss that Iran had plunged into, then nothing would prevent him from attempting to track Roger down and seeking retribution.

Chapter Two
Friday, May 3
Energy International Headquarters,
Richmond, Virginia

Brian Matkins had been president of Richmond Nuclear for nearly five years. He had held executive positions at two other utilities before finally ending up as Roger Cowling's trophy during a headhunt. Cowling had sought an exec with the type of operations experience that could bring profit to two nuclear units that at the time were labeled by Wall Street as being money pits. Brian had not liked Cowling from the moment they met. That aside, however, he had been eager for the challenge Richmond Nuclear presented and had accepted the job.

Cowling spoke of his loyalty to his employees and his commitment to nuclear safety first above profit. Instinct, however, had told Brian from the beginning that Cowling was only interested in the bottom line. Alas, his instincts had proven correct. Tonight, however, Cowling was more callous and reckless than ever. He was hell bent on a course of action that would sacrifice both personnel and nuclear safety for profit.

"Have a seat," said Roger Cowling in a tight whisper. He knew what Brian Matkins thought of him. He had known it when he hired Matkins. However, hiring a "yes" man would never have achieved the profitability that hiring Matkins had. He had been the best choice for the job. Without the increase in performance achieved under Matkins, selling Richmond Nuclear would only be a pipe dream.

Like Matkins, Cowling did hold to the fact that the people in his company were his greatest asset. However, assets were for one to use to produce a profit, and often that meant getting rid of ones no longer needed and acquiring ones more useful. People that worked for him were property and property was something bought and sold every day. In this case, they simply produced a product that he could sell, electricity. In the days before de-regulation, it did not matter in Virginia how efficiently they produced it because the Virginia State Corporation Commission, the SCC, guidelines guaranteed each utility a certain percentage of profit. Now, however, the power generating industry was like any other business in that it had to compete to sell its product. Bottom line; employees were overhead. Cowling now needed every margin of profit he could squeeze and that meant dispensing with overhead.

Cowling took his seat behind the desk and fixed his eyes on Matkins. Matkins had performed beyond Cowlings' highest expectations in turning Richmond Nuclear around. If not for Matkins, the opportunity to sell Richmond Nuclear to the California Energy Commission would not exist. However, Matkins' ethical notions were getting in the way. This was a critical moment for Energy International and Cowling needed all that he could get out of EI's subsidiary companies. Most important of those subsidiaries was Richmond Nuclear. An opportunity existed for EI that would reinvent the power industry. It was an opportunity, however, that required resources that EI did not have, nearly five billion dollars in liquid assets. Nevertheless, that would not stop Cowling and his fellow board members. California was screaming for affordable power and Cowling had a near deal with its Governor and legislature. He would sell them Richmond Nuclear and Richmond Fossil, EI's stateside holdings. With de-regulation of the electric industry, the state of California would be able to free-wheel nearly 5,000 megawatts of power across the United States from its nuclear and fossil units to its own troubled electric supply grid. It was a free-trade solution that he knew the Bush administration could readily support. The East coast currently had a surplus of power, thus, there was little chance that the SCC would oppose the sale.

Nothing, however, was ever simple. The deal with California was supposed to be kept in strict confidentiality by both parties so as not to affect the stock of EI. If the news leaked, it would undoubtedly affect EI stock and employees would get the jitters. It was also vital that Brian Matkins not be aware of the plan too soon. If he did, he would likely crusade against it. Already, CNN was quoting anonymous sources that a major deal was in the works for California to buy an out of state utility.

Brian, seated in the black leather chair in front of Cowling's desk, returned his CEO's icy gaze. The richly lacquered mahogany desk that separated him from Cowling was large enough for Brian to have huddled his old Virginia Tech football team on. On several occasions, he had come close to asking how they got it in here. If Cowling fired him tonight, Brian made up his mind at least to walk out of here with the answer to that question.

Fine paintings hung from the walls on either side. If asked, Brian would not have been able to identify a single one of them. He was sure, however, none were reproductions. A rug adorned the office floor. As a college student, Brian had worked in an Oriental rug store in Blacksburg, unloading shipments of rugs and carrying rugs out for customers who bought them. The Iranian, Amir, who owned the store had been quite a task master and had been obsessed with ensuring that Brian new each rug that he had lain a hand on. Brian had developed a strong appreciation for the artistic value of rugs. Here was a rug that was like none Brian had ever encountered. He recognized its fine detail of floral patterns, woven of silver and gold thread into fine Persian silk. Though he had never actually seen such a rug, he would have bet his next paycheck that it was from the city Nain.

"Brian, we don't seem to be moving forward together on this," said Roger. "Our industry faces enormous change. That means challenges. Now is when we need to move to meet those challenges. If we wait, then we'll be in no better position than our competition. Richmond Nuclear is Energy International's most valuable asset. If we can get it, along with our fossil stations, ready to be competitive in a deregulated environment, we can ensure its survival. That means your employees don't have to hunker down, worrying about some buy out or merger that's going to cost them their jobs. Instead, you'll enable us as your parent company to be in a position to acquire nuclear utilities that aren't preparing right now like we are." Roger paused, trying to gauge Brian's reaction. He could sense the disdain. "Come on, Brian, I know that you want to look after your people, but there's a need to trim down or a great many more are going to suffer."

"I'm in a position to see what's needed," said Brian. "There's no reason to make any cuts right now, especially fifteen percent across the board when you don't even know what the results will be. I know what's going on in the industry and I know that there's not a single competitor that's better positioned for de-regulation than we are." Cowling had cleverly engineered a board vote that required reducing Richmond Nuclear's operating budget by fifteen percent. Several board members had pulled with Brian, but it seemed like Cowling had a core majority that he could always count on to vote as he willed. Brian himself did not have a vote, at least not unless there was a board member absent. In that case, he would vote if it was a matter that affected Richmond Nuclear. In the case of a vote affecting the fossil units, Paul Marcini, president of Richmond Fossil, would cast the tiebreaker. The fifteen percent had affected the fossil plants, as well. Marcini had done nothing more than look over at Brian and subtly shake his head.

Brian, however, had decided to commit professional hara-kiri by speaking out harshly against Cowling's move to reduce the nuclear utility's operational budget. Thus, here he sat, facing Cowling, perhaps only seconds away from having his head handed to him. Brian was not particularly worried. He knew that any number of nuclear utilities would offer him a position. Problem was, only layoffs could achieve the budget cuts. They would negatively impact nuclear safety and people's careers. He could not understand why Cowling was so damned intent on destroying what worked so well.

"Brian, many a CEO would ask for your resignation at this point..." said Cowling, immediately cut off in mid-sentence.

"Ask for it if you like," said Brian. "When there's a need to sacrifice jobs, then I'll do it. But, there's no way in hell that you can justify the jobs that are going to be lost because of this. There will be an immediate risk to nuclear safety at the power station and eventually it will erode our ability to efficiently operate and thereby defeat your purpose."

"Please, let me finish," said Cowling, sounding like a patient father. Brian, without knowing the reason behind the cuts, could hardly be expected to endorse them. He would take one last gamble to win his nuclear VP's support. "I'm not going to ask for your resignation. There is a certain investment opportunity that I'm not free to discuss with you. We need additional cash flow to make it happen. I will also need the best damned operating executive to succeed with this opportunity and that happens to be you, regardless of differing points of view. However, I need to rely on you to support me when I'm forced to make decisions that make no sense at your level."

"What you're asking for doesn't make sense at any level if it degrades nuclear safety," continued Brian. He had already called Cowling a "dangerous heretic" whose bureaucratic meddling would degrade nuclear safety and lead to disastrous consequences. "This is fifteen percent on top of last December's ten percent. I brought operation costs down by thirty-three percent over the past five years. We are one of a few nuclear utilities that produce a profit. Right now we are number five in the nation for profitable generating stations. Only one other nuclear utility besides us is on that list."

"What's wrong with us taking their place?" asked Cowling. The effort to control his frustration in having to deal with Matkins was enormous.

However, he had to be careful. If Brian Matkins went to the SCC over the budget cuts, it could be dicey. Dealing with him was problematic from all perspectives. Only by convincing him that there was really a need to cut costs could he manage the exec. "If we can move up it would certainly raise our stock value. I can't tell you how much that would help us in raising capital for this new opportunity."

"Mr. Cowling," said Brian, "there is no opportunity in the universe that is going to convince me to risk the nuclear safety of my units." With that said, Brian rose and left the office. He had nothing further to say and would not listen to this depraved tyrant continue.

Cowling watched him leave, not saying anything. From his desk, he took out a folder. Bob Orton had long been one of Cowling's greatest assets. Orton had years ago worked for the government, mainly running black ops, doing things that Uncle Sam would never want to admit to. He was a man who could find dirt on the Pope if asked to do so. As with all of his hiring decisions, he had had Orton run a thorough background check on Matkins.

Orton's idea of a background check differed from the norm. It did all the standard checks to make sure that an individual was reliable, but there were other interests, as well. Most importantly, he searched for potential character flaws that his employer could use in a particular time of need.

Well, this was a particular time of need. Cowling was not the least bit surprised that Matkins had refused his counsel. In fact, he had anticipated months ago, as his plan for selling Richmond Nuclear had been forming, that he would require such leverage. He had had Orton put the wheels in motion. Matkins had no idea to the extent that he had already compromised himself. In a short matter of time, Matkins would heel to him just like a well-trained canine.

Yorktown, Virginia
Friday, May 3, 2002

All she really wanted to do was leave. Instead, Fatima ordered another round of beers for her and Lenny. For a while longer, she would listen to sailors swearing macho curses and marines yelling, "betcha goddamn ass, marine." Almost as bad, were the high school girls giggling at the bar, elated beyond ecstasy that their fake ID's had worked to get them in. Moreover, of course there was the cigarette smoke. It stung her eyes and made her throat feel like someone's hand was squeezing it to within a few centimeters of occlusion. She knew what that felt like, for real.

More than the physical agitations of smoke and noise in the Hoisted Anchor Bar and Grill, were the many unwanted eyes and ears that doubtless existed here. Rather than merely being sources of annoyance, they were extremely dangerous. Such was always the case in a bar this close to a military base. The U.S. government had given the FBI and the intelligence agencies a lot of power to monitor civilian activity in order to seek out and uproot terror cells. Many of the al Qaeda cells were in disarray as a result. It was not easy for Middle Eastern men to be covert and blend in. Let a Pakistani walk into a lawn and garden center to buy a bag of fertilizer and alarms bells sound. That was why the al Qaeda cell that she and her uncle were working with tolerated her. Al Qaeda was entirely a male organization. With her pristine, Americanized English skills, she could go anywhere without arousing suspicion. Her uncle's fluent Italian and forged Italian passport was equally effective.

The Hoisted Anchor Bar and Grill was close to the Yorktown Naval Weapons Station. It overlooked the beach and the York River and attracted an interesting mix of customers. There were, of course, the sailors and marines, but also a good many well-to-do tourists balanced by an equal number of bikers. Locals visited the place, too, but generally chose the weekdays to avoid tourists.

Over the months, in ways that no one would notice, not even a trained watcher, Fatima had studied the varied assortment of humanity that surrounded her here nightly. Which of these almost falling down drunken customers were actually stone sober and a Naval Intelligence Officer? She had narrowed her choices on that matter. There were two, a man and a woman. The woman tended the bar, providing excellent opportunity to observe and mingle. The locals did not seem to know her, meaning she was not a local herself like the others who worked here. The man was a regular, always arriving early enough to find a seat quietly nestled in an obscure corner with a great vantage of the rest of the bar and grill. He interacted well with the locals, something she would expect of an effective intelligence officer. The American intelligence apparatus had won her respect many years ago. It's current theme of working with other US law enforcement agencies made it even more formidable.

Lenny Allen was not NIS, of that, she was certain. Fatima knew just how falling down drunk he really got, practically every night. In no way was his condition a matter of make believe inebriation. Often, he drank so much that he could not respond to her most intense efforts at arousal. She was thankful for those nights. He was vile, he was scum, he was repugnant, and he was the most putrid form of excrement that she had ever met. To fuck him night after night required an effort nearly super human. It made becoming a suicide bomber seem appealing.

Lenny Allen, Weapons Technician First Class, United States Navy, should have made Chief a few years ago. His drinking kept him from it. After a typical night, he could not possibly sober up by the time he showed up for duty in the mornings. Now there was a frightening thought, Lenny handling live ordnance, some of it nuclear, after one of his binges on the town. The six beers that he had consumed thus far tonight had already made him belligerent.

"So." Fatima touched his arm, her slender finger, with its long acrylic nail, tracing like a tease over the anchor tattooed on his forearm. She felt as though she were spending eternity in purgatory suffering Lenny's drunken stupors and rages. It was, however, nearly time to bring her torture to fruition. The thought brought her comfort. Carefully, over the past months, she had massaged his dissatisfaction with his wife, spreading her legs with enough regularity to destroy their marriage. His sexual dependency upon her was absolute, his financial situation a total cataclysm. "What did the judge say?" she asked, knowing that she was dropping a match into gasoline.

"Shit, gave her the goddamned house, the car. The bitch's got the kid and I have to pay a goddamned fortune," spat Lenny, throwing his cigarette butt to the floor and stamping it out with unrestrained fury. Perhaps he was imagining the butt being the face of either the judge or his wife, or maybe both. He then took a long swig of beer. "Me, I got fucking nothing. Absolutely fucking nothing! I'll be eating in the fucking chow hall and sleeping in the fucking barracks."

"At least you've got the Navy to fall back on," she said, certain of his reaction. What a kick in the ass it would be, though, should he suddenly feel that the Navy was all that he had! A lapse into patriotism would hardly reward her efforts. That, however, was not to be, she quickly noted. His face immediately began to darken. Fatima threw more gas onto the fire, "It's not like you're out on the street or something."

"Let me fucking tell you something, babe," said Lenny, his voice rising, the veins in his neck pulsing. "This fucking goddamned Navy ain't jack shit.

You know what they're fucking threatening to do? The fuckers will send me to Captain's Mast if I'm late on a single, goddamned child support payment. They called me into the Chief's office the moment I got back to base from court just to fucking let me know that. And goddamn, fucking judge ain't left me jack shit to survive on, let alone make car payments." He drained the beer, looking as though he might crush the bottle with his bare hand. Glancing over at one of the bartenders, he held the empty up, signaling for another.

Lenny, she could tell, was in a mood to feel no pain. He was fixing to get stinking drunk. Then he would be shooting his mouth off, loudly, attracting attention.

"Come on," said Fatima. "Let's check out your new wheels." Just before the judge was obviously going to take his last cent, she had still been able to suggest that he go sixteen grand into debt on a '99 corvette. *"Do it,"* she had convinced him, *"before the separation agreement ruins your credit."* And he had.

"We'll go when I'm fucking ready, god damn it," said Lenny, pulling out another cigarette. He picked up his lighter sitting on the table in front of him, beside his keys.

"Fucking fine, then," said Fatima, suddenly, loudly. A number of heads turned to where she and Lenny sat. Even a couple of the girls stopped giggling to see what was happening. Before Lenny could react, she snatched his keys up. "Just fucking sit there and enjoy your own fucking company. I can find someone who knows what I need."

"Baby, I can give you what you need!" shouted a large, baby-faced marine from the bar. He and his buddies began laughing.

"Bitch, what the hell's your fucking problem?" hollered Lenny, rising from his seat. He was an impressive figure with broad shoulders, standing over six foot tall, and with hair blacker than her own. He wore a moustache that richly accentuated his well-chiseled features. At first glance, his looks sent women into distress. A Clark Gable clone was what Lenny Allen was. At least until he opened his mouth. Unfortunately, once his lips began to move, the Clark Gable image was history.

Lenny caught up to her before she made it to the door. Viciously, he wrenched the keys from her hand and then shoved her out the door. He always handled her rough, like baggage tossed into the cargo hold of a plane. Patrons of the bar watched, sailors and marines who fancied that given the chance, they could show her how a real man would treat such a beautiful woman.

"What the hell's your fucking problem?" Lenny's question, screamed at her, was cut off in mid-stream as Fatima whirled herself onto him, covering his mouth with hers, one hand on his crotch.

"Shit, babe. Only needed to say what was on your mind," said Lenny, finally breaking away from her kiss. "But I ain't got no money for a place."

"We don't need a room," said Fatima with feigned impatience. She could feel him growing, responding to the need in her voice. That was good. It gave her control. "Where's your car?"

"Here, over here," said Lenny, pulling her towards the '99 Corvette parked in the poorly lit lot. "Not new, but one hell of a beauty. Hot like you, babe." The anger of chasing her into the parking lot had sobered Lenny for the most part.

"Oh, it's gorgeous!" Fatima cooed. Suddenly, she found herself yanked around to face him. Like so many times before, she feigned a moan of delight as he pulled her close, covered her mouth and filled it with his thick tongue. Soon, though not tonight, Lenny would find out just how hot she really was.

When Lenny finally released her from his disgusting embrace, Fatima went through the process of running her fingers across the Corvette's brilliant, luminous blue finish. She gave the girlish squeals of delight that he would expect. The Shah had once owned 3,000 automobiles. Her own father, a member of the Shah's government, had owned over a dozen. The sleek fiberglass frame and its powerful engine were more important to her than Lenny would ever have guessed. He thought he had purchased it with credit and smooth talk. Soon, he would realize that its sticker price was his soul. The final payment would come much sooner than he expected.

"Lenny, can you afford this with what the judge is making you pay your wife?" Fatima turned her face upwards so that he was looking into her eyes, showing him her feigned heart rendering compassion. Her entire face was a perfect mask, mocking genuine concern. What she saw in Lenny's eyes delighted her. Beyond the smug, macho façade that was Lenny, were eyes filled with both terror and anger. Lenny knew that he was financially adrift in unfriendly seas. It was only a matter of time before his creditors caught up with him. The military, she knew, dealt unpleasantly with debt-ridden personnel.

"Want to ride?" asked Lenny, meaning it more as a command than a question. His voice bore a strong hint of irritation. Her question had found its mark.

"Ride and be ridden," she purred. There was the clicking of the doors unlocking as he pushed the button on his key chain. Opening her own door, she bent her tall, lean frame close to the earth as she slid into the richly upholstered seats. The smell of the leather was heady.

Lenny was quickly around the car and sliding into the driver's seat. He never bothered to open or close doors for her. "Listen to this," he said, turning the key in the ignition. The engine came to life with a deep throaty roar, one that demanded respect. "Ain't that just the sweetest sound?"

The terror and anger that had filled him only seconds ago, was gone. Lenny was intoxicated, not only by the beer he had drank, but by the smooth flowing power of the Corvette and the thought of screwing his brains out. He was a simpleton, Fatima knew. It was the kindest thought she could remember ever having about him.

"I love it," she shouted above the noise of the engine and squealing tires as they spun out of the parking lot.

They had had sex on the beach along the James River several times. Lenny steered that direction along the Colonial Parkway. He drove recklessly with impatience at speeds well above the posted limit. Lenny barely slowed going into turns, trusting the car's extremely low center of gravity, more so than what Fatima was comfortable with.

The parkway provided Lenny with the opportunity to hang winding curves at exhilarating speeds. They only came upon one car that slowed them down, and that was only for the brief time that it took Lenny to be sure that it was not the park police. Flooring the gas pedal, he left the offending slow poke in a cloud of smoke as he burned the rubber of his tires against the road's surface.

"There!" yelled Fatima, feigning enthusiasm. She pointed to one of the more secluded parking areas along the James River. They had used this one before. Immediately, Fatima felt herself lurching forward as the corvette decelerated in a flurry of downshifting.

Idling into a parking space, Lenny killed the engine. "You are so fucking hot, babe," he said, sliding a hand up her skirt, his calluses rubbing against her bare thigh. In a few seconds, his fingers would explore her dampness, causing her to fake a splendor that he could never arouse.

Fatima gave forth the expected slight moan, and then lightly touched her fingers to his cheek. The tip of her glistening tongue briefly flicked across the top of her upper lip, its suggestion, unmistakable. She moved away, her eyes still locked with his. Then, with one swift motion, she opened the car door and escaped into the fresh stillness of the night.

For just brief seconds, Fatima allowed herself to block Lenny Allen from her mind. It was necessary to do this, creating a barrier that protected her from insanity. She gazed at a splendid moon that hung high over the river, casting an elegant brightness across the sky, reflecting across the river. The air was damp and cool. For but a moment, she took this all in, certain that she was already insane. And why shouldn't she be?

They had the overview to themselves. That was normal at night. A series of highly publicized murders, years ago, had made the secluded Parkway stops little used after dark. Her reverie, however, was short-lived as Lenny came around the Corvette to stand beside her. His large arms surrounded her, pulling her close so that she had no choice but to inhale his pungent cologne and the smell of stale cigarettes. His cologne, for whatever reason, made her think of mustard gas. Fatima remembered with a cold chill how she used to smell it in the clothes of the wounded soldiers at the field hospital in Ramhormuz. As a teenager, she had spent what seemed an eternity in that field hospital, trying to comfort young men her own age, mere children ravaged by Saddam Hussein's crude weapon of mass destruction and the land mines; a war machine aided by the U.S. It was there that the news of her beloved little brother had shattered the final, fragile thread of her sanity. That was why she was here. She comforted herself with that thought.

There was justice to be meted out. It had begun September 11 last year, but the Americans had been uncharacteristically strong in their response. They had broken up many cells that would have continued the battle. Now, however, despite the warnings of the politicians, Americans had relaxed. They were ready to be hit again. This time, harder than before.

"Want to walk along the beach," asked Lenny, already tugging her in that direction.

"No," said Fatima, putting her hand against the bulge that swelled beneath his Levis. "I want you, right here, on the hood of this car." With those words spoken, Fatima re-entered her private hell.

Chapter Three
Monday, May 6
Richmond, Virginia

Fatima glanced around, one more time, more slowly than before. Generally flawless in her planning and research, she was unaccustomed to such surprises. Not only were there no tables free, there was a long line waiting to be seated, as well. By the time she was seated, Frank Baker would be finished eating and on the way back to his office. That would not be catastrophic. She could wait until next week. However, Uncle Abdul was a stickler for timetables.

Like the others, she had easily obtained his name from Energy International's web site. Fatima had the entire list of Energy International board of directors' names. She knew more about each of them than they probably knew about each other. They were all high profile enough that a search on their names had turned up a wealth of information. She could not imagine the amount of research and risk it would have taken to come up with the same information without the Internet. The World-Wide Web was as vital to terrorism as it was to e-Business.

As was typical of American society, several of the board members had been involved in scandal over the years; none more so than the lawyer, Frank Baker. Obviously, from the newspaper accounts, he was a no holds barred womanizer. Reading about him had been entertaining. It had been easy deciding on him out of all the others on Energy International's board of directors.

Twenty-eight years ago, a Richmond detective had caught him in bed with his wife. The detective had shot both his wife and Frank. The wife died. Frank, by sheer good fate, had survived. The bullet miraculously grazed Frank's head and knocked him unconscious. When he woke up, the man had already turned the gun on himself, taking his own life. Despite all of that, Frank Baker's law firm had continued to prosper. Energy International apparently tolerated sleaze, and sleaze always made Fatima's job easier.

Fatima had intended to seat herself at a table directly across from Frank. Unfortunately, today's lunchtime crowd was not typical of her previous visits here. She had eaten lunch here twice a week, varying the days that she did so, allowing herself to feel comfortable and to have some idea of the restaurant's flow. However, there had been no way to know that nearly thirty office workers would be cramming the restaurant to celebrate a co-worker's birthday. She opened up the copy of the POST that she held, exposing the advertisements for legal services.

Stepping past the waiting patrons in front of her, Fatima moved confidently past the hostess. She walked slowly among the tables, carefully and obviously scanning all of the tables from side to side. She was just another patron, searching for someone that she was to meet for lunch, gambling that the Hostess was too busy to come to her rescue.

Out of the corner of her eye, Fatima saw Frank Baker glance up at her. She glanced down, gave him a half-hearted smile and then continued to search the tables. With practiced subtlety, she pulled her mouth into a pouty frown, showing her frustration at not finding who it was she looked for. Glancing back down at Frank, she put on the smile of the helpless and the distraught.

❖❖❖

Frank Baker surveyed the lunchtime crowd with a certain amount of glee. Eventually, one of his past conquests would show up, see that there was no seat available and come sit with him. Sorry to say, but his sex life was apparently down to such devices. Before the heart attack, he had never given growing old much concern. The younger women now, however, were giving him wide berth. The fiftyish clan of bored housewives gave him heartburn and barely a hard on. They seemed, however, his only respite. If this was how life would be from now on, better another heart attack and be done with it all. He did not believe in life in the hereafter. There was only life in the here and now.

He carefully studied the young woman standing next to his table, obviously searching for whomever she was to meet. She was an exquisite beauty he had seen here a couple times before. On both occasions, she had been alone, looking somewhat preoccupied, almost distressed. On her ring finger, she wore an aqua. Somehow, he could visualize a very large diamond and wedding band set recently removed.

Suddenly, without warning, she glanced down and caught him watching her. Somewhat apologetically, he gave her a casual smile. She smiled back, a polite, hurried smile. Immediately she returned to scanning the room, looking more distressed than before.

The same hand that was likely once adorned with an expensive wedding set, also held a newspaper. With a certain amount of disdain, he looked at the legal advertisements. It was scornful that lawyers had lowered themselves to such mush. Not his firm, and not ever. Good law firms did not need to stoop to such practice. It had been just ambulance chasers at first. Now, however, it was darn near everyone. Likely, she was searching for a good divorce lawyer to go after a very rich and influential husband. Rough waters for a woman, especially if she did the leaving. Obviously, it was she who had left. Why else would she be new to the club?

The ravishing dark beauty again turned her head to survey the tables in his direction. She was close enough to reach out and touch. He cleared his throat. At once, she glanced down at him. "Miss, can I help you find someone?" he asked. "I know pretty much everyone regular here."

"An attorney, Thomas Woodhaven III," said Fatima. "Maybe he couldn't get a table and left. I'm very late I'm afraid."

"I'm Frank Baker, Attorney at Law," he said, rising. She extended her hand. This woman had manners and was willing to give him a moment. "Seen you in here a couple of times. You must be new to the area." When she nodded, he continued. "I was getting ready to order lunch. Have a seat and join me. Looks like being stuck with me might be the only way to get a table in here today. I haven't seen Tom. His misfortune for not being more patient." He gave her a warm, reassuring smile, one he had perfected in his many years of practicing law and philandering.

"Thanks very much," said Fatima. "But I feel I'd be intruding." She had researched the connection between Woodhaven and Frank Baker thoroughly; and there was none. Tom Woodhaven was an attorney with an organization that helped women get free from abusive relationships. He was not someone that Frank would likely call up and chat with about meeting Fatima.

"Not at all," said Frank. "I hate eating alone." Frank moved easily, gracefully around the table to seat her. She seemed to hesitate, but as any lady with good upbringing, she accepted.

"You're very kind," she said, reaching over and lightly touching his hand. Though nothing more than a polite gesture, she discerned the carefully hidden look of delight in Frank's eyes. She would not have any difficulty baiting the hook for him.

"So, what brings you to Richmond?" asked Frank.

"What makes you think I'm new to the area?" asked Fatima.

"I can tell that you fit very well into this environment," said Frank. "If you lived here any length of time, I'd have seen you here before."

"My, so perceptive," said Fatima with a flattering smile.

Frank smiled broadly, giving only a very slight nod. "Looking for a good divorce attorney?" he asked. If she wanted perceptive, he would give her perceptive.

Fatima feigned a look of mild disbelief. "Most certainly am," she said with just a brief delay.

"You said I was perceptive," said Frank. "And I'm well qualified. The law firm I own has been handling divorces for years. If your husband intends to fight, I suspect he can and will hire some big guns. Woodhaven is not in that league; you'd be eaten alive." From a pocket in his warm-ups, he pulled out a business card. On it was printed the name of his law firm Baker, Baker and Anderson. "Tell me what's going on. The consultation and lunch are both on me today. After this, I'll make it my point to collect from the unlucky fellow who no longer has you."

"My name's Laura McClish," Fatima said with a slight, uncertain smile. With feigned reluctance, she told her story to Frank Baker, one well prepared. Hers, she told him, was a marriage filled with psychological torture by her husband, an extremely successful plastic surgeon in New York City. She had fled to Richmond to find escape from her painful situation. One of her problems was that she had just discovered that her credit cards, all in her husband's name, had been cancelled. Her money would soon run out.

"I was supposed to meet Mr. Woodhaven here," said Fatima. "Somehow, I think fate has smiled down on me, meeting you instead."

"Best for you," Frank assured her. "I don't have to make up stories where my work is concerned. I'm as good as they come. Hire me and you have my word you'll never pay a dime and will walk away a wealthy woman."

They ordered, talked, and then ate. Frank asked her if she played racquetball. Fatima explained that she did, but hadn't found anyone to play with since joining the club.

"So how are you affording all this at the moment?" Frank asked, indicating the country club.

"I put the membership on his American Express before he got to the cards," she smiled.

"I can't imagine why he possibly could have wanted to pull the plug on those credit cards," said Frank with a hearty laugh.

"Guess I probably should do some job hunting, huh?" said Fatima. She knew that Frank was the fisherman, and feeling very good about his chances at a big catch.

"Got a place to stay?" asked Frank. He appeared to be thinking.

"Rented a small place out in the country," said Fatima. "It's close to the nuclear power station."

"A year's lease and all paid up on hubby's American Express, right?" asked Frank.

"Visa Platinum," she smiled. "I didn't manage to gather a year's worth of gas, food and electricity before he caught on, however."

"Seems like it might be in his best interest to divorce you rather quickly. Any thoughts on a job?" She shook her head. "I can take care of that, too." With that, Frank Baker rose from his chair, looking in the direction of the much younger man she had seen him playing racquetball with earlier.

Travis Harding met Frank Baker at the country club on a very regular basis. Also, on a very regular basis, he always let the member of Energy International's board of directors win. Never by much, knowing that patronizing too much, could have nearly as undesirable an effect as winning.

Frank Baker was the biggest pain in the ass member of the board. Unfortunately, he was second only to Roger Cowlings in the amount of stock that he owned and power that he wielded. Thus, he was a member with clout. Travis wanted as much of that influence on his side as he could get. After all, such influence was responsible for picking the vice-presidents of its subsidiary, Richmond Nuclear. Travis Harding was currently vice-president, Administration-Security. Over the past year, he had been working in quiet subterfuge to get to senior vice-president, Richmond Nuclear. He had grown tired of existing in his old college buddy's shadow. Now, however, that position appeared meager to the prospects that Frank Baker and Roger Cowling were presenting to him.

Travis was discussing the menu with his secretary when Frank motioned him over to his table. Cindy Johnston, his personal secretary, did not come to the club often. This was one of the few times. Travis could only bring her when his wife was out of town. She had flown to Houston for a medical conference, so it was safe. It also required good tips to ensure that none of the staff would have any reason to say anything when it was his wife accompanying him to the club rather than Cindy.

"Damn it, Travis," Cindy spoke in a whisper. "What does the old fart want?"

"Hell if I know," said Travis, a fake smile spread across his face as he waved acknowledgement to Frank.

Travis had grown used to seeing Frank with one of several bored housewives, none of them particularly attractive, most in their mid-fifties. The old fart, as he normally thought of Frank, had once held quite a reputation when it came to the ladies. Age and a bad heart, though, had taken their toll. However, the woman sitting next to Frank at the moment was stunning.

"Laura McClish, this is Travis Harding, V.P. of Administration and Security for Richmond Nuclear," said Frank.

"Ms. McClish, very pleased to meet you," said Travis. In his mind, he could not avoid rhyming the words together, *"Ms. McClish, oh what a dish!"* The woman did not offer her hand, so he offered his instead, unable to resist the temptation to touch at least a part of her.

Fatima obliged by coolly taking Travis Harding's hand. She had not planned on meeting the V.P. of Administration and Security. Luck, Allah, one or the other was her shadow today. "Pleasure meeting you," she said. For a mere instant, she gave him her eyes.

"Miss McClish is in need of a job," said Frank, placing his hand over Fatima's. Inwardly, she smiled. Frank Baker was marking his territory, telling the younger womanizer, *"hands off."* "Laura, Travis oversees the security and administration of our nuclear units at Jefferson Davis Nuclear Power Station."

"That's so impressive," said Fatima, once again meeting Travis' eyes with her own. Then quickly, she switched her attention back to Frank. He, after all, was the real power here. Travis Harding would do whatever Frank Baker wanted him to do. And there was little doubt that Frank Baker would have him do just about anything to please her. "You didn't tell me that you're in the electrical industry as well. More than just a great attorney, huh?"

"I dabble in many things," said Frank.

"I'm certain that we have something available at our corporate headquarters," said Travis eagerly.

"Well, if you don't, then make something. That's why you're a V.P.," snapped Frank, making sure that he stayed in control. "What type of job would you prefer, Miss McClish?" he asked, turning to her.

"Actually, the place that I'm renting is close to your nuclear power station," said Laura. "I really hate rush hour traffic and having to get up early."

"If we're going to make a position it'll have to be at corporate," said Travis as diplomatically as he could.

"No, no, no. Her goddamned husband's just screwed her life up and has taken nearly every last cent she's got," said Frank, reproachfully. "She doesn't need the expense of driving that distance every day."

Travis suddenly looked like someone had kicked him in the balls. Fatima had no doubt that she would get what she wanted. She decided to play the circumstances for all they were worth.

"I used to supervise the records department for a police precinct in New York City," said Fatima, turning to Travis. She gave him her most innocent smile. "It was a long time ago, but I really liked it. Since you're in charge of security, maybe that's what I'd be best at."

"Actually, we can't really get you a job in security," said Travis, shifting uncomfortably. "That requires a background check. Takes at least three months. We can find you something in administration while we take care of getting you a security clearance."

"God damn it! Don't be so fucking useless," said Frank, loud enough that several heads turned their way. "She hardly looks like she's going to be blowing things up. If you care to be a part of Energy International's future, then you better show that you can take some fucking initiative."

"Yes, sir," said Travis, looking like a little boy severely whipped by his father. He gave Fatima a nod and headed back to his table. Pretty near the entire club had heard Frank dress him down.

"Now, Laura," said Frank, once Travis had left, "seems to me that you could use a bit of legal assistance. If you'd like, I can get some paperwork moving to help your husband decide to send you some funds. Like I said, don't worry about my fee, he'll pay it when we're finished with him. That and much more, I promise."

Chapter Four
Saturday, June 1
Hanover County, Virginia

Fatima left Green Top Sporting Goods Store in the early evening, making her way down Route 1 and then taking I-64 East. Traffic was tedious. That was because it was now officially sun and surf season, time for the interstate to become one big parking lot, from Richmond to Virginia Beach. Fortunately, she did not have to pass through the Tunnel. She would have plenty of time to get to the Hoisted Anchor and meet Lenny. For once, she looked forward to their evening together. It would be memorable. Moreover, it would be their last.

Three days, the salesperson had told her, to take care of the background check. That was for the .45 Colt, a purchase that Abdul had tried to persuade her to avoid. He always worried about getting tripped up with any type of background check. However, she knew what was involved in the background check for purchasing a weapon. As long as she had no known criminal history, she was covered. She would never have passed the type of background check required for her job at Jefferson Davis Nuclear Power Station, but Travis Harding had fudged the paperwork, at least for the time being.

It was almost two hours later that she parked her '96, paint-faded Firebird in front of the Hoisted Anchor. Inside the smoke filled bar, she spotted Lenny with no difficulty. He was in his usual booth. Nevertheless, what else she saw made her blood run cold. The female bartender was sitting across from him. Was he simply trying to make time with her? Or, were they setting her up? How pathetic if Lenny did, after all, turn out to be an intelligence agent. She shook the thought aside. He was, she was certain, the ultimate oxymoron to intelligence. The bartender, however, was at the top of her list for being an intelligence officer. At this point, though, there was too much at stake to pull out. She would continue as planned.

Cigarette in hand, Lenny muttered an "Oh shit," and motioned the bartender away as soon as he saw Fatima. The bartender rose from her seat, faced Fatima and rolled her eyes in disgust. Question was, mused Fatima; did she find him truly disgusting or a wealth of information? Should she call Abdul and warn him, cancel this evening's final episode? Well, if the two of them were working together, then certainly the phone lines here would be monitored. Besides, Lenny had no idea of what was in store for tonight. No, it would have to be chanced.

Cigarette ash had fallen on the table in front of Lenny. Fatima found it revolting. He smoked constantly. With a rare perspective of dry humor, she thought that if she and her Uncle Abdul did not work quickly, the cigarettes and the booze would kill him before they did.

"How's it going?" asked Fatima, sliding into the seat across from Lenny. The question was pure rhetoric. How it was going was written all across his face in hard lines. The effects of half a dozen empty beer bottles that sat upon the table already dulled his eyes. This allowed her to put her suspicions to rest. When Lenny was drunk, he hit on anything vaguely resembling female.

His financial crisis was catching up with him. The timing was more or less, as she expected. Now it was important to get him out of here before he became totally wasted. Though the alcohol was necessary to dull his perception of what was to come, it was also necessary that he have total recall of tonight's events.

"Well let me put it to you this way Laura, babe. Like to take one last fucking ride in the 'vette before the fuckers come and tow it the hell away?" asked Lenny in a loud voice, throwing a cigarette to the floor and immediately lighting up another. Throwing his hand into the air, he gave a shrill whistle to attract the bartender's attention. It was not the woman, but an older, grizzly looking man wearing a stained apron. He reluctantly headed over.

"Lenny, let's go for a ride," said Fatima, reaching and touching his arm. He paid her no attention. She stood, and with one hand hidden from Lenny's sight, motioned the bartender away. Suggestively, she kissed Lenny on the ear and tugged at his elbow. "Come on. My period starts tomorrow. You know how hard I like to fuck when it's this time of the month," she whispered.

"Fucking going to ditch me after I lose the vette, ain't 'cha?" demanded Lenny, his words an angry slur. He stared up at her with glazed eyes. "That's about all you goddamned babes care about. Nothing but a man's goddamned money and his wheels. It's all fucking shit."

"Come on Lenny," said Fatima. In another hour, he would become sober in the blink of an eye. That was if she could get him the hell out of this place. "Come on. We can come back later for a drink. Better yet," she paused for effect. "We can go to my place and spend the night. It'll be better there. We'll have all night."

"Your place?" asked Lenny with obvious surprise. There was at first a sudden glimmer of anticipation in his eyes. It dimmed away, however, as quickly as it had arrived. "What about that flipped out ex of yours. You told me he shot some dude he found at your place. Even after you fucking divorced him. Shit if I want to deal with that!"

"He got in a fight in Richmond a couple nights ago," said Fatima. "He's going to be in the slammer a while." She was losing count of the number of times that she had used the flipped out ex as an excuse not to show a john where she lived. It always had the desired effect.

Half pulling him, she got Lenny from his seat. As he removed a ring of keys from his pocket, he staggered to one side. Instinctively Fatima glanced towards the bartender. He caught her eye with a very brief shake of the head.

"Give them," said Fatima, jerking the keys to the 'vette from his hand. Without giving him time for protest, she headed to the door, knowing that he would follow. Angry perhaps, but he would follow. The last thing that she needed tonight was for the bartender to get dutifully concerned and notify the police that a drunk was taking to the road.

"Just shut up and get in," she snapped at Lenny as she heard the first attempt of protest pass his lips. He grabbed her wrist and attempted to jerk her towards him. With a smooth, deliberate twist of her wrist, she pulled free of his grasp and jerked the passenger door open. Using her knee to buckle his own from beneath him, she shoved him into the seat and slammed the door closed.

"Fucking, shit, babe," said Lenny, a look of disbelief on his face.

"Just shut up," she told him.

"What the fuck...?" he started.

Fatima explained nothing as she guided the Corvette down the winding Colonial Parkway. They rode in silence. Lighting up a cigarette, Lenny simply stared out into the darkness. He looked questioningly at her when she idled the Corvette into the same overview that they had used at other times on the parkway.

Fatima killed the engine and opened her door. "Get out," she said.

"Shit, Laura," Lenny protested as he glanced over at the Mercedes parked at the opposite end of the scenic overview. "There's people here. Thought we were headed to your place." He obeyed anyway, stepping out into the sobering coolness of the night.

"I lied," said Fatima. "You're meeting my uncle instead."

Lenny was quickly starting to sober. He remained silent as a man climbed from the Mercedes and came towards them. Fatima's finger never left the trigger of the .45 Colt hidden in her purse. Unknown to Lenny, she aimed its barrel at his rib cage. It was, she knew, an unnecessary precaution. From the darkness of the surrounding trees, the barrel of a high-powered rifle was sighted on the unsuspecting sailor's heart. Should he surprise her with an unexpected moment of patriotic indulgence, his life would end very suddenly.

"You must be Lenny Allen," said Abdul, reaching out for Lenny's hand. His words bore a heavy facade of Italian accent. Most likely, out of reflex, Lenny took the outstretched hand, shaking it with zeal. He seemed unable to take his eyes off Abdul. A full foot and a half shorter than Lenny, Fatima's uncle nevertheless posed a commanding presence in his white blazer and matching Franco hat.

"Yes, sir," Lenny answered, sounding suddenly very sober.

"My niece has told me quite a lot about you. All very complimentary, of course. I am made to understand, however, that you've suffered significant setback lately. That your fiscal means has fallen below your level of need. My name is Lou Carlotti, Mr. Allen. Laura has asked me to help you."

"Glad to meet you, Mr. Carlotti," said Lenny, totally entranced by Abdul's spit and polish. "I wasn't expecting to meet anyone out here."

"I realize that," said Abdul. "But our conversation is best conducted here, where we are assured of privacy."

"Why?" Lenny's voice bore the first hint of suspicion.

"Because I'm a man of discretion." Abdul paused a second, studying Lenny's reaction. "I have come to offer you, Lenny, the solution to all your financial problems. I will see to it that you keep your beautiful car. You will not have to worry about living from one paycheck to the other. Does that sound like something that you'd like?" Lenny merely nodded. Abdul continued. "From you, I need what only you can provide."

"What do you mean?" Lenny stiffened. "Drugs?" His question had a frightened ring to it. He had the look of a rabbit about to flee.

"I find drugs extremely distasteful," said Abdul. "In fact, such an assumption insults me. However, I forgive you. For you are in a unique position to provide me with a service that will greatly put me in your debt.

33

And, for that, I'll pay you handsomely. Lenny, do you know who I am?"

"She said you're her uncle," said Lenny, timidly.

"Lenny, my family runs the entire mid-Atlantic region of the United States. I am uncle to many," said Abdul. He pulled a cigarette from a gold case, offered one to Lenny and then lit both. It was a moment of silence, allowing the sailor to absorb his words.

"You mean like Mafia?" asked Lenny, awe and uncertainty crackled in his voice.

"La Cosa Nostra, Lenny," snapped Abdul like an impatient father chiding his child. "Don't say it as though it's an organization of hoodlums. It's a business. I'm a business man. And because I want to stay in business, when I give my word, you can depend on it."

"Yes sir," said Lenny very quickly.

"It's all right," said Abdul. He gave Lenny a reassuring smile. "I know, the movies. They make it so ...so evil. Nevertheless, we're a business, ran by honorable men. Please appreciate that."

"Yes sir," said Lenny one more time.

"Lenny, I need three Hellfire missiles," said Abdul. Fatima could never fail to be astonished at her uncle. He could mouth such a bold request, spoken as though it were a perfectly reasonable expectation.

"Shit, you're trying to set me up," Lenny suddenly spat at the ground near Abdul's feet. Fatima could feel the tension as the muscles tightened beneath Lenny's shirt. "I wasn't born yesterday. I know how bad you fucks want a reason to get rid of me. You're fucking Navy Intelligence."

"Is that what you think, Lenny?" asked Abdul in his heavy fake Italian accent. He sounded extremely hurt and disappointed at the response. Then quicker than a blink of the eye, Abdul had a pistol in his hand, its barrel leveled at Lenny's chest. Fatima heard Lenny suck his breath in at the chilling sight of the barrel pointed at him. "Well, I actually appreciate your caution. Working with someone who is careful is always preferable."

"Wait, now. Shit... what exactly you going to do?" asked Lenny. There was still a touch of skepticism to his voice. It was still possible that this was a set up. The gun, however, did make him reconsider that possibility.

"Navy Intelligence has its limitations, don't you agree?" asked Abdul, smiling as Lenny warily nodded. "But, you shall notice, I have no limitations." Abdul suddenly swung the weapon to point at Fatima. Without hesitation, there was a flash and the deafening roar of the gun's discharge. Fatima bucked backwards onto the Corvette, her hands clutching her chest, her face set in pain and surprise. She made a gurgling sound as she slid to the ground. Abdul ejected the weapons clip, letting it fall to the ground. Lenny was frozen stalk still, the smell of his urine scenting the air. Abdul then fired the round remaining in the chamber into Fatima's collapsing body. She bucked again, and then lay there, her body quivering.

Before Lenny could react, Abdul's foot shot out, the pointed toe of his boot coming up to catch Lenny expertly in the groin. Then he grabbed Lenny's hand, slapping the grip of the pistol into it.

"Choice, my friend," said Abdul, his voice flat. "Take the rap for this, or come, and let us go somewhere more congenial to conversation."

"Fucking shit!" Lenny's scream was hoarse. He barely was able to stand. "You just killed your own fucking niece for god's sake."

"I am who I said I am," said Abdul. "However, she wasn't. Just some prostitute who could do a little acting. Now, do you want my men to take care of this mess, or should I just leave it with you to explain to the police?"

Lenny looked up. From out of the darkness came two men, both carrying rifles. "I'll go with you. Oh, fuck. Oh, fucking shit."

"Hurry," said Abdul. "There are people living nearby. Someone is bound to have heard the shots and called the police. We'll see to it that the blood is cleaned from your car and get it back to you. Everything will be fine." Then he guided Lenny quickly towards the Mercedes.

"They're gone," said Ali as the Mercedes' tail lights faded into the distance. "You died very well for the whore that you truly are."

"Shame that your uncle didn't use real ammo," said Rajani.

Fatima looked up into the faces of Ali and Rajani. She got to her feet and brushed off the grit from the parking lot. They were both al Qaeda, and believed the only role in Jihad for a woman was to be strapped with a bomb. What they did not understand was this was a new kind of Jihad. It was being fought in a manner that their enemy did not expect. Both the FBI and CIA thought as they did, that the women of Jihad were relegated to blowing themselves up in market squares.

"So," said Fatima, staring for a moment at Lenny's car, "who's brilliant plan is it that leaves three of us to ride back in this?" Neither answered. "I'm driving," she said, opening the door of the Corvette and sliding in behind the wheel. Ali and Rajani started for the passenger side. Before they could reach it, however, Fatima had locked the doors. Quickly, she started the engine and sped away, leaving them to find their own way home.

"She is an unrighteous whore," said Ali in Arabic.

"I will kill her when this is through," swore Rajani.

Chapter Five
Thursday, July 14
Hanover County, Virginia

Fatima sat across the table from Frank Baker. Racquetball and then lunch at the country club was now a once a week thing for her and Frank. He was rambling on about some brilliant legal maneuvering that he had used years ago in a courtroom battle. She nodded and smiled whenever it seemed appropriate.

Frank was oblivious to the fact that she paid only enough attention to prevent him from realizing she had no interest at all in what he said. She had to admit, however, Frank's posturing to be her knight in shining armor was amusing. Once she had heard an American phrase, *"playing him like a fiddle."* For months now, she had managed to do that with Frank. Abdul had hired an extremely capable law firm in New York to represent him as her husband, Donald McClish. It was an expensive façade, but necessary as Frank had wasted no time researching the law firm representing Mr. McClish. An American attorney, Muslim by birth and an al Qaeda supporter, ensured that Abdul had all the necessary background documentation to demonstrate both a marriage and a business practice.

Today, Frank was displaying an unusual amount of agitation. At first, she thought that it might be his frustration with her. On numerous occasions, he had tried to bed her. She sensed, however, that it was something else. Could that "something else" be connected to the rumors that buzzed through every department of the Jefferson Davis Nuclear Power Plant? There were layoffs and cutbacks everywhere. Everyone was sure that the power station was being poised for a sale. It was no rumor that the station's Senior VP Brian Matkins was in a slugfest over the cuts. The battle was even in the local news.

Whatever Energy International's plans were, they could not have timed them any better for Abdul's operation. America's commercial nuclear power plants had always been prime targets for al Qaeda. However, the extremely high level of security and the tough physical barriers protecting the reactors, made them nearly impenetrable. That security was now fragmenting at Jefferson Davis as budget cuts and layoffs demoralized and reduced the security staff. If she had been a Believer, she would have thought this was Allah's plan. Abdul certainly did.

Abdul's plan had been two-fold, hit the U.S. with an attack more terrifying than that of September 11, and personally destroy Roger Cowling. They could achieve both in one swift and in horrifying operation. However, was it possible that Frank's unusual state of agitation was in response to the imminent sale of Jefferson Davis Nuclear Power Plant? If that occurred before they struck the power plant, then Roger Cowling would walk away unscathed. She and Abdul could not permit that.

The waitress interrupted them to take their lunch orders. Frank allowed himself to display his annoyance at the distraction.

"Frank," asked Fatima, "has there been any progress with my situation?"

"I spoke with your husband's attorney yesterday," said Frank. He eyed the dark haired beauty sitting across from him. Even with her being forty years his junior, he had easily beaten her at racquetball. It was a matter of skill, knowing how to strategically place himself and the ball. He wished that his progress report were more positive. "They seem intent on dragging this thing out. Most likely, they believe the financial stress will make you settle for a fraction of what you'll eventually win in court."

"That's not what I needed to hear," said Fatima, patting her forehead with her cloth napkin as though over-heated and exhausted from their game. "You kick my ass and then give me bad news? Frank, I thought I meant a little more than that to you!" she teased. It was easy to stroke Frank's ego, especially where his physical prowess was concerned. He could certainly beat most players his own age, but his wins against much younger opponents was a matter of corporate courtesy, nothing more. She could have beaten him with little difficulty.

"Everything working out all right at the job?" asked Frank, wanting to turn the conversation from his lack of progress on her legal issues. Fighting an out of state battle put him at a disadvantage. In addition, the fact that his client had left on her own free will did not make his job any easier.

"It's great. Good folks to work with. Thanks for helping," said Fatima, her eyes locked with his. She touched her fingers to his hand just long enough to say, "I couldn't have survived for long without that job. You're a friend that I can't do without."

"Well, I worked hard all my life to get where I'm at," said Frank. She pulled her hand away just as he was about to grasp it. Her touch had sent a jolt of sensual excitement through him that he would be thinking about for the rest of the day. "If I can take advantage of my position to do something worthwhile for people who need it, then that makes it rewarding." He could not remember the last time that he had bedded such a lovely young thing as her. This was the closest they had been to sharing an intimate moment. That momentary touch and gazing into her eyes made him aroused in a way that he had not experienced for decades. This was not the type of woman a man simply wanted to bed, she was the type that he would walk through fire to place a diamond on her finger. That such a thought would even enter his head astounded him. Hell, a woman like Laura might be the end of him if he ever did get her in bed, let alone marrying her. He could not think of a better way to leave this world.

"I'm so happy that you didn't let Travis stick me in an office shuffling paper downtown," she said. "You seem to have such control. You know what you want to make happen, and you make it happen." She paused a second and added, "You know, control and power are definite turn-ons."

"Well," said Frank, jokingly, "fighting off hordes of beautiful young women does occupy a great deal of my time."

"I'm sure there's more truth to that than sarcasm," said Fatima.

"When you get to be my age, you learn to choose carefully," said Frank. If she knew the true definition of "choose carefully" over the last several years, she would be laughing and rolling in the floor.

"So, what's special about Brian Matkins, that you tolerate him stepping out of line like he does?" she asked. "There's certainly a lot of gossip at the power station about a power struggle between him and Mr. Cowling. It must be tedious managing a loose cannon like him. I hear though that he's one of the best VPs in the nuclear industry. Guess that's why you keep him around."

"He's the one son of a bitch who thinks he's above doing what he's told," said Frank. Cowling had told him this morning that Matkins was going to meet with the Region II Nuclear Regulatory Commission in Atlanta to discuss the cutbacks at Jefferson Davis Nuclear Power Station. Frank had been telling Cowling for a couple of months that they needed to deal with Matkins. Cowling now agreed, it was time to bring Matkins down, hard. Hopefully they were not a day late and a dollar short at this stage.

"I'm surprised that he's still working for you," said Fatima.

"The utility business is regulated by government agencies that can really crimp your style," said Frank. He stopped for a moment, realizing that he should not be talking about any of this. There were not many opportunities at his age, however, to have a woman with these looks and oozing with such sexuality. Things were starting to gel with her. She was a woman who appreciated him, the kind of woman who found power superior to the hard muscle of younger studs. All he had at this stage in life was that power and control that she admired. What had she said; it was a turn-on? Besides, she was extremely intelligent and he could certainly find a useful position for her in Energy International, one more suited for her than working in the security department.

"You see," said Frank, continuing, "Energy International owns Richmond Nuclear. We're not state or federally regulated, but Richmond Nuclear is. It's very tricky for us to fire one of the executives there, especially if it looks like it has an effect on nuclear operation. Brian Matkins is bantering about, telling the State Corporation Commission that we're cutting costs in ways that affect nuclear safety. He's wrong and he's out of line. But the rules that govern how we do business don't let us deal with him like we could if he worked directly for Energy International."

"Why's all the cost cutting going on?" Fatima saw the uneasiness in the way Frank moved his eyes and shifted in his seat. What was going on behind the scenes at Energy International? This mission had two objectives. One was to injure the American psyche beyond its ability to mend. Their plan was firmly in place to do that. The other was to personally destroy Roger Cowling. The key to the second objective was in destroying his wealth, not killing him. Abdul had assured her that for Cowling to live without his wealth would be a Hell beyond anything physical they could do to him. The financial fallout of the first objective was expected to accomplish the second. However, what if the first objective failed? As solid as their plan was, nuclear power stations were not easy targets; they could fail.

It was at that moment the waitress arrived with the food. Fatima made a deliberate act of glancing at her watch, an indication to Frank that she needed to leave. She had baited the hook by making it appear she liked him and giving the smallest hint that it could turn into something more. He was going after the bait, but she could sense his caution. She needed to apply a little pressure to encourage him to swallow the hook.

"You know," said Fatima, "just from the time that I've been working out at the power station, it really seems like you guys are making cuts that are going to hurt your company in the long term. Is it a stock value type of move?

I understand that you really can't say too much," she said, setting her sandwich down and wrapping it in her napkin as though to take it with her. "It's just that I find the financial strategies required to manage a corporation such as this, intriguing." She scooted her chair just slightly away from the table.

"It's just a matter of weighing things," said Frank. He wondered where she needed to be. Maybe he was reading too much into her comment about power and control being a turn-on, but it really appeared that she had an interest in him with at least some romantic potential. How long before someone else, maybe someone with power and control plus young and handsome, caught her eye?

A sense of mild panic swept over Frank. She had created an opening for him, perhaps intentionally, perhaps not. It occurred to him that her subtle signals of preparing to leave were staged. Why? If you took the comments about her being attracted to a man who exhibits power and control, combine them with questions pertaining to corporate operations and strategy and subtle hints to leave, it added up to one thing. She wants to get on the inside of Energy International, he thought.

Frank was not under any illusion that she saw in him the person that she wanted as her life partner with which to make a family. More likely, she saw him as a partner with whom she could build an empire for herself through a marriage of convenience and opportunity. If that was what she was about, he had no problem with it. However, what if she were working undercover for the government? The Bush administration was certainly waging war on corporate fraud. Perhaps Matkins had already talked to the Nuclear Regulatory Commission or some other agency and Laura was working the case. No, that did not seem likely. He was handling her divorce, dealing with an established law firm in Manhattan and going after a person who had real accounts and a business practice. All of that was too real. If she wanted in, he would open the door. All he required was to be the one to carry her across its threshold.

"Actually, what we're doing is really quite extraordinary," he said. "The cost cutting is about a new future for the American utility industry." He felt as though he was uncorking a bottle of very fine wine as he began divulging the new course that he and Roger Cowling had set for Energy International.

"What do you mean?" asked Fatima. "At the power station, they really wonder where Cowling is headed with the company."

"Roger Cowling isn't the sole entity guiding the company," Frank responded. Her reference to Cowling agitated him. However, that was not her fault. As CEO, Cowling's name was synonymous with Energy International's image. For that to be the perspective of the rest of the world was fine. It was not, however, the perspective he would continue to allow Laura to have. "A lot of what we're doing, I'm responsible for. I've got a law practice to operate and I'm not interested in the day-to-day running of Energy International. Roger wears the CEO hat because he manages companies and is good at it. We're a cohesive team."

"Interesting," said Fatima. "Are you getting ready to buy another power company? Cutting operating costs to build up your cash reserves; that's what you're doing, isn't it?"

"You've got a good mind for business, Laura," said Frank. "I don't plan on leaving you out at the power station."

"Really," said Fatima, unfolding the napkin from around her sandwich. There was still a lot of work left before they could execute the attack on Jefferson Davis Nuclear Power Station. She needed to remain there. Was this conversation backfiring and now Frank was wanting her closer? Another possibility was Travis Harding's concern about her lack of a security clearance. Perhaps Harding had bypassed Frank and gone to Cowling. "I don't want to make any changes until things are settled with my husband. I'm into the routine at the power station and the stress level is low. In the future, however, I would like to view the workings of Energy International from the corporate perspective."

"Don't worry," said Frank. "I was referring to some things down the road a bit." He was leading Energy International into the twenty-first century as one of the premier utilities. There was no more holding back. "Fact of the matter is I enjoy building empires. That's what I'm all about. If you're interested, there could be a place for you in that empire. Along with being very beautiful, you're also intelligent and confident."

"What kind of empire?" asked Fatima. "You already have an empire." So indeed, they were building up their cash reserve to fund the purchase of another power station. She was not sure that this was necessarily news that would be of great benefit to Abdul. It had been worth a try.

Frank glanced around and carefully lowered his voice. "What we're doing is cutting our operational costs to the absolute minimum. We've worked a deal to sell our two assets, Richmond Nuclear and Richmond Fossil to the state of California. My God, Laura, don't say a word of this to anyone. Not even CNN knows what's going on. Fact of the matter is, once this is finished,

I can find a place in the organization for you. I'm a man of good judgment and I see in you the ability to manage. Travis is likely going to be our Senior VP. You like security, how does VP of Security and Administration sound to you?"

Laura said nothing. Her body language did it all for her. She scooted her chair closer to the table and lightly placed her hand on Frank's. "I'm listening," she said.

"We have a majority of the board of directors who have secretly invested substantial sums of money in a land lease in Mexico," said Frank. No longer was he pensive about talking. His words flowed easily. "With the proceeds from the sell of the Jefferson Davis Nuclear Power Station and Richmond Fossil, we can build a number of state-of-the art nuclear generating units there. The simplicity of the regulation in Mexico will allow us to move quickly. Seven years from now, we plan to be free-wheeling electrical power directly into the U.S.

"You see, the U.S. is deregulating the electrical generation industry. We already have the North American Free Trade Agreement. With what it will cost to build nuclear generating units in Mexico, we'll be able to send power to any part of the U.S. far cheaper than anyone else. It'll be a monopoly south of the border that no one can touch. Not without nullifying NAFTA, and that would take years. Besides, with rolling blackouts in California more common than getting a cold, who'd want to stop us?"

"And Matkins can't see the wisdom in this?" asked Fatima.

"He knows nothing about it," said Frank. "There's precious little he can do to stop it, regardless."

"What do you mean by precious little?" asked Fatima. Her hand was still on Frank's. Somehow, she imagined that as long as it remained there, he would answer anything she asked.

"Like I said, it's precious little. If one of the board members is unable to vote, the Senior VP votes in that member's place." Frank stopped. The fact of the matter was, he thought of that potential eventuality a lot.

"With so much at stake, I'm sure that you have enough of a majority that he wouldn't be able to sway the vote," said Fatima. She saw the hesitation in Frank's eyes. Almost always, an op rested on finding the smallest chink in the enemy's armor. Intuition said she had found one.

"I'm not really sure to tell you the truth," said Frank. The warmth of Laura's touch was nearly intoxicating. In fact, he had become aroused almost immediately. Common sense dictated that he say no more about this vulnerability of Matkins voting. He had, he was sure, said much more than he would ever want Cowling to know about. Frank, however, had spent his entire professional life looking clients and witnesses in the eye and determining his next move. In Laura, he had a true confident; she could be trusted. "We've got a couple who are in their seventies and several who we know will vote against the project. See it all has to have Board approval. Right now, those of us with money invested make up the majority of the board by only one vote. Something happens to one of us, Matkins can destroy us."

"Frank, that's so scary," said Fatima making a long face. She gripped Frank's hand harder to show her concern. "It's such a huge risk."

"It's under control," said Frank, suddenly anxious to ease Laura's alarm. "We helped him get hooked up with a young lady down in Atlanta where he's going to meet with the NRC. He goes down there an awfully lot. Call it blackmail, but it's going to get the job done. He will vote the way we tell him to vote. Make no mistake about that."

"How do you find out all this? Own stock in the CIA?" asked Fatima in her most admiring tone and showing her relief.

"Ever hear the term, 'buddy fucker?' laughed Frank. "When you met Travis Harding, you met the king of them."

They sat in the corner of the Dairy Queen. Quite a change in venue, Lenny thought. It was certainly a change from those nights that he had spent in the Hoisted Bar and Grille with Laura. The girl sitting across from him was not a Laura, not even close. Petty Officer Janelle Thompson was plain Jane. Raised in rural Indiana farm country, she had joined the Navy to flee a father that preached hellfire and brimstone on Sunday and beat the love of Jesus into his children the remaining six days and nights of the week.

"So, what happened to her," asked Janelle. She was afraid to ask the question, but even more afraid not to ask it. Though she had never seen Lenny's old girlfriend, she had heard others talk about her. From the sounds of it, she had been as beautiful as a model.

"Dumped me," said Lenny. He glanced around. There was nothing but teenyboppers in here, but a couple of them did not look too bad. He could certainly have had a better time with them than he was having with Janelle.

"That's mean," said Janelle. Lenny was as handsome as any man she had ever met. However, she had always kept her distance from him. He had always come across as a Godless, mean-spirited person who drank and took the Lord's name in vain constantly.

"Best thing that could have ever happened to me," said Lenny. "God has a strange way of doing things. I thought losing Laura was my world coming to an end. But you know, once she thought I was losing the 'vette, she was through with me. Made me start thinking and looking at my life." He was itching to light up a cigarette, but that would not have been well received.

"I thought you were teasing me when you asked if I'd take you to the Bible study at the chapel with me," said Janelle. Lenny had just suddenly ceased his raucous behavior. It was mentioned that he was no longer seen hanging out at the Hoisted Bar and Grille. His much talked about Laura seemed to have vanished. Then, out of the blue, he had picked up her Bible from her desk and asked what church she belonged to. For the past two weeks now, they had attended church and Bible study. There was no more of his foul mouth. Almost no more, anyway; he had let out some pretty harsh words when he smashed his thumb a couple of days ago working on a missile engine. However, all of God's children slip now and again.

"The opportunity that the Lord has given me isn't something to tease about," said Lenny.

"You didn't lose your car, though," said Janelle. It was beyond her that something like a car would determine whether a woman loved a man or not. It did not matter to her whether Lenny drove the Corvette or a broken down pickup truck, she would feel the same for him. Of course, that in itself was an issue, was it not? She had started feeling something for Lenny right from the beginning. Not in her entire life had she ever dated, thus the almost constant attention that she got from Lenny was difficult to adjust to. Her father had home schooled her and she never really had an opportunity to be around boys. Contact with the boys at church had always been carefully supervised. However, now that she was experiencing it, she liked it. Without a doubt, she was starting to like him a lot.

How would Lenny feel if he were to go into her room at the barracks, not that she would have ever invited him? He would see where she had written his name on the front of the *TV Guide*, scribbled it across the notepad next to the telephone and any number of other places.

"No, she left me and suddenly I wasn't spending money on her," said Lenny. "Then, I suddenly realized that drinking and smoking was such a stupid waste of my money. Getting rid of her and the booze basically solved my money problems." He did not add the fact that Mr. Carlotti had paid the

Corvette off for him and was allowing him to stay in a furnished apartment that he owned, rent-free. Thinking of the apartment reminded him that there was a bottle of Jack Daniels under the sink. He would really welcome a drink of it later on. He kept it hidden in the eventuality that he found it advantageous to invite Janelle over.

"Have you thought about going back to your wife and child?" asked Janelle. This was the real question that she hated to ask. If Lenny had broken up with his girlfriend, then there was a good chance that he would go back to his wife. Sally was a Christian who had dated a lot. Janelle thought of her as knowledgeable when it came to relationships. Sally had warned her sternly that men usually do go back to their wives and you could not trust a man until he was divorced for at least three years.

"If I tell you something, will you promise to never tell anyone else?" asked Lenny.

"Sure," said Janelle.

"I didn't leave my wife for Laura," said Lenny. "My wife cheated on me. The child's not mine. But I want him to always think of me as his father. I could never go back to my wife, though. You can't imagine how something like that feels."

"Oh, Lenny, I'm so sorry," said Janelle. Immediately she felt the guilt sweeping through her. She was not really sorry, but covertly ecstatic. Marriage was for life but for a few exceptions. A spouse's adultery was one of them. Lenny left his wife for a legitimate cause. If this continued, and they really loved each other, they could marry and be right in God's eyes.

Chapter Six
Friday, August 20
York County, Virginia

The music had been just right, the lights low and overall, it had been the perfect atmosphere for romance. Lenny and Janelle had made it to the hand holding stage a little over a week ago. As they left the steak house, they held hands as they walked to the car. The last few days had been abnormally hot and humid. However, during their dinner a cold front moved in, delivering a violent spat of wind and rain. It was over now, the air smelled clean and fresh and the temperature was down in the sixties.

Lenny moved to open the car door for Janelle. He deliberately moved across her, his face passing only inches from hers. When he rose back up from unlocking it, he did so again, this time stopping, locking his eyes with hers. Their lips were only an inch or so apart. He could see her tremble ever so slightly. There was desire written all over her face. Of course, she probably did not have a clue about what it was she desired and what she was feeling, but that was likely to his advantage.

Janelle could feel Lenny's hot breath for the brief moment that he had paused so close to her. For a brief instant, she feared he would kiss her. When that did not occur her relief turned into disappointment. She had never been that close before.

"A really beautiful moon tonight," said Lenny. "Let's drive the parkway before I take you back."

"The what?" asked Janelle. Vaguely she knew something about a parkway. She had heard others talk of it. It had something to do with the historic parks in Yorktown and Williamsburg. Ever since being stationed at Yorktown Naval Weapons Station, she had never ventured much beyond going to the Patrick Henry Mall in Newport News.

"It runs along the James River," said Lenny. "It's one of my favorite places lately to be alone with the Lord. I sometimes take the car and drive it to help keep my mind clear."

"Let's do it," said Janelle. It was important to encourage Lenny to strengthen his relationship with God. If he had a special place, a special thing to do that brought him closer to the Lord, then she wanted to experience it with him. Besides, she did not want their evening to end just yet. Once she was back to her room, she would lay awake the entire night thinking about what if Lenny had kissed her. It was sinful to think like that, but she knew she would.

Lenny left Newport News on Rt.143, heading towards Williamsburg until he came to Rt. 199. This he followed to an exit for the Colonial Parkway. He took the exit towards Jamestown. Even before Laura, he had brought his dates here. They generally required some extent of reassurance the first time, as most had heard of the parkway murders that had occurred years back. Somehow, he did not think that would be the case with Janelle. He did not think that she had heard of much outside of her own little world. When he came to the parking area where he had met Mr. Carlotti, he pulled in. It was empty, as it normally was at night.

"What are we doing?" asked Janelle. She felt a strange mixture of fear and excitement.

It was the first time that he had come here since Mr. Carlotti had killed Laura right in front of him. That moment was probably the closest he would actually ever come to really getting religion. He had peed his pants right on the spot. Numerous times he had tried to think of ways to get out of this. Stealing something like a Hellfire missile would pretty much put him behind bars for the rest of his life. However, as he stared at the spot where Laura had died from two rounds pumped into her, he realized that his odds were far better if he simply stole the missiles. A million bucks and a new identity awaited him if he succeeded. A place in the dirt with a bullet in his brain was the alternative. Every minute he spent masquerading as a happy born again Christian for Janelle made him want to puke. It was, however, the only way to pull this off.

"Lenny, what are we doing? Why are you so quiet?" asked Janelle. He seemed to be totally lost in his thoughts. That bothered her more than the unplanned stop.

"Just reflecting how lucky that I am," said Lenny. "I could have stayed angry after Laura left me. Continued drinking and chasing around. But I saw your Bible on your desk that day... I can't tell you how much a difference having God in my life has made. And the fact that He brought us together makes it even more wonderful."

"I feel the same way, Lenny," said Janelle. She hoped that they were going to stay in the car because her legs suddenly felt weak. She might not even be able to stand.

"I come out here sometimes and watch the fiddler crabs run along the beach in the moonlight," said Lenny.

"Oh, I don't think I've ever seen a fiddler crab," said Janelle. "What do they look like?"

"Really want to know?" asked Lenny. "Come on, I'll show you." He opened the door and stepped out. Here along the river, it was cooler and much more pleasant than it had been in town. He reached behind the seat for the jacket that he had brought.

Janelle carefully extracted herself from the car. She was excited, but also uncomfortable. Everything seemed very surreal and something deep within was telling her that this was dangerous. However, she knew that she could trust Lenny. Anyone who believed as strongly in the Lord as he did could be trusted.

"What's the jacket for?" asked Janelle. She had stepped around the car to where Lenny was. She did not hesitate to place her hand in his when he reached for it.

"Sometimes it can feel chilly down by the river," said Lenny. "I thought you might need it."

"Lenny, you're the sweetest guy," said Janelle. "I can always depend on you to look after me."

"That's because I love you, Janelle," said Lenny. "You are the most wonderful thing to ever come into my life."

Janelle felt like electricity was flowing through her body. Maybe she could vaguely remember hearing her mother say that, but she was not sure. Her mother had died when she was six, so it was hard to remember. Certainly, she never heard it from her father, and never from any other man.

"I like it when you say that, Lenny," said Janelle.

"I like to say it," said Lenny. She had turned to face him. The timing was perfect. He bent down and gave her a brief kiss on the lips. So that he did not frighten her, he made it light and quick, not allowing her any time to react.

Janelle did not move for a second. She could not believe that he had just kissed her, and on the mouth. What she felt now was difficult to describe. It was good, but certainly it was bad. Lenny's hand moved to her lower back and he was guiding her along toward the river. He had never placed his hands on her before. However, she liked his touch there, enjoyed the strength that she felt in him. Still, it scared her how it made her feel.

They walked silently along a path that led to a narrow, sandy beach of the James River. It was a bright moon and they had no difficulty in making their way. Lenny took great care not to make her overly concerned with his romantic overtures. He could read her like a book. She had never experienced love and once she got a taste of it, she would gulp it like lemonade on a hot July day.

"See them?" asked Lenny, pointing to the dozen or so fiddler crabs that scrambled away from them.

"Yuck!" said Janelle, startled. "They look like spiders. Oh, they give me the shivers." She drew up into a fetal position as much as a person standing could.

"They can't hurt you," said Lenny. He quickly put his arm around her as reassurance. "Come over here and sit down and let's watch them for a while." He gently guided her to a tree that had fallen ages ago.

"But they've all gone," said Janelle, beginning to relax. Though the cause of her anxiety had all scurried away, she made no attempt to pull away from Lenny's arms. She was feeling all kinds of things that she had never before felt.

Lenny placed the jacket over the log and guided her down onto it. They sat there for a few minutes and watched the first few fiddlers re-emerge from their burrows in the sand. She had placed her hand subconsciously on his thigh.

"They really are funny," said Janelle. She turned her face to Lenny. He returned her glance, his gaze suddenly locked onto hers. Funny how it made her think of A School, it was a class on radar detection systems how they were used to warn pilots when enemy missiles were locked onto them. This was definitely a lock on, but she was not pulling out and she was not going to eject. Nothing in her life had ever given her this level of excitement and she was not about to let go of it.

Lenny had been careful not to be too aggressive from the beginning. Now, he had intended to hold her gaze just long enough to have an effect. He did not properly anticipate what that effect would be. When Janelle rose from the tree and lightly put her lips to his, he nearly fell into the sand, it surprised him so much. It had only been a peck, a questioning one. He held her eyes, despite his astonishment. Carefully, slowly, he bent down and delivered a kiss to her lips. As the excitement of the conquest heightened, he hardened. As unattractive as he found her, there was something wild and erotic about the way he felt she was ready to give herself to him. Keeping the kiss gentle, he let it linger, waiting for her to break away. She did not, rather pressed harder towards him.

The taste of Lenny on her mouth was the most wonderful taste that she had ever experienced. Janelle hungered for more of him. She wanted to swallow his mouth into hers. There was an instant of panic as she felt him breaking away from her kiss, but it faded into oblivion as he began kissing her neck. The fire that was burning became an inferno as Lenny treated her neck with one kiss after another. Then she felt his hands upon her breasts. That was a definite no-no, but she never made a move to stop him. It was the same when she realized that he was undoing the buttons of her blouse. Enemy missiles had not only locked on, but she had been hit. She was spiraling down into the depths of a sea of passion.

Chapter Seven
Friday, September 1
Richmond, Virginia

To avoid Frank Baker, Travis took Laura McClish to the Bottoms Up restaurant in Shockoe Slip. It certainly would not do for the old fart to see him making time with what he considered his woman. Travis grinned. Laura was clearly playing Frank for all she could get, and not doing a bad job of it. He could tell, however, that she was not giving it up for the old fart. Therefore, if Frank was not getting it, then Travis might as well.

Laura was at the Corporate Center to attend one of the new employee classes. She had called him the preceding afternoon, wondering, she said, if they could meet for lunch. Obviously, she wanted to play Travis for a little extra. Well, he would let her play, but she had to pay, too.

Laura seemed to purr when he placed his hand across her back to guide her to their table. During the meal, she reached over and touched his hand or arm countless times. And always, she blazed holes straight through him with those dark, seductive eyes. She was sending all the messages that she was available to him. He was not under any illusions. Laura McClish was simply a power grubbing, gold digging little bitch that knew how to play all of the angles. However, she had a lot to offer and that certainly made it acceptable.

"So, you got class this afternoon?" Travis asked. He knew that she did not. It was a morning class only.

"No," said Fatima. "Got any place that you have to be?"

Travis felt her ankle brush against his calf. He could not deny the charge of electricity that traveled up to his groin with that touch. "Marriott's not far from here," said Travis, looking into her eyes.

Travis wondered what Laura's price tag for this afternoon would be. He did not really care. He had plenty to offer. He could arrange to boost her paycheck. On the other hand, if she was eyeing some other position, he could make that happen, too. How he wished she would ask for that. He would gladly double her paycheck to get her out of Security. Frank Baker was one hell of a dumb ass for insisting on putting her in that position. If the Nuclear Regulatory Commission made a surprise audit, heads would be rolling; likely his own among them. She was working in an area that handled sensitive security information. Frank was right, she was not going to be blowing anything up, but it was breaking all the rules. He had gone ahead and initiated a security check, but that she was already working was a major violation. The Nuclear Regulatory Commission would eventually uncover that fact during a routine audit. Hopefully, by that time, Richmond Nuclear would be someone else's headache and he would be in Mexico directing the construction of multiple nuclear generating units.

Travis paid for the room while Laura waited for him near the elevators. Once they got to the room, he shut the door and displayed the "Do Not Disturb" sign. Last thing he wanted was someone barging in to clean the room. As he loosened his tie, he watched Laura undo the buttons of her blouse. Next, she seductively let her skirt fall to the floor. He followed suit; they were both able to enjoy each other's natural assets. And assets she did have. God must have denied beauty to other women to give Laura more. Her features were long and elegant. It was evident that she worked out, obviously more than he had seen her doing at the club. She could have passed for a female bodybuilder back in the early days before they started bulking up.

Travis took a step towards her. Suddenly, she took a seat in one of the leather armchairs, crossing her legs as if she was in a meeting. Her eyes, one second filled with passion and seduction, were at once cold, harsh and penetrating in an unsettling sort of way. Travis was too stunned to speak, trying to determine if she was doing some type of role-playing. It was immediately, and disappointingly, obvious that such was not the case.

In front of Fatima was a round, glass topped table. Directly across from her was a matching black leather chair. "Sit down," she said.

Travis was a VP of Richmond Nuclear, Laura merely a clerk that worked in his department, processing guests and contractors into the station. Clearly, he was the one to be in control here. Instead, he felt exposed, vulnerable and angry. He had never been one to imagine his audience without clothes, an age-old technique taught in speech classes, meant to increase a speaker's confidence. Confidence was not something he lacked, at least not normally. However, standing naked in front of his employee, who had positioned herself authoritatively in the chair across from him, his confidence was seeping away. Laura's sudden and complete metamorphous before his eyes frightened him, and being frightened made him angry. He had brought her to screw her, but suddenly, it appeared that she had similar intentions.

"What the hell is this?" Travis demanded. He fought within to find the toehold that would bring him back into control. He attempted to overpower her by staring hard into her eyes. Instead, he found himself met by eyes like cold-rolled steel.

"Sit down, Travis," said Fatima. So easily, she had crushed his ego. It would have been well within her ability to have stood and physically forced him into the chair. To do so, however, might mean hurting him; and that was not her objective. "Please, I want to talk about Mexico. And, I want to know all about the flight attendant that Brian Matkins sees when he goes to Atlanta. You know, the one that you helped them set him up with."

Now, Travis had to sit down, else his legs would simply give way and let him collapse to the floor. "What are you talking about?" said Travis, his voice rattling with both anger and fear. This woman knew everything. She had obviously opened up Frank Baker as though he was a can of beans. That she knew everything was obvious. What if she was an undercover agent? Had he done anything that he could go to jail for? Nobody had attempted to extort Matkins' cooperation yet, so he was still clean, right?

"Don't worry," said Fatima. "I'm not a Fed. I'm sure that's what you're thinking. I'm the competition. I'm here to offer you a win-win situation. Everything Cowling is offering and more. My company is going after the property in Mexico. Here's the deal, help us, and we'll give you everything Cowling has promised you. Perhaps I can provide some fringe benefits that he can't." With that, she uncrossed her legs. "If Cowling wins, you're in, if we win you're in and in the meantime, you're in." She moved her legs to subtly expose her vagina and uncrossed her arms. It was amusing to see how Travis' eyes glued themselves to her anatomy.

"How do I know for sure this isn't a trap?" asked Travis, unable to take his eyes from between Laura's legs. Even under the circumstances, she was the most beautiful woman he had ever seen. True, Frank was a fool for spilling the plan to her, but, he mused, this woman could persuade the Pope to break his vows and hand over the keys to the Vatican.

"Well, you chose the location, so it's obviously not bugged," said Fatima. "And I think it's obvious that I'm not wearing a wire. My purse, my clothes, their on the floor beside your feet. Check them if you'd like." He raised his eyes to hers. The logic of what she said was registering.

"That's okay," said Travis. "Who do you work for?" His fingers were beginning to hurt from digging into the arms of the chair. He forced himself to try and relax. His gaze kept drifting back down to the thin line of pink that was exposed between her thighs.

"I work for a firm that has plans to take over what Energy International is doing in Mexico," said Fatima. "Unlike Energy International, we have the cash on hand."

"We've got a firm lock on the building sites," said Travis. Personally, he disliked Frank Baker enormously. However, Frank was meticulous in handling legal matters. It was not imaginable that Laura's company could buy the site out from under them, regardless of their available funds. "I think I should simply let Roger Cowling know what an idiot Frank Baker is. Where does that leave you?"

"Without your help and consequently, without any gratitude to you" said Fatima. "You've only got a lock on those sites for so long. Energy International needs to sell off Richmond Nuclear. If the buyer backs out or Matkins gets a chance to hose the sell, Energy International loses big. You're the only one involved without a financial interest. It should be very obvious to you that we don't approach takeovers with a Wall Street approach."

Travis was silent. Did they know the identity of Richmond Nuclear's buyer? Were their tactics limited strictly to what he was now witnessing? Somehow, he thought not, though he could not imagine what other means could be at her company's disposal.

"So, let's say that you had a guarantee of Senior VP, regardless of who won," said Fatima. "And a financial interest. If we're unsuccessful, you're Senior VP with Energy International. If we win, and we're going to, you're still the Senior VP, but with a large enough financial share to make it really count."

"It's an impressive offer," said Travis, the lack of enthusiasm evident in the echo of his words. He had a feeling that this was an offer with limited choices. Either you signed up to be a team player or find yourself forced into cooperation. In the same manner that he had played Brian's weaknesses, whoever Laura was working for would no doubt do the same to him. "Somehow, I think it's pretty much along the same lines as in *The Godfather*. An offer I can't refuse."

"Not an inappropriate comparison," said Fatima. Had she expected it to be this easy? Yes. Travis had set his 'best friend' up to be blackmailed for personal gain. She would not have expected anything more of him, now.

"Travis, would you be a gentleman and hand me my clothes?"

"Why…?" Travis stopped short of asking as Laura stood. Obediently he picked them up and handed them over. "I thought I was in."

"You are darling," said Fatima, taking her clothes. "But not today." She laid the clothes on the bed and picked up the hotel stationary. "Start writing. I need every detail there is about how Matkins is being set up. Names, addresses, phone numbers and I want to know how it's being executed. Finish that, then you can get dressed." She dressed as Travis began to write. It was somewhat amusing to watch him sit there naked, writing on the sheets of paper like a school child doing homework.

Lenny had pointedly convinced Janelle that they had to play it cool at work. With him being a first-class petty officer and her only a third, the Leading Petty Officer, LPO, in charge of their weapons maintenance shop, Senior Chief Petty Officer Joe Smith, would have been sure to make out the watch-bill so that they did not pull night duty together. There was another benefit as well, to keep her from clinging to him like a leech. Ever since they made love on the parkway, she had morphed from being runner up to Mother Teresa to becoming a Heidi Fleiss clone. She wanted to fuck until she was silly in the head, all the time talking about how they were already man and wife in God's eyes. It was driving him insane.

Two weeks after the night on the parkway, Lenny and Janelle had pulled a nightshift together. However, it would require more than pulling duty together to accomplish the job. There also needed to be an order for Hellfire missiles to be distributed to one of the commands designated as authorized to receive them. One did not simply waltz into missile storage and grab three of them. A complex security system consisting of electronic locks and video cameras protected all the weapons. There was no way to fool or override the system. He needed a legitimate reason for access so that the Officer in Charge, the OIC, would program the access control system to allow the night's duty personnel into the storage vault. That night, it had been maintenance on Tomahawks for delivery to one of the fast attack subs moored in Norfolk.. It was the same the next two times that he and Janelle had pulled duty together. Weeks were going by with no window of opportunity presenting itself.

As time went on, the risk grew that his superiors would grow wise to his relationship with Janelle. Some of those that they worked with were already aware. If they were split apart, it would be impossible to steal the missiles. A two-man rule was strictly enforced for weapons handling. Not only was there a complex security system to contend with, but also a requirement that two people remove and store the weapons. Lenny had to have someone's cooperation to pull this off. That someone was going to be Janelle; no other possibilities existed.

"So, Lenny when is all of this going to be accomplished?" asked Abdul. They had a conveniently isolated corner booth. Abdul had slipped the maître d' a twenty to give them some privacy. He noted that Lenny did not look nervous, but seemed frustrated. Nervous men had something to hide; frustrated men were those desperate to accomplish something. "I mean, you have your car and the apartment. I've provided what I said I'd give you."

"It's not something that I can plan like a scheduled job, Mr. Carlotti," said Lenny. He had honestly done the best he could so far. He was certain that when the opportunity arose, Janelle would play along. "There's all kinds of security surveillance and any access to something like what you want requires two men to present their access card and pass a retina scan. Even if I got real ballsy and broke in, there would be a platoon of Marines on me like flies on shit in less than three minutes. The only way I can get those missiles are to be patient and wait for a perfect opportunity. That's why I told you it would take so long."

"So," said Abdul. "Are you telling me that it might not even happen?" He asked the question rhetorically. Leaving nothing to chance, he had kept a surveillance team on Lenny whenever possible. Lenny's new romantic interests were known. He only wanted to hear it from Lenny and to reinforce the importance of succeeding.

"It will happen if we give it time," said Lenny, somewhat forcibly. "I've been working hard on this girl. Sometimes we pull duty together. I'm sure that she'll do it when the time comes. Problem is, we have to pull duty together on a night that there's an order for these things. With things the way they are in the world, that's sure to happen soon enough."

"I'm in rather desperate need of them," said Abdul. Lenny was right. America's president would soon find some of his brethren and order a hailstorm of the missiles to take out their bunkers and camps. However, Abdul had something in store for America that they would remember for a very, very long time. They would remember for fifty thousands years, according to the science books and Periodic Tables.

56

He had planned to put some pressure on Lenny, to apply some of his time-tested motivational skills. However, this was delicate business, obtaining the Hellfire missiles. If he forced Lenny's hand and he was caught, he had no other options for getting them. From Fatima's accounts, though, there was not a lot of time. Richmond Nuclear would soon be sold. Though it would still be viable target, it was much the more so while still in Roger Cowling's possession.

"However, Lenny, I understand that one sometimes must wait if one desires a fine Chianti. Do what you have to, but remember, the price of failure is not something you can afford."

Chapter Eight
Monday, September 10
Yorktown Naval Weapons Station

Lenny was processing the orders. They were electronically generated. The customer, usually a Weapons or Missile Technician or a Torpedoman, generated the order on a secure Web-site. The entire web site resided on the SIPRNET, the Secret Internet Protocol Router Network. All transmission was encrypted using secure socket layer. Access to the page, as was the case with all high security access needs, was with the user's Public Key Infrastructure digital certificate on a smart card and use of a retina scan. Once the order was submitted, it was routed to the command's weapon's officer who used the digital certificate on his or her smart card to digitally sign the order. It was then routed to the command's CO for a final digital signature.

This order was from the USS Iwo Jima, a helicopter carrier stationed nearby in Norfolk. Lenny studied it and clenched his fist. It was the perfect order, a request for 35 Hellfire missiles. Only problem, Janelle had the duty tonight, but he did not. On duty with her was WT2 Brad Hanson. Brad was Mormon and generally very methodical about planning his time with his family. It would not be easy to talk him into switching duty nights. Making it doubly hard was the fact that he seemed somewhat aware that Lenny and Janelle had something going on. He was a goody two-shoes and Lenny had to play it cool with him. This looked like another near miss.

Lenny started to acknowledge the order and forward it to Lieutenant Williams, the shop's department head. Williams would then verify the order, ensure that the inventory had the weapons requested in stock and then program the security system to allow access. Once the request was digitally signed, Lenny would print a copy of it off that would be used by the crew working the order. It was 1000 hours, if he submitted the request right now, it would likely be processed and delivered this afternoon. If he waited until 1500 hours, Williams would assign it to the duty crew to take care of after normal working hours.

He processed several orders, submitting them to the Lieutenant, printing them off and then handing them off to others to pull the weapons or firing system parts from stock and prepare them for shipment. The whole time, Lenny's mind contemplated how he might suggest to WT Hanson that they swap duty nights. Not only did he need to get Hanson to agree to the swap, but it also had to get signed off by the Senior Chief. If he simply said that he wanted to be on duty tonight, it would arouse suspicion, a lot. He needed a good reason, but that did not seem promising at the moment.

Everyone in the department was amazed by Lenny's spiritual transformation. Along with Janelle, he now attended a short Bible study during lunch on Thursdays. Brad attended with his always, unpopular Mormon point of view. Janelle's friend, WT3 Sally Fern was always there, as well. All were amazed at how Lenny had walked away from the booze straight into the loving arms of Jesus. During these discussions, Lenny only spoke when he had an opportunity to tell them how God was working in his life and he could never have imagined how sweet the love of Christ was. Lenny had always despised these people. That their habits were so irritating, gave him the familiarity he needed to act out the part, to pretend to be one of them.

It was during the Bible study that Sally brought her new CD by a Christian group, *Savior's Rock*, for them to listen to.

"They're going to be at the Amphitheater in Norfolk next month on the 24th," said Sally. "Maybe we can all go as a group."

"I'd love that," said Janelle, glancing discreetly over at Lenny.

"Lenny, come with us," said Sally. She knew that Lenny and Janelle were dating. Janelle had confided in her. Something deep inside of her, however, did not trust this rebirth that Lenny claimed to be experiencing. If exposed to enough of the Christian life, she was certain he would unravel. "Experiencing this in person will be an uplifting that you'll never forget."

It was the last damn place on Earth that Lenny wanted to be, surrounded by thousands of Christian teenyboppers and listening to this stuff. He realized, after counting up the weeks, that he had duty that evening. As a First Class Petty Officer, he was on an eight-day rotation. The concert was three full weeks plus four days and since he was on duty tomorrow night, that meant he had it then.

"You know, Lenny," said Brad. "There's a Parent Teacher Conference this evening I'd like to attend. Take my duty tonight, and I'll stand-by for you on the 24th."

The weight of Brad's offer took a moment to register. "Brad, that works for me," said Lenny. He would sit on the USS Iwo Jima's request another hour and a half and then turn it over to the Lieutenant. That way, it would for certain get on tonight's list. "I need to run back to my apartment and get a clean uniform for tomorrow and my shaving kit, then I'm all set."

Lenny walked the chit through to get the permission for swapping duty nights. The Chief did not give it a second thought. Swapping duty nights was a common practice. As the second highest enlisted in the shop, it was no problem for him to explain to the Senior Chief that he needed to run home to get a clean set of dungarees and his shave kit. The Senior Chief was happy to okay it. After all, WT1 Lenny Allen had made one hell of a dramatic turn-around. He had gone from the scumbag of the US Navy to someone that the Senior Chief was now proud to serve with.

Lenny rushed home. Once there, he immediately logged into his computer. Along with the apartment, Mr. Carlotti had provided him with the computer and furniture. Janelle had asked him why he had his computer at home password protected. Quick on his feet, Lenny had told her that it was because he did his banking on line and his internet browser was set up to save passwords. His excuse passed.

The real reason he password protected his computer was because deep into his personal documents, he had a folder. Its properties were set to "hidden" to make it even more difficult to find. Since he had to change his folder view to show all hidden folders it took a few more seconds to open it. Inside of it was one file. Quickly, he double-clicked it. The electronic weapons request forms were fillable PDF files. Lenny had obtained one by copying one of the weapons orders at the shop and then emailing the file to his home email account.

"Son-of-a-bitch!" hissed Lenny. He then slammed the palm of his hand down on the desktop with such force that it sent excruciating pain up his arm. He had not thought to print out a copy of the USS Iwo Jima's weapons request to bring with him.

"Okay, relax and just picture the form in you mind," he told himself.

The first line was easy, requesting command. He typed in USS Iwo Jima. Next was a field for the ship's hull number. He did not know it, but that was not a problem. He opened up Internet Explorer and did a search with Google for USS Iwo Jima. That was easy. He typed in LDH-2. He continued on, typing in the name of the Petty Officer, WT2 Mike Thompson, making the request, the Weapons Officer that authorized it and finally the ship's CO that had given final approval. Lenny had dealt with these individuals for the past two and one-half years. He was able to remember their names and contact numbers. He grinned. It was all no sweat. Next, he went out to a Web-site that allowed you to download a digital certificate for a free 30 day trial period. He registered three certificates, one in the requestor's name, one in the Iwo's Weapons Officer's name and the third in the Commanding Officer's name. Almost instantly, he received confirming emails with instructions on how to download the certificates and the appropriate identification number for each one. All of this took about fifteen minutes.

Using the downloaded certificates, Lenny digitally signed the appropriate fields on the request form. It would not have passed muster for generating the authentic request, but it provided the needed 'digitally signed' for the fields on the copy that he printed out. The only person that would see this was Janelle. She was dumb as a rock and would not be able to tell the difference.

After carefully double-checking his work, Lenny folded the request and placed it in his pocket. Next, he took out his cell phone and dialed a number that he had committed to memory, one that was too risky to write down.

"This is George," said the voice answering Lenny's call.

"George, if it's not too late, I'd like to still attend dinner," said Lenny.

"Never too late," said George. "See you at 7." There was a click and George was gone.

Lenny double-checked to be sure that the request was in his pocket, grabbed a clean set of dungarees and his shave kit and headed out the door.

In less than 50 minutes, Lenny was back on base and at the Aerial Weapons Maintenance Shop. Everyone had left, only Janelle, who shared the duty with him tonight, remained.

"Guess we'd better get turn'n and burn'n," said Lenny as he walked into the shop. "Thirty-eight warheads to check and load before we quit tonight. There's also some preventive maintenance that's scheduled. Thought I'd have you begin with that while I get the missiles out of storage."

"You know you can't get them out by yourself," said Janelle. "We both have to card in."

"I know," said Lenny. "We'll card in together and then I'll move the weapons into the shop while you work on the preventive maintenance."

"That's not how it's supposed to work," said Janelle, a look of concern sweeping across her face.

"If we always go by the book, then shit just doesn't get done," said Lenny. Too late, he caught himself letting the four-letter word escape.

"Lenny, why did you say that?" asked Janelle. "You've done so well for weeks. Is something the matter?"

"I'm sorry, honey," said Lenny, attempting to sooth her. "This is a really big order and I'm letting it get to me. I know I shouldn't. Maybe a little prayer time when this is finished tonight."

"It always works for me," said Janelle, feeling better at hearing that. "Thirty-eight? That's an odd number to request isn't it?"

"Not really," said Lenny. "I've seen the odd-ball numbers come in from time to time." She was asking too many questions. "Come on, help me get into the store room so we can get cranking."

"Sure, okay," said Janelle. This was violating procedures and she did not care for it at all. "I just think we should follow the rules."

"Come on, girl," said Lenny, feeling exasperated but trying not to let it show. "Someday you'll make officer and then you can tell me how to do it."

"I won't do that," said Janelle. "Officers can't marry enlisted and in God's eyes, you and me are already man and wife."

"Yes we are," said Lenny, doing his best not to choke on the thought. Once these missiles were delivered it would be time for him to disappear. He could not wait for that moment to arrive. And that moment would be real soon.

Reluctantly, Janelle swiped her card and went through the retina scan, allowing Lenny to access the storage area for the missiles. It was admirable of Lenny to be so determined to get everything done tonight, but rules in the Navy were written in blood, meaning that somewhere along the way, someone got killed because of how something was done and so a rule was made to keep it from happening again.

The missiles were stored in boxes that sat five to a palate. Using a battery-powered forklift, he would move a palate at a time through the big double doors that he and Janelle had just unlocked. Each metal box would then be opened and the missile inspected to ensure its reliability if and when it should ever need to be fired. Now a days, that seemed to be a "when" question rather than an "if."

An armored vehicle similar to those used by Wells Fargo for transporting money was used for such deliveries. Two men in the front, three in the back were always heavily armed. Unmarked escort vehicles both proceeded and followed the shipment. The vehicle was also rigged with a switch both in the front and in the back that would allow any one of its crew to disable the fuel pump. Though anything was possible, stealing a missile by ambushing the convoy would be a desperate act.

A Chevrolet van sat beside the transport vehicle. It was typical Navy, plain white except for the black stenciling on the back and front doors identifying it. It was used to transport people and parts. The transport vehicle completely overshadowed it. He would be able to place his first palate of missiles right in back of it out of sight of the camera. That first palate, coincidently, held only three Hellfire missiles.

Someone from the shop typically made a parts run each day to the nearby bases. Lenny had always been an eager volunteer to do this. When he volunteered to make the run tomorrow, no suspicions would be aroused. As of tonight, there was only one such request. From the computer, Lenny kept an eye on Janelle in the back room doing preventive maintenance on the high-pressure hydraulic system. Hopefully she would not blow the damn thing up while he was in the middle of all this. She had a reputation of being quite fickle when it came to working on anything with more than one moving part.

Quickly, he reviewed the request for EP-2 grease and silicon lubricant to be taken to the Missile Technician's school at Damneck Naval Base. Then he added three AGM-114B/K/M Hellfire Missile Engines, No Fuel. It was not a frequent, but nor an uncommon request from the school. It would also account for the three containers that would be in the van if anyone should ask. Since no warhead was involved, it did not require the same level of authorization that the live missiles did.

He had several palates moved out of the storage area and into the shop by the time Janelle finished her work on the hydraulic system. The first palate near the back of the van held the three missiles that he would ultimately load into it. She began the job of checking the missiles internal circuitry and verifying that each missile had fuel and a live warhead that was in the safe position. It was standard, though tedious work.

It was nearly 0200 when they completed the task. They would not load the missiles on the transport vehicle. That would wait until they had more manpower in the morning.

"Let's signoff the paperwork and wrap this up," said Lenny. He went to the desk where he had placed the fictitious order that he had created in his apartment. "Here, sign it." He handed her the form. To his chagrin, she started reviewing it, top to bottom. Oh well, that was no problem. He had done a first rate job and she would never tell the difference. In fact, watching her scrutinize it amused him.

"There's something fishy here," said Janelle. "Or else someone's just plain stupid." She handed the form back to Lenny. "The Iwo's hull number is LDH-7. This has it as LDH-2."

Lenny took the form from her and did his best to maintain his composure. "No, I'm sure it's LDH-2," he said.

"I know it's not," said Janelle. "It was my first duty station before I came here. LDH-2 is the hull number for the first USS Iwo Jima that was decommissioned. How could that get past both the Weapons Officer and the CO of the ship?"

Lenny tried his best to keep his voice steady and his hands from shaking. "I'm sure the requestor just screwed up. A 2 and a 7, if you're in a hurry probably doesn't get noticed."

"Maybe, but we need to report it to LT Williams," said Janelle. "You never, know, maybe there are terrorists who have somehow gotten into the system, generated the request and plan to hijack the shipment."

"Darn," said Lenny. "You could start writing Tom Clancy novels! But I'll show this to LT Williams tomorrow morning before the shipment leaves. We can call the Iwo and verify the request. Cool with that?" His anger was growing by the second, both at her for suddenly showing a smattering of intelligence and at himself for such an idiotic foul-up.

"Sure," said Janelle. "That's cool. Just let me know what happens. Next time I see Thompson I'm going to ask him what he's smoking."

"Must be the good stuff," said Lenny, forcing a laugh. "Hey, you look beat. Get out of here. I'm going to put this in the computer and close up the storage area, then I'm heading to the barracks."

"I can close up the storage area while you do the admin on this," said Janelle.

"I've still got to put the forklift back," said Lenny. He had left it out, knowing that even though she was qualified to operate it, she was scared to death to do so.

"In that case, I'm out of here," said Janelle. "Good night."

"Good night," said Lenny. He watched as she went out the door. Quickly, he finished with the information that needed to be entered into the computer. Next, he took out the real copy of the request. For weeks he had practiced

Janelle's signature. He glanced at it on the fake copy and then with great care, signed the real one for her. Next to his desk was a shredder. "DON'T FORGET – SHRED ALL DOCUMENTS!" said the sign above it. Lenny ran the fake copy through it.

There was one last thing to do. Lenny moved the forklift back into the storage area. Instead of parking, however, he went to the cage holding the non-fuel missile engines. He loaded three containers onto the forklift and moved them into the cage containing the actual missiles. There he removed their contents. Once he did that, he then used the forklift to take the empty containers back into the shop.

He placed the palate on top of the three live missiles. Anyone studying the security video would likely become curious about all of the maneuvering around, but the only reason that they would do so was if there was some concern that things were amiss or if there was an accident. Lenny was confident that Janelle would let him handle the screw-up on the Iwo's hull number. However, what if she spoke to WT2 Thompson about it?

Lenny got off the forklift and loaded the empty containers onto the van. He was now out of sight of the security camera. He next opened all three containers that held the live missiles. These, one by one, he loaded into the van and placed into the containers meant for the non-fueled engines. Each missile weighed approximately one hundred pounds. It was not the easiest thing to do, but he broke only a small sweat with it. Now, there was one last thing to do that could hang him if he did not perform it perfectly. He climbed onto the forklift and adjusted the forks until they were the approximate width of the missile containers. Climbing back off, he carefully balanced the containers on the forks so that they protruded to the front instead of the side.

The other missile palates blocked the camera's view as he backed away from the van. As he passed them, he slowly made a sharp turn to minimize any exposure the camera would have of the missile boxes. By having them protrude to the front, at least they were not obviously sticking out on both sides as he passed through the double doors into the storage area. It was tricky. If not real careful, he could spill them onto the floor during the turn.

He made the turn with no problem. After twelve years of handling weapons, he was able to maneuver the forklift with an expert touch. Back in the storage area, he placed the non-fueled engines into the containers and placed them with the actual missiles far in the back where they would be the last ones pulled out.

Once a week, the missiles were inventoried, but it did not involve opening each container. Eventually, however, the swap would be discovered. Tapes would be reviewed, paperwork would be examined and the trail would point to Lenny. By that time, however, he would be out of here. Mr. Carlotti had a plan for faking his death in a fiery crash of the corvette. It was a sad waste of a good car, but there would be plenty of money to replace it and a new identity to use while driving it around. It was also a way out that would not arouse suspicion.

Lenny parked the forklift in its appropriate spot. He took his time checking everything he had done. It was a job well done, a Bravo Zullo for WT1, soon to be a millionaire, Lenny Allen. Once he was confident that everything was in order, he locked up.

❧ ❧ ❧

The next morning, after quarters, Lenny supervised the loading of the missiles onto the transport vehicle. Part of Lenny's job was to help the senior chief to make assignments for the day. He suggested Brad Hanson and one other to the transport vehicle. The remaining three individuals would be Marines. The senior chief had already requested a detachment for the detail yesterday.

"Any suggestions for the run to Damneck?" asked the senior chief.

"I'll take it," said Lenny, without appearing too eager. "Just some grease and dummy missile tubes."

"Go for it," said the senior chief.

"I'll go ahead and get it out of here now," said Lenny. Out of the corner of his eye, he saw Janelle approaching. "Catch you later, Senior." With keys in hand, he headed towards the van. Janelle had cast him glance after questioning glance as they had loaded the missiles onto the transport unit.

"Lenny, did you talk to the Lieutenant about the discrepancy on the missile order?" asked Janelle.

"Senior Chief and I called WT2 Thompson on the Iwo before quarters," said Lenny. Janelle and the senior chief had never hit it off well and he knew she would be hesitant to mention anything to him. At least that was what he hoped. "Everything's on the up-and-up. He was pretty damned impressed with you catching that."

"Still, when I see Thompson at church Wednesday night, I'm going to ask him what the heck he's been smoking," said Janelle.

"I hear you, " said Lenny. He had totally forgotten about the Hampton

Roads Naval Chapel Fall Dinner that was taking place Wednesday evening. Thompson was a Bible thumper, too. He would have to let Mr. Carlotti know about the situation. It had the makings of a major disaster.

Lenny made his way past the gate leaving the weapons station and leading to Rt. 143. He showed the authorization and shipping manifest for the items he was carrying. The guard waved him on. Rt. 143 gave him access to I-64 and from there he headed east.

Considering the enormous complexities involved, stealing the missiles had gone very well. The only fly in the ointment had been his screw-up with the Iwo's hull number. Mr. Carlotti had cautioned him from the beginning not to underrate any of his peers. He would need to reassure Mr. Carlotti that he would never do so again in hopes of doing future work for the Mafia boss.

He exited off I-64 onto I-264, which took him towards Virginia Beach. He then took the Birdneck Road exit. Birdneck Road was windy and ran through a rural area until it connected to General Booth Boulevard. Before he reached General Booth, however, he made a turn past a Christian school that took him into a wooded area. Here he found the address that Mr. Carlotti had made him commit to memory.

No sooner had Lenny pulled into the driveway than the garage door began to open. Inside was someone that Lenny had never seen, frantically waving him inside. Beside him was Mr. Carlotti. Without hesitation, Lenny drove straight into the garage. Mr. Carlotti's was an impressive operator. One of the SEAL teams from Damneck would likely not fare well against him.

"Hello, Lenny," said Mr. Carlotti. He ran his finger across his throat, a gesture to Lenny to kill the engine. "Giuseppe, unload the gifts that this fine man has brought us. Come inside, Lenny, let's talk. I think in the military they call it a debrief."

Lenny followed Mr. Carlotti up the steps and into the kitchen. From there, they proceeded into the living room. A tray with a carafe and two small cups sat on a coffee table. That explained the strong aroma he smelled in the kitchen.

"Please, have some coffee," said Mr. Carlotti. "The cups are small, but it's Turkish coffee. Very, very strong."

"Sure," said Lenny. "Thanks." He had guessed that it was espresso. This was the first time he would try Turkish coffee.

"Any complications?" asked Abdul, his steady had pouring the thick, dark liquid. He studied Lenny intently for any sign that he was attempting to hide something. He could see some hesitation in his eyes.

Lenny did not want to admit that he had screwed up. However, Janelle was a big problem. Somehow, he was sure that not owning up to the problem would have very severe consequences.

"Yeah, a small one," said Lenny. He picked up the cup and sipped it. It was obvious why the cups were so small. A regular cup of this gritty fluid would have anyone bouncing off walls.

"In this business, small complications can cost men their lives," said Abdul. He listened as Lenny explained the problem with Janelle seeing the incorrect hull number on the fake request.

"Lenny," said Abdul, once Lenny had finished explaining what had happened with the hull numbers, "you may not realize this, so let me tell it to you. By being straight with me on this, you've shown me that you have honor. Though the Mafia is a family of criminals, we have honor. You have honor. Lenny, I want you to consider joining my family. You will be an extremely valuable asset to me."

"I'm honored to do that," said Lenny, feeling the adrenalin rushing through his veins.

"Now, here's what I want you to do about Janelle…"

Lenny sat in his car until he saw Janelle pull into the parking lot. They had agreed to meet next to Cheddars at the mall. It was already dark, so there was little chance that anyone would see or remember them.

"Hungry?" asked Lenny. Janelle was climbing into the passenger seat of his Corvette.

"Starving," said Janelle. "Where we going?"

"Really good Chinese place in Williamsburg," said Lenny. "I used to eat there a lot…"

"With her?" demanded Janelle.

"No, she didn't like Chinese at all," said Lenny. Janelle's confidence level was certainly growing. At first she never challenged him over anything. However, she had been quick to challenge him last night about procedure, about the hull number, and now about Laura. This was getting tiresome, but not for much longer.

"Sorry," said Janelle. "I think I'm tired. Maybe going out tonight was a bad idea." Though she was indeed tired, Lenny's behavior last night bothered her. She had felt like he was manipulating her. It was something they would discuss later.

They drove the twenty minutes to Williamsburg in Lenny's car and pulled in front of the Peking Restaurant off By-Pass Road. Tonight they were able to get in easily since it was the off-season for tourists. The Peking often drew long lines then.

"I don't know where to begin," said Janelle. There was an enormous buffet, plus a Mongolian Barbecue and a Sushi bar.

"Just dig in," said Lenny. He scooted from the table and headed for the Mongolian Barbecue.

Janelle followed suit. She had never heard of Mongolian Barbecue, let alone ever tried it. As they sat down to eat, Janelle tried to get the conversation rolling about last night. It seemed however, to stall at every point.

"Is something wrong?" asked Janelle. Maybe things were getting ready to fall apart between them. Upon recalling Lenny's slip of the tongue last night and how frustrated he had seemed, it was that he was either getting tired of her or perhaps having a spiritual crisis. Or maybe he was hiding something. Last night's activities bothered her tremendously. What had Lenny really done after she left him to lock up? WT2 Thompson was a good friend. Tomorrow night, at the Fall Feast, she would get him aside to make sure that everything was on the up and up. Thirty-eight missiles was an odd order. She was surprised that the Lieutenant had not questioned it. There was also the hull number mistake.

"No," said Lenny. "Maybe a bit tired from duty last night." Mr. Carlotti's instructions made it difficult for Lenny to really swallow his dinner. He remembered the horror of watching him kill Laura as she stood right next to him.

"I'm scared that you're getting tired of me," said Janelle, hoping to hear him say that was not the case.

"No, no," said Lenny. "To be honest, I've really slacked off on prayer time and reading scripture. I guess it's kind of like exercise, if you don't do it, spiritual flabbiness is the result."

Janelle laughed at that. It made sense that the source of Lenny's strange behavior was a spiritual crisis. That could be mended. If he dumped her, she doubted that her heart could be. As she thought about her concerns from last night, she realized that she was making a mountain out of a molehill. She was letting her insecurities affect her ability to see things clearly.

On the way out to the car, Lenny said, "Let's go down the Parkway, I want to talk."

"Okay," said Janelle. She glanced up at the sky. Though the evening was chilly, there were a lot of stars out and a brilliant half-moon. The haze that made them difficult to see during the summer was now gone. A twinge of desire shot through her. This was what she needed.

They said hardly anything as Lenny guided the Corvette down the parkway. He slowed as he came to their normal spot. Once he parked, Janelle gave his hand a quick squeeze and then eagerly exited the car. It was almost cold, but she was certain that it was going to get warmer, much warmer.

"Let's wander down to the beach," said Lenny. "Here, put this on." He handed her his wool peacoat from behind the seat. Fortunately, it was too dark for her to see his shaking hands as he gave it to her.

"I can think of better ways to beat the chill," said Janelle, smiling.

"And I can think of better uses for the coat than having you wear it," said Lenny, grateful that she played along so easily. He would be very glad to get this over with. He took one final glance at his car. It was the last time he would see it.

Janelle slipped the coat around her shoulders. When Lenny offered to take her hand, she accepted. Being with him felt so wonderful. If she lost him, she would not be able to survive. Together, they walked down the path towards the river. As they reached the sandy banks, Fiddler crabs scattered in all directions.

Lenny looked in all directions. Mr. Carlotti said he was going to use a hit woman for this, someone who could get in close without Janelle being scared.

"Lenny, what's wrong?" asked Janelle. "You seem so tense."

"I don't want to continue sneaking around," said Lenny. "I want to come out in the open about us. I want you to marry me."

"Oh, Lenny," said Janelle. "This is the happiest moment I've ever had." She began crying, gripping Lenny's hand and pulling as close to him as she could.

Fatima's feet hurt. She was wearing a pair of men's shoes that Ali had purchased. They were a size too small. The tracks that they left in the sand would, however, serve to throw off the forensics team. She saw Lenny and the girl come down to the beach. They were sitting on a fallen tree. Standing in the shadow of a tree in the darkness, it was not possible for them to see her.

Once they were situated, she started walking towards them.

Lenny saw the woman approach. His heart beat so fast that he was suddenly concerned he might simply have a heart attack and never enjoy the spoils of his hard efforts.

"Have a light?" he heard her ask. It was the question he expected, but not the voice. On cue, he dove his hand into his pocket for his lighter.

"Lenny, don't!" hissed Janelle. She felt creepy having this woman coming up to them in the darkness like this. Plus, why was Lenny carrying a cigarette lighter? He had quit smoking.

"Hello, Lenny," said Fatima. She watched them both jump as she spoke his name.

"What the hell!" yelled Lenny. "You're dead. You're fucking dead!"

The moon showed her unmistakable features clearly enough as she leaned down for the light, a cigarette in her left hand, held up to her mouth. There was no mistake. It was Laura. Then this was a set up. He attempted to pull his hand free of his pocket to defend himself, but it was too late.

Fatima smiled as she let the cigarette drop so that she could grab Lenny behind the neck. With her right hand she plunged the knife into the left side of Lenny's chest. She held it sideways so that it slid unimpeded between the ribs and through his heart. be. He sunk down and fell backwards from the fallen tree. She held the knife firmly, letting his weight do the work of freeing it from his torso.

The woman had murdered her Lenny with lightning speed. Janelle jumped up. Her scream was lodged in her throat. No matter how hard she tried to let it out, it just stuck there. She was powerless to resist as the woman grabbed her and she felt the unbelievable agony of the knife entering her just to the left of her navel. Her attempt to scream became an anguished moan as the woman rotated and twisted the knife inside of her. Sinking to her knees in the sand, she felt the knife jerked free of her abdomen. Glancing up she saw the woman poise to plunge it into her again.

It was unlikely that the girl would be able to survive the first grievous wound that Fatima had inflicted upon her. However, it was foolish to take any chances. She shoved the knife into her stomach and twisted it towards the liver. Jerking the knife down, she open her up in a way that allowed her intestines to spill out. The fiddler crabs would have a feast tonight.

Fatima looked down at the girl. This double murder would not have any resemblance to a premeditated hit. It would look like the work of a crazed, woman-hating psychopath. No one would tie this to the fact that these two worked in a sensitive weapons facility for the Navy. It would instead simply be the revival of the legend of the Parkway murders.

Chapter Nine
Tuesday, December 1
Energy International Corporate Center
Richmond, Virginia

"Yes," said Roger Cowling, speaking at the telephone on his desk.

"Sir," said Edna, his private secretary. "Mr. Harding is on the phone. I told him that you had someone in your office, but he insisted on letting you know that he needed to talk to you as soon as possible. I know you don't like being disturbed when you're meeting with Mr. Orton."

"Is he still on the line?" asked Roger, glancing at Bud Orton, sitting across from him.

"No, sir," said Edna. "I told him that you'd have to call him back."

"Please, ring him back right now," said Roger. "It pertains to what I'm discussing with Mr. Orton." He clicked off the phone. "Showtime?" he asked Bud.

Less than two minutes passed before Travis Harding's voice was coming across the loud speaker of Roger's phone. "Good morning, Travis," said Roger. "I've got Bud Orton here in the office with me. What's going on?"

"Matkins is making his trip tomorrow," said Travis. He was thankful that he was doing this over the phone and not in front of Orton. Orton was one scary son-of-a-bitch. He was not sure he could pull this off with the former mercenary staring straight into his eyes like he had done the other two times they had met. It was like he was looking right into your mind when you spoke to him. Spooky, very spooky.

"This is a bit short notice," said Roger, glancing at Bud to see if he displayed concern. He did not.

"They had a cancellation of another meeting and contacted him this morning since he said his business was urgent," said Travis. "I've been helping him get the facts and figures that he needs to show the Nuclear Regulatory Commission how our budget cuts affect Security at Jefferson

Davis. I think the Operations Department has given him some stuff that can help his case, too."

"Well, in a few months we might all get our hands slapped by the NRC," said Roger. "The state of California will probably want to sue us for what it costs to bring things back up to par. But the fact of the matter is, when we bring those new units on line in Mexico, we'll walk all over the competition. We won't feel any pain."

"I hear you loud and clear," said Travis. "By the time the NRC validates his concerns, we really won't need to be concerned."

"I believe our friend Bud, here, has everything in place," said Roger. Orton gave a slight nod. Matkins was an irritating nuisance, one that he did not need at the moment. Unlike the cost cutting at Richmond Nuclear that could result in a fine, with Matkins they were committing blackmail, something that could mean jail if things took a turn for the worse. This, however, would not be the first time for such risk. He could feel the adrenalin moving through his veins as he contemplated what they were about to do. There was nothing like a dose of larceny to keep a man feeling young.

"There's a new element that concerns me," said Travis. This had to sound convincing and was the part that made him very glad that this was not face to face. "Matkins has been talking the last several days about telling his wife that he wants to separate. He's the type to get noble. I think we need to dice things up a bit as a precaution," said Travis.

"Fuck," said Bud Orton. "It's too damn late to change the game plan. Matkins is a family man. Would he put his kids through the embarrassment?"

"This day and age, getting caught having an affair doesn't exactly have the impact that it did. His daughters aren't that old and he might not think that the impact would be that much. But I was thinking, what if we got him doing something really over the edge with this Madison woman. I mean more than just a cigar trick. Something that he'd be certain not to want his daughters to know about. Let's make it kinky beyond what he's able to deal with publicly. Can we get her to cooperate?"

"Damn it, Harding," Roger yelled into the phone. "Why the hell wait until the eleventh damn hour to let us know this?"

"Mr. Cowling, I understand how this impacts the situation," said Travis. He felt a warm glow. Cowling's anger was evidence they were buying it. "But, this isn't the kind of thing that Matkins just sat down and discussed with me. It's been tidbits over the past few days. Only today did I realize that this was an 'oh shitter'. He was making arrangements to meet Madison and said that he was tired of doing it behind his wife's back."

"Kinky?" asked Roger. "What kind of kinky?" Orton looked real concerned. If he was concerned, then Cowling knew he needed to be, as well. Harding's approach made sense.

"Something sadistic. Have the woman convince him to take her at knife point," said Travis. "Brian would do it. He used to do some really wild shit back when we were at Tech together. Make sure she knows to really play it up, all the way. Make him look like one hell of a deviate. Something that would really threaten both his career and his chances in a custody battle over his kids if it got out."

"Bud, what do you think?" asked Roger, looking across the desk at the six foot four, 220 pound retired mercenary. Bud Orton was a scary man. He even gave Roger the shivers. But he was real handy when it came to dealing with some special problems that crept up from time to time.

"I like it," said Bud, smiling. His German accent filled the room. "Mr. Harding, quite good. I believe that I can find a toy that will introduce quite a thrill into their evening together. I'd even go so far as to suggest that when this is all done, we meet here for movie and popcorn. But then, I know how picky you are, Roger, about your rug. No popcorn on the rug, right?" The German's hearty laugh filled the office. "I think we should offer her a bit more financial incentive for this."

"Maybe we could pay her a little extra to castrate the son of a bitch," said Roger, failing to see the humor in Bud Orton's joke. He knew the story behind the rug. But it had been many years ago since Bud had sought out information on Abdul Hazdiz for him. Nothing had ever turned up. Perhaps he had been killed in the war with Iraq, or had been taken out and shot in the head by the revolutionary council. Still, he treated the rug as though it was something borrowed, not something he owned. He never stopped loving and admiring it, and he also never stopped wishing he had never laid eyes on it.

"Afraid she wouldn't be up to anything quite that intense," said Bud. "But blackmail isn't the only solution, here. Atlanta has a high crime rate. Maybe he could get killed in an armed robbery."

"No," said Cowling after a moment's pause. "There have to be limits. We've discussed this before, Bud. Don't bring it up again."

"Fine," said Bud. "So you want to add the knife, correct?"

Travis was stunned at how casually Orton had suggested killing Brian. He had suggested murder in more or less the same way a doctor might suggest an antibiotic for a patient's infection. Would Cowling's limits apply if Travis was successful in helping the other side procure the property in Mexico? What Laura had described as a win-win situation for him seemed much more like a lose-lose.

"Yeah, a nice touch," said Roger, thoughtfully. "Alright, Travis. Keep me informed if you find out anything else." Roger clicked off the speaker phone.

Chapter Ten
Wednesday, December 2
Atlanta, Georgia

Tanya Madison pushed her jet black RX-7 to twice the twenty-five mile per hour posted speed limit. She was entering Hartsfield International's sprawling array of terminals and parking areas. Repeatedly, she glanced in her rearview mirror. She was running late and could not afford getting pulled over. That, however, was trivial to what really bothered her. Each time she glanced up, it was with the fear that she would see that one, single headlight in her rearview mirror of the rat-faced kid with the Harley-Davidson motorcycle.

His visit to her apartment earlier flashed across her mind, despite her best efforts to forget about it. Without a sound, rat-face had entered through her locked and chained door. He had simply appeared in her make-up mirror, standing behind her as she prepared to meet Brian. *"They sent me,"* he had told her. He set up the hidden camera in her bedroom. All the time he was there, he looked and leered at her. She had felt naked and afraid under his gaze. To hell with what he might steal, she decided to just leave.

Tanya decided to forego the free parking to which she was entitled as an airline employee. By the time she parked and caught the shuttle to the terminal, she would be a good twenty minutes late. She chose to pay, instead. At the entrance to short term parking, she hastily jabbed her finger at the button on the ticket dispenser. There was a silent, sickening sensation of her red lacquered fingernail breaking.

"Shit," she said to no one, angrily tossing her ticket into the cup holder. When the hell would the Valium start working? She had taken it as she was leaving the apartment. It should have already started taking effect. She wished that she had taken two. By the time this was all over with, she might wish that she had taken the whole damn bottle. As much as she hated being frightened, she also hated what she was about to do to Brian.

Tanya sped between the rows of cars closest to the terminal. She came within inches of smashing her RX-7 into the front of a green Ford Ranger as she raced him to a spot that someone was pulling out of. He had not budged and there was no time or energy for a confrontation, so she backed up and kept looking. Finally, she ended up parking at the far end of the lot. Emerging from the warm interior of her car, she shivered violently in the chilly, December night air. Vaguely, Tanya remembered something about a cold front moving through the Atlanta area. Well, it was certainly here and she was dressed like it was July.

Long flowing strands of blonde hair dropped down to below the middle of her back. In the glow of the halogen lamps, lighting the parking lot, her hair highlighted the short, bright green dress she wore. It clung tight against her curvaceous hips, molding around her narrow waist. It was not, however, doing a damn thing to keep her warm. Her well-muscled thighs, nude of hose or stocking, carried her quickly towards the terminal.

Tanya glanced nervously from one parked car to another. Was there someone here, in the far corner of this parking lot, watching her every move? But there really was no reason for them to be, was there? The paranoia was impossible to shake off, however, no matter how logically she viewed her situation. All she had to do was what Mr. Orton had told her. Tonight it would be over and she would have the money she needed to leave the crappy, uncertain job she had as a flight attendant. She would leave, change her name and use the money to enroll in an acting school in Hollywood and start searching for small parts until she was ready for better roles. Already, she had contacted several schools and was waiting to see which ones accepted her.

Tanya hastened her pace towards the terminal's closest entrance. She was beginning to shiver painfully hard from the combination of cold and anxiety. The entrance to the terminal would be her refuge from the dark cold of the parking lot. The closer she got, the more rapid the clop-clop-clop of her heels became. There were only several more long strides to go. Despite her cold and her shivers, beads of sweat stood out above her brow, sending an icy chill directly into her skull. The skin across her forehead felt stretched tight as a drum. Her head ached miserably.

U.S. Global Airways Flight 797 touched down at Atlanta at precisely 7:47 PM. Brian Matkins immediately crowded into the plane's narrow aisle. Normally, he stayed seated until the first wave of passengers to scramble from their seats, had finished pulling their bags and coats from the overhead compartments. This evening, he was in a hurry. More like a heated rush, he mused to himself. He had wanted an earlier flight, but today was his daughter Stephanie's 10th birthday. Try as he had, he had not been able to persuade her to either celebrate a day early or wait until the weekend. He had even made her lucrative offers. Reserve the roller rink, rent horses at the Up-Up And Away Dude Ranch. Name what you want, he had told her. But it had been no deal. She wanted her birthday on her birthday. So it was birthday party first, flight last.

It had been cheap and selfish to attempt to bribe his daughter into delaying her birthday. He had no remorse, however, about what he had going on with Tanya. His wife, Abby, had contributed much over the years to the chasm of issues that fragmented their marriage. But he should not have let his plans with Tanya interfere with his responsibility to his daughters.

Brian's carry-on consisted of his briefcase and an overnight bag. In his briefcase were all of the document submissions to the Nuclear Regulatory Commission. These would show that the cutbacks at Jefferson Davis Nuclear Power Station were a threat to nuclear safety. He had stayed awake the last two nights compiling this data. It would have been impossible to get it all done, however, had it not been for Travis' help; especially the security related information. Travis was putting his career on the line to help Brian in his fight against Cowling and the board. It was good to have someone he could trust and confide in.

Brian's exit from the plane, and those behind him, was brought to a complete halt by a couple of women directly in front of him. They were taking an eternity to get their bags from the overhead and get moving. There was no room to squeeze around them. One was having difficulty with an oversized bag that he had watched her literally jam into the overhead when they boarded and was now hopelessly stuck there. They seemed oblivious that they had the aisle completely blocked.

"Here, please. Allow me," said Brian, forced to fight back his impatience. He sat his baggage down and wrestled the woman's bag until he had it free. In his effort, he maneuvered himself in front of the two women. Once he handed the bag over to her, he leaned across the seat, grabbed his bags and headed for the plane's exit.

Nearing the plane's exit, he heard sharp protests from the two women that he had just assisted. Glancing back, he saw them giving the what for to a young woman, probably a college student. She had rudely shoved her way past them. Brian did not slow. The flight had landed twelve minutes late. He was headed for the gate.

"Brian!" The shrill voice ranged a couple of octaves above the rest of the anxious friends, relatives and lovers who waited patiently and impatiently for the disembarking passengers.

"Tanya," said Brian catching her in an embrace as she jumped into his arms. He smelled the herbal shampoo in her flowing blonde hair and the cologne she wore. The moist stickiness of her lipstick made him discretely reach for his handkerchief.

There was something, however, a bit stiff in her manner. He wondered if having to catch the later flight had upset her. If so, they would have to talk about the reality of their relationship. He was willing to leave Abby, and would eventually do so whether Tanya was in the picture or not. However, as for being a father to his daughters, there could and would be no compromises.

"The flight was late," said Brian as he guided her towards the baggage area.

"Don't worry about it," she said, feeling the tightness in her voice.

"I hate keeping you waiting even for a second. But it's my daughter's birthday, today. I should never have planned the earlier flight. Sorry," said Brian.

"As for your flight being late, to tell you the truth," she bumped up close to him, forcing her schoolgirl like giggle that would normally have been spontaneous. "I just pulled into the parking lot maybe seven minutes ago. I practically ran to the terminal. If your flight hadn't been late you'd have been waiting for me. And as far as catching a later flight for your daughter's birthday… I'd be disappointed in you if you hadn't."

"You even broke a sweat," teased Brian, observing the droplets running across her brow. He had wondered over the last few weeks how Tanya felt about him already having children. It was one of those serious discussions they would need to have. Her reaction now was reassuring.

With his hand riding along the comfortable slope of her buttocks, they headed out of the airport. He enjoyed the firm feel of her buttocks. Tanya worked hard to take care of herself, much like he did. Abby, on the other hand, had simply accepted her middle age spread without any attempt to battle it. That was only one of many disappointing aspects of his marriage.

As they made their way out of the airport, Brian remained very aware that something was not quite right. Tanya's normally fluid gait seemed stiff, her attention somehow distracted from him. He had a wife and kids. She was tired of sharing him. Perhaps she had not meant what she said about understanding that this was his daughter's birthday. Would this be their last time together? It just had that feeling. "What kept you?" he asked.

"Hey, takes time to prepare a worthy main course," she said it with a laugh that she hoped did not sound as hollow as it was. She was thinking of how rat-face had arrived late. He had brought the miniature camera and meticulously set it up in a spider plant that he had also brought along. Then there had been his instructions, spoken as though to a three year old. If she had not been so frightened of him, she would certainly have lost her cool.

To divert Brian's attention, afraid her lie was written across her face, she playfully squeezed at his love handles through his wool jacket. There wasn't really anything to get hold of. Like her, Brian was fanatic about keeping fit.

"We talking food, or something much more interesting?" he asked, pressing against the solid muscle upon which he rested his hand. Brian, now an athletic 52, found himself captivated by her youthful exuberance and the carefree manner in which she gave herself to him when they made love. The thought that this might be coming to an end, hurt. He wanted this to last forever. Maybe it was time to make some decisions about his life.

They had met six months earlier on one of his trips to Atlanta. Tanya was a flight attendant for U.S. Global Airways. It was not on the flight, however, that they had met. He was sitting in one of the airport coffee shops, also doubling as a bookstore. The place was packed. She had purchased a book, a cup of coffee and a sweet roll. Along with that, she was carrying a jacket and an overnight bag. After stumbling and dousing his jacket sleeve with hot coffee, he jokingly told her that her sentence would be sit with him so as not to endanger the rest of the shop's patrons. She had. Then she happened to be working his flight back to Richmond. And she happened to spill a coke in his lap. For that, he had told her, it was capital punishment, meaning that she now had to hand over her phone number. She had.

Dinner was at a narrow fronted Italian restaurant that, from the outside, looked to be one of Atlanta's poorer choices for fine, romantic dining. However, the lighting was low and the bent over Italian widow who owned it made her own sauces. Getting in required reservations. It was located just off of Peachtree. Tanya had suggested it their first night out.

"So, you sounded real secretive about your trip here," said Tanya, considering her own unpleasant, secret agenda. Her head was pounding. She had swallowed three, extra-strength Tylenol while in the ladies' room. They had not served to cut the edge off of her headache in the least. "Is everything all right?"

"You're as perceptive as you are beautiful. Do you know that?" said Brian. He had told no one about the nature of his trip to Atlanta except Travis. There was absolutely no one else that he dared trust. Even the NRC officials that he would be meeting with tomorrow had only a vague idea of his agenda.

"Just don't want you to be in any trouble or anything," said Tanya. This was what she had been dreading ever since she took the cold, hard cash that Bud Orton had handed over to her. He had paid half before, and the rest of the money would come after she provided what he needed. She had no idea why she was being used to destroy Brian. It was eating at her. She needed to know.

"Not in trouble, yet," said Brian. "Actually, what I'm doing is making trouble. Making trouble for a very greedy CEO and some of his cronies. But I'm sure I'll be in plenty of trouble after I've finished explaining to the NRC what's been going on at Richmond Nuclear. I don't really expect to keep this job much longer."

"Brian, don't say that," said Tanya, gasping. "What's going to happen to us if you end up... well, you know, if you end up getting fired? You wouldn't have any reason for coming to Atlanta. This is awful!" Her head pounded with increased intensity. This was the last time they would be together, regardless. She was helping to blackmail a man whom she really loved. When Brian found out, he would hate her more than any other person on the face of the earth. That was a very painful thought. Still, she knew that she would go through with it. And what if she was successful in Hollywood? Brian would recognize her and it would become one of those stories on *Entertainment Tonight*. But no, he would not expose himself. He would simply find a way to confront her. The whole damn thing was too complicated. Likely, she would become nothing more than a small part actress and would never be noticed and end of story.

"Yeah," said Brian. "I've thought about that. Before I go back I want to talk about us, and what we see the future holding. I don't want this to be all that we have. But let's make that for tomorrow night. I need to have my mind clear for the morning's meeting."

"I agree," said Tanya. "Let's enjoy the night. We can talk tomorrow. Tell me what's going on... I mean if you can, if you want."

"A very tense situation's developing between Richmond Nuclear and our parent company, Energy International," said Brian. "I'm not making myself a popular person with our CEO and he's a son of a bitch about extracting vengeance and getting what the hell he wants."

"Oh God, Brian. This is… how horrible." She heard her own words echoing meaninglessly between the two of them. It was as if she was part of this conversation but was not really in it.

"It is a difficult situation," said Brian. Tanya was like a coin. One side of her was like a hormonal teenager, giggling as she had met him at the airport. The other was her sitting at the table with him, able to intelligently discuss something as serious as the compromise of nuclear safety. "Energy International's attempting to force us to meet financial goals that is making it impossible to safely operate our nuclear units for a sustained duration. Basically, they want us to get rid of a lot of good people and take shortcuts in maintenance and security."

"Well that's the new corporate credo," she said, welcoming the chance to add some humor, even if it was mildly sarcastic. Working for an airline provided her with clear insight on such things. Her industry had been decimated in the months that follow the 9/11 attacks. "Cutback until it hurts; all except for the stockholders, of course. They cut our staff, cut our flights, over book the ones we have left and then tell us it's our job to ensure passenger satisfaction." She ended it with a forced laugh, hoping for a smile or laugh from Brian. But there was none.

"Re-engineering is a damn virus that's spreading through corporate America like the clap through a whorehouse," said Brian. "Right now I've got one of the most efficient, most profitable, and safest nuclear stations in the U.S. But that's not good enough for Cowling. We've got to make it more profitable. He's ordering cuts beyond what I'm willing to make. Now it's a legal issue. I'm here to get a Nuclear Regulatory Commission ruling that our parent company doesn't have the technical expertise to dictate staffing and operational matters." He sat his glass down a little too hard; making enough noise to cause the maitre d' to turn their direction.

Even in the dim light of the restaurant, Tanya could see how Brian's face had darkened. His blood pressure was probably up ten points. What would happen if he decided to back down? Would this Bud Orton still be intent upon blackmailing him? Why did he not simply let them do with their company what they pleased?

"Why do you say it's a legal issue? They own your company. Isn't it their right to make what ever decisions they want, right or wrong?" asked Tanya. "You don't have to fight. Just let them worry about it. I don't want us to stop and I'm afraid that what you do tomorrow will destroy us." She had to fight to keep her tears from coming.

"No, it's not their right. And we don't have a right to put ourselves first. Not if it degrades nuclear safety. Nuclear power can't afford another Three Mile Island. It's just the same with airline passengers, you consider their safety before your own," said Brian, taking another sip of Chianti. "The charter under which the parent-subsidiary relationship is set up stipulates that Cowling and Energy International don't have the expertise to make operational decisions. For them to do so is a violation of the corporation by-laws and also federal regulations. However, it's going to be up to the NRC to determine that the cutbacks in staffing affect nuclear safety and that they are meddling in operational matters."

"Ah, Brian," said Tanya. "I just wish you could leave it alone. We've got us." But was there really an "us"? Maybe it really was like Orton had said, that she was merely his plaything.

Bud Orton had had an interesting perspective on why she should cooperate on blackmailing Brian. He had asked what would happen when Brian's thrill of banging a young flight attendant had gone. Who did she think would have Brian in the end, her or his wife? Who would end up with a Mercedes and a big wonderful house? Tanya had only been able to grimace. She was, unfortunately, experienced enough at affairs with married men to easily answer those questions. But Brian had talked about not wanting this to end. Tomorrow he wanted to talk more about them. It was, however, too late. That discussion would never take place.

"I've tried to convince the State Corporation Commission that the cuts pose a threat to nuclear safety," said Brian, acknowledging her comment with a smile. "But at the same time, Energy International tells the SCC that nuclear safety is not affected and that our customers will benefit from lower production costs. At the moment, the so-called 'nuclear expert' that evaluates this stuff for the SCC, has ruled that nuclear safety is unaffected by Energy International's financial goals. I need to get it from the NRC that this nuclear expert is full of shit."

"Why isn't the SCC more concerned about safety?" asked Tanya.

"Personally, I'm suspicious of money changing hands, bribes," said Brian. "Of course I can't prove it and won't waste my effort trying. But if I can get the NRC to agree with me, then I can get a court order that will bar their interference. I can even make it difficult for them to sack me and replace me with someone who'll do their bidding."

❖ ❖ ❖

Rachel Lambert apologized as she crowded past the two ladies in the plane's aisle. Her job was to maintain surveillance on Brian Matkins. If he was meeting a woman here, it was important that she get documentation of the fact. There was a mini-digital camera fitted into her purse. As soon as Brian had stood to disembark, she had turned it on and aimed it his direction. Continuous footage of him getting off the plane and walking into the arms of whatever bimbo he was seeing would be difficult to refute. Otherwise, there would be cries from Brian Matkins' divorce attorney of tampering with the video file.

So, as her subject met and embraced an attractive, much younger female subject, she caught it on video. Yeah, this was a Kodak moment, she thought, her mind racing back to an old commercial. Then she followed them out into the blustery night air, headed to short-term parking. The camera was still running. What it recorded, no judge would buy as two good friends getting together for an innocent evening together. There would not be much challenge to this trip. It was just more of the same, boring routine, which was the norm for spousal infidelity cases.

Rachel smiled as Brian Matkins removed his jacket and placed it around the blonde Bambi. Bambi in the short green mini was freezing her ass off and it was Rambo to the rescue. Good, that would teach her to flaunt her tight buns and gorgeous legs. Bambi was a Barbie doll.

Without warning, Bambi suddenly glanced back. It was, however, unlikely that she could have realized that Rachel was studying her. As she had been taught, Rachel always shadowed with her gaze cast downwards at the heels of whomever she was following. She simply kept her subject in her peripheral vision. It was effective, and it also made one more situationally aware of the operational environment. Such as a car coming up slowly from behind, shooting photos to try and identify a possible tail.

Rachel kept her cool, donning the image of a weary traveler returning home. Bambi's eyes were locked on her a lot longer than should have been the case for just a nervous glance. It happened a second time, and then a third. Rachel's mind raced, back stepping and evaluating everything that had taken place since she disembarked from the plane. She was good at what she did and there was no reason to believe that her cover was compromised. So she continued to follow, simply acting disinterested.

Perhaps Bambi was merely suffering from acute guiltanoia. Perhaps it was not a term that Webster or Freud would endorse, but it was more fitting than paranoia. It was the rational explanation. After all, there was bound to be a certain amount of anxiety associated with screwing someone else's husband.

They stopped at a sleek, black RX-7. Though the lighting was poor, her camera had been continuously running from the moment she disembarked from the plane. Not once had she let Brian Matkins escape the prying eye of its lens. It was definite overkill, but it made disputing the validity of her footage doubly difficult.

Rachel slowed her stride, giving Rambo time to open the door for Bambi, tuck her safely inside, and then make his way around to the passenger side. Rachel timed it so that she was directly behind the RX-7 as he was just pulling his door shut. Though neither of her subjects was positioned to see, she dropped the hanky that she carried in one hand and stooped to pick it up. In those brief seconds, she aimed the camcorder at the license plate.

Providing that the car was Bambi's, and not borrowed, Rachel had all that she really needed now, to I.D. Brian Matkins' lover. And most likely, she had enough evidence on her video to consider Brian Matkins bagged and tagged for Mrs. Matkins' divorce attorney. But she was not one to take chances. It would be the destination of Rambo and Bambi that would provide absolute certainty in a court of law that this was not merely an innocent, affectionate meeting of old friends.

The miniature camera was attached to the end of her purse, camouflaged by ornamental brass work. To anyone watching her move through the airport, only a trained eye would have had any chance noticing that she was deliberately aiming her purse. There was not even a problem getting through airport security with it.

Not until she was far past the RX-7 and lost in the shadows, did Rachel stop. There no was no sense of urgency. And even if there were, she would have been helpless to address it. She had no way of following Rambo and Bambi. And even if she could have made all the right guesses and had a vehicle in the right place, ready for her to jump in and take off, there was little point to it with this type of surveillance. Rachel would use the RX-7's license plate to get a name and address. Most likely, they would stop off for dinner somewhere and she would be waiting for them when they arrived at Bambi's residence. If that were not the case, then she would at least be in place when they crawled out of the sack and emerged for fresh air.

Suddenly, a car, just several spaces down, switched on its engine. Rachel, not easily startled, nearly came out of her shoes. She was a model of situational awareness whenever she worked. A chapter, devoted to the topic, was in a handbook used at the CIA's training academy at Camp Perry; she had written it. There had not been anyone else nearby, no sound of a car door opening or closing. Whoever was in that car had been sitting there, not making a sound and not having the interior light on. And, they had been in perfect position to spy on Brian and the woman. Coincidence?

The Honda Accord had been backed into its spot, providing a perfect vantage point. There was no hesitation as its driver pressed the accelerator and lurched forward with no headlights. Like the RX-7, it sped towards the lighted exit sign, waiting until nearly reaching the booth before switching on its headlights. Was Bambi married? And if so, was that her husband or another private investigator in the car that just pulled out? So much for the idea of just another boring stakeout. If she and the other, unknown, party were not careful, they would be like bad dancers, all over each other's toes before the night was over. Still, maybe it had been someone just getting back from a long flight that had decided to take a nap before leaving the airport. Perhaps Matkins and his Barbie-like girl friend had awakened them.

Rachel had a rented Chevrolet Astro van waiting for her. Unfortunately, she had to trudge back to the terminal and wait for a shuttle bus to carry her to it. She had called ahead to ensure that such a vehicle would be available. She had specifically requested the Astro, one with an 8-cylinder engine to give her the power she needed to discreetly keep up with a subject. Its height gave her sight advantage over most other vehicles, another valuable asset.

Whoever had been in that second car, had been in position to get good footage of Rambo and Bambi getting into the RX-7. Its driver could have followed her to the airport and then parked in a convenient location for surveillance. Perhaps a second person had conducted operations inside the terminal, or maybe they did not consider footage within the terminal important. Especially if it was Bambi's husband or a jealous boyfriend in the Accord who could not have gone into the terminal without a significant chance of being seen by Bambi. Then again, perhaps she was being too paranoid; it was probably just another traveler. Still, she would be heads-up.

Though, she tried, she could not shake her suspicion of the driver in the Honda. The husband/lover possibility created one definite complication that Rachel could easily have done without. Would they be going back to her place or to the Atlanta Embassy Hotel where Matkins had reservations? Matkins' job brought him to Atlanta frequently, as it did other Nuclear Industry officials. He would likely opt not to take her to where he was staying, as he would risk being seen by another colleague also in town on business. If there were a husband, then Matkins would have to take that risk. Now she did not know whether to find out where Bambi lived so she could stake it out or go to the hotel.

Rachel eventually trudged back to the terminal, caught her shuttle to the rental agency and then wasted no time guiding the Astro van out of the Hartsfield terminal. At the same time, she was punching numbers into her cell phone. She would try to cover all her bases. First, she needed to get Bambi's address.

"Hello," a male voice answered after several rings.

"Hello, yourself," she said.

"Sis, I thought that you were flying to Atlanta," said Les Lambert. He was pensive, and not without reason. He knew intuitively where this was going. He had told her *"no,"* a thousand times before. However, she never listened.

"That's exactly where I am. Real quick, then I'll let you go. Need you to run a Georgia plate for me." Rachel knew that she would get the brotherly lecture, but that was simply the price of a necessary short cut.

"Real quick and I'll let you go, my ass," said Les, his tone admonishing. "How many times have I told you that it's illegal for you to call me up and ask me to do this? Just because I work for the sheriff's department doesn't mean that I can be calling them up for someone's license plate whenever the hell I feel like it."

"Just tell them you ran out for groceries and that you saw a suspicious vehicle," said Rachel. As a private investigator, Rachel did not have easy access to the Department of Motor Vehicle files, not even in Virginia where she lived. Normally, she avoided asking Les to do this, going instead to DMV and filling out the forms and waiting for the information. But that was not an option in situations like this. She needed to find out where Bambi lived so that she could be there when they arrived. Otherwise, her surveillance was finished unless her subjects turned up at the Atlanta Embassy Hotel, which did not seem likely.

"Couldn't you have just flagged a cab and told the driver to follow that car?" asked Les, irritated.

"My subject's girlfriend was picking him up. I had to follow them out to the parking lot to I.D. her car," said Rachel. "You can't flag a cab out in short term parking. You watch too many movies. Try a reality check."

"Oh, Christ, sis..." Les paused, then added. "I'll get back to you as soon as I have something."

"Try to make it quick will you?" she replied. "Just think of your sweet little sister driving aimlessly through Atlanta, not a clue where she's going."

"You're not sweet, but with no clue… yeah," said Les.

"And you're off my Christmas list if you don't hurry up and run that plate," said Rachel.

Rachel waited another ten minutes and then called the hotel. If they had gone straight there, then they should be there by now. She had obtained Brian Matkins' itinerary from his wife. The clerk, however, informed her that Mr. Matkins had not yet checked in.

"Would she like to leave a message?" the clerk had asked.

"No," she had told him.

Ten minutes later, Rachel Lambert's phone rang. She was sitting in a Burger King, grabbing supper. "You got it?" she answered the phone.

"Anybody ever tell you you're a pain in the ass?" asked Les. "Okay. The license plate comes back to a Tanya V. Madison, twenty-nine years old, Billings Court Apartment 3A, 8013 La Sarde Avenue, Atlanta. Blue eyes, blonde hair and five foot, two inches tall. Maybe I should come down there and follow her around."

"No problem," said Rachel. "Just put my sister-in-law on the phone and we'll see. Next of kin to contact?"

"Hell, she might send me," said Les, teasing. "Next of kin is her mother. I didn't write the name down. You planning on her having an accident or something? Or have you been promoted to an assassin for hire?"

"Never know," said Rachel, clicking off the phone with her brother. She pulled out a map of Atlanta, found the address and hit the road. If Tanya Madison were married, then she would most likely have listed her husband as the person to notify on her driver's license. Then again, it didn't mean anything. Maybe she got married and simply never got around to changing it. And one did not generally list jealous boyfriends as next of kin. Rachel arrived at the apartment complex on La Sarde in less than twenty minutes. She was nothing short of ecstatic at finding a visitor's space that gave her the best possible view of the front of Tanya Madison's apartment building. There were two dark colored Accords sitting in the parking lot. It was impossible to determine if one of them was the Accord at the airport or if anyone was in one of them right now. Both were parked in spaces designated for other apartments and neither was located so as to provide a decent vantage point of the Madison apartment. She would discount them for now, but memorized the license plate numbers of both.

Rachel left the warmth of the van to walk up to the building's front entrance. Had it not been necessary, she would not have done so. If one of those Accords was the one from the airport and its driver saw her here, he or she would then certainly know that she was tailing Matkins and Madison. However, she needed to figure out, if possible, which apartment belonged to Ms. Madison so that she could tape them entering the building and then the apartment lights being switched on a few moments later.

It wasn't Atlanta's highest-class neighborhood, but it was not shabby, either. Bambi lived in one of those places that Rachel had several years ago termed yuppieville.

The front door allowed general access into a foyer where the resident's mailboxes were located and a courtesy phone hung on the wall. It was the standard setup that enabled guests to call up and request a resident to electronically unlock a second door, one which likely gave access to the elevator and the ground floor apartments. Residents got in by using an electronic access card. Not nearly as secure as something more posh and actually manned by twenty-four hour security agents, but it hinted at security and was affordable. And of course there was a security camera. Smile and say cheese, thought Rachel. She wondered if the camera merely provided the resident with a visual of who was in the foyer, or did it also provide a recording of who came and went. A copy of the two walking into the building together, provided by an independent security service, would be a nice addition to the package of evidence that she was putting together. Of course, getting access to the footage would involve enormous legal effort. Subpoenas running out the ass, literally.

Comparing the size and shape of the building to the number of mailboxes, gave her some idea of how the apartments were laid out and how many per floor. Back in the van, Rachel studied the third floor of the building. There were four apartments on each floor. Since Madison was in 3A, hers should be in the front of the building. Since there was obvious activity in the apartment on her right, but no sign of the RX-7, Rachel was certain that Tanya Madison lived in the darkened apartment to the left.

Of course, there was still a chance that they might go back to Brian's hotel room. Once more she called the Atlanta Embassy Hotel. Still, Brian had not checked in. Obviously, they had stopped off for dinner. All she could do now was wait and watch as people occasionally came and went from the building.

It was another hour before one of several sets of headlights to pull into the parking lot turned out to be Madison's RX-7. Then it was several moments before the two finally emerged from the car, clinging to each other like muskrats mating.

Through the viewfinder of her digital camera, equipped with infrared night visibility, Rachel watched and grinned at Bambi and Rambo as they kissed and groped each other. Eagerly, her fingers snapped several shots of their tender moment. The moment had certainly been worth the wait. There was no sign of another Honda Accord.

Rachel finished snapping her stills and switched to motion mode. Fumbling with buttons and zippers, Bambi and Rambo made their way towards the entrance of the apartment building. As soon as they disappeared through the door, she swung the camcorder up to the third floor. She would continue to let it run until the lights came on then stop when there really was nothing to record. Suddenly, a tiny flash of light passed across one of the apartment windows. It was so minute, so unexpected, that had she not been studying the apartment through the camcorder's lens, she would never have noticed it. Then it appeared a second time, coming back across the room. Holding the camcorder steady, she waited to see if the flash of light returned for a third time. It did not. It was several minutes later when the lights in the apartment went on.

There was no way that the flash of light could have been her two subjects; simply impossible. They had barely entered the second door of the foyer. Bambi's husband? A jealous lover? "God, please don't let somebody get their fucking brains blown out," Rachel muttered, thinking of the paperwork that she would be involved in.

As the moments passed, there was no screaming or yelling, no sound of gunfire. Finally, she shut off the camera. Again she scanned the parking lot, searching for anything out of the ordinary. Nothing. Just the two Accords. She was certain that the one at the airport had been dark blue. The lighting here, however, was much poorer than the airport parking lot. She could not tell exactly what color these two cars were.

There was nothing to do now, but wait. Waiting was the part of being a private investigator that movie audiences were never shown. Those who thought PI work was glamorous, had simply not experienced sitting in a car in frigid temperatures, unable to start the engine for heat because it could attract attention. The long hours of sitting were not enjoyable.

Some music would go nicely. She dug through her camera bag looking for her Norah Jones CD and heat pad. It was hard to understand why the Jazz singer had turned to country. Rachel liked country, too, but she preferred

Norah's work as a Jazz artist. She positioned the heat pad behind her. Its heat would keep her comfortable during what would likely be a long wait.

Glancing up, she saw a man appear in the apartment building foyer. Unshaven, black leather jacket and ragged jeans, he was leaving. Her mind went back to the light that she had seen earlier and the dark colored Accord in the airport parking lot. Snatching up her camera, Rachel took several pictures of the man as he exited. Would he climb into one of the Honda Accords and speed away? She watched, feeling a tinge of disappointment, as instead, he climbed onto a motorcycle. It immediately roared to life with the throaty roar of a Harley. There was no opportunity to get the license plate number as man and machine accelerated out of the parking lot. Probably there was no need for it.

Half an hour later, a couple exited the apartment foyer. They were dressed up in a casual sort of way, looking like they were headed to the movies, or perhaps out for a late, romantic dinner. Rachel shot several frames of them. They further drew her interest when they climbed into one of the Accords, backed out of the parking space and drove off. This time, however, the driver used his headlights and there was seemingly no hurry. Then Rachel studied the apartment number stenciled onto the space vacated by the Accord. From where she sat, it took a moment. It belonged to an apartment in the same building as the one Madison lived in, simply one floor down. Nothing to it, she was sure.

Two pizza deliveries arrived and left. Once again, Rachel took pictures, leaving nothing to chance. Would Rambo spend the entire night here? By pulling a few strings and copiously spending her client's money, she had managed to get a room right next to his. She really, really, wanted to make use of it, at least for a few short hours. For damn sure, she did not want to spend the night in the van.

❦ ❦ ❦

"It's two o'clock in the morning," said Brian, looking at his Rolex. At the moment he wasn't the least bit sleepy. In fact, just the opposite; he was hyped. But he was certainly all fucked out. If he woke up impotent in the morning, he would not care. He'd had enough sex tonight to warrant celibacy for the rest of his life with no regrets. "I've got to be able to stay awake tomorrow. There's too much riding on the outcome of my meeting."

"Sleep here, Brian," Tanya pleaded quietly. "Please don't leave me alone tonight."

She thought of rat-face who had stole into her apartment to set up the camera. It scared her that he could just enter at will. Numerous movie plots played before her eyes, innocent young women being murdered to cover up high corporate or political crimes. The fear disappeared long enough for her to feel a thrill at the idea that her life had taken on aspects of a Hollywood thriller. The fear that she felt now would be an experience to help her when she began her acting career.

Still, she preferred never to see rat-face again. Perhaps he would have an accident and never come back. Tanya pictured a large, red tractor-trailer crushing the Harley and its rider under the truck's huge wheels. Wishful thinking, she knew. He would be back. Suddenly the money that she was being paid to do this did not seem so significant; nor the experience so beneficial.

"Can't," he said. Brian pushed himself up from the bed, his hand touching the handle of the knife. Picking it up he shook his head. "Tanya, are we extremely perverted, or are we simply just sick human beings? Realize what Lorena Bobbitt could do with a blade this sharp."

"I like thinking we're just kinky in a classy sort of way," she said, biting playfully at his neck. "Sure you wouldn't like to ravage me just one more time at knife point?" She had fantasized about such rough love, but never dreamed it could be the rush that it had been. For much of the time she had been oblivious to the camera and the thought of rat-face.

"No, no, I don't have any more ravaging left in me. Believe me!" he said. But even as Brian said it, he could feel himself grow slightly hard. Tomorrow, however, was vital to his company; he had to get at least some sleep. "How about if I call a cab. No sense in you going back out this late."

"Nonsense," she said, feeling disappointed. "I'll be dressed in a minute." Maybe he would let her stay at the hotel. Rat-face could return, retrieve the miniature tape from the camera and rob her blind if he liked.

Finally, at about a quarter past two, Rachel had her answer as to whether or not Brian would spend the night here. What she did not have was any heat from her heating pad. Most likely, the rental agency had removed the fuse to the lighter's circuit since the van was a non-smoking rental. That was no longer important to her as Bambi and Rambo emerged from the apartment's foyer. By now, the couple in the first Accord had returned from their evening out. There was no sign of the young man on the Harley. Best of all, however, no jealous husband or lover had popped a cap in her subjects. She had as damning footage of the two together as Mrs. Matkins would need. There really was nothing else necessary, though she had planned a little electronic eavesdropping for the coming day. Though chances were slim that she would catch anything to make this case tighter, it would give her a great chance to play and practice a little trade craft of the electronic variety. It was something she truly enjoyed.

Fatima's view of the lights in Madison's apartment was limited from where she sat in her rented Honda Accord. There were too many other players in this game for her to risk parking in the apartment complexes parking lot. She would have to rely on simply seeing them come out of the apartment building. Then it would be necessary to move fast, not knowing if the Harley rider would come back immediately for the camcorder or not. If he did, it was going to get messy. It was far better that she arrived first.

Chapter Eleven
Wednesday, December 2
Atlanta, Georgia

Rachel waited until the car was pulling out of the parking lot before she started the van. Without turning her lights on, and careful not to touch her foot to the brake pedal and activate the brake lights, she pulled out to follow. The van's automatic transmission groaned in protest when she forced it from reverse to drive while it was still moving backwards. Earlier, she had put black electrical tape over the backup lights. Such precautions were overkill, she knew. But they were spy craft that she had been taught, and had once taught, herself. The one time she decided not to take these precautions could well be the time that she would need them.

There was really no rush. It was only logical that Madison was taking Brian back to the hotel. Rachel regretted that she had not brought a device along to eavesdrop with. If she had, then she would know for sure where they were going. She was not sure, however, whether it would have been worth sitting through all the grunting and groaning that she would have had to listen to. It was certainly not evidence that she would try to use. The legal implications of violating these cheaters' privacy would undoubtedly be enormous. Regardless, she would not have any difficulty following them in the early morning hours.

There was absolutely no moon, which made it really dark, despite the lights in the parking lot. Madison and Matkins were speeding away in the RX-7. Rachel reached for the headlight switch. The instant she turned the headlights on, she slammed the brake pedal with all the force she could muster. The sound of the van's skidding tires broke the cold silence of the early December morning.

The van came to a halt within feet of a tall, slender woman who had come out of nowhere. It all happened fast and the woman quickly stepped out of the glare of the headlights. Rachel was already moving again before she pondered the thought that the woman wore dark glasses and a headscarf. Looking up in her rear view mirror, she was sure that she could make out the figure of the woman, standing there, staring vehemently after the van that had nearly plowed her over.

Fatima had not noticed the van, not until it was right on top of her. For a fleeting moment, she thought that she would be robbed of all that she had worked so hard to attain. Mainly, the opportunity to extract revenge worthy of what Roger Cowling had taken from her and to make America pay for its debauchery towards God. Noise from the apartment complex's heat pumps had drowned out that of the van's engine. That was why she had not heard it approach. Its driver was obviously following Matkins and the Madison woman. Why else would she not have her lights on? Perhaps she had been focusing too much on when the rider of the Harley might arrive, to pay attention to someone leaving. She did, however, have time to get the license plate number. It was a typical rental plate, making the vehicle and its driver all the more suspicious. She would give it to Abdul to have checked out first thing in the morning. The van's driver had seen enough of her to make for big problems.

Who had been driving the van and why were they following Matkins and the Madison woman? The only logical conclusion was that it was the same people that Roger Cowling and Frank Baker had hired to blackmail Matkins. So why follow them back to the hotel? It made more sense to go up and retrieve the videotape. What had just happened, made her all the more certain that she should finish her business and be out of here.

Keeping her face hidden from the camera, Fatima used the smart card to unlock the door to the stairwell. Travis had had the good fortune to find the card that Madison had given Brian. It had taken little effort to persuade the perverted wimp that maintained the power station's smart card driven access control system to break into the card and copy its codes for her. His talents were becoming increasingly important to everything. That made him increasingly a liability that she would need to remove as soon as his usefulness was finished.

Her duplicated card unlocked this door and the one to Madison's apartment. Brian Matkins had kept it in his Franklin planner, an item that Travis looked through whenever he had opportunity. It was unlikely Brian had ever noticed that it had been missing for a couple of days. Travis had been a hesitant convert at the beginning, but she had managed him well. Which was precisely the reason why the others accepted her as a soldier and not just another female to which a bomb could be strapped.

Fatima took the stairs to reach Tanya Madison's apartment. The elevator was too risky. There she used the card once more to let herself in. All the while, she could not stop thinking about the Astro van that had nearly ran her over in the parking lot. Who was following Tanya Madison? And why? It had to be the same woman that she had seen in the airport parking lot.

The smell of sex was strong, even in the living room. Then again, Fatima had an extraordinary sense of smell. Just standing in a MacDonald's on a Saturday afternoon she could smell the cordite from a hunter's hands and clothes several feet away. Such sensitivities were important assets in a world where staying alive was based on noticing what most did not.

The bedroom was easy to find. It was also a predictable scene, with the bed unmade and articles of Madison's clothes scattered about. On the floor, beside the bed, lay the combat style knife. She imagined Matkins, attempting to act the villain, holding the knife to her throat to force himself upon her. Had they even bothered to use it, or, had they simply played, broke into laughter and then fucked each other's brains out? For a brief moment the razor-edged blade mesmerized her. There was an arousal as she considered how easily its point would incise the skin and muscle, allowing the length of blade to penetrate her victim's organs with near sexual ecstasy. She had only killed three times using a blade of steel, whereas she had lost count of the number of targets that she had dispatched with a firearm. Four times she had left explosives, once as a bag of groceries in an Iraq weapons lab where she had spent a year cleaning floors and working as a general housekeeper, a car bomb outside a hotel where a prominent Israeli diplomat was speaking and twice with a briefcase in Zionist business establishments. Nothing, however, made you feel the kill like sinking a steel blade into one who did not expect it. There was that look of astonishment, of knowing that they were mortally wounded.

Fatima shook herself loose from the fixation. Travis knew the general details of the plan, but it would not have been practical for them to clue him in on the finer aspects, such as where they hid the camera. Madison was being paid to set Matkins up. The semen droppings on the sheet were on the same side of the bed where the knife lay. Thus, it had to have been captured from this side. Not from the head of the bed, however. That would not have provided a wide enough vantage. Definitely from the end, but enough to the side to really get good shots. She turned to see the table behind her. Without hesitating, she parted the runs of a large Spider plant. There was the camera, a low-tech affair that captured the image on a miniature cartridge. She removed the tape and placed it in a pocket on the thigh of her trousers. The pocket had a flap that she buttoned securely. There was only one last piece of business.

It was ten past three in the morning when Tanya returned from taking Brian to his hotel. Silently, she cursed herself for agreeing to see him tomorrow afternoon before he left Atlanta to go back to Richmond. What if the people who were hiring her to blackmail him contacted him today? What would it be like to face him once he knew of her treachery? Surely they would not be likely to contact him so soon. However, once he knew what she had done, Tanya wanted to be certain that she never crossed paths with Brian Matkins again. Not so much because she was scared of him, but because what she was doing to him was so awful and so wrong. She would not have the stomach to face him.

In retrospect, $100,000 was not worth doing something like this to a man who had treated her so well. The older guy, she never learned his name, had been so convincing though.

"How many affairs have you had with married men like Brian Matkins?" he had asked her. When she was slow to answer, he had answered for her; six. "What did you ever get out of any of these affairs after they were over?" Again, when she hesitated, he had answered for her. One had wrecked her car, letting her suffer the charges and going high risk on her auto insurance; one had given her a sexually transmitted disease. The gentleman had listed several other laudable events that had terminated her various relationships; all of them, she realized with some dismay, that had been with married men.

"What I'm offering you," the man had told her. "Is the opportunity to end this thing with Matkins and come away the winner for once. You know it's going to eventually end anyway. Change your name, take some time off in Acapulco or some such place and go to work for some other airline. Tell them you changed your name because you were being stalked. They'll buy it. In fact, I'll create a paper trail to prove it." And she had said yes. Rather than Acapulco, it would be Hollywood, but all the same, she had said yes. Maybe he was right. But it just felt so dirty.

Tanya went up the steps and let herself into her apartment. Setting her purse down, she went straight to her bedroom, her legs wobbly from the late hour and the alcohol that she had consumed. Brian had acted very ill at ease with her driving, insisting numerous times that it would be better to get a cab. Damn, what if she had gotten another DUI?

The miniature camera was hidden in the spider plant on her dresser. If it worked, and there was no reason to suppose it would not, it would have caught a broadside view of all that she and Brian had done on her bed. Including the knife thing. Just the thought of that made her shiver. But it had been good. Hell, she had never come so violently hard in her whole life as she did when Brian held the point of the knife against her belly, pressing himself harder and harder inside her. It was another of her experiences that she would one day draw from, shaping her into the actress that she knew she could be. Hell, this ordeal ought to shape her into Academy Award material.

The young man on the Harley had been very precise with his directions about how to handle the camera. "Keep your fucking hands off of it and just don't touch a goddamned thing," he had told her in a chilling tone. Careful not to touch it, she brushed back a leaf for just a look at how he had placed it in the pot. That was when she noticed that the little red light was not blinking. He had told her it would be, and that it would stay on and continue to record for up to ten hours. Something was wrong! Maybe it had not worked. Maybe the man on the Harley was not as competent as she had given him credit for. It was an almost pleasant sensation to think that it had not worked. She really did not want to do this to Brian. Screw the money. It was not worth it. She was glad the fucking camera did not work. Brian would help her get to Hollywood; he would support her aspirations. No, she reminded herself, it would end with her having nothing, just as Mr. Orton had described. Whatever, she was tired.

Glancing at her watch, Tanya realized the time. She did have a flight tomorrow evening and there would be Brian to contend with in the afternoon before he flew back to Richmond. He wanted to talk about them. He had given her the impression that perhaps he was thinking of leaving his wife and starting over with her. That made what she had done all the more painful. Sure, all the other married men had left her high and dry, but that did not mean that this time had to be the same.

Tanya decided not to concern herself with the camera. As she had been told, she had not touched it. Whether it had worked or not was out of her hands. She was going to bed.

Tanya stepped out of the faded blue jeans she wore. She watched herself in the mirror, noting that few women could boast of an ass like hers, full and firm and a flat stomach to go along with it. She resembled Sharon Stone, she realized. There were a few red lines where Brian had carefully run the blade of the knife across her. Yeah, she would be a natural for a Sharon Stone type of role. Maybe a year of acting lessons and she would be on her way. As she went to pick up the bra that had been tossed on the floor when she and Brian first arrived at the apartment, she realized that the knife was no longer lying where they had left it. It had been lying on the floor beside the bed. That explained it all then. The man on the Harley had been here while she took Brian to the hotel, explaining why the camera's light was not blinking. So, why had they left the camera? Regardless, they had the tape and the knife. What concerned her the most was that this meant they were in a much bigger hurry to use the video than they had led her to believe. Perhaps they would show it to Brian before his scheduled visit to the NRC in the morning.

"Too late now," she said to nobody in particular. When she got up in the morning she would pack some stuff and leave. One of the other girls would clear the apartment out for her later on. One thing was for sure; she could not take a chance on them using the tape to blackmail Brian today while she was still in town.

Tanya glanced around for her robe. It was probably in the closet. Her mind was processing all the necessary items that she would need to take care of before skipping out of town as she slid open the double-mirrored doors. Foremost, she needed to collect her money for the dastardly deed that she had just performed. As she thought about the significance of a hundred grand in her life and Hollywood, what she was doing to Brian seemed all of the sudden much less significant.

Tanya was imagining her first audition when she realized that she was staring at the knife, and the hand that held it. She attempted a scream, but with savage swiftness, the gloved hand plunged the knife into her, just below her navel. She felt the blade of the military style knife as it was jerked upwards, slicing through the firm six-pack of which she was so proud. Tanya felt all that was happening to her, but it was not pain, it was something else, too bizarre to describe. Vaguely she was aware that her intestines were falling to the floor and the room was swimming around her. There was a smell, like alcohol and rotting food, the contents, she realized, of her own bowels. Helpless, Tanya fell back onto the bed, looking up into the face of the woman who held the knife. She had never seen a picture of Brian Matkins' wife, but this woman's eyes were so full of hate that she was sure that this had to be her, having followed Brian to exact her revenge on the other woman. In less than a minute, everything around her faded away. Faded away into nothingness.

Chapter Twelve
Thursday, December 3
Jefferson Davis Nuclear Power Station
Hanover County, Virginia

Ray stood silent and motionless for the seven seconds that it took to compare the pattern of his retina with the pattern that was contained in the computer chip on his smart card. The retina scanner and smart card were used to verify that he really was Raymond Jackson Cisco, Security Shift Supervisor at the Jefferson Davis Nuclear Power Station. At least for today he was a Security Supervisor. Tomorrow he might be back at the position of Security Officer, or perhaps standing in the unemployment line. What was the unthinkable had already happened to Richmond Fossil where several hundred people had been laid off. Two years ago, no one could have envisioned layoffs in the electric power industry where job security had been akin to being in the military.

Richmond Nuclear and Richmond Fossil were both subsidiaries of the much larger Virginia based firm, Energy International. Up to a third of both operational and support staffs had been sliced away at the fossil fueled electrical generating stations. Engineers, power plant operators, maintenance staff and administrative personnel; no department had been spared the sharp edged scalpel of Roger Cowling, CEO of Energy International. Ray "the kid" Cisco knew that there was no longer any telling what the future would hold. People had rationalized that the nuclear side of the house would be more protected from the cutbacks because there were nuclear safety requirements that dictated that a certain staffing level be maintained. That assurance, however, seemed to be holding little water as of late.

Electric utilities, once thought to be elusive to corporate takeovers and massive layoffs, were now as vulnerable as any other business. Word was leaking down from corporate headquarters on an almost daily basis of infighting between Richmond Nuclear's executives and Energy International's

Board of Directors. The strife was even beginning to get attention in the newspapers and on local news channels.

The big rumor was that Energy International wanted to sell the nuclear operation. Duke Power or CP&L, according to these rumors earlier on, would be likely buyers. However, stories leaked through CNN rumored that the California legislature was in the process of obtaining a major utility to end two years of off and on rolling blackouts and sky-high prices for electricity. Regardless of who bought them, a buyout would mean a reduction in force, an unavoidable result of any corporate merger. Smart cards, retina scanners and, just recently, surveillance cameras in place of guards in the towers, had reduced the size of the security force through early retirements. Using smart cards for access control reduced the need for two security officers per shift. Once upon a time, it had been security officers who verified the identities of plant workers and handed them their badges and key cards as they entered and exited the plant. Now it was a computer.

Surveillance cameras had been installed at strategic points along the double chain link fence surrounding the facility. This alone eliminated four security positions per shift that had manned the guard towers with high-powered rifles. Corporate called it progress that would reduce security costs enormously without reducing effectiveness. However, the idea of camera's replacing men who could shoot bad guys was not Ray's idea of effectiveness. Especially so in an era where a guy name Osama bin Laden had symbolically drawn a bull's eye on every nuclear power plant in the U.S.

A Productivity and Cost Enhancement Team had been formed of both corporate and plant security staff. The purpose had been to come up with cost saving ideas that would not degrade the nuclear power station's security. Using smart cards for access control had been Ray's suggestion. In the Navy, they had been used successfully to free personnel for more important duties than pushing a button to open a door. Here, it would have freed up two security officers per shift, officers who were really needed to meet security objectives in the plant. Money would have been saved by not having to pay out overtime for double shifts. This was especially true during repair and refueling outages when maintenance required several hundred extra workers that security had to process into the station.

The company installed the smart card system, gave Ray $500 plus recognition for his suggestion and then promptly gave early retirement to ten security officers, two from each of the five rotating shifts. Ray had been living in silent rage ever since, avoiding his co-workers out of guilt, constantly searching the web for a job that would take him away from here; at least until recently. With the arrival of Laura McClish at the Jefferson Davis Nuclear Power Station, his rage remained, but his desire to leave had faded significantly.

To make matters worse, the Security Department was bypassed in the purchase of the smart card access system. Travis Harding, Vice President of Security and Administration, had his purchasing department go out and buy a system based on low bid. That had created a nightmare. It was necessary that the system run on the same computers as the Central Alarm System. Those computers were installed when the plant was built, six years ago. Moses himself would have thought them too slow. The software for the system was a hash of something put together by a company that was new to the smart card world and lacked the experience to build a secure system. There was real potential for the system to screw up and let the bad guys in. And there were fewer Security Officer to shoot them. The whole thing was FUBAR, fucked up beyond all recognition.

As far as cameras replacing armed security officers in Guard Towers, well, a six-year-old playing toy soldiers would be able to tell you that cameras cannot shoot a rifle. There were scenarios where an expert marksman in one of the towers could make all the difference in the world if an enemy attempted to penetrate the station's protected area. The protected area was the fenced in portion of the plant that contained the nuclear reactors and all the related systems needed to keep those reactors operating safely. Anyone entering it had to have either a security clearance or be escorted by someone who did, or clear the fence. Clearing the fence looked like a task next to impossible. However, a skilled commando could be over the fence in eleven seconds. Ray had done it himself several times to test the site's security.

And now there was talk about further cutbacks. Reducing the number of security officers actually in the plant. Once upon a time, the NRC would have bristled at the mere thought of such cuts in security. But the Republicans controlled both the House of Representatives and the White House, and they were very sensitive to the complex needs of teary-eyed stockholders. They now made it clear to regulatory agencies like the NRC and the EPA that they needed to be empathetic and sympathetic to cost cutting in large corporations. Even the Agency for Homeland Defense turned a blind-eye.

"Hey, Ray, how's it hanging," asked Jed Turner, the superintendent of maintenance. He was entering the door of the Administration Building for the morning meeting.

"Rather limp for the last couple of days," said Ray as he unlocked the door to his office. "Donna's been out of town. Visiting her mother up in New York."

"I thought that it was limp because the girl out front has been gone," Turner said it in a near whisper; a large grin was spread across his face.

"Yeah, whatever," Ray entered his office, shaking his head, trying to appear as though there was nothing at all to Turner's comment. Hell, he had not had sex with Donna for so long, he really could not remember what it had been like and did not care. The fact of the matter was, he also could not remember the last time that she had been sober enough to make it to bed on her own.

With Laura, on the other hand, things kept getting hotter and hotter. If not for the job uncertainty, he would leave Donna, whether things worked out with the temporary Security Administrator, Laura McClish, or not. It was a damn shame that she had to go see her mother the same week that Donna had gone away to visit her family. Laura was due back today and Donna would not be home until tomorrow evening. That created some real nice possibilities at least for tonight.

The morning meeting would start at 0805 hours. That gave him time to browse the various security logs and Operations Shift Supervisor entries that were made through the night on the computer network. Ray shook the image of Laura from his mind and logged onto his computer, placing his smart card in the reader and his forefinger on the biometric reader. Employees no longer had to scribble down half-a-dozen passwords for all the various programs and hide them about the desk. A hacker would play heck trying to break into the plant's network. He just wished physical security was that tough.

Suddenly, a tall, lean form appeared in his doorway. Her dark features ripped at his insides in the most pleasurable sort of fashion. She was back.

Laura was a temporary, one of the contract personnel that the company liked to hire so they could lay them off as quickly as they needed to and not have to pay them benefits or severance. That someone in Corporate Security had decided that there was a need for a second Security Administrator while at the same time laying off much needed security officers, was beyond him. Out of nowhere, this charming, beautiful flower of womanhood had arrived at the power station. Laura wore the customary gray blazer with a black dress that came down to just above her knees. A red tie added the final degree of required professionalism to her attire. As Ray's eyes started at her slender, well shaped ankles and made the erotic journey all the way up to find her large black eyes looking into his, he decided that at least not all corporate decisions were bad ones. She could not shoot very well, but somehow it simply did not seem to matter.

"Brought you coffee," she said, her words seductive, whether she meant for them to be or not. The dark shadows under her eyes simply highlighted this seductiveness.

Ray stared at her without apology. Her eyes were the same glossy blackness of a black widow spider. Her skin had a golden richness that came from the Mediterranean. She had told him once that she was Italian. Laura was like autumn in all of its glory, like brightly turned leaves caught in the morning's first glinting rays of sunshine. Autumn was his favorite season and having Laura enter his life was like its coming. His life with Donna, for the past ten years, had been like a long, uncomfortable summer.

"Did you stick your finger in it to sweeten it?" he teased.

"I think you're sweet enough without it," said Fatima, purring the words the way she knew Ray liked. "Missed you."

"Missed you, too. Your mother picked a terrible time to get sick," said Ray. "Donna's been gone, visiting relatives. She's supposed to be back tomorrow. Feel like driving into Richmond for dinner tonight?"

"Let me call you this evening after I've had a chance to assess just how bad my house is," said Fatima, flashing a smile of distress. "There're still dirty dishes sitting in my sink from before I left. God knows what might be growing there. Let me get some time sheets over to Sharon. Talk to you later, okay?"

Fatima quickly made her way from the office. There were actually dirty dishes sitting in her sink, waiting to be shoved into the dishwasher. More than that, however, there was unexpected business to attend to.

With some sense of alarm, she realized that she would like to have been with Ray tonight. She had liked him from the moment they had met. Where had this sudden weakness come from? Never before had had feelings for a man. It could not, however, be allowed to interfere with the mission. As unexpected as this attraction to Ray was, she would be able to keep it under control. To make it all worse, she felt that unexpected warmth between her legs that always came with thinking about Ray being inside of her. Her sex was a weapon, a powerful one provided by Allah that she had used since she was a budding young woman of fourteen. To suddenly feel pleasure was frightening, and also dangerous. And she was so very, very tired.

Ray did not take his eyes off Laura until she had disappeared through the door. He had known that he was in trouble the second he had laid eyes on her.

106

If God had said to him, "Ray, tell you what. Here's Moses' stick, knock it against that rock over there three times and create the most beautiful, most seductive woman that you can imagine," something about three-quarters the beauty of Laura would have been created.

Three weeks after she had started working here, he had run across her at Green Top Sporting Goods. He had been buying ammo for his forty-five and his AK-47. Laura had been shopping for a handgun, one for personal protection. The salesman nearly hooked her up with a .38 Smith & Weston, but Ray had been in time to intervene. A 9 mm Beretta, "a real ladies weapon," Ray had told her, was by far the better choice. She had bought it. Then she had asked the sales clerk where she could take a class on how to use it.

Ray had listened to the clerk give her several suggestions, including the target range in the back of Green Top. None of the suggestions were objectionable, but intuition told him that there was a better option. Out in the parking lot, Ray had opened the floodgates. He told her that he had his own target range on some woodland owned by his father. If she would not think it too forward of him, he would be happy to take her there and teach her to shoot. After all, he had assured her, he was a certified firearms instructor for Richmond Nuclear's Security Department.

The following weekend, they had gone out to his firing range. Ray meticulously, and it should be added, most professionally, instructed her on how to safely use her new weapon. He did more than just teach safety and how to fire and aim. Ray had taught her about how and when to use the weapon, where to keep it, and how to move through the house with it if she suspected an intruder. Then they had banged away at targets. He with his .45, and her with her 9 mm. When she looked like she had the hang of it, he had pulled out the AK-47, fully automatic as well as fully illegal. Laura had really liked that. And when they finished banging away at targets, they had ended up with the tarp out of the back of his Ford Ranger, on the ground banging each other. Ray had really liked that.

Glancing at his watch, Ray shook himself from his reverie. There were two security logs that were kept on the local area network, or the LAN as the Instrument Techs who maintained the computer network called it. The first one that Ray punched up was the Security Turnover Log. It would make mention of any security related problems, officers who did not show up for work for one reason or the other, and just about any heads up info that needed to be passed along.

Two officers had been out with the flu. There was a lot of that going around. Ray suspected that the flu bug was likely being passed from every dedicated worker showing up with a fever to those still healthy. It would probably account for some holes in his day shift. The ominous threat of corporate mandated cutbacks in station manning had nearly everyone, even the IBEW union workers, scared to call in sick. Management probably called that a good thing, Ray called it scary.

The only other item in the turnover log was a recommendation from the off-going Security Shift Supervisor to put a work request in to troubleshoot circuitry for the Central Alarm System on the Emergency Diesel Generator Rooms. There were better than half a dozen spurious alarms received of attempts to gain unauthorized access. None of the alarms had checked out as valid. There was also one spurious alarm on the Control Room access from the Normal Switch-gear Room. Ray wondered what kind of bug was in the low-bid smart card computer system this time.

All doors to security related areas were tied into a central alarm complex. Unlike the smart card access control system and the surveillance cameras, replacing the central alarm system had not shown promise of reducing the size of the security staff. Thus the plant was stuck with an antiquated system sorely in need of replacement trying to deal with the tasks for which it was originally designed and a that of the smart card system as well. Both he and the company installing the smart card system had argued that the present computers would not allow the new access system to function the way it was designed to operate.

There was a knock at the already open door of his office. Even before Ray's grunt of acknowledgement cleared his throat, Pete Burns was walking through it. He was the off going Security Supervisor of B shift.

"Looks like you had a good night chasing down alarms," said Ray, glancing at his watch to let Pete know that he was in a hurry. There was only seven minutes until the morning meeting in the Attack Room. His mind drifted back to Laura. He sure hoped that she would call him tonight.

"Nothing but a piece of outdated garbage," Pete leaned against the doorframe. He looked exhausted. "Had to chase down some of them myself. Two officers out sick and one on vacation."

"Do you good. You eat too damn many donuts. Need to run them off." Ray was only half joking. The midriff on the guy was beyond being just noticeable. It was only sixty days or so until fitness testing. These days of corporate uncertainty were not a good time to have to answer an Undesirable

Fitness Report. Not when the company could at anytime be looking for the best candidates for the 613 shuffle. The 613 shuffle was what everyone joked they would find themselves doing if they were one of the layoffs. Shuffle out the main gate, get in your car and shuffle down Route 613 to look for another job.

"Fuck you, but thanks for caring," said Pete. "Do you mind putting in a work order to have that piece of shit that you talked the company into buying looked at so that I can get the hell out of here?"

"Got you covered," said Ray, ignoring the derision that he had become so accustomed to hearing. "Reckon it requires a Station Deviation Report since it's equipment not operating as designed."

"I'd say no on the Deviation Report," said Pete. "I mean we can only assume that it's a malfunction. Never happened with an officer standing right there to watch. There's enough damn paperwork around here as it is. Let's not make any we don't have to have. Save a tree for Christ's sakes."

Ray listened as Pete quickly finished up his face-to-face turnover. Pete was obviously happy to make it brief and hit the road for home. Ray then hustled on down the hall of the power station's administration building to the Attack Room.

Everything had a gimmick these days. The Attack room was one of many.

The Attack Room is where we will meet as professionals and attack problems that threaten the quality of Richmond Nuclear's operation and mission of carrying out safe and reliable electrical generation using nuclear power.

Catchy names for conference rooms, mission statements out the ass, and bull sessions on how to mean what you say and say what you mean. And it all added up to the same thing, his officers doing double time to chase down the problems of low bid and antiquated systems.

Ray eased into one of the few available plush velour chairs at the long oval table. He felt a slight relief at not being the last one to show up. The assistant station manager and the operations superintendent had not arrived yet. It was not Ray's normal function to attend the morning meeting and he felt very out of place being there. But since the superintendent of security operations was on vacation in Orlando, it fell to him as the senior security supervisor to play the role. He wished he were in Disneyland.

Unit 1 and Unit 2 Control Rooms are actually one large operational space. Each has its own control panel, perhaps fifteen feet in length, bending in the middle to make it into a chevron. One half of this panel operates primarily nuclear systems. The other half operates mostly the turbine generators and related support systems directly responsible for producing electricity.

The major difference in design between nuclear power electrical generating plants and fossil fuel electrical generating plants is the heat source. A fossil plant burns coal or natural gas to boil water, creating high-pressure steam to drive the turbine-generator. In a nuclear plant, water is turned into steam using heat produced by the fission process between neutrons and atoms of uranium. The turbine-generator and its support systems of a nuclear station, however, are very similar to those of a fossil fuel plant.

In front of the control panels are instrumentation boards that are literally covered from floor to ceiling with over a thousand indications of what is happening in the plant. Most of these, of course, were for the nuclear systems. Behind where the operator stands, facing his or her control panels, are more of the same, though for systems requiring far less scrutiny. All of the important components vital to safety and operation are located on the chevron shaped board. Anyone having opportunity to visit such a facility would likely find an immediate comparison to a scene out of Star Trek. One would expect to hear Captain Kirk ordering Scotty to beam someone aboard.

Dick Trane was Operations Shift Supervisor for Jefferson Davis Nuclear Generating Unit II; he had the Captain Kirk job. This was the second of two units at the power plant, both of which were capable of individually producing a thousand megawatts of electrical power. Jeff Clark, a licensed reactor operator, was at the control panel.

Trane had taken over with his C Shift at 0700. His turnover, as was required, had begun at 0630 with the Shift Supervisor of B Shift. They had discussed thoroughly the operation of the unit while Trane had his first cup of thick black coffee, just the way he remembered it as a Machinist Mate Chief aboard the numerous nuclear submarines he had served. There had been, actually, very little to discuss during the turnover. Unit II, as was Unit I, was operating normally at 100 percent power. Several minor nuisance problems existed, of course, but nothing substantial that would impact the safe, reliable operation of the nuclear reactor.

A horn from the unit's Annunciator panel sounded, bringing Trane's head up to see which alarm it was. There are over two hundred alarms on the Main

Annunciator panel. Several inform the operator that a reactor trip has occurred, an automatic shutdown of the nuclear reactor. Others let the operator know that a reactor trip is imminent. Most of the alarms, however, inform the operator of conditions in the plant that, if left uncorrected for a considerable length of time, will lead to a reactor trip or deterioration in the unit's safe operation. The last do not constitute any sort of urgency and constitute the bulk of alarms that sound from day to day.

"Unit II reactor trip." Jeff Clark announced the automatic reactor shutdown and calmly pressed the acknowledge button to silence the alarm.

Trane stood, staring at the panel, his eyes carefully scrutinizing every gage and meter available to him. Then he focused on his operators.

"Inserting a manual reactor trip," said Clark, reaching for and turning the trip lever. It was an extra precautionary step to ensure that the reactor did indeed properly shut down. "All rods indicate on the bottom. Entering AP-1, Reactor Trip Procedure."

"Acknowledge rods on the bottom and that you're entering AP-1, Reactor Trip Procedure," said Trane. AP-1, Reactor Trip, was the abnormal operations procedure used whenever the nuclear reactor automatically or was manually tripped. Trane watched as additional operators entered the operational area of the control room, as orderly as priests going to communion. One operator read each step of AP-1 while other operators verbalized a repeat back of the step and then performed the required action.

Trane's job was to stand back and look at the big picture, not to get drawn in on the details. He would step in only if necessary. Trane picked up the gaitronics, the plant's announcing system.

"Unit II reactor trip, Unit II reactor trip."

The announcement would be heard in every nook and cranny of Jefferson Davis Nuclear Power Plant. To workers and supervisors in the plant, it would mean that a very long day was ahead.

Right now, the big picture showed nothing to indicate why the reactor trip had occurred. Some unstated intuition told Trane that the picture was amiss.

"Dodson, check the P-250 Plant Monitoring System and see if there is any indication of what brought the unit down," said Trane to his assistant shift supervisor. "Williams, send someone to the Rod Drive Room and check the area."

Almost always, a reactor trip is either preceded or accompanied by one or more other alarms indicating the cause. This time there was nothing. There was only the constant blare of new alarms resulting from the trip. All of them were to be expected and even listed in AP-1 along with the correct operator action to be performed when the alarm sounded. Trane had been involved in operating nuclear reactors for thirty-one years and was a veteran of more reactor trips than he could keep track of. Somehow he had an uneasy feeling about this one.

Five years ago a reactor trip occurred, one that this seemed to replicate exactly. Now and again, the Training Department would present each shift of operators with the scenario of that trip on the simulator. Not often, though, since it was so simple a scenario that it did not muster much training value. Most training scenarios were designed to make you hard pressed to save the nuclear core from melt down.

In the actual incident, a laborer, mopping the floor of the Rod Drive Room had accidentally hit the breaker trip button on the Reactor Trip Breaker panel with the end of his mop. It had caused a simple reactor trip just like this appeared to be. As was the case now, there were no accompanying alarms indicating the cause of the trip. Unfortunately, it had taken three days to get the laborer to confess; costing the company almost three million dollars of revenue. This was because the laborer, realizing what he had done, had fled the Rod Drive Room. Of course the fact that the floor was wet and a mop was lying near by pretty much told the tale itself. The Nuclear Regulatory Commission, however, would not buy the obvious. Every reactor trip had to have its cause positively identified and corrected before the reactor could be restarted. Until the laborer confessed three days later, the plant had been stuck with a perfectly good nuclear reactor that they were not allowed to restart.

"Unit II Shift Supervisor," said Williams. "Operator Baxter reports from the Rod Drive Room that it is clear, no other personnel present. And no mops lying about," Williams had felt obliged to add his own bit of dry humor to the moment.

Ray cocked his head at the sound of the gaitronics. It was just habit, listening to every communication that came into his range of hearing. He was a person who was always aware of what was going on around him. "Unit II reactor trip, Unit II reactor trip."

"Ah, shit," said Jed Turner as he wearily got up from his spot at the table. The maintenance superintendent would be reporting to the Operations Annex to coordinate any needed repairs by the electricians, mechanics, or instrument technicians to get the unit back on the line and producing electricity. Even if it were not a failed component that brought the unit down, the reactor trip would be used to repair items awaiting a shutdown. Then there would be testing of certain critical components prior to a startup.

"Got a quarter?" demanded Lloyd Ralston, Station Manager for Jefferson Davis Nuclear Power Station. He held up the "swearing off" jar. It was his effort to eliminate swearing among the various supervisors and superintendents to create a more professional image at meetings. It was not his idea, but rather one of the stupid mandates from downtown.

Banning swearing from meetings smacked of management being taken over by yuppies, thought Ray. Cussing was the language of soldiers and working men. The executives who wore the white shirts and ties did not understand that. Not that Lloyd Ralston himself was a yuppie, far from it. Ralston was a hard-nosed, mean spirited, barrel shaped version of Scrooge. But the station manager obviously was obligated to carry out the mandates of the VP's downtown. They were yuppies. The company was going to hell in a very fragile hand basket.

The meeting proceeded without the superintendents from either operations or maintenance. About twenty minutes into the meeting, it was Ray's turn to brief the station manager and other department heads about significant security matters. He reported on the problems with the alarm system.

"Last night's "B" shift was short staffed. Just like all the other departments, this flu's taking a toll on security," said Ray. "The shift met its objectives, but was stretched pretty much to the breaking point. What makes it difficult is that we had seven alarms on security doors to various Emergency Diesel Generator Rooms and one on the Control Room access from the Normal Switch-gear Room. The problem's twofold. One, the Central Alarm System's computers are old and beginning to fail more and more. Secondly, those computers weren't designed to work with the smart card system that they're tied into."

"Well," said Ralston, with no empathy to be detected in his tone. "Like you said, every one's strapped at the moment. Nothing we can do about that. But the equipment problem is Security's own fault. There's a Work Request process, use it. Get it fixed and quit whining about it."

Ray's cheeks flushed an angry red. It was obvious to all the others that he was uncomfortable and out of place doing this anyway. Now he had just been slammed in front of the whole bunch without deserving it. Around him, other department heads were shifting their eyes awkwardly about, shuffling papers or grabbing for their cups of coffee, all of them trying to act as though they had not noticed Ralston's harsh response. This was a moment of awkwardness that they had long ago grown used to, as it generally occurred at least once during the morning meeting. They felt especially bad for Ray, however, because he was not a department head. He was not being paid the big dollars to get slammed like this.

Ray's discomfort quickly disappeared, replaced by the savage wrath that had helped him survive in the jungles of Southeast Asia.

"No!" it came out as a shout. "Hold on just one goddamned minute."

Immediately, Ralston pushed the 'swearing off' jar towards Ray, appearing nonplussed at his outburst. Ray chose to ignore it. The jar was nothing but a silly game, one that he was not playing. "When I say the system's old, I mean it's degraded and no longer dependable. Sensitive electronic components like what's in the system get unreliable before they completely fail. The computers don't have the speed to hash the crypto that the smart card system throws at them. That means that you can get a rash of unexplained alarms and when you check the circuitry you find nothing. Days, weeks, maybe months later, it suddenly crashes and then you can fucking see what's wrong. That's why it's not so easy to fix.

"Corporate went out, without consulting us, bought fucking low bid equipment. CAS either needs a major upgrade or complete replacement. If we do..."

"Bull shit," shot back Ralston. He too, now ignored the jar. Cisco was the little dog barking at the big one, and if he did not back away, he was going to feel the big dog's teeth. "Corporate gave security a say on the task force when the changes were made. Harding acknowledges that there's a problem. But I remember you being on the task team for installing the system. Fact is, I remember this smart card shit being your own fucking idea."

"That's a cock and bull story if there ever was one," Ray was in a desperate battle to keep his voice something akin to a level that qualified as talking. "We only knew about what was being bought after the purchase order was approved and sent to the supplier. The smart card shit works, it's these goddamned antique computers that we have that don't. I told Harding, the smart card people told Harding, you have to replace the fucking computers if you want it to do what it's designed to do." Ray no longer felt out of place with this group of men who were positioned higher in the food chain. He had found himself a fight; he was always comfortable when there was a fight.

"Well maybe we'll just get Harding down here to the station and I'll let you tell your VP that he's giving us a cock and bull story," challenged Ralston. "How's that grab you?"

Ralston's words were short sputters as his teeth gripped harder and harder at the unlit cigar that was always stuck in his mouth. He was angry at Cisco's belligerence, but he was also frustrated. If he had to choose whether to believe Cisco or Harding, it would be no contest. He would not entrust Harding with his neighbor's pet cat. And Ralston hated cats and he did not particularly like his neighbor. But Cisco was bound and determined to back him against a wall and he sure as hell could not allow that.

Ray was about to answer when Kat Jenkins, the Station Manager's personal secretary appeared at the door of the Attack Room. She must have been able to hear the fray, because she gave Ray a scowl of disapproval that stopped him in mid-stride.

"Ray, Lloyd, Shift Supervisor requests that both of you report to the Control Room ASAP."

The room grew instantly silent. For some serious technical matter to require that Operations consult with the Station Manager was not unusual. But the request for the Station Manager and the acting Superintendent of Security to report to the Control Room following a reactor trip was ominous. Each department head thought of how unhappy the plant personnel were as the talk of layoffs proliferated and workers were called on to accomplish more and more on less and less of a budget. The same thought ran through everyone's mind. Sabotage. Deliberate act.

Ray Cisco followed the Jefferson Davis Nuclear Power Station Manager out of the Attack Room and down the long corridor that ran along the Turbine Building's Mezzanine level. Ray was never one to be out of shape. Ralston, he was certain, was one never to have bothered to try and get in shape. Yet, the short stubby legs moved the Station Manager along at a clip that surprised Ray. It was adrenaline, to be sure. Even from behind, he could see how the veins in Ralston's fat neck stood out.

At the Control Room door, they stuck their smart cards into the dual port reader and entered their PINs. There was a long pause while the computers of the access control system read each card, verified the PINs, and ascertained that they had legitimately accessed the plant earlier in the day. Ray was silently amused at how hard Ralston's teeth were clenched on his cigar during the wait. He wanted to say, *"Sure is slow, isn't it?"* But this was not the moment. On the other side of this door was likely to be some very serious business. Whatever differences had been aired earlier, they would now be put aside. Nuclear safety and security were serious matters.

There was a loud buzz and then a metallic click as the door was finally unlocked electronically. Together, they entered the Control Room. What Ray saw there was something that he had never before seen, the organized chaos that takes place in the control room during a reactor trip. The word chaos came to mind because people were moving from one panel to the next flipping switches, pressing buttons, others were barking out commands while others repeated them back in stern fashion. Yet it was organized, it flowed. It was not at all unlike how his SEAL team would rehearse going into a terrorist stronghold to free hostages. Everybody had a place, a job and there was no bullshit, just pure adrenaline and precision drill.

They both did an obligatory pause at the red line. Beyond this line not the Station Manager, not even Roger Cowling, CEO could pass without the Control Room's Shift Supervisor's approval. Dick Trane quickly nodded his permission for them to cross over into the operational area.

"What's going on, Dick?" asked Ralston as he scrutinized the scene before him. His sweeping gaze took in the sight of Licensed Nuclear Operators as they continued to complete the steps of AP-1. He himself held a Senior Reactor Operator's license. Like Trane, he had spent many years in the Navy Nuclear program, operating the nuclear reactors that provided the steam to propel submarines through the depths of cold, murky seas.

"At 0812, we received the Reactor Trip Annunciator," Trane's voice was deliberate and matter of fact as he briefed Ray and the Station Manager. To Ray's surprise, and discomfort, he directed his comments as much to Ray as he did to Ralston. That meant only one thing; at any moment, Trane was going to say that the reactor trip was suspicious or that evidence of sabotage had been found. "We had then and still have now, absolutely no indication of what tripped the unit. No Rod Control Trouble lights, nothing. I've got Jed Turner's instrument technicians running diagnostics on both Rod Control and Reactor Protection."

"Well stay on it," said Ralston sharply. "We can't afford this. If it's broke we do what we have to do to fix it. If it's not broke, then we need to get the goddamned unit back on line."

"Ray, I'd like to find out if anybody was in the Rod Drive Room when the unit tripped," said Trane.

Ray saw Ralston's teeth clench down once again. Any moment, he expected the cigar to be bit in two and fall to the floor. He processed the operations jargon the best he could. As a supervisor, he had attended a two-week class on Nuclear Plant Operations. He knew that the Rod Control System was responsible for controlling the heat production of the reactor by regulating the fission of the nuclear fuel. The rods were moved up and down in the core as needed by a system using electromagnetic coils. When a reactor trip occurs, the Reactor Protection System trips the electrical breaker supplying the power to those electromagnets, allowing gravity to be the force that brings the rods to the bottom and shuts down the reactor.

"Any reason to believe that someone caused the trip deliberately?" asked Ray.

Ray wished that Jack Evans had not picked now to take his family on a vacation to Disney World. The thought of conducting an investigation involving so much technology was by itself, daunting. The other very unpleasant aspect was that the people who worked at the nuclear station were a family of sorts. It was his job to keep bad guys out, not to go after his own people. But that was a pipe dream, he knew. This was reality.

"That's not something that I care to speculate on," said Trane quietly. "I just want to cover all angles. We need to know what happened."

"And we need to know it fast," added Ralston. His face was a beat red. "This is a goddamned million dollars a day investigation. Trane, you sure we have to do this?" Trane simply gave a nod and turned back to Ray.

"All right if I use your phone?" asked Ray. The matter was out of Ralston's hands. If it involved nuclear security, Ray, acting as Superintendent of Security had the authority to conduct an investigation however he saw fit. At Trane's nod, Ray picked up the phone and dialed the number for the Security Central Alarm Station. It was the logical place to start.

"Dale, this is Ray," he said. "How about going into CAS and check if anyone was in the Unit II Rod Drive Room, let's say, between 0745 and 0815. I'll hang on."

Alarms continued to sound and warning lights flashed. It was all handled with a smooth deliberation that Ray could not help but admire. He also decided that it was a job filled with far more stress than he wanted at this time of his life. There was, of course, the possibility that some major stress was in the cards for him. He sure hoped that the Central Alarm Systems' computers showed that no one had been in the Rod Drive Room during the reactor trip.

Finally, Dale was back with his answer. "Thanks." Ray breathed a sigh of relief as he hung up the phone. "Unit II Rod Drive Room was vacant at the time of the trip." He directed his comments to both Trane and Ralston. "Baxter entered at 0819. Before that, the last time anyone was in there was Rogers who entered at 0710 and exited at 0717. Personally, I consider that good news. If you feel like there needs to be anymore of an investigation you'll have to guide me along. Is there anything else that you want me to check out?"

"No one tripped it," said Ralston. "Keep on Turner to find a cause. We got to get this damn thing back on line. Remember, if you can't get the job done, then there's always someone who can."

At that, Trane simply turned to the action that was taking place in his Control Room. He had a damn good pension check coming in from the Navy. Besides, words like that coming from Ralston were as natural as the laugh that comes from a hyena.

Chapter Thirteen
Thursday, December 3
Richmond, Virginia

Roger Cowling had risen for work at 7 a.m. today just like he did every morning. Coffee, two local newspapers, *The Wall Street Journal*, and *USA Today* were the beginning of his morning regimen. About midway through the Journal, Rosetta brought in breakfast. It was a robust, old fashioned, stick to your ribs start to a day type of breakfast. Roger believed that strict adherence to a proven routine was necessary for success. Starting the day well fed was just such a routine. To the sixty-seven year old CEO of Energy International, a well-fed mind and pallet were equally important.

"My dear, Rosetta," said Cowling gazing down at the fare on his breakfast plate. "Are you trying to fatten me? Two eggs, I only eat one. And oatmeal? Rosetta, we may have to discuss your early retirement so that I don't become a blimp!" Such teasing was normal. He was, however, puzzled by the extra egg. The oatmeal was something that he could count on twice a week. However, this was the third day in a row she had served it up.

"Oh, but si, Señor Cowling," said his maid, her words rolling off her tongue with that flavor of old Mexico that Cowling found so pleasant. "Lately seems you no have gusto! Perhaps better you eat more. I could not bear you be ill."

"Cease your worrying," said Cowling, with a hearty chuckle. Rosetta had been his housekeeper for the past eleven years. Besides some distant cousins who he hardly knew, she was the only family that he had. She took very good care of him, and he did the same for her. "If I am lacking in any way, it certainly is not due to your dereliction. It's this new era that the electrical industry has found itself in, Rosetta. You know how they say that you can't teach an old dog new tricks? Well, if I don't learn some new tricks, I might be without a job! Imagine me, Rosetta, standing in the unemployment line. You'd have to pay me to cook for you."

"No, no, I cannot believe such," said his maid as they laughed together.

"There is no better at what you do. Besides, how can you not have a job? No less lights are needed. And you own the company. Tu es hombre mejore! Anyway, you no can cook, I would not hire you!"

"Oh, well thanks," said Roger, shaking his head. "These are new times that we're in." He launched into the topic with Rosetta as if he were a professor and she his favorite pupil. These discussions went both ways; she listened intently whenever he talked of mergers and corporate takeovers while he listened to stories of her growing up in Mexico and about why her countrymen risked their lives to sneak north across the border. "Laws are being passed that remove the stiffly regulated nature of the business. Much like with the airlines and the telephone companies. The day is very close, Rosetta, that you may be able to buy your electricity at cheaper rates from a utility in Utah, than what my company here in Virginia can sell it to you. And they'll be able to deliver it to you. It's called freewheeling. And it's muy malissimo."

"No, no, no! Be for sure, not even if they give it free," exclaimed Rosetta. "I buy my electricity only from you."

Cowling gave her a smile. Rosetta lived in the servant's quarters. He doubted that she even knew how to contact the electric company, with the exception, of course, of talking to its CEO over breakfast most mornings.

"Now, Rosetta. Your loyalty, no matter how flattering, disappoints me," said Cowling, throwing her a look of mock scorn. "Never forsake astute fiscal management to display personal loyalty. Besides, I plan to be eating my competition for breakfast, providing I have room after all this." He raised one brow at the tray laden with food. "My company will sell you electricity for a long time to come. And it will be at the best rate you can get." He wondered what she'd say to the prospect of that electricity actually coming from her own native country. But lose lips sink ships; and regardless of her loyalty, an unknowing slip could place him alongside the Titanic at this point in the game.

"Si, Señor Cowling," grinned Rosetta. "Now you talk muy macho!"

Cowling continued with his breakfast, he was digesting the additional egg that Rosetta had set before him, polishing it off with an article on the impact of numerous small phone companies that were emerging into the market arena. Established phone companies were laying off personnel to decrease overhead. Jobs were being created in the new companies, but often in different locations and at lower pay and benefits. The bleeding heart who wrote the article appeared to be crying over the worker's demise.

"It's called capitalism, you bloody fool," muttered Cowling. He looked up as Rosetta entered the breakfast room. It was an all glass enclosure, triple pane, boasting a broad expanse of spider plants, fern, coleus and other such plants that flourished in the greenhouse like atmosphere. Rosetta had added a wide variety of her country's native cactus, including the famed Agave from which Tequila is made.

"Señor Cowling, Señor Harding from Richmond Nuclear is on the phone," said Rosetta.

"Thank you," said Cowling, taking the portable from her. "Travis, good morning. What unwanted tidings are you starting my morning off with?" Was this official company business, such as trouble with one of the nuclear units? Or did he have some additional information concerning Brian Matkins' trip to Atlanta.

"Unit II at Jefferson Davis tripped just after eight this morning," said the V.P. of Security and Administration for Richmond Nuclear. "Nothing major appears to have caused it. At the moment, Ralston is not anticipating a long shutdown."

"Make sure that Ralston knows, and I want you to tell him personally, that whatever it takes, I don't want that unit down for more than two days," said Cowling, his voice as cold as the frost on the grass of his front lawn. "Understood?"

"I will pass that message along, sir," said Harding. "I'll let you know if there are any further developments."

"No," said Cowling. "That would be an unforgivable waste of my time and yours. Instead, make certain that there are no further developments. Ride with me now, and you can ride with me later. Believe me, there is some riding to be done. And you know it."

"You know that you can count on me, sir," said Travis.

"Any word from our friend?" asked Cowling, ignoring Harding's affirmation.

"Knowing him, he's been way to busy pounding pussy to think about this place," said Harding. "He'll call me after the meeting. Want me to give you a call?"

"Only if he gets some kind of real decision out of the NRC," said Cowling. "That's not likely."

Cowling clicked the phone off and laid it down on the table. Then he continued with his breakfast and paper. Harding was the worst possible trash. A college classmate of Brian Matkins and professed friend, he was selling

Matkins down the river without a single trace of remorse. As soon as it was all done, Harding would have to go. Cowling could not stand such scum. For the moment, however, Harding's perverse sense of loyalty and selfish ambition was what he needed.

At eight thirty, he was out of the house and on his way to the office, chauffeured in his Lincoln Town Car. Even enroute to the office, he continued to read his morning papers. It was unforgivable imprudence to skip over even the tiniest, seemingly unimportant article. Roger Cowling read it all. Treasure, he knew, was hidden in the most unlikely places. Though this morning, it was more difficult to focus on such articles. Matkins being in Atlanta, talking to the NRC made him nervous. The evidence he would present of Energy International's cutbacks being a risk to safe operation of Jefferson Davis Nuclear Power Station would likely be convincing. By the time the NRC began to consider how to react to what was going on between Richmond Nuclear and Energy International, the smoke should be clearing. The ignorant legislators of California that had so significantly screwed up free enterprise where electric generation deregulation was concerned would be left holding the bag. Matkins' cavalry would arrive too late. At least that was the plan. Nothing in life, however, was for certain. Perhaps he could use the blackmail tape to get Matkins to recant some of the evidence he presented to the NRC.

"Good morning, Edna," said Cowling as he entered his office. Edna, his prim and proper secretary, notoriously disliked by the entire staff, was at her desk. She sat there as though presiding over a throne. Like Rosetta, she had been with him a very long time. Unlike Rosetta, he did not care to engage in conversation with her. He kept her around simply because she had the loyalty and demeanor of a faithful watchdog. That was something he needed in a personal secretary.

"Good morning, Sir," said Edna. "Frank Baker is on the phone. He insisted on holding for you. He's been on the line for about five minutes. I explained to him that he was calling too early."

"I'll take it in my office," said Cowling, shaking his head. He continued on through the heavy oaken doors. Taking his time and situating himself in his chair, he finally picked up the phone.

"Frank," said Cowling, his tone clearly displaying his dismay at having to talk to the Board member. "If you called to tell me that we have a unit down at Jefferson Davis, I already know."

"I trust that you're also doing something about it," said Baker, his tone tense, demanding. He was real damned tired of Cowling trying to bully him around. Maybe the CEO had nerves of steel or just did not care if he went belly up, but having one of the nuclear units down at this so very critical moment could be catastrophic. "We vote to sell soon. If the capacity factor drops then they can refuse to buy or at least adjust for lost capacity. Then I lose big! We can't afford this. I've got millions of my own money tied up down there in Mexico and I'm not about to lose it."

"Frank, calm yourself," said Cowling, his voice scornful. "It would take a lot more than just being down a few days to bring the units' capacity factors to below seventy-eight percent. Even if that happened, the points we end up paying won't prevent the deal from going through, not unless capacity drops down to seventy-six percent on both units. Our fossil units are hanging in there pretty damn good, too.

"The only real threat," Cowling continued. "Is if our stock changes drastically. If it drops below thirty-four, they can decline to buy. We cannot and will not allow anything to happen which would cause that to happen. I've got it all under control."

"Roger, have you dealt with Matkins yet?" asked Frank, not at all satisfied with Cowling's answer. "What happens if Matkins gets to vote? Or if he gets the NRC to shut us down? He'll laugh himself sick watching us go down."

"Frank, do you ever do a goddamned thing besides worry?" asked Cowling in exasperation. "You'll have worried yourself to death and then, yes, damn it, Matkins will get to vote!" Matkins only had a vote if one of the regular Board members could not attend for whatever reason. There were seven Board members. Four, a majority, had large sums of personal money secretly invested in the Mexico project. The remaining three were expected to oppose any sell of Richmond Nuclear and of yet, knew nothing of the proposed sell or the prospect of building more nuclear reactors in Mexico. Neither did Matkins. Since all four of the Board members were over sixty, with one in his seventies and yet another in her eighties, Matkins was potential trouble. It was unlikely that he would be called upon to vote, but Cowling knew it would be imprudent not to have the possibility covered.

"Damn it, Roger!" Baker shot back. "We have to be ready for some unlikely act of nature. Like one of us being hospitalized. Mary Beth's been in and out of the hospital with her blood clots several times this year. God, we just can't take a chance."

"Well, it just so happens," said Cowling, a light chuckle escaping his lips as he thought of his play on words. "We already have an act of nature. But it's one working to our advantage. You know that. Matkins, if he ends up voting, will vote the way we tell him to vote. I've got work to do. Goodbye, Frank." With that, Cowling hung up.

Chapter Fourteen
Thursday, December 3
Atlanta, Georgia

Brian let the water hit him in its pulsating, soothing streams. It felt like his dick might just fall off, he had used it so damn much last night. *Damn! She is so damn fine!* Now all he had to do was show up at the NRC's Region II headquarters and convince them of how detrimental Energy International's proposed cost reduction plan was to Richmond Nuclear's successful and safe operation. There was no detriment from his nearly sleepless night. On the contrary, he was abuzz with energy, seemingly ethereal in its source.

His meeting was for 10 a.m. Glancing at his watch, sitting on the counter, he saw that it was only 8:13 am. Plenty of time to run down stairs and grab some pancakes, scrambled eggs, and fresh coffee. Last night had certainly given him one hell of an appetite.

What would it be like to be married to Tanya? Waking up next to her in the mornings? Coming home to her in the evenings? Probably an early grave for him; he laughed at the thought. And it would likely mean an early retirement, as well. There was enough animosity towards him on the part of the people who had hired him, the Energy International Board of Directors. Were he to leave Brenda for the likes of an attractive, young flight attendant, they would zealously claim that he had become unreliable and that his ethical standards were impaired. As if the group that ran Energy International had any inkling as to what ethical standards were.

Brian dried and dressed. Then he glanced at the phone. It was time to do what, unfortunately, simply had to be done. He picked it up and dialed the number.

"Hello," his wife answered. Her voice was cold. There had been three messages when he got back to the hotel, all from her.

"Hey, good morning," said Brian, struggling to generate enthusiasm.

"You said you'd call last night. Stephanie wanted to say good night to you. She wanted to thank you for such a happy birthday. Guess you had other business to attend to, huh?"

Her words stung. Not that he felt any guilt about being with Tanya. For him and Brenda, the marriage was nothing but a partnership for the raising of their two daughters; at least as far as he was concerned. That she struggled to make it more was a source of constant consternation. However, that he had disappointed Stephanie gave him genuine remorse.

"A couple of execs from Duke Power were in town. We went out for dinner and had a few drinks." Shit, how he hated telling bold-faced lies. "They seem to be having a lot of this company restructuring to deal with just like Richmond Nuclear. We just got to talking, lost track of the time."

"That happens a lot in Atlanta."

"Well, you almost always have execs from other companies in town to meet with the NRC." Damn it, another lie. It made him angry that she forced him to cheat and lie. Why did she not just accept the fact that they were through? "Anyway, I've got to get down and have some breakfast and make my meeting. Call you later?"

"Yeah, I'm used to later. Bye." There was the click and then the line went dead. It was a sound that filled him with a sense of coldness.

There was no time to sit around and ponder over what had been said and how it made him feel. But it did bother him, and that, of course, was cause for concern. Maybe it was not as dead for him as he made himself believe. Or perhaps it was quilt. How does the song go? *You don't know what you've got until it's gone?* He shook his uneasiness aside and made sure that his tie was straight. Then, checking that the contents of his briefcase were as they should be, he left the room.

At the elevator, he pressed the call button and waited. By the time he heard the 'ding' of the elevator stopping at the eighth floor, two other passengers had joined him. One was an aged, white haired gentleman who looked to be in his eighties. They exchanged "good mornings". The man had two plastic probes sticking up his nose from a long clear tube connected to a portable oxygen caddie that he pushed in front of him, and a pack of Camels in his shirt pocket. Brian shook his head. It amazed him how people could display such utter disregard for their own health and well-being.

The second passenger was a brunette, probably in her early thirties; she wore a black outfit designed for the business-minded woman. She appeared fit and he speculated how she might look in a more revealing dress. The dark sunglasses she wore unfortunately hid her eyes. *"Must not be a morning person," thought Brian.*

It was just as the elevator reached the ground floor that he felt his phone vibrate. He pulled it out to answer as the elevator stopped and the doors opened. The phone had been in his jacket pocket instead of on his belt and it must have been buzzing before he noticed it, because as he pulled it out, it stopped. He made his way to the nearby hotel lounge, deserted in the morning hours and sat down at one of the tables. There, he quickly checked his voice mail. It was a message to call the Station Manager at Jefferson Davis Nuclear Power Station. Quickly he dialed Ralston's number. An unexpected call from the station could only mean a problem, likely a big one. The line rang twice before it was answered.

"Good morning. Station Manager's office. How may I help you?" answered Kat Jenkins.

"Kat, Matkins. Good morning," said Brian. "Got a message to call Lloyd. Have you broken one of my toys?"

"Well… he's in his office waiting for you, Mr. Matkins. I'll let him tell you what's broken."

There was that slight pause where one holds their breath, waiting to see whether they actually get transferred or disconnected. Kat had a habit of doing that. Computers and phones, you would think the proficiency of their use would be job requirements for the personal secretary of the Manager of a nuclear power station. He did not have time to get cut off this morning. This was cutting into breakfast.

"Brian." Lloyd's voice was raspy from years of smoking and yelling at people. "Unit II came down at 8:12 this morning."

"What brought it down?" asked Brian. The pancakes and scrambled eggs were starting to look like a long shot.

"Gravity, I guess," said Ralston. "There was nothing indicating the cause. And still nothing. Instrument techs are doing diagnostics but it's starting to baffle us all. Call you as soon as I know something. Harding says that Cowling ate his butt good a few minutes ago. Demanded that we get the unit back on line right the fuck now. What the hell's going on, Brian? Why is Cowling getting his panties all in a wad over a unit going down? He knows how business has to be done."

"You know Cowling. The bottom line is always what's up with him," said Brian. He paused for a moment, considering whether or not he should tell Ralston at least something of what he suspected. But it was not proven, and he would be doing the company a disservice plus destroying his credibility if in the end, he was wrong. "I've got to get going. Any ideas at all on what brought it down?"

"None."

"Well, keep me up to date." Brian hung up, not wasting precious breath to tell Ralston to get the problem fixed. There was not another man alive more competent. Nor was there another Station Manager more loathed by those that worked for him. The man was relentless. However, it was that same relentlessness that had increased Jefferson Davis' generation capacity higher than nearly any other electric power plant in America, fossil or nuclear. And he did it with a commitment to the safety of the nuclear core that resembled the Pope's commitment to daily prayer.

Ralston was also perceptive. He knew something was going on. Cowling never bothered himself to apply pressure to get a unit back on line. Doing so could be construed as interference, something that was forbidden under the rules that the State Corporation Commission applied to the Energy International - Richmond Nuclear relationship. This was just one more thing that Brian could bring to the attention of the Nuclear Regulatory Commission. It was also another signal that what he had been suspecting all along was indeed a fact; that Energy International was planning to sell its generating units. And God forbid that it would be to those nut cases in California.

Across the lounge he noticed that the brunette from the elevator had taken a seat at one of the tables and was on her phone as well. Must be a rash of early morning crises, he mused. Her dark glasses were sitting on the table, but she was turned just enough that he could not see her face. He could not help but think that something about her seemed familiar. Perhaps, like he, she traveled to Atlanta often for business and used this same hotel.

Rather than hang up when Brian Matkins did, Rachel kept her phone to her ear. Good spy craft relied on not assuming that minor details would go unnoticed by amateurs. Where Matkins was sitting, he could see her every move. For another thirty seconds, she laughed into the phone, she then interrupted the imaginary audience on the phone's other end and argued good naturedly. Then she hung up.

Brian Matkins' phone going off when it did had been perfect, allowing her to verify that she was intercepting his phone traffic. She had been aware that his phone was ringing by her own buzzing in her pocket. This particular phone call had been of absolutely no interest to her. She had no interest in his business dealings. This was all just in case Bambi needed to contact him during the day. A mid-day fuckfest was sure to be necessary before Brian flew back to Richmond and she wanted to document it. The phone calls themselves would be of no use to her client, as they constituted a violation of Mr. Matkins' privacy and would have resulted in her losing her PI license if they came to light.

Rachel put the phone down and began gazing at the stack of papers before her, keeping an eye on her quarry. It was at that moment that a waiter showed up to offer her coffee, fully blocking her view of Brian. It was, after all, he said, on the house. But she declined. She would follow Matkins. If he showed up at Region II NRC headquarters, fine. Then maybe, she would come back to the hotel and get a nap. Who was to say, however, that he would not meet Bambi again, or perhaps even a second woman? Maybe there was no meeting with the NRC. Unlikely, she knew, but if it did happen, she wanted it documented. Matkins had proved himself to be slime, and it was her job to prove just how slimy he was.

Matkins was suddenly up and moving towards the restaurant. Then he stopped, glanced at his watch, shook his head and headed for the front desk. Rachel wished that he would simply go on into the restaurant. An omelet and coffee would have been nice. But breakfast was not to be. Most likely he would go to the front desk and request a cab. Rachel had been up and out of her room earlier, had had the valet bring her van to the front of the hotel and then paid him twenty dollars to let her leave it there. Wherever Brian Matkins was going, she was ready to follow.

Chapter Fifteen
Thursday, December 3
Nuclear Regulatory Office, Region II
Atlanta, Georgia

Brian left the Region II Office of the Nuclear Regulatory Commission frustrated, angry and frightened. The only thing positive to come out of the meeting was that the Region II Director of the NRC appeared concerned at the cost cutting measures that Energy International was forcing upon Richmond Nuclear. He was assured that an evaluation would be forth coming, timely and thorough. That meant no immediate steps by the NRC to stop Roger Cowling's meddling. By the time the NRC evaluated the situation and was ready to step in, Brian felt certain that Richmond Nuclear would belong to someone else. The damage would be done. The only thing that he would be able to do would be to use what resources he had to keep the nuclear station safe.

The receptionist for the Director's office called a cab for the Richmond Nuclear VP. Brian thanked her and then stood near the door, waiting for it. Out of earshot, he dialed Tanya's number on his cell phone. There was no answer. Not even her answering machine picked up. This, too, was frustrating. Hopefully by the time he got to her apartment, she would be back.

If it came to a vote among the board of directors to sell Richmond Nuclear, Brian knew that Cowling would have the votes. A majority of the board belonged to Cowling, lock, stock and barrel. Only if one of them could not be there, would Richmond Nuclear have a chance to survive, because then, Brian would be called upon to vote in the missing member's place. That scenario, however, was highly unlikely. Richmond Nuclear, he was sure, would soon be an entity of the past. Worse yet, would be the wrecked lives of many of his employees as a new owner decided to replace them. That always happened in buyouts. It was very likely that his position would be in jeopardy.

Brian dialed a different combination of numbers. It rang twice before a familiar voice answered, "Hello, Richmond Nuclear. Travis Harding's office..." Brian was impatient and cut off Travis' secretary before she could go through her entire spiel.

"Valerie, Matkins here. Travis in?"

"Good afternoon, Brian," said Valerie, not seeming to notice the VP's agitation. "Yes, he is."

"Thanks, I need to speak..." Brian heard himself put on hold in mid-sentence. Travis' secretary qualified for her position merely by the fact that she would assume any position that Travis wished of her, in bed. And she looked stunning at his table whenever he took her to the country club. Brian had hinted to Travis on many occasions, especially on occasions that Valerie had screwed something up, that he should replace her. Travis simply made excuses for her.

He knew that he should have forced Travis' hand in the matter. Brian should have long ago flatly told him to get someone in as his secretary that he would not end up sleeping with. It did not matter to him who Travis slept with, but it should not be an employee. A couple of times, he had thought about getting rid of Travis, but it was hard to do that to his old college buddy. Perhaps it was good that he had not gotten rid of him. Now was a crucial moment and he needed the loyalty of his friend. Brian was certain that some stormy weather was sure to break.

"Brian! How goes the mission?" asked Harding.

"Not well, actually. They promise to evaluate and take action if necessary," said Brian. "Problem is, if Cowling is fixing us for a sell, the NRC will never get to the matter in time. Any information on why we lost Unit II?"

"No," said Harding, relieved that he would have something positive to tell Cowling. Maybe that would take some of the heat off on the unit being down. "I wanted to check with you before we ask for permission to restart it. We've been through all possibilities for the reactor trip, top to bottom. Not a damn thing. I don't know what Cowling's problem is, but he's seething. Wants it back on line right now." Of course, he did know what Cowling's problem was and Travis would very much like to have ordered the unit put back on line. But it had to go through the NRC first and if the Senior VP did not make the request, then it was unlikely that the NRC would say yes.

"Continue looking," said Brian. "They'll want a definitive cause for the reactor trip. If we don't have anything further by tomorrow morning, then we'll ask permission for a restart. I don't think that it's any plainer than the nose on your face why Cowling's screaming. He's got a buyer. If the capacity factor drops, then so does the value."

"Yeah. Well, on a more interesting note, how's Tanya?" asked Harding. Cowling was going to be pissed to hear about the delay. He wished someone else could convey the message to the old goat. "You staying awake today?"

"Barely," said Brian, answering his friend's second question first. "I don't think I could survive too many trips to Atlanta. She's getting fucking wild. I'm not sure that I'd even tell you what she had me doing last night!"

"Come on! That anyway to treat a frat brother?" teased Harding. "Couldn't be anymore awesome than what we did with those three cheerleaders at Tech after we kicked Virginia's ass at homecoming. You and me buddy, you threw the long one and I was there for you. God, I'll never forget how great that felt."

"The girls or the touchdown? Shit, Tech pales in comparison," said Brian, shaking his head. "Hey, my cab's here. Push hard on finding the cause of the reactor trip. Talk to you later."

When the cab pulled up front, Brian gave the driver Tanya's La Sard address. He tried her phone one more time on the way over. Still there was no answer. When the taxi came to a stop in front of the apartment building, he saw that her car was parked in its spot. He felt better. Likely she had just stepped into the shower or a relaxing bath when he had started calling. Her voice mail was probably full, too.

Brian used the smart card Tanya had given him to get through the foyer and then rode the elevator up. He rang the doorbell three times and waited. When nothing happened, no sound of footsteps as Tanya rushed to the door to let him in, he used the card once more to let himself in.

"Tanya?" he spoke her name in a normal tone of voice as he stepped inside. There was no answer. Brian was not sure whether he was angry or worried. Maybe she had had to make a quick trip to the store. There was a small convenience store within walking distance.

"Tanya?" again he called her name, this time his voice was constricted with his uneasiness. A smell was setting him on edge. It had hit him the moment he had stepped inside, but it was only now that he realized how much it frightened him. It was a stench that he knew from somewhere, sometime in his past. He simply could not remember what it was.

Brian was startled to find his legs weak as he moved towards the bedroom. Its door was slightly ajar and from it emanated the sickly, repugnant odor. The stink was stronger the closer he got. Strong enough to bring back the elusive memory it had triggered. He had been eight years old, coming home from a day with his parents at the amusement park. Rascal, the families German Shepherd had not come out front to greet them. Brian had gone to the backyard to find him. Rascal was nowhere to be seen. It had been a hot, July day, and as young Brian had approached the doghouse that he and his dad had built together, he had for the first time in his life, smelled what he now smelled.

Brian felt his legs warning him that they were shutting down, refusing to take him another step closer. He lunged through the doorway, knowing that if he did not, he would collapse into a heap on the floor. The door banged hard against a nightstand with a loud crash. And there she was.

Tanya's eyes were frozen wide open with the terror that she must have felt as death had come to her. Her nude body lay partly atop the bed, covered with her own blood, which had clotted and coagulated all the way down her legs and to the floor. Like once molten lava, it was now congealed, finally mixing with what could only be feces. Intestines emerged from the gapping wound, lying on the bed beside her and hanging over the edge of her bed.

It was only a second later that this pungent mixture of death sent Brian stumbling towards the bathroom, his vomit staining his suit before he could direct it otherwise. He tripped and literally fell into the bathroom, gagging violently. For five minutes he retched unceasingly. Finally, he collapsed, exhausted, near the base of the commode which had caught very little of his vomit.

Brian's stomach was knotted up into a tight ball. Moving seemed to be out of the question, there simply was not the strength for it. But he had to move. He absolutely had to. Because, in the room next to him, was the shredded body of a woman, his lover.

He thought of shielding his eyes from the gory scene as he made his way out of the bathroom. But he could not do that. Brian leaned against the doorway, studying the grotesque scene in disbelief. The stench no longer had its nauseating effect on him. It was there, but it had already given him his worst. His mind seemed to clear. Rational thought seemed to come back to him.

A multitude of thoughts flooded his mind. Leave. Call 911. Was the killer still in the apartment? The first gelling thought that came was that as soon as he called the police, his life would never be the same. That, however, was what he must do. Tanya was dead; his life was in ruin. The Board members of Energy International would finally have their justification for voting him out, his marriage would be over and perhaps he would even be convicted of

Tanya's horrible death. What this would do to his children and to Brenda was staggering.

Glancing at the phone on the dresser, he steadied himself for the call to 911. Despite his many fears, he knew that to do otherwise was foolish, that it would simply make him look guiltier. Before he grasped the receiver, he suddenly thought of fingerprints. Perhaps the murderer's fingerprints were on the phone. That almost made him laugh it was such a stupid thought. A killer rips Tanya's guts apart and then picks up the phone to make a call. Unlikely, as hell, though he still needed to be careful.

Brian took out his flip phone. Using it would make certain that he did not destroy any prints on the phone, however unlikely they might be. He dialed 9-1- and then stopped cold. Finger prints. The knife, what if the killer had used their knife? Would it still bear his fingerprints from last night? Brian sat the phone down. How would he ever explain his fingerprints on the knife? What would he think if he were an investigator, listening to the story that he would have to tell? He stuck his phone back into his pocket.

It was at this moment that he saw the unusual device sitting on the dresser beside the phone. Crumbling bits of earth dirtied the dresser top and the device. With a rattling jolt of horror, Brian realized that it was a miniature camera. Undoubtedly, it had been hidden in the flower arrangement. The knife game had been her idea. Had their tacky, bizarre sex-game been taped? By Tanya? Cowling? Who? What the hell was going on? Brian felt his legs begin to give way once again.

"Shit, Jesus," yelled Brian, jumping back as his flip phone in his jacket pocket vibrated. It vibrated a couple of times before his trembling hands could extract it.

"Matkins," the voice was heavily accented. "I'm sure that this is a difficult moment for you. Do you see the camera on the dresser?"

"Yes," Brian struggled to get the answer out. "Who the fuck is…"

"I have a most interesting video of your performance from last night. Especially the footage with you and your toy," said the voice.

The knife had been the only 'toy' that they had used. There was no doubt as to what the voice referred to. Panic swept through Brian as he considered the implications of the police viewing a tape of him fucking Tanya, holding her at the point of the very knife that had obviously been used to slaughter her. Occasionally, he had experienced the same horrible dreams everyone has; those in which you have killed someone and now must face the consequences. But this was no dream, no mere nightmare. It was a living, hellish reality.

Could Cowling have…? Would Cowling have done this? Who else would have reason? His fright made room for anger.

"Listen carefully, Matkins," said the insidious voice. "Walk out of the apartment and call for a cab. Just do as you're told when the time comes and you will save you and your family unsurvivable torment and consequences. You will get instructions and they will come from me and only me."

"Did Cowling do this? You fucking bastard…" he screamed into the phone. But there was only a click, terminating the connection.

Rachel followed Matkins to the NRC Region II headquarters. Why she bothered would have made other private investigators roll their eyes and shake their heads. Her career had been built on following cold war spies while there was still a Soviet Union. One element of good surveillance was to never assume. Thus, she watched as he exited the taxi and entered the Atlanta Region II office of the Nuclear Regulatory Commission. Only then did she go to find breakfast. She was tired, but she needed coffee and something to eat.

It was unlikely that any meeting that an executive would fly from Richmond to Atlanta for would last less than two hours. Besides, to post herself outside the NRC for any length of time would be inviting trouble. In these days since September 11 and the final war with Iraq, there would, without doubt be trained watchers looking for any sign of surveillance on a federal facility. The threat level was currently Yellow, but that was high despite being normal. The Homeland boys would be on their toes and Rachel would rather not have to explain what she was doing to them.

Brian's call to Travis Harding had woken her as she napped, fully dressed in her hotel room. Within moments, Rachel had her shoes on and had been ready to leave the room when she heard him leave. The conversation was recorded and would make for a nice piece of leverage by Brenda Matkins if she chose to use it the right way. It was not something she could use in court because she had no permission to place a wiretap on Brian Matkins' phone. Though there was no physical wiretap, it amounted to the same thing in a court of law. However, playing it back to Matkins at the right moment would likely yield valuable concessions that a divorce attorney would charge thousands for.

The reality was, she had gathered enough dirt on Matkins last night and could have slept late this morning and taken a convenient flight home. Now, however, she sat in stunned silence in her rental van, parked outside of Tanya Madison's apartment. Rachel was monitoring a phone call that Brian Matkins had just received on his flip phone. This was unbelievable. Her subject was suddenly, out of nowhere, a victim of blackmail. Her very straight forward, easy to make case for marital infidelity had just blasted off into a high orbit without giving her time to strap in.

Matkins was inside the apartment. Rachel knew that, because she had returned here rather than try guessing when he would leave the NRC building. She had been sitting here about forty-five minutes. Tanya Madison's car was parked in its normal spot. From the cell phone conversation, however, it sounded like Tanya was not in the apartment. Was Tanya Madison part of an elaborate setup to compromise Brian Matkins? There had been no mention of money, rather an explicit warning for Matkins to do as he was told. The caller's purpose was vague, but he had seemed extremely focused in the delivery of his message.

Rachel fought to ward off the effects of the adrenaline that pulsed through her veins. Three times in her career, she had worked extortion cases. Twice had been for political gain, and once for monetary. The victims had each been prominent embassy officials, all of them, serving in Bonn during the cold war. Two of them had been swept up in romantic liaisons specifically meant to compromise them, much like this. East German agents convinced the third that he had committed vehicular homicide while driving drunk one night after a party. No one, in fact, had been killed. But the diplomat, though not scared of prosecution due to his diplomatic immunity, had been fearful of being booted from the Diplomatic Corp. Thus, he had resorted to handing over state secrets.

Tanya Madison was no longer Bambi to Rachel, not if she was part of this. Instead, she had to be a real pro to play her role so well. Tanya had given every appearance of being a young woman caught up in lustful, illicit love. From the sounds of it, she had quite effectively sold Brian a bill of goods that he could ill afford.

Matkins' first call had disgusted her with all the good old boy back slapping that had gone on with Travis Harding. She assumed that Harding was most likely another one of the company's executives. Clearly, there was too much testosterone in Richmond Nuclear's upper management. That conversation, however, now faded away. Brian Matkins was being blackmailed, here, right in front of her. What did she need to do about it?

Nearby, most likely in this very parking lot, was someone watching Brian

Matkins as she was. Rachel scrutinized the vehicles around her. She did not expect to see the Harley, but looked for it anyway. A motorcycle was not the vehicle of choice for someone who had to watch and wait; especially not a Harley, with its thunderous roar. There were, of course, the other apartments, and the cars that were parked out on the street.

In her mind, Rachel could see that flash of light in the darkened window from last night. Someone had indeed been in the apartment. Most likely setting up the camera that the caller had referred to. Thus, one of the individuals that she had photographed leaving the building was the blackmailer. The voice on the phone was male. She thought of the man on the Harley. He seemed the most likely.

Rachel watched a terrified Matkins emerge from the apartment building. In one respect, the avid look of fear that showed on his face was fitting; she had, after all, no sympathy for cheaters and liars. "Play around with fire, asshole, and you will get burned," she muttered under her breath while watching him blink at the brightness of the sun, glance in all directions and then quickly turn away. With an unsteady, yet rapid stride, he rounded the corner of the apartment complex and disappeared from sight.

Rachel watched and waited; hoping that whoever was blackmailing Matkins was careless enough not to consider that this game had another player. She was tempted to follow him, but that would expose her to anyone watching. And they must be watching, or how else would they have known to call while he was in the apartment? It was better to see if someone else moved to follow him. She sat for a reasonable amount of time and realized that no one was going to do so.

There was, of course, the million-dollar question: *Was the blackmailer also watching her?* She had taken minimal precautions in that respect. With a basic operation involving a cheating husband, one simply avoided being seen by one's subject and attracting attention. Elaborate avoidance simply was not necessary. With the circumstances as she now knew them, however, she was butt-ass naked. Anyone watching Matkins had likely observed her.

Abdul would like to have had a better vantage point with which to see the blue van. As it was, his vantage point was not the best. Though not one to overlook potential complications on a mission, this strange new player was most unexpected and unappreciated.

The Madison woman's body had to have been a gruesome sight. Abdul's niece always took a perverted pleasure in a kill. Her use of sexual enticement and thirst for blood were valuable tools to the fight. So much the better, however, had she grown up knowing how to love and to have a family. Life, though, was what circumstances created. In Fatima's case, it had taken a young girl and created a killing machine. Perhaps, he should have smuggled her from Iran to get psychiatric help instead of taking her to live with her aunt and uncle. It was, however, much too late for retrospect. He never stopped wondering if she had any memory of that horrible day in Tehran. Were all those memories blocked out? Pray to Allah that such was the case, and may a thousand camels shit and piss on Roger Cowling's soon to be grave that that day had ever happened.

Finally, the blue van pulled from its parking space and drove off. His view of the driver was but for a mere instant, but all that he needed, praise Allah. His hands deftly clicked several shots with a digital camera, its telephoto lens pulling her image in close. Within moments, these pictures would be down loaded to his handheld and then emailed to his men in Richmond. If his intuition was correct, and rarely did Allah allow it to fail, this woman would be going back to Richmond. Perhaps she would fly on the same plane as Brian Matkins. At any rate, his men would be watching for her. When they found her, they would kill her. It had to be done, to allow otherwise would be very foolish. Thanks be to Allah that he had spotted her.

Chapter Sixteen
November 12, 1979
Tehran, Iran

Abdul raced through the narrow streets, crowded with its rampaging, chanting masses. Damn Sahed. His soul, if he possessed one, would burn forever in the fires of hell. Maybe the phone call had been in error. Perhaps his family was safely onboard the plane, entering Turkish airspace even now. His mind continued to seek hope. His heart, however, was close to bursting in his chest. The part of him that was still rational knew that catastrophe awaited him.

On every street there were angry mobs. He avoided them when he could, and when he could not, forced his way through as they chanted their anti-Shah, anti-American slogans. Occasionally, they stopped their verbal attacks in order to praise the name of Khomeini. Their thinking was mad; they were capable at this moment of performing acts so horrifying that their conscious minds would someday disassociate the memory of them entirely, or else they would face insanity. A mad man galvanized by fear, Abdul was aware of hitting several of his fellow countrymen with his car, knocking them to the pavement.

Mohammad had called him from the airport as Abdul had requested, letting him know that Roger Cowling had arrived and that his plane had departed safely.

"Did he get his property safely loaded onto the plane?" Abdul had asked, anxious to know that his family was safely out of the reach of the fanatics. He had earlier explained that Cowling was his good friend and that he was only interested in seeing him safely out of Iran.

Despite the tremendous anti-American sentiment, many of the most fervent Khomeini supporters had American friends whom they were anxious to see out of harms way. Many, like Abdul, would like to have seen the hostages in the American Embassy released as well. But once these people, many who were loving and with generous hearts, were together in the streets, stirred by the foment of the religious wrath that Khomeini encouraged, even inspired, their individual nature as human beings disappeared entirely. They had become savages, nothing unlike wild boar, hungry and enraged.

"No," Mohammad had told him. "Cowling came by car. He had only the rug. He appeared very frightened and he left quickly." Mohammad had helped him load the rug onto the plane. There was nothing else. The plane flew away with only Cowling and the one package. Abdul was in a rage that he did not know was possible. His state of mind was as deadly as that of the angry mobs. It had been his father's prize Nain, done in silk, inlaid with gold and silver along the borders and with pearls and small diamonds woven into each corner. It had been a gift to his father from the Shah. His father had given it to Cowling as a gift to symbolize the special friendship that Cowling had with the Hasdiz family. He himself had helped Cowling stick it through the back and across the folded down front passenger seat of the Volkswagen Rabbit.

His hands were shaking as he down shifted. The Bradford Oil Building was on the right, just ahead. He could see it now. His stomach twisted and turned in abject terror as he saw that the throng of Persians in front of the building had formed a circle like a pack of hungry wolves surrounding prey. He jumped out of his car. The street and sidewalk was one solid mass of human flesh. Violently he elbowed his way through the wall of humanity gone mad.

When Abdul got to the center, what he saw froze his blood. Men, women, even children were carting stones to the edge of a circle. In that circle were his mother and father, his sister and her nine-year-old daughter.

Abdul felt as though a monstrous hand had ripped through the wall of his chest and was crushing his heart within its grasp. His father sat there, clutching his mother's arm, stoic against the horrible, painful death that he knew would soon come. His mother wept. Ghetti, his sister, held her daughter tightly to her bosom, as though to perhaps shield the young Fatima from what would be slow, agonizing death from the stones. Fatima, her eyes wide with fear, stared back into the angry crowd, gazing at her family's tormentors in confusion. There was little to be done. A mob such as this was a carnivorous creature with no conscience, no empathy. Only spilt blood would satisfy.

Only two days ago, Abdul had denounced his family. Publicly, he had called them infidels, servants of the American Satan, doers of the Shah's misguided policies. Then he had worked feverishly with Cowling to develop a plan to get his family to safety. Now, his father stared at him with eyes filled with fear. But Abdul knew that it was not for his own life that his father feared, but for his. His father would fear that Abdul would sacrifice his own life hopelessly trying to save them. That Abdul would have done without hesitation if it were possible to do so.

Assistant Minister of Taxation for the Shah, his father had never cheated, never lied. But he was a symbol of what had once been the Shah, and Khomeini wanted, encouraged, all that represented the Shah, to be destroyed. Both his mother and his sister had been at the forefront of seeking higher status for women in the nation of Iran and all Islam; they too, represented a freedom that threatened the Ayahtolla's ability to wield his sword of power. Even now their faces were bare of the chador, the veil that Allah required a woman to wear. He was powerless to do anything; yet he could not allow the innocent to perish. How could the crowd, even in its fury, ignore the innocence of young Fatima?

Then, he caught sight of Sahed. Sahed the devil! It was not really for their crimes that Sahed had dragged them down here into the street. Instead, it was an attack on him. Abdul had a strong influence among many who were being called upon to make up Khomeini's Council of God. Sahed wanted that influence for himself. This was all his doing, his attempt to destroy Abdul. It had nothing to do with seeking justice, of blessed service to the Ayatollah. If Abdul were to now so much as raise a finger to plead for these who had been pronounced guilty, he would sacrifice all influence, which was precisely Sahed's desire. And that influence was important; not on a personal level, but for the sake of the Iran he loved. Left to his own devices, Khomeini would lead the nation into an age of darkness. Perhaps he could not stop that from happening, but he could eventually help bring it back into the light when Khomeini died, and maybe even manage to keep that plunge into darkness from going too far.

Fatima was calling out to him. Though her words were lost upon the din of the mob, he seemed to hear her say "Uncle, take us home." He could not let this mob kill her. Nor could he allow Sahed to goad him into an action that would prevent him from helping Iran find its road to the future. And certainly, he could not die without first seeing Roger Cowling pay for his treachery. Roger Cowling, lover of money, faithful to none, would pay a devastating price for his treachery.

Already stones were being hurled. One struck his sister in the mouth, barely missing Fatima. Another hit his father in the chest, knocking him backwards. Quickly, Abdul stepped forward. He would do what only could be done at this point. Several ordered him out of their way, as they prepared to cast their stones. From the holster at his side, he pulled his pistol. Sahed, raised his hand and the stones stopped coming as the crowd now looked on with curiosity. Abdul knew their fervor too well, however, to believe that they were cowered by his drawn weapon. This pause would last merely seconds.

"Abdul, have you come to save your father, a collector of our money for the Shah?" taunted Sahed. The crowd had grown momentarily quiet, the air about him vibrated with their silent rage. "Or perhaps it is for your mother and your sister, who disgrace Islam with their wicked ways."

Abdul knew that in an instant, the enraged mob would once again begin hurling their stones; at him as well. What was to be done had to be done this instant.

"Stoning, Sahed," declared Abdul to Sahed and the crowd, "is for the crime of adultery. From hence forth, Persians shall live by the words of the Prophet, not the whims of man.

It was brutal, but it was mercy. Walking up to his father, Abdul aimed the weapon at his head. His father stared into Abdul's eyes. Abdul saw the gratitude, the knowing. Then he fired. His mother placed a hand over her mouth as he pointed the gun at her, choking back whatever it was she wanted to say. He pulled the trigger. His sister, whose arms cradled Fatima, screamed, "You're mad, you're mad." Her words ended as his bullet shattered her brain. The crowd was absolutely silent. Abdul then aimed the gun at Fatima. "For what crime do I take the life of this young girl?" he demanded, his eyes fixed on Sahed. "Has she taken your money? Has she robbed us of our Godliness?"

"Not the child," yelled someone in the mob. Other cries joined in. Fatima lay upon the bloodied body of her fallen mother, her eyes staring dully up at him. He stood for a moment, letting the crowd grow insistent on sparing his niece. Finally, he holstered the weapon and picked up the young girl. Praise Allah, no stone had touched her. He had saved young Fatima's life in the only manner possible. For this day, Roger Cowling and his people would pay a huge price.

Fatima wanted to cry, but did not. She was afraid that it would make the people angrier. Earlier, when the men had ripped the crate apart, it had scared her so bad that she had to cry. The nails had squealed loudly and the banging of the hammers against the crowbars had been deafening. She thought that her mother would be happy to be let out of the crate, but now, she could see why she was not.

Fatima did not recognize any of these people, but they were just like the ones who had burst into their home just nights ago, and had taken her daddy away. She had cried then, regardless of her mother's attempts to stop her. She had cried even louder when one of the men hit her mother because of her crying. Not even her wonderful grandpapa could make the tears go away.

With frightened curiosity, Fatima had watched as the people about her and her family, had gathered the stones. She could not imagine why they were doing it, but it had scared her. In stunned silence she had watched as men kicked and banged to loosen bricks from a wall, pulling stones from pathways. Never had she seen such madness. Never had she heard such awful noise, so many angry voices. And then, the people had begun hurling the stones at them, hitting both her grandpapa and her mother.

Then she had seen Uncle Abdul. He would make them stop throwing the stones and quiet the people. No one would treat her family bad if he was here. Fatima felt relief; a sense of protection engulfed her. Then Uncle Abdul stepped forward, pulling his gun. Guns were something she was not use to, and they normally frightened her. Now, however, there was a sense of hope at seeing the weapon in her uncle's hand.

The noise stopped, as did the stones and bricks. Fatima felt confident that her Uncle would take them home, that he would keep them safe. Then she watched with confusion as he pointed the gun at grandpapa. She saw the flash, she heard the powerful bang, but it was her uncle who held the gun, her uncle who would protect them.

The loud crack of the pistol shot seemed suddenly to transport Fatima into another world. Now she was not afraid. It was not her grandpapa that fell backwards, his head exploding. It was nothing more than a doll, being knocked down backwards in play by her uncle. Then another doll was knocked down. Now the one that was holding onto her, it fell over, too. And finally it was her turn. Fatima, too, was simply a doll being used in play. Uncle Abdul pointed the gun at her doll face, and she waited, without emotion. But he did not pull the trigger, he asked the people if he should, and they said no. So the game ended. Uncle Abdul picked her up. She guessed that he would put her away until it was time to play again.

Chapter Seventeen
March 1980
Ramhormuz, Iran

It was the time of year when the weather was pleasant. Temperatures were mild, cooled by early morning rains. The fresh scent of budding flowers filled the air everywhere. These were days when Fatima and her little brother spent hours with others, battling over a soccer ball in good-natured fun.

Inside the house, however, the air was stiff with tension. Spring flowers were forgotten. There was nothing good-natured about the icy looks exchanged between the two men. Such was always the case now when Abdul visited his brother, Hussein, and his wife, Khadija. Hussein had at first attempted to prevail upon Abdul to never again cast his shadow upon their doorstep. The murderer of their father, mother and sister was not a welcomed guest. Those attempts stopped abruptly when Abdul took his brother outside, beyond earshot of Khadija, and Fatima. When the two men returned, nothing more was ever said about Abdul's visits. He came and went as he pleased. Still, the uneasiness, the anger remained.

As with all visits, Fatima was sent outdoors to play. As always, Abdul brought gifts for the family. They consisted of candy, trinkets, and other items difficult to find outside of Tehran. But these days, even the basics were getting hard to find in the city of Khomeini. His real purpose in coming, however, was to get the answers to the same questions he always asked. How was Fatima? Does she talk? What does she say? Does she study? Is her learning ability normal?

On this visit, as on all others, he watched in silence from the window as Fatima and the neighbor's son, Hasan kicked the soccer ball back and forth. In a few more years, she would be considered a woman, and then she would not be able to go out and play. How sad, that such was the life in Iran. The Shah had been glutinous, he had been extravagant and he had been foolish in so many respects. But he had brought hope, and he had brought a sense of freedom to the people of Iran. Now, that was just the past. Abdul had once

144

hoped to lead Iran from this darkness. However, that hope had long ago died.

Today, Abdul watched Hasan, not Fatima. He watched the youngster with a certain amount of jealousy and a certain amount of gratitude. For it was not until she met young Hasan, that she spoke her first words. She had remained mute since the day she watched her him kill her mother, grandmother, and grandpapa. Still her words were few and stiff to Hussein and Khadija. To Abdul, they were non-existent. What ability she had to find life, seemed linked to Hasan, whom she called her little brother.

Abdul thought of the night that he had arrived here with Fatima. Three days it had taken to get from Tehran to Ramhormuz. During that time, Fatima spoke not a word, had uttered not even a single cry. Abdul was not even sure that she had so much as blinked during the time that they were together. She simply did as he told her, ate when he said to, sat when he told her to sit and moved when told that it was time to go. But when he implored his nine-year-old niece to speak, seeking to understand the thoughts that filled her mind, she simply stared listlessly ahead through glazed eyes. Now was still the case. He feared that her mind was damaged from the trauma of seeing him kill her mother and the others, that it had permanently unhinged her. And if she should ever recover, what would she say to him? What seething hatred was locked away in her heart for him? He knew how hatred affected people. Abdul feared greatly what she might become. It was the true purpose of coming here, to find out if there was any sign of her releasing her anger, her hatred, her grief. Oh, how he wanted her to speak, even if it was to say how much she hated him. He only wished her soul to be whole.

Hussein and Khadija had taken Fatima in eagerly. They had showered her with all the love and affection possible. But Fatima had remained inanimate. Then suddenly, one day, they saw her in the street, kicking the soccer ball with Hasan, calling him little brother and laughing. She spoke not a word to them, however, when she finally came inside. Little by little, she had began communicating with her aunt and uncle. Never, however, with Abdul. It was worse than a dagger through his heart. He loved her so much. Forever he would hate the traitor responsible for destroying his little Fatima. Never would he rest until Roger Cowling had paid for his deed in full.

Fatima was a year younger than Hasan, but a full head taller. Together they played, always on the same team. "Little brother, give me the ball," she demanded. There were four of them against five. She could kick the ball as straight and as hard as Hasan or any of the other boys. The space between the two cars, which made up their goal, was wide open for her to shoot.

"Fatima."

Looking up, she saw her Uncle Abdul standing at the gate, preparing to leave. The soccer ball shot past her without her making any effort to stop it. Fatima found herself moving with almost robot like stiffness while her eyes became nothing more than lifeless orbs. In a mere instant, she had become a being transported to another world.

Fatima attempted to speak as she neared her uncle.

"Yes, Uncle Abdul?" she wanted to ask. But the words simply did not come out. Attempting to smile, her facial muscles refused to obey. She was oblivious to the other kids yelling at her for missing the ball.

"I must leave, Fatima," said Abdul, studying her doll like expression. She was staring at his uniform. It was the uniform of the Revolutionary Guard and this was the first time that she had seen him wear it.

"Here. Some candy," he said, handing her a packet of plain brown paper, "for you and Hasan, your little brother."

At the mention of her little brother's name, her eyes seemed to flicker with a hint of life. Fatima turned towards the street, watching as Hasan chased down the ball.

When Abdul left, he did not, unfortunately, manage to leave the tension behind him. All through his nation, a new tension was rising, nearly eclipsing the revolution. It was only a matter of time before Iran and Iraq would be at war. This was a war that Abdul dreaded, for he sensed it would be bloody. Iran would, he feared, be plunged further into darkness at the hands of its neighbor, Saddam Hussein.

Chapter Eighteen
May 1986
Ramhormuz, Iran

A heavy rain was falling. No matter where Fatima moved her bedroll to, a leak still found her. Neighbors had tried to persuade her to move in with them, though none had homes completely unscathed by the attacks. They all knew how she had suffered the loss of her parents, and now she had more suffering, and they winced to see her with no one to cling to when the bombs fell. When Fatima declined the offers to share their homes, the old men and the women helped repair her home the best that they could. The husbands, the young men, were now all committed to the war. Building supplies were scarce, limited mostly to scrap removed from dwellings that had been completely destroyed in the air raids and the missile attacks. The home once owned and lived in by Hussein and Khadija Hasdiz would have been a prime candidate for seeking scrap materials if Fatima had been sensible and had abandoned it. There was little hope of rebuilding it now that its owners were dead.

Both her bedclothes and her blanket were hopelessly soaked. She lay shivering, staring into the darkness. Did Hasan feel the cold? She placed her hand to her lips. Sweet memories came, along with the pain of Hasan's last day in Ramhormuz. Her tears joined the rain as she remembered him turning away and walking out the door. Only fifteen, he had climbed on a bus with other young men, all seemingly eager to be taken to the battlefront.

They had sat quietly together in the Hasdiz living room on that day. Hussein had already left to fight on the front, rumored to be leading successful forays into the heart of Baghdad. Khadija, sensing the need to allow the young teens a moment of privacy, had gone into the kitchen, closing the door behind her. Fatima and Hasan had gone to each other, taking one another's hands. It had been some time, now, since they had been kids, banging away at the soccer ball together. Fatima had officially become a young woman, wearing the chador and no longer allowed to play soccer in the streets. They had never touched in a manner such as this. Time was short. Hasan reached up and swept the veil from her face and they stared for an eternity into each other's eyes. Then, he leaned over and touched his lips to hers. It was sweet, tender and so, so brief. Fatima, would, she knew, remember the touch of his lips for a lifetime.

Finally, the first light of day showed. Fatima was thankful. The nights were so full of loneliness that she eagerly awaited each day, this, despite the fact that it would likely offer more misery in one form or another. It seemed that sleep was illusive. No matter how tired she was, she would lie awake, most of the night, thinking of Hasan, willing in her mind and heart that he be safe. Her Uncle Abdul had sent word to her that Hasan would not be serving with those charging across the minefields, but assigned to an artillery unit. That was some relief, but not much.

Last night, before the rains had arrived in the early hours of the morning, Fatima had fallen into a sound sleep. Not a restful one, but a sleep filled with a series of unsettling dreams.

In these dreams, she stood before a pile of broken dolls. These were dolls from very long ago, dolls that she had forgotten about, but dolls that she loved. One was her grandpapa, another was her grandmother and the third her mother. But there had been a forth doll, laying face down on top of the pile, looking as if it had just been added. Fatima had not been able to see its face. The dream filled her with dread. She did not want to go to the hospital today. The wounded soldiers on the cots looked too much like dolls, broken dolls with their legs pulled off and their faces scarred from the mustard gas.

Fatima arose despite her reluctance and folded up her wet bedroll. There was really no way for her not to go to the hospital. If she failed to show up, the worried women would send the hobbling old men to find her. She would be asked a myriad of questions, she would be offered waves of advice and she would be reminded for days that she had a duty to the wounded of Iran's army.

As she did every morning, she offered up prayers to Allah for her little brother's safe return from the war. She did so this morning with a sense of urgency, backed by her fear and dread.

After a quick breakfast of flat, soggy, unleavened bread and cold, stale tea brought home from the hospital, she trudged through the narrow streets, ignoring the rain that seemed determined to drench her both in her sleeping and in her waking. The downpour was so intense that it hid the hospital, even when she was close enough to it that she could hear the wails of pain that came from within its walls. Fatima cringed as she always did at those cries.

They were all young men. Most had lost one or both legs. It was young men like these that the Revolutionary Guard encouraged to go to the front, to charge across minefields. They were told that Allah would bless them for their bravery. And they did so, exploding the hidden devices and thus allowing the seasoned soldiers to pass safely after them. And so, they were blessed. However, Allah did not provide morphine to ease their suffering nor antibiotics to prevent infection of the stubs that had once been proud limbs.

Though she was only a teenager, any and all help was needed in these makeshift hospitals. Like all of the others in Ramhormuz and the other villages and cities along the border with Iraq, she had suffered her loss. Her Uncle Hussein had been killed in an air attack by poison gas. Aunt Khadija had died when Iraqi planes had swooped without warning from the sky, bombing the town indiscriminately. Saddam Hussein's war machine, along with the help of his American friends, was butchering Persians by the thousands.

She and the other women of the town went daily to the hospital, comforting the wounded, both soldiers and neighbors. Fatima would wash their infected wounds and whisper useless prayers to Allah for them. And of the young men, listen to their incessant, insane praises of the Ayatollah Khomeini.

The stench from the soldier's rotting wounds and the mustard gas residue in their clothes greeted Fatima as she entered the hospital. Already, even at such an early hour, some of the young men were already chanting "Praise Allah! Long life to Khomeini! Death to Iraq! Death to America!" Their chants were like a morphia. As long as they kept them up, they seemed oblivious to their pain. Eventually, a young soldier might get better. More often than not, however, one would suddenly stop his chanting, lay quiet for an hour or maybe two and then go to Allah, a martyr, and a victorious hero. "Allah be damned," she muttered to herself at the thought.

Fatima hurriedly spread her coat out on the floor in a place where it was the least likely to be stepped on. It would not be completely dry by the time she left, but the less soaked the better. The evenings were becoming somewhat chilly and her coat would have to keep her warm through the night as well as on her way home. She quickly donned one of the aprons hanging from a nail on the wall. As she tied it behind her back, she began walking down the rows of cots.

Thus Fatima began her dreaded morning search. Not a day went by that new faces did not appear. But would there be one that she would recognize?

Such had been the case several times, as she would see the piecemeal form of a boy that she had once played soccer with. In the back of her mind was the constant dread that one day, she would find Hasan here.

From one suffering young soldier, to another, each in the agony of realization that he would never again walk, Fatima moved mechanically, drone like. She offered what comfort she could. It was all that they would get. There were no antibiotics to fight the infections, and there was no morphine to stem their pain. Now and again, a young man, no longer crying chants to Khomeini or Allah, would peer past her chador and into her eyes. What she saw was always the same haunting stare. It bespoke of one who realized that Allah did not wait on the other side to bless them into paradise, after all, and that Khomeini was simply another politician sending boys to fight in a war.

A young boy, Bahram, merely fifteen, raised his head slightly as he saw her approach. This was his second week here. Both legs had been blown off just above the knees. Like so many others, he had arrived strong and fervent despite his pain. He had ignored Fatima's gestures of caring, preferring to shout his praises to Allah and to Khomeini. But infection had set in and now he burned with its fever. Like many, his suffering had become so great, that his vision of paradise had faded into oblivion. Just yesterday, for the first time, he had reached for her hand, his eyes helplessly fixed upon her own.

Fatima started towards Bahram. She would take his hand and speak whatever words of comfort that she could. Today, most likely, would be his last.

"Fatima." It was a whisper, accompanied by a hand clasped around her arm. Instantly she recognized the voice, one that she had not heard for nearly two years. She turned, looking down at her uncle's boots.

Abdul touched his hand to her chin, lifting it until she was forced to look into his eyes. Fatima fought to avoid his effort, moving her eyes first to one side and then to the other, determined, and fearful. There was, however, nothing she could do. For as long as she could remember, he had never touched her, and she had never looked into his eyes. What she saw now was someone very different than she imagined him to be. There was not the cold, menacing glare that she expected. Instead, there were tears.

"Fatima," said Abdul, softly. He stared into her eyes with an unnerving presence.

A cold chill swept through Fatima. This was a look that she had seen too many times. An army Colonel had worn the look when he came bearing the news of Hussein's death to Khadija. It was the look of neighbor telling neighbor of a son's death on the battlefront. Now it was on the face of her uncle. There could be but one meaning, and there was but one person that he would bring news of. Curse Allah.

"Hasan!" she cried. Immediately, the powerful arms of Abdul surrounded her, pulling her tight. Fatima had lost everything. There was nothing left in her life.

Chapter Nineteen
Thursday, December 3
Hanover County, Virginia

Ray was nearly two hours late pulling into his driveway and he was flat-assed tired. Standing in as Superintendent of Security and dealing with the politics was stressful enough. Today, however, arguing with Lloyd Ralston and having to spend the entire day investigating the reactor trip, had taken it all out of him. Would the real Superintendent of Security please step forward! It was high time for Jack Evans to shag it from Disney World and get his butt back to Jefferson Davis Nuclear Power Station.

The concern about a deliberate act shutting down the Unit 2 nuclear reactor was not the least bit plausible. However, simply because the question had been posed, Ray had ended up spending hours working on a report that would have to be presented to SNSOC, the Station Nuclear Safety Operating Committee, tomorrow morning. SNSOC would decide whether or not his report adequately explained away the possibility of a deliberate act. If they decided that it did not, then the investigation would continue. Continue where, he did not have a clue. He would simply have to think of creative ways to waste a few reams of paper to say what he had already said.

Now, to make his day all the more enjoyable, Donna's car was sitting in the driveway. His wife was home a full day early. Perhaps she hoped to catch him doing something bad. He wished he could have been caught doing something bad. With Laura away at the same time to visit her sick mother, there had been no opportunity. Ray had counted on making up for some lost time tonight before Donna's return.

Maybe he would just have to find a way to do it anyway. Truth of the matter was, it was high time that he and Donna simply laid their cards on the table. Once they did, only one conclusion would be possible; this marriage was dead, a rotting corpse in need of burial.

"You're home late," said Donna. She was sitting at the kitchen table of their doublewide. A half-empty bottle of Coors in her hand and two empties on the cabinet showed that she was hard at work doing what she did best. Her drinking was the reason they rented a cheap doublewide, rather than living comfortably in something nice, something that they owned. Like always, she had meant to toss the empties in the trash and put something on top of them so that Ray would not see them. However, like always, she had forgotten about them until he was in the door. The best she could do was put him on the defensive.

"So what? Your home a day early," said Ray, opening the fridge to get himself a cold one, if there were any left. "We had a reactor trip today. Jack being gone, I had to take care of an investigation report."

"Get me one while you're up, please," said Donna in the sickening sweet voice that Ray had grown to loathe.

"Looks to me that you've had more than enough, already," said Ray, returning to the table with only one. Damn if he was going to cater to her sickness. How many times had she gone into treatment centers for her alcoholism? Four? It was too damn many if he had to actually stop and count.

"Your supper's cold," said Donna. She got up and stuck a casserole dish filled with macaroni and sliced up hot dogs in the microwave. As always, she ignored his comment about her drinking. She had meant to fry up some chicken, do some sweet potatoes. But she simply did not have the energy. She had needed to sit for a moment with a beer, hoping that the motivation to cook up a good meal would come to her. But it had not, as it never did. One beer had turned into two, and then the third one that she had been nursing when Ray got home. Life had been like that for years. Anyway, why bother? He was a jerk. Before she sat back down, Donna took another beer from the fridge.

Ray Cisco had been a jerk from the day they were married. Three hours after they left the altar, while actually checking into their honeymoon suite in the Florida Keys, his pager had gone off. At the time, he was in command of a Seal Team that specialized in hostage rescue. It had been during the time of the Iranian revolution with Americans being held hostage in the over run US Embassy in Tehran. Three weeks, three fucking very long weeks she had waited for some word from him. There had been no word, however, not even a hint of whether he was in the states or abroad.

Finally, when she did hear something, it had been dramatic. A black sedan had pulled up in front of her parents' home in Virginia Beach where she was staying. A young Marine officer had come to the door and requested that she go with him. Scared half out of her wits, she had climbed into the back seat.

Donna had arrived at the Naval Base at Little Creek. There, she was quickly, but courteously escorted into a very plain, tan brick building with no windows. Next, she was taken to a room where maybe a dozen or so other women sat. All of them wore grim faces. At first, she could not remember ever having seen any of them. But they, however, immediately seemed to know her. Then it came to her, in perfectly logical fashion. Each one of them had been at her wedding. They were the wives and girlfriends of her husband's comrades. Already frightened, this realization had taken her to the brink of total hysteria. What horrible thing had happened? The subdued chatter in the room had stopped. An awkward silence had ensued before they realized who she was and invited her to sit with them. And then they all waited. And speculated.

Four and one half-hours after she had arrived there, a Navy Captain entered the room. He, too, was grim. And his story was even grimmer. The Seal Team had been part of a multi-service effort to rescue the American hostages from Tehran. The operation had gone awry. There had been an accident, and men had been killed. Names were not available. The Captain had been kind enough to have food and drink brought to the wives. Donna had sat with the others the whole night through, drinking one beer after another, watching special reports on television and listening to frequent updates from the Captain.

Ray, and the others, thankfully, had returned home safe. But there was always another mission, always another wait, and always another beer. Yes, Ray Cisco could despise her for her drinking and for what she had become. He could not, however, deny his part in it. How could he fail to understand that she had loved him too much to face the sober reality of what their life was? She had lived in daily terror of a phone call, of his pager going off, of some international crisis abroad.

"How's your folks doing?" asked Ray, taking a long sip of his beer. It slid down his throat, cold and soothing. Nothing quite hit the spot like a cold one after a day like this had been. He no longer concerned himself about drinking in front of Donna. Earlier on, he had tried not drinking when she was around, but it had never made a difference.

"Fine. Daddy thinks if I don't go back on the wagon and lose some weight you're going to divorce me," said Donna. Of course, that had been nothing new. She would not even bother going into all that her mother had said about the matter. "I told him not to worry about it. I'd probably die of cirrhosis of the liver first. Hey, then you and he could split the insurance money and both buy new bass boats and live happily ever after." She hoped for at least a smile if not a chuckle. Neither came. Well, no one had ever suggested she make a living doing stand-up. Disgust spread across Ray's face.

"You just plain don't give a shit," said Ray. The timer on the microwave sounded. He ignored it. Once upon a time, she did give a shit and so did he. Remembering that made the inevitable so difficult. If only he could simply erase the memories of the good years, of what it was about her that had made him fall in love. Then he could move on. When they had met twenty years ago, she had been forty pounds lighter. The first time they made love, they had been on a deserted stretch of private beach. He could not forget how her eyes had danced like fireflies in the light of the moon. Now, it seemed like just so much irrelevant history. Across the table from him, sat an entirely different person.

"And you don't give a shit either," she said, taking yet another swig of beer. Fishing a cigarette from her purse, she lit it up. Smoking in the house really annoyed Ray. But what about her did not annoy him anymore? "So, is the unit going to be down long?" she asked, wanting to avoid trouble. The conversation had been moving into dangerous territory. It would not be long before Ray decided to leave. That had become obvious over the past couple of years. Over the past months, it had become even more acutely so. He had had affairs in the past and she could see all the signs again. This time, however, something was disturbingly different. She got up and took the casserole from the microwave and sat it down on the table beside him.

There was a Laura somebody who had started working in the Security Department just a few months back. McClish, that was her last name. She had heard someone from the plant make a comment about the new girl in Security. They called her "McClish the Dish". The timing would be about right for the change in Ray's attitude.

"I don't think for long," said Ray, dishing food onto his plate. His mind was processing all the possibilities as he made conversation of the day's events. He needed a good excuse to leave so that he could call Laura. "More than the unit coming down, management has everybody teetering on the edge of their seats about getting laid off. It's getting to people. Not everybody there's wrapped as tight as they ought to be with all this lay-off talk going on. I just hope Jack Evans gets back real soon. There was actually some concern today that maybe someone had brought the plant down deliberately."

"Sabotage?" asked Donna, horrified, momentarily forgetting their domestic upheaval. The people that worked at the Jefferson Davis Nuclear Power plant were very much like a family. That one of them might do such a thing shocked and frightened her. A nuclear reactor was not something to be vindictive with.

"That's what it would be," said Ray. "It wasn't though. Something technical instead. Something they haven't figured out yet."

"Good grief, I'm glad," said Donna. "Ellen and the kids have been looking forward the whole year to their trip to Disney World. Would be such a shame for something like that to happen and Jack have to come back early." Immediately she saw the reaction in his eyes. Slight, yet noticeable. Shit, why had she said something about the kids?

Ray took another swig of his beer. How many times, years ago, had he envisioned traipsing through Disney World with some little blonde haired girl tugging at his hand, begging him to play some silly game to win her a teddy bear? Or a son that he would teach to hunt and bait a hook? He remembered that for a long time he had been angry about Donna's inability to bear him a son or a daughter. Now, however, it was just a piece of their history that added to the emptiness. Considering the state of their relationship, perhaps he should be thankful they had no children.

Ray finished his supper in silence and then went to take a shower. It felt good to step out of his uniform and into the hot pelting spray. As he lathered himself, he thought of different reasons he could give for going out. He needed to get out of the house. No, what he really needed was to see Laura. He felt himself thicken and grow hard at the thought of being with her. She was his black magic lady, always staring deep into his eyes when they made love. He had never had a woman before who became so out of control in bed, one that he had such an affect on and had such an effect on him.

Ray thought as he showered. There had to be some excuse that would sound valid to Donna for him getting out of the house. However, none came to him. The Hell with excuses, he decided. Plain and simple, it was time to tell Donna that they were through.

The hot stinging spray massaged away the tension that tightened the muscles between his shoulders. Ray reached for the shampoo. He stopped short, however, realizing that someone had just stepped into the bathroom. Through the opaque glass doors, he made out Donna's form. She hollered his name and banged against the shower door. Immediately, he switched off the water and slid the door open.

Ray had little doubt of what she wanted. It was typical of what he did for a living. He no longer needed an excuse for getting out of the house. Donna held his excuse in her hand, the portable phone. However, it was not an excuse that would land him at Laura's doorstep. It was, rather, one that would have him back at the plant for hours, perhaps the rest of the night. Had he been wrong when he had earlier ruled out sabotage? Had the technical investigation uncovered evidence of a deliberate act? He had an uneasy feeling that he had long ago learned to respect.

"Pete Burns from the plant," said Donna. "Told him you were in the shower. Said he needs to talk to you right now." She handed him first a towel, and then the phone.

"Yeah, Pete, what's up?" asked Ray, drying as he talked. He listened for a moment before answering. "Okay, be there quick as I can." Then he clicked off the phone and handed it back to Donna.

"Unit 1 just tripped," said Ray. "Shift supervisor thinks someone deliberately mis-positioned some switches."

"Does it sound serious?" asked Donna as she studied the hard lines etched about his eyes.

"Yeah, it's fucking serious," Ray snapped harshly. "A nuclear reactor's just tripped and it sounds like from what Pete's telling me that somebody made it happen and tried to fix things so it would fucking melt down. I don't know what 'serious' is in your book, but in mine, that's real fucking serious." He moved past Donna into the bedroom. His anger, he realized, was frustration. He needed Laura, needed her some kind of bad. Instead, he had Donna home a day early and a nuclear reactor shutdown under suspicious circumstances.

Ray pulled a fresh shirt and trousers, neatly pressed by him, from the closet. Still damp from the shower, he dressed. He was no longer thinking of Laura as he hurriedly laced his boots. Instead, he was considering whether he needed to go ahead and try to contact Jack Evans. Not to call him back, but just to give him a head's up on what was happening. He decided to wait until he knew more. Grabbing his cap, he headed for the door. Suddenly, the phone rang, stopping him midway through it. Something told him that this call was for him. He waited as Donna picked it up. She cast her eyes towards him with a look that was unsettling. It was her look of trouble. What now? Something yet more serious at the plant? Maybe someone going off the deep end, shooting fellow workers? He took several long strides to where Donna stood with the phone pressed against her ear.

"He's already on his way to the plant," Donna was saying into the phone, as Ray got closer. He stood waiting for her to hand it to him. However, she seemed reluctant. "Can't you talk to him there? ... Well, okay, here." She placed the receiver against her body to mute her words. "It's Laura McClish. Do you want to talk to her? Why can't she wait until you get there?"

Ray glared at his wife, grabbing the phone from her hand. He was filled with the flutter of anticipation and annoyance both at the same time. Mostly annoyance. He was annoyed with Donna for simply being there and even more so at the misfortune of whatever it was that was happening at work.

"Yeah, Laura," he said into the phone, his tone as professional as he could possibly make it sound.

"Damn it, Ray. I'm so sorry," came Laura's voice over the phone, her tone apologetic. "I thought your wife was still gone. I'd never have called otherwise."

"I understand," he said, using his best work voice. "Yeah, Operations has called about the Unit I trip. I'd appreciate it if you'd have the duty shift run the CAS reports so that I'll have them as soon as I get there. Give me two copies so that I can make notes on them."

"That's a shame," said Laura. "I was really hoping to make your last night of freedom memorable."

"Sounds like a scheduling problem," said Ray. Just talking to her and thinking about the possibility was making him hard. He turned slightly so that Donna would not look down and notice. Laura had an effect on him that made him feel like some horny teen. "When I get to the office I can take a look at it. Perhaps if this doesn't turn out to be serious, we can take care of it tonight."

"Ray Cisco, I'm going to make your butt drag tomorrow!" said Laura.

"Well, I certainly appreciate you letting me know that," said Ray. "Talk to you when I get to the office." Ray hung the phone up. "Looks like a long night. Get some sleep, you look tired." Then he turned and left, saying nothing more. His mind should have been on what lay ahead of him at the plant. Instead, however, it was on the idea of Laura McClish making his butt drag tomorrow.

Fatima hung the phone up. Her hands shook. The shaking was from exhaustion. Also, it did not help that she had eaten nothing more than a banana during the past twenty-four hours. She longed for Ray. While in Atlanta, she had thought of him continuously. Never before had she experienced such distraction. Had her mind not been on him, it was unlikely that she would have missed seeing the van before it's driver turned on the headlights. That blunder had potentially exposed her. It could have been worse, though. Had the driver not had quick reactions, or had delayed turning on the headlights; Fatima could have been face to face with Allah. A sarcastic smile broke across her lips. Allah was not likely in a hurry to claim her, for when He did, she had some tough questions to put to Him.

Never in her life had she felt the need for a man to satisfy her. All her life, sexual satisfaction had been synonymous with ending someone's life. Certainly this was some type of mental illness. But, like her uncle had once commented, it made her a highly motivated assassin. It was impossible to count the number of times that she had achieved her sick pleasure from driving a knife into the torso of an unsuspecting victim or while strangling him with her hose or garter. Men were surprisingly weak and vulnerable when in the middle of their own orgasm. That was always the moment that she pulled the knife from beneath the mattress, or pulled her garter tight around her victim's throat. Almost always, the victim at first thought her attack was play. The smile she wore and her passion filled eyes were certain to always mislead them.

Then along came Ray Cisco, with his dark Mediterranean looks and eyes that reminded her of Hasan. For that very reason, she should have never involved herself with Ray. Her relationship with him added nothing to the mission. Jack Evans, the Superintendent of Security would have been a far more valuable target. Or she could have simply stuck with screwing Travis Harding. After all, Harding would sell his mother's soul if he could use it to buy a moment of gratifying passion. From the moment she met Ray, however, she had felt an inescapable attraction.

Uncanny, was the resemblance; at least as far as her mind conjured. Never had she considered what Hasan might look like as a grown man. The moment she had laid eyes on Ray, however, she knew that Hasan would have looked like him. Ray's every touch, every kiss, his every penetration, took her, in her mind, back to what it would have been like with Hasan.

Uncle Abdul, perceptive as always, quickly questioned the need for her involvement with Ray. However, he had not been quick enough. Ray was as drawn to her as she was to him. It would have been impossible for her to terminate the relationship without creating chaos and suspicion. She did her best to assure her uncle many times over that she was fully focused on the mission. In reality, Ray did provide useful insight into the security and everyday operation of the nuclear power station.

Well, regardless of her entanglement with Ray, the operation was continuing. Because of her work, they now had control of Brian Matkins. He would provide the means to destroy Roger Cowling. Cowling's destruction was, of course, no concern to the Jihad. However, she had long ago discovered his role in the murder of her mother and her grandparents. Cowling loved nothing in life other than his empire. And that, she and Uncle Abdul, would take from him.

Two unexplained reactor trips in one day. A great deal of suspicion had surrounded the Unit II reactor trip earlier in the day. Nothing, however, had been discovered to support the concern of it having been a deliberate act. Ray was now going in to investigate the second one. Though certainly a distraction, her relationship with Ray was useful. From him, she would discover the details of this latest incident. If her assumption was correct, Ray would not find anything to explain this reactor trip, either. That would mean that the second phase of their plan was ready for implementation. If it unfolded as planned, then Roger Cowling and the entire Mid-Atlantic region would feel the wrath of the Jihad. And it would happen soon, real soon.

For the moment, however, everything seemed so out of balance. Less than twenty-four hours earlier, Fatima had plunged the military style K-bar knife deep into the belly of Tanya Madison, gutting her like a slaughtered animal. She had had to wait nearly an hour and a half in the closet for her to return from taking Matkins back to his hotel. Even now, the memory of the kill's stench and the feel of the knife made her pulse race.

Her only sleep had been during the flight back to Richmond. Other than that, she had been awake for far too long. She should sleep. More than sleep, however, she needed Ray. Both, she realized, should have been low on her priority list. They would certainly be low on her uncle's. There was, after all, the private investigator to be dealt with. And how about the two suspicious reactor trips? Had it been Danny? If so, how long could she trust him to keep his mouth shut about it? Fatima answered that question for herself, not long. He was in constant need of people's attention. In a day's time, at the most two, he would need to make mention to someone that he had accomplished something special. It was up to Fatima to allow him to get it out of his system, to help him feel recognized. Perhaps it would be best to get it out of Danny's system for good. That was, of course, if he had indeed accomplished what she suspected.

The phone began ringing. Fatima let it ring a couple of times, staring at it with a sense of dread. It was most likely Abdul. Could it not, however, be Ray? Maybe the situation at the plant had been a false alarm and he was calling to tell her that he would be there soon. That thought perplexed her. It was a bad idea to have him over tonight. She had known better than to call him. But she needed him. He was like morphine to the pain that had lingered deep in her soul all these years. Now that she had experienced what he could give her, she was totally addicted.

"Hello," she answered, knowing that she had no choice but to answer.

"Laura," said the heavily accented voice of her uncle. Immediately, Fatima could tell that he was on edge. After so many years together, there was little that they could hide from each other. "Your sister's flying in from Atlanta tonight. Landing in Richmond at 8:50. Can you pick her up and bring her home?"

Disappointment quickly swept through her. Uncle Abdul was referring to the private investigator, Rachel Lambert. He had become extremely anxious upon learning about someone tailing Matkins and Madison. The private investigator's appearance was like an unknown constant in an algebraic equation. In their business, there was never room for unknowns. Missions were often aborted due to unexpected developments. This one, however, was different. Together they had spent years planning this moment of revenge. Risking failure because of her involvement with Ray was unimaginable; she would not allow that to happen.

Fatima's tone concerned Abdul. Certainly she was exhausted from handling things in Atlanta; that was to be expected. There was, however, an unfamiliar weariness in how his niece answered the phone. He had sensed this change when she started working at the nuclear station. Though he had never met Ray Cisco or had had an opportunity to observe him, he knew a great deal about him. Nothing that he knew explained the affect Cisco had on his niece. At another time, in another place, he would have championed the idea of Fatima experiencing love, even with an infidel. However, this was not the time or place for it to occur. *"Oh, Allah, why now?"* Why when they were so close to achieving the retribution that they had sought for so long? Not only for he and Fatima, but for all of Allah's faithful. This was an opportunity like no other to bring the Great Satan to his knees.

Abdul too, was tired. He was still in Atlanta had been relentless in scrambling his every resource to identify the driver of the blue Astro van. It was not a simple thing to accomplish on such short notice. Every avenue he tried turned up as another dead-end. Finally, however, the answer had been obtained in the simple old-fashioned way. He had taken a taxi to the airport, caught the shuttle to the rental agency and then walked up to a young attendant who was working the return line. He explained that he was from the rental agency's corporate headquarter and was there to verify that vehicles were not being misappropriated by employees. It had been determined, he continued to explain, that one of the Chevrolet Astro vans was not accounted for. The attendant wasted no time using his hand held computer to show what was in stock and what was being rented. Abdul examined the information on the computer, memorized Lambert's information and thanked the lad. He was then on his way.

What Abdul had discovered was not as disturbing as it could have been. Rachel Lambert from Richmond, Virginia had rented the Astro van. She listed her company as Lambert Enterprises. Entering that into the search window of Google had turned up the web page advertising her services. She was merely a private investigator, which translated into her being nothing more than a nuisance. If she had posed as a schoolteacher or salesperson, then, in all likelihood, she would have been an Intelligence agent. Still, she posed a danger and he needed Fatima to help eliminate her.

Why was Lambert following Matkins? Her web page, unfortunately, did not answer that extremely important question. There was, of course, a host of possible answers. The most likely being that Matkins' wife had hired Lambert because of her husband's suspected infidelity. Another possibility was that someone at Richmond Nuclear had hired her. That was not likely, however, since Fatima had garnered a thorough working knowledge of Roger Cowling's blackmail operation from Travis Harding. She knew the cast of players. It did not include a Richmond private eye.

Whatever Lambert's role, she was an unknown variable and had to be eliminated. There was no telling what she knew. Maybe she even knew about the murder of Tanya Madison. After all, Lambert was not expected back into Richmond until tomorrow morning, but evidently had changed her plans. Something had caused her to do so. He had people working for the airlines. Finding out that she had changed her flight had been very simple.

Abdul had turned to Fatima to take care of Lambert simply because she was the best for the job. The others, though efficient killers, lacked her skill at setting up and conducting a clean kill on the spur of the moment like this. They had been in the U.S. as long as she had. However, they still spoke with a Mid-Eastern accent and failed to dress in a manner that made them inconspicuous. They stood out like sore thumbs. Fatima, on the other hand, blended in with natural ease. She could dance words off the tip of her tongue, sounding like she was from the back woods of Georgia or the busy streets of the Bronx.

"Call my brother," said Fatima. "Ask him to go. There are some problems at work and I might have to go in to do some reports."

"I was really counting on you," said Abdul, his voice immediately communicating his frustration. "You know how your sister and brother argue. I have to insist that you take care of this."

"Please don't mention this to anyone," she said. Fatima and Abdul always had to assume that someone knew about them, that every phone conversation was monitored. It was highly unlikely, but caution was vital. "There's unexpected trouble at the plant. They believe that there's been some sabotage."

There was a brief silence, then, "I see," said an attentive Abdul. This was good news and her tending to it made sense. Still, he was certain that she had another, underlying agenda. He decided that it was best not to press the issue. Dealing with her unwillingness to do something was not familiar territory. Perhaps he was too tired and misjudged her. Perhaps she truly needed to handle things at the power station. "That's very troubling to hear. Then I must get someone else to meet her. Could you be free for dinner tomorrow evening? With your sister's arrival, I think it would be nice."

"That sounds good," said Fatima. "I'll call you tomorrow about it."

"Fine," said Abdul. "I hope that you don't have to work too late. Good night."

Fatima breathed easier after her uncle clicked off, thankful that he had not insisted on her handling the private investigator. There was a tinge of guilt at disappointing Abdul. The prospects of success at the plant, though, seemed to have offset his disappointment at her not taking care of matters at the airport.

The clock was ticking. With Abdul's coaching and the promise of significant financial reward, Lenny had been able to supply the missiles and plastic explosive that were needed. It would be months before an inventory turned anything up as missing. Lenny was already dealt with. Now, there was only Danny's part that they needed. The whole thing hinged upon his technical success. That was frightening, that Allah's plan rested on the talent of a sexual pervert.

⋘ ⋙

Ray reran the CAS program, this time himself. He glanced up at Ralston. The plant manager stood in the Main Security Area, biting down hard on his unlit cigar. He was awaiting the CAS results that he had ordered reran. Meanwhile, he stared with venomous fury at the two mechanics through the glass enclosure of the Security Shift Supervisor's Office. Ralston was certain that they were guilty and that the officer running the first CAS printout had missed something.

The mechanics sat there, waiting to see what indignity would follow. One was quiet, the other loud and boisterous. The heavyset Italian, his hair graying, mouthed his disdain for station management. But he was always doing that. His voice carried easily beyond the bulletproof glass walls of the office for Ralston to hear. George Vincente was infamous at the power station for his loud mouth and he never hesitated in directing it towards towards management.

Mike Forrest, the other mechanic, said little. People in the station knew him to be a devout, evangelical Christian who probably spent more time sharing the Word of God than he actually did turning a wrench. Several times now, Ray had watched as Forrest bowed his head and closed his eyes. Together, George and Mike made a very unlikely team. They had, however, worked together as a pair for years. George was forever breaking Mike's balls about his religion. Mike, forever undaunted, fervently worked to save George's soul. Both had one thing in common, tolerance for the other's choices in life. The two were known to work well together and were a good team.

Today, their careers and future were on the line. If they were found guilty of bringing the reactor down, they would likely spend the rest of their lives in prison. Each attested to the honesty and integrity of the other, standing beside one another like brothers. People at the power station often saw them as a pair who constantly argued and harangued each other about religion and morals. However, it was as if such carrying on was the glue that held them together. Ray had served with SEALS and on Special Operations teams; he knew what strange recipe of personalities made for cohesiveness. These two would enter the gates of Hell for each other, if needed.

Ralston was grasping at straws by going after these two. George and Mike had been the only two workers in the Emergency Switchgear Room before the reactor trip. It was from there that the Auxiliary Feedwater Pump electrical breakers had been mispositioned. Those switch positions were verified every hour by a roving watch stander who made rounds through the power plant's Emergency Switchgear Room. Mispositioning the breaker switches would also be apparent in the control room. Neither the roving watch stander, nor the operator at the Control Panel, however, had noted the switches out of position. Operations personnel concurred with Ray that this made it unlikely that the switches had been mispositioned for very long. Certainly not long enough to have been tampered with nearly two hours earlier. The CAS readout showed the two men entering Emergency Switchgear at 1913 and exiting at 2010. The trip had occurred at 2206.

"What do you think?" asked Ralston for the third time, nodding at the two mechanics.

"I don't think they did it," said Ray, his voice matter of fact. "They both say they were together the whole time that they were in Emergency Switchgear. They're vouching for each other. And the time line makes it almost impossible. Those switches would have to have gone unnoticed in the wrong position for two hours for it to be them. Plus, we know they weren't in Normal Switchgear when the breakers for the Main Feedwater Pumps tripped. They were logged into Emergency Diesel Room 2H. I think it's a technical problem of some kind. No sabotage involved."

"Somebody did it, goddamn it," Ralston was nearly shouting at Ray. He knew his plant, and the equipment in it, too well. This was no quirky malfunction of equipment. This was planned, was deliberate. Some sick asshole, fed up with corporate's downsizing and cutbacks, was trying to get even.

"At 2206, the breaker for the electrical supply to the Unit One, B Main Feed Water Pump tripped," Ray read from his notes. He was doing his best to get the Station Manager to see the obvious. "Within seconds, the breaker for C Main Feedwater Pump tripped. Since those breakers are located down in Normal Switchgear and we don't have CAS installed to monitor that area, there's no record of who might have been in there at the time. We know these two were in the 2H Diesel Room. They couldn't have tripped the main feed water pumps. "

"What now? How do we proceed as far as their concerned?" asked Jed Turner who had been called in and had been sitting back, quietly listening. "These are damned good boys. I can tell you right now, they don't have a thing to do with all this bullshit."

"Lloyd, if you want me to give them a polygraph it'll have to be in the morning," said Ray. "Need to send them home now, though. Keep them here all night to finish up their shift and it's going to make the polygraph results less reliable and that can become a fucking worst nightmare for all of us. I can have one of the corporate investigators bring in the equipment and do it about midmorning." There was no question about the two consenting to take the test, as they themselves had suggested it out of frustration from the very beginning.

"What do you think, Jed?" asked Ralston.

"Screw the damn lie detector. These guys fucking didn't do it," Jed's voice was emotional. He was known for taking care of his people. Because of that, his people did good work for him. "Morale in this plant is already at fucking rock bottom. Everyone's had it with talk of layoffs. We start pointing fingers at good people then I'm scared shit will really get out of hand."

"Morale's not the issue, damn it," Ralston became red in the face. "We pay people good money to get in here and get the job done. They don't have to feel warm and fuzzy about it, just do their job." Ralston turned to stare out the window, towards the Reactor Containment Buildings. Jed was right, but he could not bring himself to acknowledge that. He had his job to do. Right now, it was to show the boys upstairs and the NRC that he was above knowing and trusting his people, that he was open to all possibilities.

"Jed," said Ralston, once more turning to the Maintenance Superintendent after a pause. "Give them the rest of the night off with pay. Tell them to be here at ten tomorrow morning so that we can give them the test and clear this thing up. If they pass, then we'll write it up as a mis-positioning incident by operations. Unless Ray here comes up with something else."

"God damn it, I need these guys to help investigate the trip," said Jed. "I'm telling you they didn't do it."

"And I'm telling you to send them home so they can take the polygraph in the morning," said Ralston. It was time to go back to his office, because if he didn't, he'd end up firing somebody. He did not know who, but just that it would feel good to do it to someone. At moments like this he felt that the greatest de-stressor of all would be to get in someone's face and scream, "get your fucking ass out of my power station."

When Brian Matkins' flight landed, Rachel Lambert once again departed the plane after him. And again, she was dressed as a college student, her hair tied back. It was a simple disguise, one requiring only some alteration in how she wore her hair, the right sweatshirt and faded blue jeans. Making it complete was the donning of just the right attitude. He had seen her close up in the elevator, dressed in business attire with her hair hanging lose. Under normal circumstances, it really would not matter if he were to recognize her as the same woman in the elevator. However, it would certainly arouse his suspicions under these new circumstances that involved blackmail and deceit.

Her intention had been to take a later flight; one that left after Matkins was already back in Richmond. In the original plan of things, there had been no need to tail him on his way home. But that had been before simple surveillance had turned into blackmail. During the flight, she had looked for any sign of the young man that rode the Harley or anyone who appeared to be watching Matkins. Neither was apparent.

There was now the question of whether or not she could ethically offer Brian Matkins her services. She certainly wanted to. Not because Matkins deserved her help; after all, he was slime. The lure of working a blackmail case was more than she could resist. However, unless Mrs. Matkins sanctioned her telling him why she had had him under surveillance, it would be very awkward. Turning her material over to Mrs. Matkins would be her first priority; she was the client and it would be unethical for Rachel to do anything that could tip her husband's hand without her authority. And then there was another tricky issue; should she tell Brenda Matkins that her husband was being blackmailed? That was not information that her client needed to know.

Rachel hung back until Matkins had cleared the gate area. Once he had done so, she proceeded on. She had been running late for the flight to Atlanta, so she had opted to leave her car in regular parking rather than in one of the satellite lots. It would cost more, but Mrs. Matkins was picking up the tab. So at least now, she would not have to wait for a shuttle bus to carry her to one of the long-term lots. For the moment, she put aside thoughts of blackmail and infidelity. She was off the clock and had a myriad of personal matters to think of. There was mail to be picked up from her box at the Post Office, she needed to check and make certain that the gas, electric and water bills had all been paid. In the back of her mind, there was a nagging suspicion that she had written all the checks but had forgotten to stick them in the mail. Perhaps this week she would start paying her bills on-line. There had not been a meal served on the flight so she would have to either stop at a grocery store or maybe run by Taco Bell. The latter sounded more appealing than shopping and cooking.

An old, familiar feeling came upon her suddenly, without warning. Someone was following her. One does not really 'feel' being watched. The 'feeling' is the subconscious mind processing something seen, heard, or, perhaps, even smelled. She had experienced being followed many times when stationed in East Germany before the end of the cold war. Her cover had been that of a sales representative for an American textile company; her employer had been the U.S. Central Intelligence Agency.

Immediately, she turned full circle, feigning a disoriented traveler searching for something. Rachel then went to the nearest bank of pay phones. The maneuver gave her a 360-degree sweep of her surroundings. Now, she had a mental picture of each person she saw. Picking up a receiver, she held it to her ear and dialed in some meaningless numbers. Something had triggered her instincts. What? One by one, she examined each one of those mental images, looking for something useful. There was nothing.

Rachel Lambert's days of herself being a subject of surveillance had ended, or so she had thought at least, with the Iron Curtain coming down. What had been celebrated as victory for the free world had been for her, as well as many others, a pink slip. Uncle Sam had simply informed her one fine day that he no longer needed her services, ending her tenure with the CIA as an operations officer.

People were no longer required for intelligence gathering. There were now 'watchers' in the sky, satellites that could practically focus well enough to make it possible to determine whether a person's contact lenses were in or not. The mindset among the CIA's bureaucratic leaders was to rely less on people and more on electronic intelligence. Unfortunately, though a satellite might be able to read the license plate off a car, it could not read minds and engage in meaningless chatter in a bar where a country's pulse could really be felt. Such a lack of human intelligence had allowed Saddam Hussein to surprise the world when he decided to vacation his armies in sunny Kuwait and did not tip off anyone in Washington as to why Osama bin Laden was bankrolling flight lessons for men from the Mid East.

Rachel Lambert had never kissed ass a day in her career at CIA. Thus she was among the first to leave the world of international espionage when The Company downsized. She was sent out, left to catch cheating spouses and crooked business partners. Though financially more lucrative, it certainly was not the same level of challenge. The missing excitement was like air pumped from a chamber, leaving behind a vacuum; at least until now. As this simple assignment of getting the goods on a cheating hubby turned into blackmail, it filled her with new energy. The possibility of being followed added all the more zest to the game.

Pretending to leave a message on someone's answering machine, Rachel hung up. There was really nothing else she could do but continue on to the parking lot. Maybe someone had spotted her outside Madison's apartment. They would naturally be concerned that she was working for Matkins and want to check her out, find out who she was and for whom she worked. Hopefully their interest in her would be no more benign than that. Just in case, she would need to stay on her toes.

Rachel was thankful that she had been running late for the flight to Atlanta and had chosen to park in short term. There were more people around, giving her some sense of security. Once in the parking lot, she deliberately walked up to a car a couple of rows over from her own. Pretending as though she was trying to unlock the car's door, she studied the area around her vehicle. Nothing drew her suspicion. Regardless, she was still being watched. It was an assumption, but the only safe one to make. Around her, a sparse number of people were getting in and out of vehicles, standard airport traffic for a weeknight.

Reza knew the game well. He had followed many CIA and SAS agents through the streets of Beirut and its airport. His query had surprised him with what appeared to be a counter-surveillance tactic. He had not stopped when the Lambert woman suddenly turned and went to the bank of phones. Now, however, he doubted that it had really been a counter-surveillance tactic; most likely she had forgotten to make a phone call and that was simply what she was doing. Though it seemed odd that a private investigator would not be carrying a cell phone. Regardless, she was merely a woman and thus nothing to be overly concerned about. Very soon she would be dead. Did she suspect that she was being followed? It was hardly likely. A man might be intelligent enough to pick up on such a thing, but never a woman.

He had already located her car in the parking lot. That had taken a while since he had begun his search with the two long-term satellite lots first. Stupid woman, did she not realize how much more expensive it was to park over night in short term? Oh well, Reza would save her the trouble of paying anything. Reza was tired and wanted to get this done. This was not his job anyway. Where was Fatima, why was she not taking care of this? Fatima was another case of a woman in a world where she did not belong. Of course, he would never say this to Abdul.

Reza had entered the airport in order to watch Rachel Lambert get off the flight. This allowed him to match her with the photograph that Naim had managed to hack from the Virginia DMV files. Having her hair tied back had been unexpected, though, making it difficult for him to pick her out. However, he had. Now he would just return to the parking lot and wait for her. He would kill her as she was getting to her car. Not quickly, however. Reza liked to see his prey cognizant of the fact that they were going to die. A 9mm hollow point to the stomach followed by one to each lung would give her some painful moments to reflect on the fact that she should be raising kids and taking care of a husband rather than try to do a man's job.

The stupid Lambert woman, she was going to the wrong car. Allah, why are women so ignorant? Several rows over, she was attempting to unlock the door of an altogether different car. A sudden feeling of panic swept through him. His English was not that good. Sometimes, he misread things and maybe he had misread the license plate. If only he could see the license plate of the car she was about to get into. In a few seconds, she could be in the car and driving off. He had no opportunity for a shot from where he was. It was imperative that he move quickly.

No sooner had he began moving rapidly towards her, than she simply left the car she was at and started walking his direction. Now, nearly too late, he realized that though female, his query was very street savvy. Abdul had warned him often not to underestimate women. However, he had always thought Abdul's warnings were mere rhetoric, an attempt to justify Fatima's usefulness to the Jihad. Curse the woman for realizing that she was being followed. If he attempted to go for his weapon, she would see and have opportunity to run. No, he must let her pass. He would cut back through the vehicles to his right and then come back around from the other side. The van and pickup parked there would provide good cover. Though he would have to hurry, this Lambert woman was as good as dead.

The weather in Richmond was far colder and windier than it had been in Atlanta. Rachel could feel her fingers getting numb by the time she arrived at her car. Using caution had been the sensible thing to do. However, she now wished that she had just come directly to her car and got the heck out of here. Bending over, she attempted to insert the key into the door lock of her '91 Nissan 300ZX. "Damn it," she muttered as her ring of keys slipped from her grasp, falling to the ground. She kneeled to pick them up.

There was a *plop! plop! plop!*, mingled with the sound of shattering glass above her head. Chunks of her driver side window fell down into her hair. Adrenaline instantly coursed through her limbs, bringing about the urge to spring up and run. Her instructors at Camp Peary, however, along with years of field experience, had taught her to reject that urge. They had instead, taught her how to calmly evaluate the moment, consider her resources and then act with deliberate desperation.

Rachel shook off the paralysis that accompanied the shock of the unexpected and nearly lethal attack. She drew a deep breath, then forced it out in a long, deliberate hiss as she sought her center. Somebody had just tried to kill her with a silenced weapon! Had she not dropped her keys and then bent down to pick them up, she knew that she would now be lying upon this cold surface of the parking lot, gasping for her last breath. And frighteningly enough, that yet could very well be the case.

Oh, but Allah! This woman was either uncanny to a frightening degree or else extraordinarily lucky. He had been too close to miss. Yet all three shots had failed to hit their target. She had ducked as he was pulling the trigger. Now there was no time to lose. Though equipped with a silencer, the noise of his weapon could be heard, not to mention the shattering glass. Someone with a cellular phone could be alerting the police even now.

Having just gotten off a flight, there was no way that the Lambert woman could be armed. Besides, caution was no longer an affordable luxury. Reza dashed towards her vehicle where she was hiding, anxious to end her life and be out of here.

Continuing with her slow, deliberate pattern of breathing, Rachel reached up over the broken glass, and unlocked her car door. Without pause, knowing that her life hung precariously by the mere thread of seconds, she opened it and dug her hand beneath the driver's seat. No interior light came on to make her a target. Long ago, she had rendered the door switch for the light inoperable. Her attacker would consider her unarmed, having just debarked from a flight. In frantic desperation, her hand searched for the holster that was velcroed to her car seat.

There was the sound of a shoe scraping against the ground and the sound of labored breathing. Her attacker was nearly on top of her. The cold, numbing her fingers, had saved her from the first shots. Now that same cold, along with the adrenaline made it nearly impossible for her hands to properly grasp the weapon in its holster. The holster was situated to allow the weapon to be drawn while sitting in the driver's seat, not on the ground reaching into the vehicle.

Only as he closed in, did Reza realize that the Lambert woman's car door was open. Allah, damn her, she was going for a gun. The door shielded her from his line of fire. He charged forward, in between the cars that she was nosed up against with her own. His heart raced, but he knew that he had her. She would be dead in just a few more seconds.

Rachel knew he was there, that he was rushing towards her. Ripping the velcroed holster from the seat, she thumbed the safety to fire, dug her finger around the nylon of the holster and hooked it in the trigger. She came up, swinging the weapon through the shot out driver's window and at the silhouette of the short, thick torsoed man, his weapon pointing towards her. He had a clear shot on her. She knew he would get a round off before she could. It was all over for her, but she would not give up until his bullet tore through her, ending her life.

Only hours earlier, a middle-aged man and woman had parked in the space in front of the 300 ZX. At the nagging of her husband, who did not want the odor of stale coffee in the car when they returned from Pittsburgh, she had dumped it out on the ground. It had formed a somewhat slick coating of ice beside her car door.

Reza brought his ten-millimeter to bear on the Lambert woman. Though her weapon was swinging around to take aim at him, he knew that he could get a shot off first and finish this. He squeezed the trigger. Suddenly, his foot slipped on the small patch of ice where the coffee had frozen into a small puddle. His shot went wild, just over Lambert's head. In the space of half a second, he was staring at the barrel of Rachel Lambert's pistol while attempting to get his own weapon back on target.

The Lambert woman's first shot tore through his chest as he attempted to leap aside. The retort of her gunfire blended into one continuous salvo of sound. Bullets hissed in his ear as they passed by, all but the first one, missing him by merely fractions of an inch. "Allah curse the fuckers," he muttered, wishing that he could kill whoever had poured the coffee on the ground. He knew that it was coffee. The smell of it permeated his nostrils as he lay on the ground beside it. There was also the odor of cordite in the air. Fortunately, the van beside him allowed enough space for him to roll beneath it out of harms way.

Letting her breath ease out between pursed lips, Rachel squeezed off four rounds, splitting the quiet of the parking lot with her fire. The first of her shots definitely found its target, spinning the man violently around, making her unsure of whether the next three rounds found their mark or not. Whoever he was, he was hurt and scrambling to escape her line of fire.

Rachel wasted no time. Perhaps there was more than just one gunman hid in the darkness of the parking lot. Sliding behind the wheel, she started the engine and threw he "Z" into reverse, holding on to her nine-millimeter as she did so. Once out of the parking space, she did not stop to shift into forward gear. Instead, she careened through the parking lot in reverse, dodging the few people not intelligent enough to seek safety on the ground between parked vehicles at the sound of her gunfire. Already she could see the flash of blue lights as police cars rushed towards the lot. She avoided the urge to flee towards them. Her safety was in disappearing, especially since she did not know who her enemy was.

Near the guard gate, she threw the vehicle into a power slide, spinning around and shifting to second and gunning the engine. A hundred feet in front of her was the tollgate where she was expected to stop and pay for her parking. "Sorry," she muttered as she crashed through it at nearly sixty miles per hour. Though the gate gave way, it creased the sloped hood of her sports car and cracked the windshield. With her foot holding the accelerator to the floor, the 300ZX continued to accelerate in a flurry of gear shifting.

Reza was aware of the frothy bubbles forming in his nose and mouth, leaving behind a metallic taste. He was angry at whoever had dumped the coffee. After all, they had helped the Lambert woman kill him with their carelessness. Damn people who do shit like that. But they had damned him instead and now he was dying. Allah would not receive him with an approving embrace, either, considering that he had failed to finish his mission. The least he could be granted was a martyr's death, but he knew it was not to be.

The 300ZX's engine roared and its tires squealed. The Lambert woman was not moving in for the kill after all. Unfortunately, however, he knew that her one bullet had been enough. He was dying as his life's blood poured freely into his chest cavity, making it nearly impossible to take a full breath. Reza struggled to his feet, each breath becoming more and more difficult. He realized that his partner, Ebi, was moving towards him in the rust colored Ford. Moving quickly, adrenaline surging through his veins, he stepped out from between the parked cars so that Ebi would see him. He knew he was going to die, but he did not want to do it here.

Blue flashing strobes and sirens flooded his senses. It would be the airport police. They had to get out of here. His feet and legs were heavy chunks of lead as he stepped out into the open where Ebi could see him. Everything occurred in less than a second. Reza expected the Ford to slow in a screeching hiss of brake upon cold blacktop and a heavy groan of down shifting. Instead, the Ford whined as though it would fly apart as it accelerated and there was no sound of braking as it swerved towards him. The impact of the car hitting him, shocked him into blackness.

His last conscious thought was, *"Damn that Lambert woman, damn her all the way to fucking hell."*

Ray Cisco stared at the unfinished paperwork and decided that he would add the finishing touches in the morning. Laura's phone number danced from his fingertips as he picked up the phone. All the pertinent facts of the investigation were documented. He would put the formal report together in the morning. That would take another couple of hours. At the moment, there was a more pressing matter to be attended to; one threatening to press right out of his trousers. Laura's rural country home was only twenty minutes away. When she picked up on the other end, he told her to expect him shortly and hung up.

This time, Ray made a point of parking his Ford Ranger in front of Laura's house. Always before, he had parked around back, out of view of anyone from the power station who might be passing by. Tonight, he no longer cared about who saw his truck and what they might think. Carrying on behind Donna's back was not fair to her, Laura or him. Even if Laura was to suddenly disappear into thin air, it really was time to start over.

Exhaustion was quickly over taking Fatima. During the past two weeks she had noticed that she tired more easily than normal. She was tempted to walk straight into the bedroom, strip out of her clothes and go to bed. She wisely resisted the temptation. If she were to curl up in her bed this tired, it would be morning before she woke, regardless of how many times the phone rang or if someone were pounding on the front door. Better, she decided, to run a hot bath and relax, perhaps a short nap. Short naps sharpened the mind and recharged one's energy, at least for a short amount of time.

While the tub filled, Fatima laid out her robe and panties. The overnight bag of toiletries that she had taken to Atlanta still contained her shampoo and soap. Opening it up to remove them she saw the two Tampons. She was as regular with her period as she was methodical about carrying out her missions. She should have required these before returning from Atlanta. That she had not, swept her with a sense of terror. Protection was something she had never used. Her first sexual experience had been Sahed raping her. She had not conceived then and had never bothered with protection henceforth. Praise Allah that there was no chance that it could be Lenny's child. Neither could it have been Danny's. She despised him so that she did require him to where a condom. A surge of exciting pleasure filled her. If she were pregnant, it could only be Ray. Excitement, however, quickly turned to fear. She was accustomed to setting her fear aside and not allowing it to hinder her performance. This, however, was a different level of fear.

Fatima shook uncontrollably as she lowered herself into the tub. What was that pill called that could abort a pregnancy in its early stages; RU thirty something? Either she would have to see a doctor to get a prescription or else ask Abdul if he could use his connections to obtain it. It surprised her that the thought of aborting turned her stomach. She found herself drifting off to sleep with the troubling thought that if she were pregnant, how ironic that the father would likely be killed when they attacked the power station.

Her nap was disturbed by ugly images that she could not control. People at the power station were playing soccer. Her little brother was there and she was frightened that he was about to be killed. The ball was a bomb and was going to explode the next time he kicked it. But he never kicked it. Instead, Abdul stopped the game and directed their attention to her grandfather, grandmother and…instead of her mother holding her, it was Ray. She watched in horror as one by one, Abdul shot her grandparents and then pointed the gun, not at Ray but at her. "You are Sahed's whore!" he was yelling at her. He pulled the trigger and she watched as the bullet seemed to make a slow motion trajectory towards what was her swollen stomach.

The bullet never reached her. The ringing of her phone woke her before that could happen. She reached for it, fumbling to push the button to answer it. "Hello," she said, realizing that her voice was trembling.

"Reza missed your sister at the airport," said Abdul. He paused, listening to the irregular breathing on the other end of the phone. He had noted the tremble in Fatima's voice. Certainly she was tired, but fatique had never affected her in the past. Something was not right about her. As sure as Allah was the True One, he knew it had to do with Ray Cisco. It had occurred to him to eliminate the man before things got out of hand. However, he was now down a man and it appeared that things were already out of hand in several regards.

"Your sister is fine, though. She took a cab. Reza is back home," continued Abdul. "We can talk more tomorrow. You sound very tired."

"Yes, call me tomorrow night," said Fatima. "Good night," and she hung up the phone. The Lambert woman had escaped and Reza had been killed, had been the message encoded in Abdul's phone call. Fatima drifted back into her restless sleep.

Fatima had still been sleeping, beset by disturbing sequences of twisted dreams when Ray called. He was on his way to her house. She had suggested that they should not see each other tonight, but he was not listening. Now she saw the lights of Ray's pickup truck as he turned into her driveway.

She opened the front door as Ray stepped onto the porch. Behind her, a fire blazed in the gas-fueled fireplace. Fatima had started it to ward off the chill that she felt, rather than for its effect. Now, however, the flicker of its flames reflected in his eyes as he stood in the doorway, studying her with anticipation. Beneath the white chenille bathrobe, she wore nothing and could feel her excitement at having Ray here. She failed to notice the cool December air sweeping into the room across her bare feet. Rising only slightly on her toes, she pressed her lips to Ray's.

"I've missed you, lover," she said, feeling the heat from their bodies suffusing together as they embraced. Never in her life had a man aroused her in a normal way. Not until Ray Cisco. There was a sudden urge to tell him that she thought she was pregnant. However, she needed to think more about that. What would she do when it was time to complete the mission and it perhaps became necessary to kill him? It was a thought that she had to avoid. There was no way that her happiness could last, just as with Hasan it had not been allowed to last. Her mind drifted back to the streets of Tehran, the blood flowing from the lifeless bodies of her grandparents and her mother. She remembered Hasan, dying at the hands of the U.S. supported Iraqi Army. Ray only looked like Hasan; he could not replace him. Roger Cowling and America had to pay for what they had done to her and her country.

Still, Ray's kisses fed a hunger inside of her and she could not resist tossing aside all thought of the mission. Never before had Fatima been in love. She never even conceived of it as a possibility. What it would be like to have his child? *Stop it! she demanded of herself. He's not Hasan, he's the enemy.* However, if her child were a boy, she could name him Hasan. He would, she somehow knew, be a boy. And with Ray's looks, he would always remind her of Hasan. Allah was returning Hasan to her! This enlightenment thrilled her with unexpected energy. She was no longer tired.

"Missed you, too," said Ray sensing a sudden intensity in her kiss. Immediately, he grew hard as he pressed against her. Slipping his hands inside her robe, he spread them around her delicate waist and slid them upwards until they found the swell of her naked breasts. A soft heat came from her skin, telling him that she had just climbed from the tub. The skin cooled to the touch of cold air. Teasing her nipples against the callused surface of his thumbs, he forced a moan from her pursed lips. At once, the sound made him harder, thickening his excitement.

"Oh, Ray. My god, I love you. I want to feel you. All of you," she cried. Fatima felt so damningly wanton and swathed with passion. Ray was Hasan, touching and caressing her, and he was also Hasan, forming inside her womb. Such thoughts were madness, but she did not care.

"Sweetheart," he said. "I've missed you. So damn much." He stepped inside, shutting the door. Her perfume, coupled with the smell of her freshly bathed body made him want to devour her.

With a hand tucked in his belt, Fatima pulled Ray towards the alluring warmth of the fire. They sank to their knees upon the thick, lamb's wool Bokhara rug. With unfeigned desperation, she began working him free of his shirt, taking his nipple in her mouth. Gently she squeezed it between her teeth, caressing her tongue across it to the sounds of his pleasure.

Ray gripped her raven black hair, balling it up hard within his clenched fists. Laura's touch, her tongue, the clever graze of her ivory teeth against his flesh, forced him to cry out. Ray loosed his grip of her hair, and sought her firm, taut breasts. They were total perfection. Now her moans joined his in a magnanimous toast to their passion. He fell on top of her as she pulled him towards her.

Hungrily, Ray took one of her dark nipples into his mouth and probed below until his fingers found her wetness. Thus he lingered, until obliged by Laura's invitation to fill her, to stretch all that was inside of her. Then together they built a rhythm, structuring their passion into a wild crescendo. Finally, no longer able to hold back, they exploded in each other's embrace until only oblivion remained of their universe.

"Oh my God, Ray," moaned Fatima, spent with a passion that she had never felt for another man. "I can't believe how powerful you are inside of me. You make me love you so much. I want to hold you in me for the rest of the night."

"And I want us like this for the rest of our lives, Laura," said Ray, closing his eyes. "Just let me. I'm leaving her. Not because of you, but because it's the right thing for me to do. Tell me to stay."

"Not like this," said Fatima, wanting desperately to tell him to stay the night. She was torn between wanting to lay in his arms the rest of the night and fulfilling her duty. However, if Danny had caused the reactor trips at Jefferson Davis she had work to do. And there was a crisis at hand with Reza dead and this Lambert woman suddenly entering the equation. "Not right now. Don't let the wonderful moments we give each other cloud your vision," she answered, looking into eyes that were truly Hasan. "I'm serious that I want you here all night. I feel like second best, a loser every time you walk out my door to go back to your wife. But I refuse to let you make a decision while we're both under the power of whatever it is that makes us crazy for each other." It was lie, but that was how it had to be.

It was what made Laura so wonderful, thought Ray. She was not afraid to love him, even though she could not have him; not yet anyway. He imagined how much it hurt her to continue loving him, knowing that he was not hers to reach out to on a cold lonely night when she needed someone. She gave him her love, shared with him her passion, only for him to go home and share his life with Donna. He wanted her to realize that that was the past; that he was hers if she wanted.

Ray looked into her eyes, feeling his soul falling into them, as though they were enormous caverns. Their power transformed him, feeding new energy into his core. He entered her again. Eclipsing the pinnacle of passion that they had just experienced, he brought Laura to another climax, then several more. He loved her until she screamed out that she could take no more. With one final release, he collapsed upon her in total, but ecstatic exhaustion.

The crackling flames glowed against their naked bodies. Contented, they lay, lost lovers, entangled in the flesh, united in spirit. For Ray, it was as a renewing of his soul. A renewing that he had been desperately in need of. What would it be like to raise a child with her? He imagined what their son would look like, adorned with the dark features that they both possessed. He had never spoken with Laura about having a family. How would she feel about it? It was best to wait and not take a chance of making their situation more complex.

Fatima lay quietly in his arms on the Bokhara. She felt reluctant to pump Ray for information. One of his hands well tanned and muscular lay across the flat of her stomach. What would he say if he knew that a life he had helped start grew inside? Maybe, she reminded herself; how disappointed she would be if her period began tomorrow, or the next day. The thought transported her back to reality. This was not Hasan, and perhaps she was not carrying a son that would grow up looking like Hasan. "Did you say something on the phone about Unit I tripping?" she asked.

"Yeah, came down about ten o'clock," said Ray, taking her hand and squeezing it in his own, brushing his lips against her fingers. "Shift Supervisor thought that there was a strong possibility that someone had deliberately mispositioned some breakers down in Emergency Switch Gear. CAS showed two mechanics down there earlier. They didn't do it though. Ops seems to be real jumpy for some reason. Had us investigating the Unit II trip this morning, as well. Thought that someone had tripped the unit from inside the Rod Drive Room. CAS put an end to that in a big hurry, too."

"How you going to stay awake tomorrow to fill out all the reports?" asked Fatima, faking her best laughter. Had Danny actually done it, tripped the units by going into safeguarded areas without registering on the Central Alarm System just like he said he could do? If so, they would need to move quickly to take advantage of the security hole before it was discovered. Now it was her turn to call her uncle. He would be very pleased, despite what had happened with Reza and the Lambert woman.

Fatima's passion with Ray had filled her anew with energy. Along with the nap she had taken in the tub, she felt fully restored. Though she felt that way now, she knew that the effects would wear off probably mid-day and she would be dragging. However, there was Danny to deal with. Not only that, what if security figured out that he had built a way around the plant's security system, if indeed that was what had been at the root of the two reactor trips?

The problem with Danny was that his stability was equivalent to that of thirty-year-old nitroglycerin. Soon, he would start sharing his secrets with others. He would most likely start by purporting theories to his friends of how it is possible to program the central alarm system's computer to not see a smart card with special codes on it. It would also be only a matter of time until he told the guys he worked with that he had slept with McClish the dish, as a lot of the male plant workers referred to her. Danny was a dangerous, loose end. She had to make sure he did not completely unravel.

"Since you won't let me stay the night, I guess I'll go home and catch a few hours sleep," said Ray. "You did warn me that you'd make my butt drag. See you in the morning."

Fatima smiled. "Yeah, I did, didn't I? See you in the morning." They parted at the door with a kiss. Watching him back out of the driveway, she wished that she too had the luxury of a few hours of sleep before the morning.

Chapter Twenty
Thursday, December 3
Richmond, Virginia

At two-thirty in the morning, Danny Miller walked out of the all night drug store with his purchase, a box containing twelve condoms. He hated using them, but she always insisted, said safe sex was very important. Well, if there was anything unsafe about sex with Laura McClish, that was how he wished to depart this world. He really hated buying the things, especially in his Richmond Nuclear uniform. Somehow it made him feel vulgar and unclean. Of course, everyone thought he was a pervert anyway, so what the hell.

Starting up his Eagle Talon, Danny sped from the parking lot, jazzed about what he had accomplished at the plant and what he would, in less than an hour, reward himself with. Same plan, same place Laura had told him. He grew hard just thinking about it.

As usual, they were meeting in the same single story, plain, white vinyl siding motel that they always used. The type that whether they have bed bugs or not, he always left feeling certain that something unwanted had attached itself to him. Hell, Danny had money, for no more often than they were able to get together, he would gladly foot the bill for a Holiday Inn or a Ramada. Laura, however, for whatever reason, seemed more comfortable with this seedy, out of the way place filled with prostitutes and drug dealers.

Danny could not believe that she had called him at the plant at two in the morning. "I can't sleep," she told him. "Tell them you're sick. Frank's here, and I got to get away. He's passed out drunk in the bed. Won't wake up until long after I'm supposed to be at work."

Hell yes, Danny was sick. Very close to dying. He fought the temptation to tell his supervisor that he was suffering from terminal lackanookie. Today had been wild. Twice in one day he had skirted by the central alarm system, tripping a nuclear reactor. Laura had told him that it could not be done. She had said that even the manufacturer of the system would not be able to create a smart card that would be invisible to the computer but yet provide access. That was why he had tripped the units, simply to prove to her that he had done it. Danny liked the way that his talents at manipulating the Security computer system impressed her. He also liked the way that his ability in the sack made her want him. Once she had told him that he was like opium to her. Danny just hoped they did not get caught, not with her ex being a lunatic and felon.

"Bring your project with you," she had purred over the phone. "I just can't believe that you were able to do it. I've got to see it. I get wet just thinking about what you do." Danny could tell how excited she had been. He patted his pocket where he had put the smart card. It had not been easy to get it to work. There had been some tense moments, as he continually set the alarm system off trying the card in the door to one of the Emergency Diesel rooms. Because he maintained Security's computer systems, he had one of their portable radios, enabling him to know when it was safe to screw around with a door. He knew which security officer was responsible for responding and simply waited until he received a transmission that let him know that that officer was not in the vicinity of the Emergency Diesel Rooms.

His dream-fantasy-come-true had begun one day when he was in the Main Security Building working on the CAS. He was attempting to sort out some of the problems caused by the incompatibility between the retina scanners and the old Central Alarm System. Because it was Fourth of July week, a lot of people were on vacation. Perhaps, for that reason, Laura McClish had been bored, having no visitors to process into the station. She had surprised him by coming over and asking questions about what he was doing. To his astonishment, she knew a great deal about access control systems. She asked intelligent questions, showing that she really understood his answers. After all, no one on site knew more about CAS than he, even if everyone did accuse him of being a pervert.

Laura had shown her appreciation for his knowledge by offering to hand him tools. He was, after all, squeezed back behind the console. To his amazement, she was able to sort through his tool kit and hand him what he asked for. In an effort to make the moment last, he had drawn the job out for as long as he could. And when she started to appear bored and in danger of going back to her desk, he told her how CAS and the retina scanners functioned. Of course, he had looked carefully around the room first, since he was divulging safeguarded information to someone who might not be cleared for it. However, she did work in Security, so certainly she had had a background check and could be trusted.

One thing had led to another and they eventually ended up here at this fleabag motel that same night. Each time they got together, Danny found himself trying more and more to impress her. A man's brain was as sexy as broad, well-muscled shoulders any day, she had told him. It was his knowledge of computers that really turned her on. She never seemed to mind that his very sexy brain was contained in a five foot seven frame that weighed two-hundred sixty pounds of multiple folds of fat. So finally, he had told her how he could defeat the CAS. She had accused him, politely, of exaggeration. Tonight he had proven himself without question. Somehow, he felt that he had achieved the ultimate feat for her; that he would never have to prove himself again, that he was now all the man that she had ever dreamed of.

The old man with no front teeth, behind the motel's front desk, gave Danny that big, everything is fine, don't worry, your secret is safe with me sonny boy, grin. It was actually a very irritating grin. No wonder the old man was missing all his front teeth. Eighteen dollars, Danny paid him the money. For a brief moment he wished that he could find a lover like Laura who was not married. He hated sleazy motels. Then he realized his chances of ever hooking up with the likes of her again in this lifetime. Put into proper perspective, the sleazy motel was just fine.

She had never allowed him to come to her home, nor would she go to his place. Though not living with her husband anymore, he was an ex-con, put away for popping a cap in someone over her. He was out on parole now and they had to be real careful. Now and then, she told him, he would come around checking on her. And she never knew when he might be following her. Here, in downtown Richmond, she was sure that he would have a hard time following her. Anyway, she said, better that he follow them here rather than learn where Danny lived.

Once again, at her bidding, Danny asked for room fourteen. Really it was room thirteen, but out of superstition, he supposed, they had skipped thirteen and named it fourteen. Regardless, it was on the end furthest from the office. Since it was the middle of the week, there was no other activity, none of the hookers and drug dealers that turned the motel into a Mecca of pleasure on the weekends.

Easing into the parking space in front of room fourteen, Danny killed the engine and then went inside. Someday, he had to tell at least a couple of the guys in the Instrument Shop about all this. Probably they would not believe him. Not unless he ended up marrying her, of course. Now would that not look grand, him showing up at next year's Richmond Nuclear Christmas party with her hanging on his arm. Yes! That would really torque Ray Cisco who seemed to be all over her at the office. What Cisco tried to get, Danny had obtained. And what about the job he had done on CAS? Shit, some terrorist organization would probably pay him millions to teach that trick!

Danny took his shoes off, turned down the bed. The T.V., he found, didn't work. Since he was getting ready to screw his brains out, he really did not care. There was no dimmer switch for the lights or lamps. So, for romantic atmosphere, Danny turned on the bathroom light and switched off the one connected to the defunct ceiling fan.

He was sitting on the edge of the bed when she knocked at the door. He recognized the light rap of her knuckles immediately. Attempting not to appear too eager, Danny slowly sauntered to the door and pulled it open. There she stood, flashing her special smile that was only for him, accenting it with eyes that made him ache deep inside.

"Hey, where's your car?" asked Danny.

"Down the street at the Seven-Eleven," said Fatima. "I had this nagging fear that he might be playing possum, might try following me. Looked all clear, though. Don't worry about him."

"Shit, Laura," said Danny, now looking past her into the night. Suddenly, he wished the weekend's compliment of hookers and pushers were about. He would feel a whole lot safer with other people nearby, regardless of who they were.

"You think I'm not worth getting shot over," Fatima said it with a pout in her eyes. Her hands brushed lightly over his rib cage. She stood close so that her perfume would envelop him.

Danny said nothing for a moment. Surprisingly, he was angry at her pout. Never before had he reacted this way to her teasing. "I shut down two nuclear reactors today," his voice shook as he spoke. "I could spend the rest of my life in prison if they ever catch me. All for... so that... I did it for you."

"Love, what you did was brilliant," said Fatima. She touched his face and then kissed him on the lips. "Don't worry, they'll never find out about what you did. They checked CAS. It showed them nothing. You're light years ahead of them."

"So, what d'ya think? Did I make them sit up and take notice, or did I make them sit up and take notice?" asked Danny, his smile smug and thick, replacing his moment of anger.

"Danny, you've really got some balls. And such a powerful mind." One by one, she began to undo the buttons of his shirt, her dark eyes watching him as her fingers did the work of disrobing him. One last time she thought. Even with him wearing a condom, the thought of him entering her, of violating the womb where a little Hasan might now be forming was unbearable.

"For Unit II, I just went into the Rod Drive Room and tripped the breaker for rod control. Me and my little phantom friend here," said Danny, pulling the smart card from his shirt pocket for her to see. He held it before her as she gingerly ran her fingers over it. "Then for Unit I, I decided to really give ops a run for their money. I tripped the breakers for both auxiliary feed water pumps and then went upstairs and tripped the breaker for both main feed water pumps."

"You really must have wanted to put the hurt on them," she said.

"Not like I could have," said Danny. "Hell, I could have gone over to the Safeguards Building and shut one of the isolation valves to keep the steam driven auxiliary feed water pump from working before I tripped the unit. Then they could have played Three Mile Island. And think, they said that they gave the Security Equipment Supervisor position to Jansen because he knew the equipment so well. Shit man, I'll be long dead and buried before he ever figures out how it was all done."

"I believe you, Love," said Fatima. Finishing with the buttons on his shirt, her fingers nimbly worked the buckle of his belt. Danny's hard on pressed tight against the fabric of his trousers. Unzipping them, she pulled his hardened repulsive flesh free and held it between her soft hands.

Gently, with seductive force, she moved him towards the bed. His legs buckled as she backed him against it. He sat, watching in amazement as she lowered her lips over him, something she had never done to him before. The mere touch of her tongue forced him to fight the urge to release. Never would he want to do that in her mouth; he would hold it back until he was inside of her.

After minutes of sheer, joyous torture, she moved her lips up the rolling folds of his belly, to his mouth. Her hands forced his pants down past his thighs until the sound of his heavy brass belt buckle thudded on the carpet. Then she stood, her leather dress came up well past mid thigh, showing miles of her lovely tanned legs. Reaching up beneath her dress, she worked her panties down, letting them fall to her ankles. Danny stared at the mound of shiny black hair, gleaming with suggestive moistness. Gingerly she stepped first one sandaled foot out of her panties and then the other.

"Lay down," she ordered. As he obeyed, she climbed on top of him, hovering over his ready to explode organ.

185

"I bought condoms, don't you want me to wear one?" asked Danny, his breathing uneven, his palms sweating at the excitement he felt. He prayed, he held his breath, please, just this once he wanted her to take him inside of her, flesh touching her flesh, nothing between them.

"No condom, Danny. Tonight is special. Safe sex would somehow spoil it for me tonight. This is how we celebrate," she said. Fatima leaned over him, her eyes, turning from their rich dark brown to almost fiery black coals as they looked, not into his eyes, but as if completely through him. Fatima held her position over Danny's cock. Reaching beneath, she cupped his balls in her hand.

Danny could not contain his moans. They came from the very center of his being. He was so close to the one thing that he knew he wanted in life above all else, to slide into her without protection and release inside of her, have her feel his hot sperm as it seared the walls of her womb. The excitement was growing. He battled to keep from ejaculating in her hand. Vaguely he was aware as she picked up the pillow and placed it over his belly. What was she doing that for? He did not have the faintest idea and doubted that he cared.

"Oh, God!" he moaned the words as he felt himself about to release. "Please, let me inside!"

From her purse, she had already removed the smooth steel of the short-barreled .22 and slid it beneath the pillow. The barrel was resting below his navel and pointed so that the rounds would pass up through his abdomen and into his lungs and heart. The gun was loaded with hollow points that would obliterate the soft flesh in their path. His eyes jerked open as he felt the cold steel against his skin. At that moment she squeezed the base of his shaft.

Her squeeze, the cold steel pressing against his stomach was making control nearly impossible. It almost felt like a gun barrel. The thought further excited him. He was going to release without being inside if she did not let him enter now. Instead, she lifted the pillow and he went rigid at the sight of the gun. It was indeed a gun and it looked real. This was fucking intense. She was achieving a level of kink that surprised him. "Oh, shit, I like that," said Danny. "Laura, I'm going to come. Let me in!"

With short rapid strokes of her hand around his shaft, she initiated his release. She could feel and smell his sperm. Placing the pillow back over the gun, she squeezed off the first round; again her finger pulled the trigger, the pillow muffling the pistol's discharge. For the first couple of shots, Danny continued to come, it was hard to tell whether he had a look of sheer terror or the most bounteous pleasure on his face.

186

Danny was still hard, his entire body, as well as his penis, quivering as she raised the pillow and gun from his abdomen. There were three small holes below his navel, each with a distinct powder burn. Only a small amount of blood oozed from them. Danny's eyes were wide open as he partially raised himself on his elbows. He was still alive, with his lips moving silently as though trying to question. Raising the pistol with the pillow still in place to muffle the shot, Fatima fired one last shot into the middle of his forehead. Danny collapsed onto his back, his eyes in an empty gaze towards the ceiling. She steadied herself with a hand on his shoulder as she took the smart card from his pocket. She stood and dropped both card and gun into her purse. Picking up her panties from off the floor, she did the same with them. And then Fatima left as she had come, with no coat, and no car.

Chapter Twenty-one
Friday, December 4
Jefferson Davis Nuclear Power Station

The phone rang at the Security Receptionist desk at Jefferson Davis Nuclear Power Station. Fatima yawned as she picked it up. Last night, coupled with her trip to Atlanta was taking its toll on her. What little sleep she did get had been marred by the weird dream in which she was obviously pregnant and her Uncle had shot her. Her mood, she realized, was not what it could be.

"Good morning, Jefferson Davis Nuclear Power Station Security Department. This is Laura, how may I help you?"

"How about you having dinner with me tonight?" asked the voice on the other end of the phone line. It was Travis Harding.

"Dinner?" laughed Fatima mockingly. "No, just tell me what you really want." The imbecile was always calling her. She endured this simply because his want of her was important and it would be a mistake to make it totally obvious that he stood no chance at having her.

"You don't have to ask," said Travis. "You know what I want. Anyway, I just wanted to make sure that your mother's doing okay." He gave an irritating chuckle.

"There were some complications with her surgery," said Fatima, annoyed that he would even think of discussing the business of Tanya Madison while she was at the power station. Phone calls were routinely monitored; something the VP of Security should have been well aware of. Would Matkins tell him about Tanya, how he had found her gutted in her bedroom? She hoped so. That would certainly help Travis to get a better perspective on his position in this game.

Travis drew a deep breath. "Is it something that we need to meet and discuss?"

"Listen," said Fatima. "I appreciate your concern, but my mother's health is family business and I don't care to discuss it."

"Wrong!" the caller's voice became louder and shook with anger. "We crossed the line and if this plan goes bad, we could go to..."

Fatima quietly replaced the receiver before he could finish his sentence. For the moment, Travis was the sole source of information from Energy International's corporate structure. He was also a liability. She really hoped that this was not one of the conversations that were randomly taped.

Travis Harding was shaking with anger. Henry Thomas and Laura McClish were treating him like some mere employee, not the partner that he was. He considered his options. There was really only one, go to Cowling and Frank Baker and let them know what was happening. It was, however, too late for that. He was incriminatingly linked to whatever had occurred in Atlanta. If he went to Cowling now, he would be out the door immediately.

There was another factor. He wanted Laura so bad that it was all he could think of every day. As illogical as it was, his obsession with her took precedence over his stake in the new power stations in Mexico. He picked up the phone and dialed his secretary's number. "Let's go grab an early lunch," he said, when she answered. There was some hesitation and then what seemed to be a reluctant "yes."

Les Lambert wondered why his sister had parked all the way over on the other side of the house. Instead of getting into his patrol car, he walked over and stared at his sister's 300ZX. Now he understood why Rachel had refused to explain her unexpected arrival at his doorstep last night. Though her own apartment was less than thirty minutes away, she had spent the night here. He had sensed that something was up. Surveying the damage to her car, his mind pieced together a scenario that sent goose bumps down his spine.

A shattered driver's side window, a damaged hood and a cracked windshield. Her car was a perfect fit to the BOL, be on the lookout, for an off white 300ZX that had crashed through the parking gate at Richmond International Airport. Shots had been fired, and a second car, described as a rust colored Ford, had run over a man who had been shot in the chest. All the police had been left with was a body with no I.D., and the stiff's weapon that had been fired. The weapon had a silencer attached to it. All the ear marks of a professional hit gone awry. And his sister right in the middle of it?

Les keyed the mike of his portable radio, "118 to Hanover County Dispatch, mark me 10-41."

"118, you're 10-41 at 0659," came the reply from the Hanover County 911 Operations Center.

Technically, 10-41 meant that Les was to be in his car, patrolling the various county roads. However, on Fridays, the Sheriff expected Les and the other six deputies on duty to meet him at the Office at eight o'clock to discuss case load. The only patrolling accomplished before the meeting would be the parking lot of the Exxon station, where the deputies gathered for coffee.

Below the shattered window of his sister's 300ZX, was a bullet hole. A very fresh looking bullet hole considering that no oxidation had yet taken place on the naked metal, stripped of its protective coating and paint by a speeding projectile. It appeared to be maybe a 9 mm soft nosed slug that had torn through it. Les opened the door and climbed inside.

Continuing to snoop, Les detected an odor, faint, but recognizable. A weapon had either been fired from within the car or placed in the car just after it had been discharged. Reaching beneath the seat, he found the vacant strip of velcro that was used to attach a holster to the front of the driver's seat. It was a self-preservation measure that he had taught her.

"111 to 118," came the radio traffic over Les' handheld.

"118, go ahead," said Les, keying his mike.

"Les what's your 20? You planning to 10-25 with us before the meeting?"

"Negative 111, not this morning. Checking out a road hazard. Nothing major. See you at the eight o'clock," said Les. This 300ZX definitely represented a hazard. The question was, to whom? He walked back to the house to find out.

Rachel was still asleep on the sofa in the living room, dead to the world. A far cry from the highly charged, wired state she had been in last night. Performing surveillance in Atlanta all night, she should have dropped off to sleep the moment she sat down. Instead, she had talked for hours about a variety of mundane topics until both he and his wife, Sandy, excused themselves and went to bed. Now, the reason for her hyper state was apparent, she had been involved in a shoot out. That was an adrenaline rush that would not soon go away. Les knelt beside her, gently shaking her.

"Hey, in there. Wake up," said Les, keeping his voice a quiet whisper so as not to wake up Sandy. A bank teller, she could sleep another hour before she had to get up.

Rachel opened first one eyelid and then the next. It was beginning to get light outside and Les was in his uniform. She had already been awake when he had gone out the front door to go to work. When she had failed to hear the sound of his tires on the gravel driveway, she knew that he would soon be back, asking questions.

"What?"

"What, hell!" said Les, his voice still a whisper so that he did not disturb Sandy. "What about you fill me in on your little shoot out. They've got a damn BOL issued on your car. With a homicide, goddamnit. What the hell is going on?"

"They couldn't have got my plates," said Rachel. "I was in excess of sixty when I took the gate out." At least she hoped that the video camera that was set up at the exit was not able to get usable footage of her plates.

"Level with me, Sis," said Les. "You're no longer government. At least so you've told me. You've got me in a hell of a situation."

"I don't know what the hell's going on," said Rachel. "It was just standard surveillance to see who was screwing who. Subject's the Senior VP of Richmond Nuclear. His wife hired me to find out what kind of business he takes care of when he's down in Atlanta."

"The Madison subject," offered Les. "Bet she's a damn stewardess he met on a flight."

"Flight attendant is more politically correct," said Rachel. "It went smooth. Standard surveillance until he gets a call on his cell phone. Sounds like he's gotten set up. Someone's using this bimbo to blackmail him."

"No shit? There's some kind of corporate fighting going on between Richmond Nuclear and the company that owns them," said Les. "It's been on the news a lot. Even on CNN."

Rachel shrugged her shoulders. "Corporate blackmail sounds like good clean fun. Somebody trying to kill me with a silenced weapon has a tendency to piss me off. Shit, so I killed the fucker, huh?"

"If it's any consolation, I'm sure he would have died."

"You said he was dead."

"He is, but it sounded like he had a partner who ran the hell over him. All I know is what I picked up over the scanner and caught on the morning news. Why didn't you tell me last night what was going on? You've got to turn yourself in."

"I needed time to think, still do."

"We're talking homicide, not speeding or drunk driving or some shit like that. You can get me into a hell of a lot of trouble."

"Spare me. Somebody with some means wants me dead. And don't offer me some useless idea of police protection. I need to be able to move around, find out who," said Rachel. Les was correct, however, she was endangering his job. But she was also counting on him.

"Make a deal with you, then," said Les. "You tell me every last detail about what you saw in Atlanta and I won't read you your rights with my next breath."

Rachel knew that she was getting the break of a lifetime. She began with her first phone call from Brenda Matkins and quickly told Les all the routine matters of the case, all the way until the first out of the ordinary occurrence. "I got to Tanya Madison's apartment long before they did. Gave me lots of time to check out the building and figure out which apartment was hers. Just as they were going up, it looked like someone walked through what I'm sure was her bedroom with a penlight. In fact..." she let the sentence trail as she opened the purse which still had the camera in it.

"I got it on camera, I hope." She went over to Les' television and quickly began disconnecting and reconnecting cables to her camera. On Les' DVD player, she played the footage of Matkins and Madison that she'd taken in the airport, Rachel got to them arriving at the apartment building on La Sarde. "They're entering the building."

"Okay, here we go," continued Rachel. "Right there." She ran forwards and backwards through the faint, very faint glint of light moving across the window. When she froze the picture, the light was nearly lost. Viewing it in slow motion didn't reveal anything. "I've got some stills. Shots of people who exited the building right after Matkins and Madison went in. Only one of them seemed interesting. A guy who left on a Harley in a big hurry and didn't come back."

"Only good guys ride Harleys," said Les. He owned one. "Maybe it was time for his girl friend's old man to get home. Anything else?" asked Les, now totally engrossed. At the moment, he was a road deputy, but he was merely biding his time until an investigator's slot opened up. He had a bachelor's in criminal science and was working on his master's. If his sister didn't get him locked up as an accessory after the fact, he would someday end up in the FBI Academy.

"They played like bunnies until after two in the morning."

"Didn't happen to get some good footage of that did you?" asked Les with a hopeful grin.

Rachel ignored his interruption and continued. "Madison took him back to the hotel. I went to bed. Damn, now I wish I'd followed her back." Suddenly she remembered how she'd almost run over the woman. "Damn, I nearly ran over some woman wearing sunglasses on my way out of the parking lot."

"Bright lights of Atlanta at two in the morning, huh?" said Les, nervously looking at his watch. He was really pushing it on the time factor. "We need to figure out our next move."

"We?" she asked, making a face of mock amazement. "Did I hear your vernacular switch to first person while referring to my case?"

"Look," said Les. "I'm a deputy sheriff. I've got your damn car shot full of holes, a BOL issued on it and Henrico County has a body in their morgue with a bullet in it from your gun. So, yeah, "we" as in you and I."

"You want to hear the tapes of Matkins' phone conversation the next day? Some interesting stuff."

"No, you didn't," said Les. "Hell, of course you did. Let me hear the tape of their supposedly private conversation."

Rachel reached into her handbag and pulled the tape player out. "Alright. First, he tries to call her. No answer." She fast forwarded the tape. "Just one of his business associates," she explained. "Okay, here we go."

"Matkins, I'm sure that this is a difficult moment for you. Do you see the camera on the dresser?"

"Yes, who the fuck is..."

"I have a most interesting video of your performance from last night. Especially the footage with you and your toy. Listen carefully, Matkins. Walk out of the apartment and call for a cab. Just do as you're told when the time comes and you will save you and your family unsurvivable torment and consequences. You will get instructions and they will come from me and only me."

"Did Cowling do this? You fucking bastard..." and then the sound of the connection being terminated.

"Nothing about money," said Les. "Just wait for instructions."

"It's something to do with this big corporate battle Richmond Nuclear has going with Energy International," said Les. "Bet on it. I just can't imagine those corporate types to be such heavy hitters as to try and kill you. They couldn't even know that you eavesdropped. Makes no sense at all." He glanced at his watch. "Damn. It's ten of eight. I've got to get out of here."

❖ ❖ ❖

Roger Cowlings walked from his chauffeured Town Car into the twenty-story office complex belonging to Energy International. More than likely that damn Frank Baker would already be on the line waiting to pester him with his incessant worrying. Baker would surely know about Unit I reactor tripping last night. Well, let him worry his damn self to death. Bud would arrive this afternoon at two with all that was needed to secure Brian Matkins vote. Then, should Baker actually worry himself into a coronary, who cares?

"Good morning, Mr. Cowling," said Edna.

"Only if you tell me that Frank Baker isn't waiting on the line to tell me that Unit I reactor tripped last night and the world as we know it is going to come to an abrupt end," said the Energy International CEO.

"Well, actually, sir," said Edna. "He is. And Bud Orton is here. He's in your office. Your calendar had him scheduled for two this afternoon. I told him that it wasn't appropriate to ignore your schedule. He just walked right past me and went into your office."

Cowling stiffened at the news. Almost certainly, something had gone awry. "You know Bud," said Cowling in an effort to sedate Edna's heightened anxiety at a breach of the schedule. The schedule was Edna's marked territory. She reacted to violators of it like they were criminal offenders. "Obviously my schedule didn't appeal to him. It's alright. You did fine."

The ancient grandfather clock that sat against the wall was chiming as he entered his office. Cowling paused, as he always did, before stepping onto the elegant Nain. The walls, the gray and black marble floor and every piece of furniture were designed for the rug. Yet, he was not really sure why he hung on to it. Lately, the Persian rug, given to him by the elder Hussein, had become annoying. Why it suddenly annoyed him, he could not figure out. Maybe it was because it reminded him that Abdul could still be out there somewhere. Persians never forgave. If Abdul were still alive, he would someday come to settle his score. It was best, however, not to think about that. Perhaps someday his car would explode with him inside of it or a bullet would end his life as he sat in a restaurant. If it happened, it happened.

Bud sat across from his desk, turning his neck just slightly to watch Roger enter. Putting his briefcase down, Cowling did not even bother to pick the phone up, choosing instead to simply turn on the speaker.

"Good morning, Frank," said Cowling, his voice level. "I'm well aware that a second reactor unit is down at Jefferson Davis. Not a damn thing that I can do about it at the moment. Go cry in someone else's beer. Good-bye." Pressing the 'End' button, Cowling terminated his connection with his fellow board member.

"Don't you kind of need his vote to push this project through?" asked Bud Orton. The sixty-two year old former mercenary turned private investigator/ enforcer, was six foot, eight inches of rock hard flesh. He had eyes, that when he looked directly at someone, could make them feel as though they were staring down the barrel of a pistol.

"I've got his vote," said Cowling matter-of-factly. "I have the vote of four of my seven board members. They've got too much of their own money invested in the project to do anything but go through with it. They are stuck with me."

"What happens if you can't come through with the money for construction?" asked Bud.

"We lose our lease," said Cowling. "I and Energy International will be swimming around in the toilet together. But in my world, Bud, I don't tolerate the word 'can't'. Never known you to, either."

"Just so you know, Roger. I'm not fucking with you just to piss you off," said Bud. "There are sudden grave developments in the operation. And that's a very literal way of putting it. I took the red eye out of Atlanta so I could get here as quickly as I could to tell you this in person."

Cowling just sat quietly, waiting for him to go on. Orton nodded towards the table next to the grandfather clock. A chessboard was inlaid in the table, composed of highly polished squares of both light gray and dark marble to match the floor. Each piece on the board was marble, hand sculpted. Rising from his seat, Orton walked over to it and picked up one of the pieces. Roger could not tell which piece, except that it was black.

"Chess is an ancient form of warfare," said Orton. "Of course it's mental rather than swords and guns. Sometimes rulers used it to settle disputes rather than actually going to war. Started in ancient India as a four person game. Then made its way to 7th century Persia. Persians changed it significantly. Then the Arabs. Finally, Western Europe. Good strategists of the game value each piece on the board. But they all fear the queen the most. Someone's taken your queen, Roger. We no longer have control of Matkins. Shit, we never even got to let him know he belonged to us. Another player's joined in this game of yours. I don't know who that player is, but it's very apparent that they've managed to take your queen without you even knowing that they were in the game."

Orton sat the piece that he was holding on the desk in front of Cowling. It was the black Queen. Cowling sat for a moment without speaking. There was a chill to Bud's words. "Any chance that you might just tell me in plain English, what has gone wrong?" he finally asked.

"Tanya Madison," Bud said the name with a narrowing of his eyes until they were merely deep slits. "She was your Queen. You depended on her for your strategy of putting Brian Matkins in checkmate. Not only for his vote, should you need it, but also because he could still derail the sale of Richmond Nuclear even after the board votes. If he starts screaming foul on nuclear safety, California could still pull out."

"Go on," said Cowling, leaning back in his chair, his hands folded in front of him. Damn, Bud did love playing the philosopher, but everything he said was true. One thing was clear, however, he referred to Madison in the past tense.

"Someone moved the black Queen and removed Tanya Madison, our Queen, from the board," said Bud, touching his fingers together as he brought his analogy to an end.

"Alright, Bud. Just cut the crap and tell me what has happened," said Cowling, running his tongue across lips that were suddenly dry. "What the hell do you mean by removed?"

"Tanya Madison is dead," Bud let the words penetrate, leaving an expression on Cowling's face that reminded him of a North Vietnamese general that he had assassinated by an arrow through the heart. It had been a look of pained surprise. "They took the tape. The scene was gruesome indeed. Someone gutted her like a pig."

"Is there anything that could possibly tie us to her murder," asked Cowling. In his desk drawer he had some antacid tablets; he pulled them out and put one in his mouth. Bud's description of the murder made him feel light headed.

"We've worked together a long time," said Bud. "You know that I'm good at what I do."

"Long enough to know that you're avoiding my question," said Cowling. For years he had used Bud's services. He immediately recognized that Bud was leading up to something that could hang them all.

"Well, depending on how the game is played and exactly who it is that holds the black Queen, we could have a problem," said Bud.

"God damn it, Bud!" shouted Cowling, suddenly coming forward in his seat. "Quit pussy footing around. Just tell me what I am dealing with."

"We've been set up to monitor calls from Matkins' home, office, and cell phone," said Bud, shifting uncomfortably in his seat. "We've known his every move. But we've paid no attention to the coming and goings of Mrs. Matkins."

"Mrs. Matkins?" asked Cowling, unsure about where Bud was taking him.

"After we realized that we were under surveillance, ..." said Bud, cut short in mid-sentence.

"Under surveillance?" Cowling roared the question. He put another antacid tablet in his mouth.

"We went back through all of the calls that we had been monitoring," said Bud, his annoyance at Cowling's interruption evident in his voice. "Be goddamned if Mrs. Matkins didn't have a private investigator tailing her husband. I always use a three-person team on a job like this. While one goes in, two others watch. My watchers observed the P.I. snapping a picture of one of my employees."

"Shit," said Cowling, shaking his head. "Mrs. Matkins hired an investigator to kill Madison? By gutting her?" This was not making any sense.

"Nothing as simple as that. The private investigator is simply an unwanted complication. Listen to this," said Bud, pulling out a miniature recorder.

"Matkins, I have a most interesting video of your performance from last night. Especially the footage with you and your toy," said the voice. *"Matkins, I'm sure that this is a difficult moment for you. Do you see the camera on the dresser?"*

"Yes, who the fuck is..."

"I have a most interesting video of your performance from last night. Especially the footage with you and your toy. Listen carefully, Matkins. Walk out of the apartment and call for a cab. Just do as you're told when the time comes and you will save you and your family unsurvivable torment and consequences. You will get instructions and they will come from me and only me."

"Did Cowling do this? You fucking bastard..." and then the sound of the connection being terminated.

"Have the police found the body yet?" asked Cowling, his hands now in his lap so that Bud would not see them trembling.

"No, I've got people with their ear to the ground in Atlanta," said Bud.

"Once they hear something about the murder, they'll call me. That is, if it gets reported. Perhaps they've cleaned up the scene and hid the body. Then if Matkins doesn't play their game, Atlanta P.D. will get a tip-off on where to find it. Along with the tape."

"Why don't you know more about what the police have found?" asked Cowling.

"Once we found her body, my people pulled back," said Orton. "Close enough to ask questions is close enough to get entangled."

"Have you any possible idea of who's doing this?" asked Cowling, appreciating that fact.

Digging through his briefcase, Bud pulled out some photos. A photo of Matkins and Madison at the airport showed a dark haired woman, dressed in blue jeans and a leather bombardier jacket in the background, a red circle had been drawn around her. Then her again, fashionably dressed as a business woman coming off an elevator behind Matkins; and finally, a night camera shot of the same woman sitting in a dark colored Astro van. She graced each of the photos that Bud laid out across the CEO's desk.

"I was hoping that she could tell us," said Bud, nodding at the pictures. "My people spotted her tailing Matkins when he landed in Atlanta. She's the private investigator Mrs. Matkins hired."

"Pretty much second rate I guess if you picked up on her so easily," commented Cowling as he studied the photos.

"Her name is Rachel Lambert. Based here in Richmond," said Bud. "If you're doing a simple surveillance like she was to hang someone's cheating spouse, you don't go to great lengths at worrying about being under surveillance yourself. She was concerned only in evading detection by Matkins and Madison. I don't consider her part of your competition. But maybe she saw something my people didn't."

"So, do you think she'll go to the police?" asked Cowling. "Does she even know that she photographed one of your people?"

"I don't even think that she knows that Tanya Madison is dead," said Bud. "The only reason we know is because my man went into the apartment to retrieve the tape and found the body."

"What did he do?" asked Cowling. This was turning into a major cluster, he could see that right now.

"I personally wasn't there," said Bud. "But my people did exactly like I've always told them to do in such a situation, get the hell out of Dodge fast before Wyatt Earp shows up."

"No one set up surveillance so that we could see who went in to hide the body, if that's what they did?" asked Cowling, truly annoyed.

"Hey, there's some heavy time involved for extortion and blackmail," said Bud, putting his hands up. "Throw in the potential to be tops on Atlanta P.D.'s suspect list for murder, shit.

"Anyway," continued Bud. "When we traced the rental and ID'd Lambert, I personally went to her apartment. I did a very thorough search of it at five thirty this morning. She wasn't home, so I naturally considered myself invited in. Seems someone else had already considered themselves invited in before me. They appear to have conducted a very impressive search and trash operation. Not to mention that they left her a little present that we took care of for her."

"The same people who killed Madison?" asked Cowling.

"That's my assumption," said Bud. "They are pro's and they are damn well organized to be able to identify her and track her down as quickly as they did. The police here are looking for a Nissan 300ZX, just like the one she owns. Seems it was involved in a shooting in the Richmond International Airport parking lot. I think the opposition tried to ice her as she landed back in Richmond. From what they left her in her apartment, they certainly don't appear to wish her well. The unfortunate gentleman who found his way to the morgue appears to be from the Middle East."

"Really?" Cowling's voice had become a mere whisper; his mouth suddenly feeling like it was filled with cobwebs. That the dead man was Mid-Eastern filled him with tremendous unease.

"She was unfortunate enough to stumble onto this mess," said Bud, noting that the reference to the dead Mid-Easterner had caused Cowlings to struggle to maintain composure. He knew of Abdul Hasdiz. Not everything, but enough to know that his client was highly fearful of the Persian. Somewhere along the way, Cowling had obviously crossed him. Not a wise thing to do considering what he had found out about Hasdiz. If it ever came down to a fight, Bud would have to pull up stakes, abandon Cowlings to his fate. In the old days, when he had a battle-hardened core group of mercenaries under his control, he could have offered a fight. However, he could not expect those in his hire these days to go head to head with Hezbollah soldiers. "The nature of her mission means she took pictures. Odds are good that she has film that shows Madison's killer. We need to find her. We need that film so that we can identify who our other player is."

"You don't think she's dead?" asked Cowling. Try as he might, he was unable to keep his voice steady. He glanced down at the Nain. Had its annoyance to him been a signal? Perhaps he was just over reacting. He should dismiss this foreboding as nothing more than the result of mere coincidences. Something easier said than done, however.

"Don't know," said Bud. "Most likely, she's gone to ground. Personally, I find her very impressive. She seems to have survived an ambush and is clever enough to drop out of sight. I think she'll surface soon. If she does, it would be well worth it to get our hands on the surveillance package that she has."

"Perhaps I need to have you put some protection on me," said Cowling. "I never worried about it before. Anyone who knows me well enough to kidnap me knows that no one would pay to get me back." He tried to grin at his own attempt at humor. Glancing down at the rug, it was as though he could hear the cries of the young girl from within the crate in the Bradford Oil Building in Tehran. Whatever had become of her? Of her family? Was Abdul still alive? A Knawing fear permeated his deepest parts. "I'd really like to stay alive to see this project through."

"You never told me why you wanted information on Abdul Hasdiz," said Bud. "But he's bad news; really bad. Unless you pay me to set up protection similar to what the President has, it's not going to matter. And if he hates you as bad as I'm suspecting, I don't even think that would stop him from getting you."

"He was once a good friend," said Cowling. He knew Bud was right.

"And you betrayed him, I take it," said Bud. The ever so slight nod of Cowlings' head was his answer. It was interesting how Cowling seemed to stare at his prize Nain with what looked to be disgust. "I've known you for a long time, Roger. You would not be happy hiding behind bodyguards."

"Perhaps it's not him," said Cowling, knowing that his argument sounded hollow even to him.

"In that case I don't think it's necessary. You don't have a vote on Energy International's board," Bud said with a shrug of his shoulders. "Why bother going after you? However, if they have Matkins in their pocket, then I would be real concerned about the health of the four board members whose votes you're counting on."

Cowling was silent for a moment. Then he spoke. "Damn it, Bud, you're absolutely right. Someone is contending for our influence on Matkins. But for the moment, he most likely thinks that it was us who killed Tanya Madison. Am I correct?"

"For the moment, probably," said Orton.

"Then, for the moment, anyway, we still have control over him," said Cowling.

Yeah, right, thought Orton.

Brian Matkins pulled into the parking space marked "Senior V.P. Nuclear" at the Jefferson Davis Nuclear Power Station. He glanced at the two large Reactor Containment Buildings, their nuclear reactors sitting idle. Normally, such a situation would have him chomping at the bit to get inside the station and rectify the problems. Not this morning, though. In fact, he thought it might have been better to send Travis Harding out here to see what needed to be done. Like a zombie, he made his way from his company car, a Crown Victoria, to the entrance of the Security Building.

"Good morning, Mr. Matkins," said an Officer who ran the x-ray machine.

"Good morning," said Matkins. Brian placed his briefcase on the x-ray machines conveyor belt. Then he stepped into the portal of the weapons detector. The detectors green light turned to red as soon as he stepped upon the platform. Upon finishing its scan, the red light blinked off and then the green light blinked back on.

Without incident, Matkins continued on, placing his keys into a small white tray that he slid across a table to where the Officer stood. He then passed through the metal detector and took his keys from the tray.

"Here you go, sir," said the Officer, handing him his briefcase. "Sure hope these units get back on line real soon."

"We all do. Thanks," Brian said, forcing a smile.

Brian passed the small cubicle where Laura McClish sat. Without fail, whenever he visited the power station, he would stop and talk with her. He had thought once about getting her phone number and asking her out, but had decided that he really wanted to get serious about Tanya. Cheating on her was not a good way to do that. Besides, Cowling, he knew, would love to find out that he was stepping out on his wife, and with a company employee at that. No, it would have been too much of a risk. And now, with what was going on with Tanya, it was no longer even a consideration.

"Mr. Matkins, Good Morning," said Fatima, her head popping up as Brian walked by. She was feeling pretty rough. She had to get some sleep.

"Good morning, Laura," said Brian, his feet ceasing their movement. Her smile, her eyes, he thought, there was just something so powerful about her. "You're looking lovely this morning." Why had he bothered? Because, he knew, someone like Laura should not be working in a nuclear power station. She should have been gracing the pages of Victoria Secret catalogs. Very quickly, thoughts of Tanya came back. Brian forced a smile and continued on through Security. He headed down a corridor lined with pictures of key company personnel and several plaques representing various achievements by the power station and its staff. Finally he arrived at the Station Manager's office.

Kat's chair was empty. Through the next door he could see the Station Manager and the Operations Superintendent. He went on through.

"Morning, Brian," said Lloyd Ralston, an unlit cigar perched between his teeth.

"Good morning," piped in Bob Livingston, the Operations Superintendent.

"Good morning, gentlemen," said Brian, taking a seat.

"Hate to get your day off any worse," said Ralston. "But Cowling is sitting up in his office. He wants a conference call with us once you arrive. I think he wants these units back on line real damn bad. What the hell is going on? Is he selling us? He knows better than to try and tell us how to do business. We hate for these units to be down as badly as he does."

Livingston had closed the door. The room was soundproof. Whatever they said in here could not be heard in the outer office. When Ralston had remodeled the conference room, he had had extra insulation and a solid oak door installed. He could chew somebody's butt at the top of his lungs without Kat ever hearing a word of it.

"First let me make it clear that this conversation isn't taking place," said Brian. Immediately he received nods from the two men. "The important thing is for you to understand that I have no knowledge of any move by Energy International to sell this company."

"Wouldn't the executives of Richmond Nuclear have to be notified if they wanted to sell us?" asked Livingston, pushing his U.S. Navy issue glasses back up onto his nose.

"No," replied Brian. "What I and the other VPs are paid to do is to ensure that these units produce electricity so as to turn the highest possible profit and to safeguard the nuclear cores of both reactors. Cowling and the Board don't have to tell me anything about their business intentions. I get to hear Lou Dobbs talk about it on CNN just like you do. Right now, we're losing a million dollars per day per unit, and that's good cause for Energy International to be unsettled. Even more so if they have plans they're not telling us about. And yes, my gut feeling's the same as yours. But there's not much to be done about it."

"All I know is that we've been in this situation before," protested Ralston. "It's the nature of our business to have generating units trip. We've proven ourselves to be damned good at getting back on line; safely I might add, and staying ahead of the competition. Even Duke Power, these days."

"And being good is a double edged sword," said Brian. "If the price is right, Duke Power, Carolina Power, the California legislature," Brian paused with a smirk. "Any number of potential buyers is out there. Especially now that our nuclear units have been granted licenses to operate an additional twenty years. On the other hand, we're good, steady income for the stockholders. It would be expensive to buy us. So who knows?"

"Cowling makes me nervous," said Ralston, staring at his phone, knowing that he wouldn't be able to put the conference call off much longer. "He and his cronies are picking up some age. I think he's selling us to California so he can retire with a big nest egg. God, I can't imagine what it'd be like to be working for those tree-huggers out west."

"I will tell you this," said Brian. It was difficult concentrating. He thought of how Tanya's death and the extortion call had something to do with all of this. "Nothing has been said at any board meeting. But Cowling has a lot of authority. He could put together a deal without me knowing it. He's got tremendous power written into the company by-laws for himself as CEO. Remember, he started Energy International. The company's by-laws were written to suit him. He can actually commit a limited amount of Energy International's capital to projects not approved by the Board. He'll still have to get the Board of Directors to finalize any kind of deal, but the majority is in his back pocket, so…Anyway, call him; let's see what's on his mind."

Ralston dialed the number. The three men sat quietly as they heard the line ringing over the speakerphone.

"Energy International, Roger Cowling's office, may I help you?" Brian quickly recognized the voice of Edna.

"This is Matkins," said Brian, speaking loudly. "Cowling is waiting for our call."

"Yes, sir," said Edna. "I'll put you right through."

"Good morning, Brian, gentlemen," said Cowling. "By the way, how was Atlanta, Brian? Do anything exciting while you were down there?"

Brian felt like he had just been slammed in the gut. The cocky, cold-blooded bastard! "A little chillier than I expected it," he said, battling to maintain his composure. "But I'll weather it."

"Good to know," said Cowling. Right now he was certain that Matkins suspected him of setting up Tanya's murder and blackmailing him. In one sense, it gave him the upper hand and he would use it to control Matkins. On the other hand, what if Matkins went to the police. Things could get nasty very fast, though he felt sure that Orton had all the tracks covered. He would feel a whole lot better once Orton had caught up to the private investigator that had been following Matkins. In the meantime, keeping control of Matkins and keeping the deal with California on track would be a fine balancing act. "I'm feeling a little chilled myself this morning," said Cowling, letting his tone turn icy. "Afraid to turn my heat up too much, knowing that my power company can't seem to produce the electricity that I need."

"Your power company has one of the highest capacity factors in the nation for its generating units," Matkins said coldly. What had Cowling meant by asking about Atlanta? Well, had there ever been any doubt about who had killed Tanya and why? "It also has profit margins to match," added Brian.

"The units' performance, past tense, doesn't concern me," said Cowling. "Our present success is a result of today's work. These two units coming down like they did; I'm wondering if my managers haven't perhaps gotten too comfortable with all these high capacity factors and past achievements. That happens. Your friend Harding, perhaps he'd like to wear that Senior V.P. hat, Brian. And I'm sure that he could find a Station Manager who can produce results, Ralston."

"With all due respect, Mr. Cowling, whatever floats your boat," shot back Ralston. "I get offers from competitors all the time trying to get me to jump ship."

"Not to mention," added Brian. "That just on the chance you should want to sell Richmond Nuclear, a major shake up in what has made the company productive, could hurt stock prices and jeopardize a potential sale." Like Ralston, he could walk away from Richmond Nuclear and step right into the Senior VP position of several struggling nuclear utilities. If Tanya were still alive, perhaps he would do so, and simply start life over. Now, however, she was dead and there was nothing to start over with.

There was a moment of silence on the other end of the line. The three men in the room held their breaths. Cowlings was not used to the likes of the barrage that both Ralston and Matkins had just delivered.

"I believe it's safe to say, my good friends," said Cowling, his voice losing none of its haughtiness. "That if a sale of Richmond Nuclear should occur, the buyer would not hesitate to replace you if it appeared that you were contrary about performing for them. And, Brian, I hold the aces in this hand, best you keep that in mind."

The thought that Cowling could have something to do with Tanya's death and the camcorder that had been hidden in her room infuriated Brian. He had just never dreamed that Cowling would stoop to murder to accomplish his goals. "Someday, Cowling, those aces will turnout to be your tickets straight to Hell."

Ralston and Livingston exchanged looks of total surprise. Neither would have been surprised if Cowling had bellowed back firing Matkins on the spot. However, that did not happen. The exchange was terminated by the sound of Cowling hanging up.

Chapter Twenty-two
Friday, December 4
Jefferson Davis Nuclear Power Station

Rachel had spent the last two hours on the phone. She had been interested in finding Tanya Madison. Her expectation, if Tanya Madison was part of black mailing Brian Matkins, was that she would disappear for a while. Such seemed to be the case as the Airline reported that she had failed to show up for work. Rachel had posed as a concerned cousin attempting to contact Madison about a sick uncle. Now she turned her attention to contacting Brian Matkins, even though she had not yet talked to his wife, her client, about the matter.

"Richmond Nuclear, may I help you," came the feminine voice over the phone.

"Yes, my name is Rachel Lambert," said Rachel, using her flip phone to prevent any possibility of a trace to her brother's home. The last thing that she wanted to do was to put him and his wife in any danger. "I'd like to speak to Brian Matkins, please. Tell him that this is in reference to his recent visit to the NRC office in Atlanta."

"Just one moment, please," said the voice. Rachel could hear herself being forwarded. Nothing she hated more than stating her business to the person answering the phone and then having to do it all over again.

"Brian Matkins' office, Mrs. Hendrickson, how may I help you?"

"This is Ms. Rachel Lambert," she said. "I'd like to speak with Mr. Matkins, please. It's in regards to a certain matter that needs clarification from his last visit to Atlanta."

"Just one moment, please," said Mrs. Hendrickson. Momentarily she was placed on hold.

"Ms. Lambert, my name is Travis Harding, Vice President of Nuclear Administration and Security," said the male voice. "Brian Matkins is going to be out of the office for the rest of the day and unavailable until Monday. We have a couple of generating units that unexpectedly shut down at Jefferson

Davis Nuclear Power Station. He'll probably be just about camping out there for the weekend. Is there anything that I can help you with? Matkins has left me, for the moment, to answer any questions concerning his trip to Region II." Travis had instructed his secretary to let him know if any calls came in regarding Matkins' trip to Atlanta. Any sign that the NRC was going to take quick action based on information Matkins supplied to them needed to be relayed quickly to Henry Thomas and Laura.

"No," said Rachel. "Thank you all the same, but I prefer to speak to Mr. Matkins personally."

"Are you with the NRC, Ms. Lambert?" asked Travis, frustrated that he might miss a prime opportunity to collect some important intelligence.

"No," said Rachel. It had been tempting to say, *"yes"*, simply to facilitate getting in to see Matkins. However, she was certain that Travis Harding would press her for more information and knowing nothing about the Nuclear Regulatory Commission, she would fail such a test miserably. "I'm with the *Washington Economic News*." She knew the editor there and knew that he would vouch for her if that became necessary. Several times she had posed as a reporter for the magazine when she was on assignment behind the Iron Curtain.

"Oh, really?" said Travis, somewhat caught off-guard. "What would be the nature of your interest in talking to Mr. Matkins?" he asked. This could be quite important. He was desperate to learn what she wanted.

"The strain between your parent company and Richmond Nuclear is catching a lot of attention lately," said Rachel, thankful for an opportunity to say something that Mr. Harding could hardly deny. "There are rumors that Matkins is trying to get the NRC to prevent Energy International from making staff cuts that could jeopardize nuclear safety." She had learned that from Mrs. Matkins.

"Well, as I mentioned, Mr. Matkins is really very busy," said Harding. This was not anything significant. Still, it was a good opportunity to get his name in print. "Let me see. I have some time between nine and ten on Monday that we could meet. If Mr. Matkins is back from the power station, there is at least a small chance that he might be able to join us."

"Nine in person will be fine," said Rachel, somewhat flustered at Harding's persuasive ability to put her off until then. She needed to talk with Matkins as quickly as possible, but she would take what she could get; at least for the moment. "Thank you." And then she clicked off.

Rachel made a mental note to contact Jim Hardy at *Washington Economic*

News to let him know that she was posing as one of his journalists. Next, she dialed the non-emergency number to the Hanover County Sheriff's Office. "Hello, this is Rachel Lambert, Les' sister. Is he in the office? Well, will you tell him to call me? Thanks." Five minutes later the phone rang.

"Rachel, what's going on," asked Les.

"Thanks for calling me back," said Rachel. "Les, you where you can talk?"

"Yeah," said Les. "What did you find out?"

"Tanya Madison is missing, Les," Rachel tried to hide the flutter in her voice. "I've been on the phone all morning it seems like. She's a flight attendant for U.S. Global Airways. She was scheduled to work a flight last night and didn't show up. I managed to talk to one of her friends. Says that she and another attendant who has a key-card to Madison's apartment went over to check on her. The apartment is cleaned out. Lock, stock and barrel."

"Well, if she was a willing and well paid partner in the extortion, it would only make sense for her to vanish," said Les. "She's probably in Cancun, like you ought to be."

"Or she was murdered, and somebody has done a good job of cleaning up," said Rachel. "Somebody was very desperate to get rid of me."

"That could either mean that you're a witness to a murder or that the financial stakes in this extortion are high," said Les. "My advice, take what you have to Mrs. Matkins, get your paycheck, and try the Caribbean. By the time you come back, they'll know that you don't know enough to hurt them. Unless, of course, something really worthwhile comes back on the enhancement of your video."

"Guess I need to give it some thought," said Rachel blandly. "Hey, thanks for the big brother stuff. Don't know what I'd do if I didn't have you to keep me on the straight and narrow." Clicking off, Rachel knew that she had no immediate plans for rum and sandy beaches.

"Yes?" asked the older woman from behind the receptionist desk. "May I help you?"

It almost scared Rachel out of her wits. She had not realized that there was a desk and a live human being hidden in the alcove as she entered the Jefferson Davis Nuclear Visitor's Center. To go any further towards the station, she would have had to pass through a checkpoint. Trying to explain to one of the security officers that she was arriving unannounced to speak with their Senior V.P. would prove more complicated than she was prepared to deal with; especially if they searched her vehicle and found her packing a 9mm. Pulling into the Visitor Center to use the phone had looked like her best bet.

"I'm Rachel Lambert. I was told that Brian Matkins was here at the station today," said Rachel. "I need to contact him."

The woman, probably in her early sixties, paused for a moment. "Yes, he is, however it's very unusual for him to take visitors when he's conducting business at the station. He is very busy. We have generating units down, you know."

"Please, let him know that I'm here," said Rachel. "Tell him that I represent Madison, Inc. and that I'm here to discuss some unfinished business from his recent Atlanta trip. I think you'll find that this is very important to him."

"Yes, ma'am," said the receptionist, her voice reflecting a certain level of annoyance.

"Kat, this is Beatrice at the Visitor's Center," she said into the phone, her eyes coldly fixed upon Rachel. "There is a Ms. Lambert from Atlanta who wishes to speak to Mr. Matkins."

"No," interrupted Rachel, irritated that the woman was not even close with what she had asked her to pass on. "It's very important that he knows that I represent Madison Inc. And I'm not from Atlanta, I'm here to discuss his visit there."

"That's exactly what I said," snapped the woman. "She insists that you must tell Mr. Matkins that she is the representative for the Madison Company in Atlanta."

Rachel walked away from the reception desk and took a deep breath. Right now, Brian Matkins was the person voted most likely to have some answers for her. Perhaps she could help him, as well. She wondered what she should do if he refused to see her. It was no longer important to her that talking to Mr. Matkins might create a conflict of interest with Mrs. Matkins. That concern had vanished when someone had tried to deep six her in the airport parking lot.

"Ms. Lambert, Mr. Matkins will come on up now to meet with you," said Beatrice, her voice suddenly sweet now that she knew that the Senior V.P. found this unannounced visitor important enough to drop what he was doing and to meet with her. "If you want to look at the exhibits in the next room, I'll go back and put on some fresh coffee."

"Thank you," said Rachel.

In the Exhibit Area, Rachel found herself surrounded by about two-dozen of what appeared to be sixth graders. They were being led around in groups, given explanations of all that is involved in the making of electricity from nuclear fuel. Rachel distantly listened to the explanation of how unused nuclear fuel is practically non-radioactive versus used fuel that has to be cooled and stored carefully for many years. A young man, probably one of the station's engineers, was giving the presentation. He looked like he was enjoying himself.

"Ms. Lambert," said the receptionist.

"Yes?" Rachel, turning around to face the woman from the front desk.

"I never introduced myself. I'm Beatrice Sturgeon. That's spelled S-T-U-R-G-E-O-N. I'm the supervisor for the Jefferson Davis Nuclear Visitor's Center. If you'll follow me, I'll take you back to his office. There is fresh coffee and some doughnuts."

"That's great," said Rachel. "I can really use some." She followed Beatrice's stiff gate. She moved with the air of someone who perhaps more belonged in the court of Queen Elizabeth than in public relations. But that was unimportant; fresh coffee and doughnuts were what mattered.

Beatrice stopped at a small kitchen on the other end of the building from where the school kids were taking their tour. "Please, help yourself," she told Rachel. "The doughnuts are on that tray."

"Thanks," said Rachel, pouring coffee from a stainless steel pot. It looked suspiciously weak as it flowed into her cup. How she hated coffee that tasted like hot water. Taking her coffee and one of the doughnuts, she followed Beatrice down a hallway. One sip of the coffee convinced her that she would need to find a place to dispose of it.

"If you'll just make yourself comfortable," said Beatrice. It sounded more like a commandment than an offer of hospitality. "I'm certain Mr. Matkins won't be long."

Before Rachel could again thank her, Beatrice was striding back up the hall at a pace that an Olympic race walker would have been hard pressed to keep up with. There was nothing to do but sit and wait. Though the coffee tasted like hot water, the doughnut was fresh. It more than compensated for the poor coffee.

"I've got the results from the polygraph on the two mechanics that were in the Emergency Switch Gear Room before everything went to shit," said Ralston. He remembered the 'swearing off jar'. If he were to put a quarter in it for every violation that he had uttered over the past eighteen hours, he would retire dirt poor. "The investigator said he had no doubt that they were telling the truth."

"The Central Alarm System shows no other possible suspects, correct?" asked Matkins. Both Ralston and Livingston nodded their agreement. "There was also confirmation from CAS that no one was in the Rod Drive Room when Unit II went down. Leads me to genuinely believe that only one possibility exists. We have a wide spread problem with electrical breakers. Could be a generic problem with the manufacture or it could be something that we're doing incorrectly during our maintenance."

"Shit," said Ralston, shaking his head. He opened his top desk drawer and removed a quarter that he promptly dropped in the swearing off jar. It was time to get back on the wagon and stop swearing. Then he took several more and dropped them in for the many times that he'd been negligent. "That's going to involve a few days down time just to check every breaker. We'll certainly have to do that if we go with that as the cause."

"I don't see how there can be any other explanation," said Brian. He pulled out a twenty-dollar bill and dropped into the Swearing Off Jar. The money went to a local Boy Scout Troop. "The rest are on me," he said, nodding at the money. "Can't imagine a couple of old Salts like you being at your best without a little off-English. With all the problems we're having with Energy International, even a hint at sabotage could cost us a great deal more in down time and stock value. The units are already down. Run tests on every Safety Related breaker. The more problems of this nature that we identify and correct, the more credible we are." Both men nodded, somewhat reluctantly. "I'll convey the official finding and our intended course of action to the NRC. I think that they'll buy it. Unit I was coming down for refueling on Sunday. I know that all of the contractors probably aren't in place, but lets go ahead with what we can. The priority will be to complete the testing on all pertinent Unit II breakers. And maybe it would be a good idea to do a system operability check on CAS so that we can respond to any NRC concerns about that. Considering that there are so many documented problems with it and the security investigations figure so prominently in our reports."

"Well," said Ralston. "The types of problems that we have had with the

Central Alarm System don't affect its ability to actually monitor when someone goes in and out of an area. And then there is a second problem."

"That is?" asked Matkins.

"An Instrument Technician, Danny Miller, was the guru of that system," said Ralston. "He evidently was screwing the wrong woman last night. Someone shot him dead. I've got a message on my desk asking me to get in touch with the Sheriff's Office and let them know when they can come out here to interview folks."

The private line between the Station Manager and Kat, his secretary rang. "Yeah, Kat," said Ralston, picking up the receiver. "Hang on. I'll see what he wants to do."

"Brian, Beatrice is on the line with Kat," said Ralston. "There's a Ms. Lambert at the Visitor's Center who says that she is with Madison Company. Says it's something about Atlanta. I hope that she isn't anyone too important. Kat thinks Beatrice is having one of her bad days."

It caught Matkins flat footed, he suddenly found himself coughing to hide his obvious surprise. His mind had lingered on the Station Manager's comment about Danny Miller getting killed while screwing some woman. Perhaps they would be saying similar lines about him soon. "Tell Kat to have her stay put and I'll be up there right away," said Matkins. It took him a moment to get his wits together. "Go ahead and begin breaker testing and get with the manufacturer to see if anyone else is or has had similar problems. Have Turner get a factory rep out here to review our maintenance program on the breakers. I'll stay in touch." He knew that he had not exited gracefully, but that could not be helped.

Putting the last piece of doughnut in her mouth, Rachel had only been in the office for about ten minutes. "Ms. Lambert?" said Brian Matkins who suddenly appeared in the doorway of the office.

"Mr. Matkins," said Rachel, wincing as part of the doughnut went down the wrong way. She quickly took a swig of the horrible coffee to try and wash it on down. Coughing and choking, she looked up at Matkins through watering eyes.

"Come on now," said Brian. "I don't know yet whether to call the paramedics or pray that the doughnut does you in."

"Gee, thanks for the warmth and support," said Rachel after a final, vigorous cough and smacking herself on the chest to get rid of the piece of doughnut.

"Blackmail rarely elicits my better qualities," said Brian. "Who are you?"

Pulling out her badge and I.D., she held it in front of him. "Not the person blackmailing you," said Rachel. "I was almost killed last night because of what you're involved with, though."

"You're going to have to explain," said Brian, seemingly stunned at her statement about almost being killed. "In what way are you involved in this matter?"

"I was hired to follow you on your trip to Atlanta," said Rachel. "Its unethical to my client to even tell you that much, so please don't ask me to identify the party; I won't. But because of what someone must think that I saw, I was almost shot in the airport parking lot last night."

"My God!" said Brian. "That was you. And it had to do with me! Just what do you know, Ms. Lambert?"

"I was monitoring your phone calls. Including the one that you got while in Madison's apartment," said Rachel. "I saw the two of you together the night before. And it's very possible, almost certain, that I have a picture of either your blackmailer or someone working for him."

"Why are you coming to me?" asked Brian. "Why not the police?"

"I should have gone to the police," said Rachel, studying the hard, blue eyes that in turn were studying her. "But I sort of acted on instinct, going to ground instead. I was an Intelligence Officer with the CIA. When the bullets started flying, I was interested in keeping myself alive. Sometimes police departments don't do a very good job at keeping people alive. Whoever we're dealing with are professionals."

"Do you believe that it was a professional hit?" asked Brian. "They couldn't have been too professional; they failed. And why are you so certain that it's connected with me. Perhaps you have enemies or you were the target of muggers. It was Richmond, you know." The wheels were spinning fast in his mind. Just how much did this woman really know? Did she know that Tanya was dead? Somehow, he did not think so.

"Don't hand me that shit," said Rachel forcefully. "I don't have enemies waiting to gun me down for sending them up the river. And muggers don't use silencers. It was a professional hit planned on the spur of the moment. Whoever is blackmailing you has organization and skill. They were able to pick up on the fact that I was doing surveillance on you and able to trace my rental plates and get an I.D. on me. All in less than twenty-four hours. Most police departments couldn't have done the same in that amount of time. These are pro's. Now just who the hell are they?"

Brian was quiet for a moment. He had already made two mistakes with Rachel Lambert. The first was assuming that she was working for Cowling, who, he was certain, was behind the blackmail. Secondly, he had assumed that he could run rough shod over her since she was a woman. "Are you aware of the publicity surrounding the infighting which is taking place between Richmond Nuclear and our parent company, Energy International?" he asked.

"It hasn't been something that particularly interested me until last night," she said. "Be assured, though, I'm becoming an avid fan. Obviously you believe that it has something to do with what's going on."

"At least it appears to me that it does," said Brian. "It's my suspicion that the CEO of Energy International wants to sell Richmond Nuclear. Probably has some great, wonderful venture that he thinks will make more money for him. Selling Richmond Nuclear would be a logical way to come up with a very large sum of capital so that he can go play some new financial game. Create whole new empires."

"Do you have the power to stop him from selling it?" asked Rachel.

"Most likely no," said Brian. "However, if someone on Energy International's Board of Directors is unable to cast a vote on Richmond Nuclear's sale, then I would vote in their stead. Most of the Board members are getting some age on them and a couple have some significant health problems. Cowling knows that I'd vote against any sale."

"Why not get rid of you?" asked Rachel.

"Next in line is Travis Harding. He's the V.P. of Administration and Security," said Brian. "Travis and I graduated from Virginia Tech together. I brought him on board here as a V.P. He feels the same way about the company as I do. Cowling would only have the same problem with him. If Cowling tried to put someone in the Senior V.P. slot lacking experience, then he could turn stock prices down, hurting whatever sale he might have in the works. He has to be somewhat careful."

"He must be extremely desperate to use murder," said Rachel. Brian Matkins stiffened at her words. She thought that he looked as though the words had struck him like a bolt of lightening.

Brian immediately realized that his shock at her words showed very clearly. For just a second he had to wonder if Rachel Lambert was referring to Tanya. To his relief, he could tell that she was referring to the attack on herself. "Actually, to find that he's done so, would come as a surprise," he said. "But one can only imagine what the stakes are in his game."

"Have you talked to Tanya Madison since you learned of the blackmail attempt?" asked Rachel.

"No, no," said Brian, fighting to keep control of his words. Thank God for Beatrice's bad coffee. Otherwise he would have picked up a cup as he passed the kitchen. It would have shown how badly his hands were shaking. "She wasn't around when I went back to her apartment yesterday afternoon."

"Any note, message on her answering machine, anything?" asked Rachel.

"Nothing," said Brian. "Ms. Lambert, would you consider trying to find the tape and the caller. I'm very certain that Cowling is behind this. I want to stop him. Not only for me, but for the sake of my company and the people in it."

"Under one condition," said Rachel, beaming inside. "You have to be honest with me about everything."

"I promise to do that," said Brian. "I promise." He wished that he had put a hundred dollars in the Swearing Off Jar. Nothing, however, could cleanse his soul. Even though he had not plunged the knife into Tanya, he felt responsible. He wanted to tell Rachel Lambert the entire story. To do so would have helped to relieve the guilt that he felt. However, despite the feeling of trust that she generated, he was not prepared to take that step. Something deep inside said to avoid the horrible story and it would eventually go away.

"I told Mr. Harding that I was a reporter from *Washington Economic News* and that I wanted to ask you some questions about the problems between you and your parent company. I have an appointment at nine to see him. Can you be there and let him know that you're handling the interview?"

"Sure," said Brian. He took Rachel's business card as she handed it to him, giving her one of his in exchange. As he watched her drive off, he wondered if he would ever survive this ordeal.

Chapter Twenty-three
Saturday, December 5

"So, what's eating you?" asked Rachel, looking across a bowl of frosted flakes at her brother's disapproving scowl.

"Sis, I think you know damn well," said her brother Les. "You never said a thing about going out to the power station when you talked to me. At least you could have let me know you'd be out and about."

"You know very well that you'd have told me not to go," said Rachel. "But I would have had to disobey you and next thing I'd know, you'd have had a BOL out on me."

"Hey, you two," said Les' wife Sandy, coming into the kitchen. "The spies and blackmailers be damned. I'm trying to sleep."

"Sorry," said Rachel. After all, Sandy had been good enough to let her use her car yesterday to drive out to the power station.

"Hey, I'm going to take Rachel into town to check out her apartment," said Les. "We'll be back in a couple of hours."

Sandy stood there, a look of worry on her face. "Hey, just be careful, okay?" she said. "I want to tell you to let the police do that, but I guess you guys sort of are the police."

"We'll be alright," Les assured her.

It was only a half-hour later that they passed the complex where her apartment was located. "Just make a couple of laps around," said Rachel. Twice they passed by, studying the area for a car or van that looked out of place. "I don't see anything," she finally said.

Les guided the Camry into the parking space that was reserved for visitors. "Think they've been here?" he asked.

"Willing to bet my next year's income on it. Want to help me get through the patio door?" she asked, not wanting to take a chance on the front door being rigged with an explosive device.

"Only if you don't intend to make me come over and replace it," Les teased. "Sure let's do it."

Rachel had found a pair of leather gloves in Les' toolbox and a roll of duct tape in a kitchen drawer. She got out of the Camry with these and a jack handle. Wary of all that was around them, they made their way to the back of the apartment.

"Do you have to pay for your own heat?" asked Les, staring at the already shattered patio door.

"Afraid so," said Rachel. "You'd think real pro's would at least pick the damn lock." It had been their intention of breaking out the door's glass. That way, if someone had kindly attached a trip wire to the door, they would not go boom.

"It's hard to tell whether someone's been turning your place upside down or not," said Les once they were inside. "Doesn't look much different from how you regularly keep house."

"Fucking ass holes," muttered Rachel. Not a drawer, closet, cabinet and not even a single picture hanging on the wall had been spared. It was all in the middle of the floor. Room by room they checked through her damaged belongings for any type of clue. It would be useless to bother with finger printing; the folks that they were dealing with would leave none of those behind.

"Hey," yelled Les. "Come check this out!" When she entered the bedroom she found him leaning over a partially opened dresser door. "Looks to me like two somebody's have been visiting. And they both seem to have impressive credentials."

Les pointed to the grenade that sat at the bottom of the dresser drawer. A trip wire was rigged to it, obviously designed to trigger an explosion when the drawer was pulled the rest of the way out. Someone unknowing could easily reach a level of frustration where they would cease being careful by the time they made it to the bedroom, yank the drawer open to put stuff back in it and ka-boom.

"It was already uncovered and the trip wire cut when I found it," said Les, picking the grenade up. "Now I know how to get rid of those damn beavers that keep damming up the creek. The bed's clean, I already checked. What's left of it, anyway."

Glancing at her bed, Rachel saw that the mattress and box springs had been sliced open and thoroughly searched. "Two different teams of heavy hitters," she said. "Go figure."

"I don't like it," said Les. "I know you're as competent as they come, Sis, but there's something big going on here. I'll tell you right now, odds are ten to one that that stewardess is dead as hell."

"Flight attendant, Les," said Rachel. "They like to be called flight attendants."

"It's not a half bad looking day to be out hitting some golf balls," said Travis Harding. He was standing at the window in Brian Matkins' office.

"Try telling that to Cowling," said Brian. "He wants to put Unit I back on line and postpone the refueling outage a week to make up for lost revenue."

"I never got a chance to ask how things went between you and Tanya," said Travis. "You haven't really been yourself since you came back from Atlanta. She's not developing a conscience about the fact that you're married or something is she?" He gave Brian a sly grin. He had to ask about Tanya. If he didn't, Brian might start wondering why.

Brian had been so busy focusing on the down nuclear units that he had spent very little time thinking about the horrible sight that he had simply walked away from in Tanya's apartment. Basically, that was because he knew that whatever was to happen, was not within his means to control. Each waking minute since he arrived back in Richmond, though, could herald the arrival of some homicide detective from Atlanta. Perhaps even with an arrest warrant, accusing him of murder. With the task of getting Unit II back on line and making sure that the Unit I refueling outage was going as it should, he had control over at least something. But now, as his long time friend mentioned her name, the heavy impact of what had happened, returned. There was nothing that he could do as he felt his face flush and his eyes cloud with tears.

"Brian?" asked Travis. He stepped hesitantly towards Brian's desk. "Man, what's going on?"

"Travis, how do you feel about taking over my job?" asked Brian. It had occurred to him on the flight from Atlanta that it might be best for him, his family and Richmond Nuclear if he were to step down. It was not good for either him or the company to continue like this. Yesterday he had felt a glimmer of hope when the private investigator, Ms. Lambert had agreed to take the case. Now, at this moment, it all seemed such a dark, hopeless situation.

"I'm sure that I didn't hear you correctly just now," said Travis. "What the hell is going on?"

"They killed Tanya," blurted Brian. "Someone butchered her with a knife in her apartment. I think Cowling is trying to blackmail me with a tape of her and I together, one that could easily tie me to her murder."

"No way... shit, you're serious. Brian, damn I don't know what to say," said Travis. He did not have to act as though he had just heard the unthinkable; blackmail and extortion was the objective, not murder. What had gone wrong? Brian was obviously telling the truth. Her death had to have been an accident. It certainly was not part of the plan. He needed to talk to Laura. "What makes you think her murder was part of a setup? What did the police say? "

"I never called the police. Someone called me on my phone while I was in her apartment," said Brian. "It was a man's voice. He told me that I would need to do what I was told or the tape would be used. There was a camera. It was obvious that someone had taped us. And they were watching me; they knew I was in her apartment, knew my cell phone number."

"This person that called you, he knew Tanya was dead?" asked Travis. Maybe Cowling would stoop to murder. He remembered how Bud Orton had mentioned killing Brian. Perhaps Laura's plan had been compromised and Tanya, somehow in the middle, had been killed. If so, did Cowling know that he had betrayed him? Maybe one of Orton's men had already been given the order to kill him.

"I think that Tanya was part of it, Travis," said Brian. He could see the shock all over Travis' face. In fact, Travis was as pale as Brian imagined he himself was when he first saw Tanya's body. "She had bought one of those military combat knives. Then she had me pretend that I was forcing her to have sex at knifepoint. Damn, she's always been wild, so I just figured it was one of those things people get into. Obviously she had no idea just how far Cowling would take it. Damn!"

"Oh, Jesus," said Travis. "You really think Cowling did this?"

"Who else and why? Thing of it is though; I know that Rachel Lambert was following me for someone. I wish I knew if she was working for Brenda or if she's connected to Cowling. Maybe she's after Cowling."

"Lambert? The reporter?" asked Travis, surprised to hear the name.

"No, I mean yes, but she's not a reporter," said Brian, surprised that Travis would recognize the name. "She's a private investigator who said she had been hired to follow me. She had to be working for Brenda," said Brian. "It's the only thing that makes sense."

"She called here and said she was with a magazine," said Travis. The whole thing was building into a plot that could be a best seller. At the rate things were going, it might. "Don't you think you should have gone to the police?" asked Travis. "You're vulnerable as hell, Brian." Travis was trying desperately to process this new angle. Lambert was a private investigator and obviously knew something about what happened to Tanya. Did Laura or her employer know about Lambert? Tanya's murder and Lambert were both adding a new dimension to the game, and it was one he did not understand.

"Fuck, I know," said Brian. "I was screwed for sure if I called the police. Reckon I'm screwed anyway. Right now, I don't know what I'd do if I didn't have someone like you to fall back on."

"Does this Lambert woman know Tanya's dead?" asked Travis. He could not bring Tanya back, but maybe he could eradicate Lambert from the picture. The more someone dug, the more likely that Travis' own culpability would be exposed. "How do you know she's not working for Cowling? Or, if she's working for Brenda, and she finds out Tanya's dead, she would have a legal obligation to report it. It would ruin you, whether Cowling followed through with the blackmail or not. Somehow, we've got to get her out of the picture."

"But, she might be the only one that can help me," said Brian.

"Yeah, maybe," said Travis. He was not too crazy about Lambert having any role whatsoever. Problem was, he could not just say that without the risk of arousing Brian's suspicion. "What exactly do you expect her to do? And can you trust her? I mean with her calling me and masquerading as a journalist. I don't like being lied to."

"Maybe…but that's just a tool to get information; all private investigators do it. I need someone who can piece all this together," said Brian. He felt better now. Just speaking about the situation to Travis was therapeutic. "It would take too long to find someone else. She's already in the picture and I sense that she is competent. Cowling has to be stopped. If he murdered Tanya and tried to murder Ms. Lambert, then he's got to be dealt with. If I'm ruined, then I'm ruined. What did she want?"

"To set up an interview with you. I set it up for next week," said Travis. "I'm not against using her, but I'm just trying to make sure we don't make the wrong move. Cowling is a ruthless son-of-a-bitch. If he finds out we're coming after him, he might just make the tape magically appear, along with Tanya's body. Once this private investigator starts stirring things up, it could put Cowling on the offensive," said Travis. "Using her could be risky; that's all I'm saying."

"I can't sit by and just do nothing," said Brian. "I want to at least talk to her and get a better feel for what she knows and what she can offer

Chapter Twenty-four
Sunday, December 6

Brian had never felt so fatigued in his entire life. He opened his eyes and then closed them again as he awoke from his first decent sleep since leaving for Atlanta. At least the situation at the power station was now proceeding along smoothly. Together, he and Travis had drafted a proposed plan of action to remedy the apparent electrical breaker failure. On Monday, the Nuclear Regulatory Commission would very likely give them the green light to test electrical breakers on Unit II and return it to service. The NRC had ruled that Unit I would remain shutdown for refueling despite Cowling's protests; a move that pleased Brian.

It seemed like a good morning to sleep in. Later on, he would get up and fix some of his world famous pancakes for Brenda and the girls. His wife evidently had stayed up late reading. That was not unusual and he had barely noticed her absence. For the first time since this nightmare began, when his head hit the pillow last night he had sunk into instant oblivion from his exhaustion.

Now as he groped the space of bed beside him, he realized that Brenda was not there. Glancing at the alarm clock, he realized that it was only six thirty. Surprised at her absence, Brian shook the sleep from his eyes and looked around the bedroom. It was obvious that she had not even been to bed. Still, he found no need for alarm. Most likely she had fallen asleep on the sofa while reading.

Navigating the best he could, considering the sleep still in his eyes, Brian left his bed and headed into the living room, pulling on his bathrobe as he went. The couch was empty. However, he could smell coffee brewing and there was the sound of a chair being scooted across the kitchen floor. Still sleepy eyed, he let his nose drag him towards the aroma of the coffee.

"Good morning, coffee sure smells good," said Brian. It was just finished perking. Brenda had already brought the Sunday paper in and seemed totally engrossed in whatever she was reading. Taking two cups from the cabinet, he felt a chill of apprehension; she had not said anything. Letting it pass, he put two spoons of creamer in his cup and then poured the rich, aromatic brew. Pouring hers black, the way that she liked it, he sat her cup on the table beside her.

"Here," he said, making an attempt to get her attention.

"Thanks," she said blandly, not looking up. Brenda continued to focus on the paper, not even pausing to take a sip of her coffee.

Brian watched her for a few minutes, sipping apprehensively at his own cup of coffee. Her eyes had not moved from that one spot. His worst fears were likely getting ready to be pronounced; Rachel Lambert's client was Brenda. That had been his gut instinct from the moment Lambert talked of having a client. Just how much, he wondered, had she told his wife?

"Perhaps we should talk before you laser a hole right through that page," said Brian. Gently he reached over and pulled the newspaper from Brenda's hands.

Brenda let go of the paper. Her eyes, dark, hard beads, now bore down on him as she reached for her coffee. "Why, Brian?" she asked, her eyes suddenly softened and became weepy. "Why do you have to be like you are? I know that there have been others. Not that I've had physical, prove it in court type of evidence, but I knew, just the same. I've always hoped that it was just something that you had to get out of your system. But I can't take it anymore. And I won't."

From beneath a section of the newspaper she removed a manila envelope. There was absolutely no doubt in Brian's mind as to what was in there. Slowly, with trembling hands, he watched her remove the photographs. In the envelope was also a CD. Could these possibly be photos of Tanya's body? Though he could not shake his concern, he was certain that it was not. He stiffened with apprehension. She pushed the photographs towards him. They were pictures taken at night, of he and Tanya at the airport, of them going into and then leaving Tanya's apartment. And then there were pictures of him arriving and leaving by himself the next day.

"Pretty much says it all, don't you think?" asked Brenda, taking the photographs from him and putting them back into the envelope. "I'm going to take the girls and go to Mom's for the rest of the week. We're through, Brian. It's up to you whether or not we play hardball. You can make it easy, or you can make it hard. But I want to make sure that these two girls get everything that they deserve."

"My God, Brenda," said Brian, unable to find words that were appropriate for the moment. With what had happened in Atlanta, there was no doubt that it was time to change. That change, however, was going to come with a heavy price. "The girls will miss school. At least wait until after Christmas to do whatever it is that you plan to do with this. For the girl's sake." By then, he could show her that he was capable and willing to change; perhaps keep this from happening.

"Couldn't you have considered being a loyal husband, if not for me, then for their sake?" questioned Brenda, her voice filled with sharp accusation. Saying no more, she rose from the table and left the kitchen.

As Brenda woke Stephanie and Arlene, and then fed and dressed them, Brian stayed in his study. Only when they were ready to go out the door did he come out. With tears in his eyes, he gave them big hugs and kisses and watched them drive off. He could sense the confusion and alarm in them; they knew something was wrong, but they had no idea of what it was. It felt as though his heart were passing through one of the document shredders at work. When they were out of sight, he went back into the cold loneliness of what was once a home.

"Just remember," said Les, giving his sister a wry look. "You owe me."

"Remember," said Rachel, glancing up from the photographs and giving her brother a mischievous grin. "I could still go looking for Jenny Peterson. What would she say if she knew that my little brother used to climb up in the big oak in the corner of our yard, and look through her window? Using my binoculars, I might add."

"Now that's a mighty unfair way to treat me," said Les, mocking a frown. "Considering all that I had to go through to get the fellows at the state crime lab to enhance your camera images."

"You're joking?" asked Rachel in disbelief as he held up the disk. Not that she doubted that Les would get it done, but she had not expected it for a couple of weeks. But there it was, in his hands in front of her. "Done?"

"Done," said Les, walking over to the television where he slid the disk into the DVD player. Using the controller, he fast-forwarded to where he wanted to start. "Okay, this of course isn't your entire original. This is an edited copy that contains the enhancement portion that they did. Check this out. Believe it or not, they're keeping a copy of this for surveillance training. Because you were using infrared night imaging, you were able to pick up something that neither you nor the lab technicians would have expected."

Rachel kept her eyes glued to the television screen as Les played the enhancement. Not only was she able to see the now distinct glow from what was most likely a mini-flashlight, but also there was a faint outline of a person moving across the room, holding the light. Reaching for the newly developed photographs, Rachel handed the photo of the Harley Davidson rider to her brother.

"What do you think?" she asked. "I'm about ninety-nine point nine percent sure that that's him."

"Well, it would be circumstantial, maybe even inadmissible in court," said Les. "But it sure as hell points you in the right direction."

"Right now, I don't need it for court," said Rachel. "I want a trail; one that I'm sure will lead me right to Brian Matkins' boss. My gut feelings are that Matkins won't handle this in a court of law anyway. All he needs is enough to make whoever is doing this to him to back off." Suddenly her flip phone was ringing.

"Hello," answered Rachel. "Mr. Matkins, I wasn't expecting to hear from…" There was a pause as Rachel frowned. Without saying anything else she clicked off her phone and laid it back in her purse.

"That was short and sweet," said Les. "I take it that his wife just informed him that she was your client."

"Yeah, and he was just informing me of who wasn't any longer my client," sighed Rachel. "Les, has it ever occurred to you how fucked up in the head you men are?"

Chapter Twenty-five
June, 1987
Iran - Iraq Border

It brought back memories of that horrible day in Tehran. He had driven like a madman only to arrive and find the mob in front of the Bradford Oil Building already gathering stones to kill his family. Once again, Abdul was driving at break neck speed and careening around corners. The same filthy bastard was to blame.

"Sahed, you will die! Sahed, you will die! Sahed, you will die you fucking pig!" he shouted his words in a frenzy of hate at the top of his voice. No one was near enough to hear his shouts of hatred towards his Islamic brother. Not unless the Iraqi pilot flying overhead could hear him.

The sun was to his back, and it was perhaps that particular mercy of Allah that had saved him once already. Abdul had heard the whine of the jet engine as the Russian made MIG circled around him. At first he had not been aware of exactly what was happening, although the possibility of an Iraqi air attack was a constant eventuality. And then suddenly, the shadow of the aircraft had appeared in the road just in front of him. Out of some instinct for survival, Abdul had hit his brakes hard. Seconds later, tar and gravel had filled the air as the pilot's cannon chewed the road up and the MIG streaked by. Abdul pressed the accelerator to the floor, mindful of the five-gallon cans of petrol stashed in the back of the Ford Pinto, along with a large amount of explosives and ammunition. Heavily laden as his car was, it did not accelerate quickly.

Now, for the second time, there was the shadow. Again Abdul hit his brakes hard. Again the plane's gun chewed up the road and tore down a tree alongside. It would only take one round to turn this vehicle into an inferno. The roar of the jet's engines shook the Pinto as the plane streak over the top. Surely the pilot would recognize that Abdul was using his shadow against him; the next attack would be frontal and impossible to out maneuver. It would be Sahed responsible for Abdul's death, rather than him killing Sahed. That, however, was for Allah to decide. And praise Allah, instead of making the tight turn needed to come in with a strafing run from the front or flank, the pilot made a lazy arc to the left and disappeared.

There were no further attacks. Perhaps the pilot feared having to explain how he had wasted precious ammo on an old beat up car. However, had anyone in the Iraqi command known about this Ford Pinto and who its driver was, every available Iraqi aircraft would have been in pursuit of it. Abdul Hasdiz was a name known and hated passionately by the Iraqi high command. Saddam Hussein had put one million dollars on Abdul's head, dead and definitely not alive.

It was another hour before he came to the makeshift hospital where months ago he had delivered the news to Fatima about Hasan's death. With great sorrow, Abdul remembered how the news of Hasan's death on the battlefront had shaken her to the core, bringing her for the first time openly to tears. Eight years ago, when she had watched Abdul shoot her mother in the head, Fatima had not even let a tear drop fall. He shuddered as he tried to comprehend the psychological torture, the emotional scars, that day must have wrought upon her.

"I am looking for my niece," said Abdul to an older woman who was tending to the wounds of a young soldier. She was changing the bandages on stumps that had once been legs. He was one more example of those who volunteered to run ahead of the troops, fearlessly letting their own bodies detonate the land mines in order to spare the more experienced soldiers of the Revolutionary Guard. It was an insane practice. One that he and most leaders of the Revolutionary Guard had attempted to discourage. The young men, however, most of them only fourteen and fifteen years old, had taken it as their calling. Stopping them from their passionate attempt to martyr themselves was next to impossible.

"We are so worried about her," said the woman. "Such a sweet child. She has gone off to Tehran saying that she would be living with Sahed Batur. None of us knows anything more about the matter."

"Thank you," said Abdul. He walked around to the side of the bed so that the young man could see him. "Were you wounded in battle?" he asked.

"Land mine," said the young soldier proudly. "If I had one good foot left, I would go back. Perhaps if I get wooden legs, I can go back yet. Praise Allah! And it wouldn't even hurt then!" The young man laughed at his own joke.

Abdul smiled. It was insanity. Now that Iran had managed to carry the war onto Iraqi soil, perhaps a peace could be negotiated. Iran needed to start rebuilding, to grow. There were too few of these precious young men to waste.

"I am Abdul Hasdiz, of the Revolutionary Guard," he told the young man. Instantly the young man's eyes widened at the mention of Abdul's name. "Heal your wounds, pray faithfully. The battlefield is not the only place where Allah needs brave young men such as you. Long live Khomeini." Then he left. It was time to kill the dog, Sahed.

Chapter Twenty-six
June 1987
Tehran

Sahed knew only their first names. They were, after all, just an assortment of young girls that he had collected on his Government sponsored visits to the heavily damaged cities near the Iraqi border. His last visit had netted him his sixth, and by far the loveliest addition to his harem. Her name was Fatima. Both parents were dead as well as her brother who had died in the fighting. She had been living in the bombed out remains of her family's dwelling. Now it was up to Sahed to see to it that she receive the security of a roof over her head and wholesome food. Or so he told the Revolutionary Council.

Her body was long and slender, her skin so milky soft. There was a quality and submissiveness to her that caused her to stand out from the others. She gave him far greater satisfaction than he received from the other five girls. In time, they would need to disappear. Their testimony of his sexual promiscuity could cost him his life in a very painful manner. As with the others, he would kill them and dispose of their bodies, telling anyone who asked that he had sent them to live with families in other villages. However, this girl, he could not imagine ending her life. Instead, he would make her one of his wives rather than destroy her beauty and the pleasure that she gave to him.

The others had been frightened and at first, less than obliging as he brought them into his bedroom. Fatima, however, had appeared prepared to share his bed. Though a virgin, she seemed filled with desire from the first moment. With what amounted to a fiery passion, she had accepted him into her body. To the relief of the other girls, he had not touched them since Fatima came under his roof.

For the third time that night, Sahed felt himself reach the pinnacle and felt his fluid shoot into Fatima's tender loins. Exhausted to the point of near collapse, he pulled out of her and rolled over onto his side. Soon he was in a contented sleep and snoring loudly.

Fatima lie beside him silently, listening as the sound of his snoring grew heavier and heavier. There would be a point, she had learned, that Sahed would become nearly impossible to awaken. Time passed, and finally, she was convinced that that he had reached that point. Quietly, she swung her legs over the edge of the beautifully carved bed and dressed herself.

With no plan, only the burning desire for revenge that had haunted her soul every day since the death of her little brother, Fatima had come here to live in Sahed's home. Tonight, Sahed would pay the price for what he did to her family. Someday, so would the American and those responsible for Hasan's death, Saddam and America. If there was any plan, it was that when she left, he would realize whom she was and why he was about to die. Then he would experience a few seconds of unspeakable horror, and then be forever gone.

Allah was with her, bringing her plan for revenge to fruition, every step of the way. Allah had brought Uncle Abdul to the market place on the side of the hill. She had spent every day there, knowing that Abdul would one day come, and when he did, the market place commanded the type of view of Sahed's property that Abdul needed to help her.

Abdul had parked his car near the market place, bought some grapes, and then had sat in the shade of the fig trees where he could look across at Sahed's house. Fatima had seen him arrive. Once he had comfortably situated himself where he could study the lay of Sahed's property, she had made her presence known to him.

"Uncle," she had spoken the word so naturally, announcing her presence. She had slid the veil from her face, allowing him to see that it was indeed she.

"Fatima!" he had exclaimed in a hoarse whisper. For an instant that felt like an age, he had sat fathoming that for the first time since that day in Tehran, she had spoken to him. And she had done it with such ease. Slowly, he had risen to his feet, astonishment clearly showing in his eyes. "Why in the name of Allah have you come to live with this monster?" he had asked. She was certain he had expected to find her distraught, in tears and a prisoner in Sahed's household. Realizing, however, that Fatima was far from that, he concluded she was here for revenge against him. He was certain she had come to live with his worst enemy to spite him. "Don't you know that it was Sahed, not I, who bares the responsibility of your family's death?" he had pleaded.

Fatima had stretched her arm to clasp Abdul's hand. There was no memory of having done so ever before. Surely, though, she had been like all little girls at one time, and had clung to this, her favorite uncle. "My dear, sweet uncle," she had replied. "I saw the love in your eyes that day. I didn't understand, but I knew that you loved us and that you were hurt just as surely as if you had been struck by the stones. Many times, I've wanted to tell you that I understood, but never could I produce the words. Nevertheless, I have found what can make me well. Already I feel the strength from what I am doing."

Fatima had been able to see that her transformation was beyond what Abdul could ever comprehend. Her words chilled him as she spoke of her new strength.

"And what is that, Fatima," he had asked. "From where is this strength that you speak?"

"In Sahed's blood," replied Fatima, matter-of-factly. "His blood that shall flow as a river, by my hands, no one else's."

"Oh, dear Fatima," Abdul had said. "You are an innocent child. I cannot allow you to defile your hands in his blood. It is for me to do. And I swear to you, that I shall not leave this place until I have done so and in a way that causes him much pain. There is yet another man who must pay a heavy price for what was done to your family. I shall tell you the whole story someday, soon. I will see to it that both of these vermin are held accountable."

"Look into my eyes, Uncle," Fatima had replied. "You will see that I am no longer innocent. I have bled upon Sahed's bed in order that I might draw his blood. His blood won't defile me, rather I shall be proud to have spilled it."

And now, several days later, standing in Sahed's bedroom with the wet of his seed running down along the inside of her thighs, Fatima knew that it was time. From the bag that she had concealed beneath her clothes, she pulled the grenade that Uncle Abdul had given her. To save time, she had already attached strong, new strings of leather to it. One piece was tied to the grenade itself, the other to the pin. The leather string from the pin, she secured to the bed, the other, she tied to the thick gold chain which Sahed wore around his neck, to which was attached a religious amulet. Using the utmost care, she made sure that the knots were reliable.

The operation required the greatest stealth. Several times, he stirred. Each time, she stroked him gently and whispered lovingly into his ear. The ties binding the grenade to him were not strong enough to survive his tugging at them for long. In this case, however, they would last long enough to see him to the gates of Hell. Abdul had removed the handle from the explosive, so there was no way to prevent it from going off. All was ready.

With the flat of her hand, she delivered a loud slap across the cheek of Sahed's face. He awoke with a yell. His eyes came wide open with anger.

"You ungrateful bitch!" he screamed. "Do you wish to die?" Sahed had not yet risen from his pillow. The pin was still intact in the grenade.

"You are an infidel swine, worse than any American," said Fatima. Then she spat straight into his eyes. "It was you who was responsible for my family's death. Go to Hell to be with the Shah." It was at that point, boiling with rage, Sahed rose from the bed. As the pin pulled free, he seemed only now to notice the weight that tugged at his neck. Almost immediately, he reached for and found the grenade. "I am Fatima Hasdiz."

There were only a few seconds with which to satisfy herself with the look of vivid fear that swept over Sahed's face. "I do this for my family!" she yelled the words. Then quickly, she was through the heavy door of cedar. She heard his scream, but it was a scream cut short by the sound of the explosion. Shrapnel ripped through the door and through the wall. Pieces of it whizzing by her face so close, she could feel them. Unscathed, she walked from Sahed's house and stepped into the Ford Pinto which drove her away into the darkness of the night.

Chapter Twenty-seven
Monday, December 7
Jefferson Davis Nuclear Power Station

"Good, Lord, Cisco," said Jack Evans. "Remind me never, ever to leave you in charge again. Jeez, man! Two reactor trips, each requiring a Potential of Deliberate Act investigation and one murdered employee. This your idea of creating job security?"

Jack Evans was back. Ray Cisco felt like getting down and kissing the ground that the Superintendent of Security stood on. Not only had Ray been forced to assume Jack's duties during the investigation of possible sabotage causing the two reactor trips, but there had also been Danny Miller's murder.

"Hell, wouldn't want you to think that I don't do anything while you're away," said Ray with a smile. "Where you want to start?"

"Start with the juicy shit first," said Evans. "Give me the scoop on Danny Miller."

"Richmond Homicide plans to be out here later on today to interview employees," said Ray. He had a copy of the investigation report that one of the detectives had given to him, hoping that Security might find some connection at the power station that would prove useful. "He was found shot to death in a hotel room, a sleaze bag place, from the sounds of the report. Cleaning maid found him at two fifteen in the afternoon. Autopsy shows that he had been engaging in sexual activity immediately prior to, or even perhaps during the time of his death. Looks like she was on top during the act of sex, and pumped three rounds of .22 cal. hollow points upwards into his abdomen where it traveled into the chest cavity and finished with a round to the middle of the forehead."

"Any idea on suspects," asked Evans. "We're talking about Danny Miller. Could have been a damn transvestite or a four-legged beast he was trying to fuck."

"Hoofs and paws have trouble getting past the trigger guard. There were dark pubic hairs. Probably picked himself up a chocolate sweetie and then told her he'd left his wallet at home," said Ray, shaking his head. "At least they concluded that it was a woman. With Danny, I was never sure."

"You're a cold hearted bastard," Evans shook his head and laughed. "Anything in the investigation that concerns our end."

"Yeah," said Ray, shaking off his sick sense of humor. "Danny was at work that night. One of the Instrument Techs took a phone call for him at 0203 hours. It was Joe Lawson. Said it was a woman. As soon as Danny got off the phone, he said he was ill, and got the heck out of here. Sounds like the fellow's hormones were in full rut."

"Damn, hope that you didn't tell the police that we trusted him to maintain our Central Alarm System," sighed Evans.

"When you think about it," said Ray. "That's so damn embarrassing, I'd have to lie to the Pope before admitting to such foolishness."

"He was a pervert, but I can't remember anyone that knew the system better. Probably sheer genius buried somewhere in that sick mind of his," said Evans. "As far as the two reactor trips, anything other than what's in your report?"

"No," Ray shook his head. "They determined that breaker maintenance is to blame. Sort of scary to think that we're so damn regimented around here that when we screw up on one piece of equipment, we do it to the whole plant. But, anyway, they're restarting Unit II today. They're going to continue the cool down on Unit I and go ahead with the refueling. We've already got a lot of new contractors on site."

"I guess management didn't happen to change their mind about us having to work this outage without bringing in contract security or at least letting our own people work overtime?" asked Jack with a raised eyebrow.

"You must have been down in Florida smoking Jamaican Gold or something to even ask such a question," laughed Ray. "Maybe I should have you report for fitness for duty testing, huh?"

"Yeah, and what if I fail?" joked Evans. "Then who'll you turn this mess over to?"

"Second thought, scratch fitness for duty testing," laughed Ray. "Hey, I had it, you got it."

Ray walked out of Jack Evans' office feeling like a new man. All he really wanted to do was to supervise his shift, collect his pay, and retire. None of this upper echelon, high visibility crap for him. Please! He walked over to where Laura was quietly going over the revised refueling outage schedule. All weekend he had tried to get together with her. Thursday night had been so wonderful. For the entire weekend, however, she had avoided him. They needed to talk. With or without her, it was time to leave Donna. Why all of a sudden she had become evasive, acting as though he was just another Tom, Dick, or Harry trying to get into her pants?

"Hey, how you doing?" asked Ray, standing in front of her desk. "I hope that you don't think that reading that schedule will tell you what's going on. It's written by the willing, who are led by the unknowing, who work for those who don't give a flying rat's ass."

"Oh, hi, Ray," said Laura. "I'm fine. How about you?"

"Not so fine," said Ray, careful to keep his voice low. "Feels like I'm getting the old cold shoulder routine today. Last few days, in fact."

"My mother's not doing well and I don't have enough vacation so that I can be with her," said Laura. "Excuse me," she said, after a minute passed by during which Ray had not moved. "I need to go to the bathroom."

Ray went back to his office. Because he was Jack Evans' second in command and because he was responsible for the Security force's training, he had his own office. It was a perk that the other Security Shift Supervisors did not have. For the remainder of the day he sifted through reports filed by Officers during the month of November, looking at them, but not really seeing them. Instead, his mind focused on Laura's sudden coldness and his desire to leave Donna regardless.

Fatima went to the ladies' room. Sitting on the toilette, she stared at the dry pad in her panties. It was the same pad that she had taken out of the package Friday evening after her shower. She had been regular as clockwork all her life. The pad should have been saturated with blood. However, there was not a drop to be seen. Neither did she have the cramping that should have accounted for her black mood. This should have been the worst moment of her life. Instead, she felt a guilty sense of pleasure at the possibility of carrying Ray's child. It was the realization that any inkling of a life with Ray was beyond the realm of possibility that made her mood so black.

Rachel Lambert had an appointment to meet with the Senior Vice President of Richmond Nuclear at 9:00 AM. Regardless of Brian Matkins' less than flattering opinion of her on the phone yesterday, she was going to be there. Her 300ZX remained parked at her brother's; she now had a leased Toyota Celica. Les had recommended that it would be a good idea not to try and get her car repaired until after the BOL had had plenty of time to be forgotten. Every auto body repair shop in the area would have been alerted to keep an eye out for the damaged Nissan.

Rachel pulled into the parking lot of Richmond Nuclear's West End headquarters. It was a nice grassy location in which probably a dozen or so other major companies had office complexes. There was a small lake and what appeared to be a driving range for noontime golfers. Even now there were corporate types in jogging suits making their way around the complex. Studying the area around her first, she exited the Celica and made her way to the main entrance of the four-story building.

"Yes, ma'am," said the Security Officer from behind his desk. "May I help you?"

"I'm Rachel Lambert. I'm here to see Brian Matkins," she said. "He should be expecting me."

"Just one moment, ma'am," said the Officer. He picked up the phone and dialed a number. There was a long pause. At least Matkins was hesitant about sending her away. "Ma'am, I've been told to have you taken up to Mr. Harding's office instead. He is the Vice President of Administration and Security. Could I just see your I.D., please? Thank you," he said after viewing it. "Gail, escort Ms. Lambert to Mr. Harding's office."

Though whoever had designed the Richmond Nuclear Corporate Center had certainly not been space conscious, they certainly had good taste. For those who were sporting of soul, the building had sleek stairways that wound to the top floor. For those needing to save their energy for the lunchtime jog, there were the escalators. There was also an elevator in a glass enclosure that reminded her of the pneumatic tubes that they have at the remote drive-thru teller windows at banks. At first glance, it was obvious that the building's design enabled people to move from one place to the other with a minimum of effort. It was both spacious and well lit by sunshine during the day, and by long, thin fluorescent bulbs that ran along the wall and over the walkway.

Gail took Rachel to the fourth floor via the elevator. She was a pleasant young woman who made sure that her charge knew which floor she was being taken to, where the water fountain was located, and as though she might have just made herself responsible by divulging that information, where the ladies' room was. Finally, the Security Officer led her through a door that advertised itself as the office of Travis Harding, VP Nuclear Administration & Security. Rachel wondered if Matkins' good friend was going to tell her to get lost, that she had already wrecked enough havoc in their lives. Harding, she remembered, was Matkins' brag partner; the one that Matkins had told over the phone of his exploits with Tanya Madison.

"This is Ms. Lambert," said Gail to the woman behind the desk. "Mr. Harding is expecting her."

"Good morning," said the secretary as she got up from her desk and rapped on the door leading into Harding's office. Without waiting for a reply, she opened it wide. "Mr. Harding, Ms. Lambert is here to see you, sir."

"Thank you, Valerie," said Harding as Rachel stepped into the office. "We talked on the phone Friday morning," he said, rising from his desk and coming around to greet Rachel. "It's a pleasure to meet you. I tried to find some of the articles you've written to get a feel for what you write, but couldn't find anything." He was interested to see if she would continue her journalistic charade.

"That's not why I'm here," said Rachel, extending her hand. This was Brian Matkins' brag partner, thus it was highly unlikely that he that he did not know her real intent. "I was expecting to meet with Brian Matkins. My appointment was with him."

"Yes, I know," said Harding. "I don't like being lied to. Brian's life has been destroyed by what you've done. He told me that he had more or less cancelled the appointment by the way of a phone call to you yesterday. At this point, if you have a clue, you'll realize that you're not welcome here."

"I realize that," said Rachel. She had not at all thought it wise to let Les know the exact language of Matkins' not too subtle message. It had ended with something like "may your mercenary soul rot in hell".

"You have to understand that though he has behaved himself badly, he loves his wife and daughters very, very much," said Harding. "In all respects aside from his infidelity, I've never known a more dedicated man to his family. I feel you've done both him and your client a huge disservice."

"Dedication is certainly a trait that women admire in a man," said Rachel, wanting to gag at Harding's endorsement of his friend. "That's why I turned over the results of my surveillance to his wife. She contracted me to do a job. She had a right to the results. Perhaps it's not so noble for a woman to be dedicated?"

"No one has been well served by your noble actions," said Harding. "Brian's daughters only know that they can't see their daddy. I don't think that Brian is likely to change his mind. Even if he did hire you, it is highly unlikely that you have the needed savvy of our business or our particular situation at the moment to really provide us with any assistance."

"Well, tell Mr. Matkins that I hope that he and his wife can work matters out," said Rachel, rising from her seat. Harding extended his hand. She ignored it, turning instead and walking out of his office and pulling the door closed behind her. Savvy her ass! She would show him some savvy. Closing his door prevented him from hearing her question to his secretary. "I need to go to Mr. Matkins' office. Could you take me over there?"

"It's the next door down," replied Valerie. She got up from her desk and led the way.

"Thanks," said Rachel, following her out the door. Valerie's phone buzzed just as the secretary cleared the door. It was most likely Travis Harding calling her to ensure that Rachel left the premises.

From Harding's office, Rachel followed Valerie down the spacious hall a short distance to the sign that told her that they had come to the office of Brian Matkins, Senior Vice-President of Richmond Nuclear. The door was open, revealing a fiftyish looking blonde sitting at a desk right outside the closed door of where she knew Matkins would be. That surprised her. With Matkins' track record, she certainly expected a sleeker, later model to fill his secretarial position. She was glad that she had brought Valerie. She would never have talked her way past Matkins' secretary.

"Hi, Valerie" said the secretary.

"This is Rachel Lambert," said Valerie. "Mr. Harding had me bring her over to see Mr. Matkins."

"He did?" said Matkins' secretary. The nameplate on her desk identified her as Mrs. Hendrickson. "There must be a misunderstanding. Mr. Matkins had me cancel that appointment. He's scheduled to address about three hundred employees in just five minutes."

Valerie looked confused. It was obvious that she still saw Rachel's request to be escorted over to Matkins' office as having originated from Travis Harding. "Can you check and make sure he hasn't changed his mind?" asked Valerie.

"Sure," said Mrs. Hendrickson. She got up from the desk and went to Matkins' door. She did not notice Rachel following her. She knocked on the door, and opened it to the sound of "Come in."

"Mr. Matkins, Mr. Harding sent Ms. Lambert over to see you," said Mrs. Hendrickson. "Did you want to speak to her before the Employee meeting?"

"I made it clear to both her and Harding that I didn't want to speak to her at all," said Brian, standing at a mirror and making a last minute attempt at straightening his tie. "I know Harding wouldn't send you in here."

"Sir, I'll notify security immediately," said Mrs. Hendrickson.

"I'm really very sorry," said Rachel, acting as though Mrs. Hendrickson wasn't there. "Mr. Matkins, I've ended up with some really promising material that I believe could shed new light on the project that we discussed. I know that you have a very poor impression of me, but I think that I could really be of great benefit to both you and Richmond Nuclear."

"Mrs. Hendrickson, she's only impertinent, not a security concern," said Matkins. "Don't call Security. You have two minutes to change my mind, Ms. Lambert."

"Yes, sir," said Mrs. Hendrickson without sounding the least deflated at being overruled. She left, closing the door behind her.

Rachel immediately opened her briefcase, removing the photograph of the man on the Harley and another of him riding off on it. Then she handed him a disk of the video enhancement.

"Brian Matkins meet your camera man," said Rachel. She watched as he stared at the picture as though at any moment, the man in it might speak up and point an accusing finger at him.

"How can you be sure?" asked Matkins.

"While you and Ms. Madison were going from the car to the apartment building, I took footage of her windows," said Rachel. "Totally by chance, I happened to catch what looked like a penlight moving across one of the windows. I went to great effort to have that footage enhanced. When you look at it, providing of course you hire me, I think that you'll agree that this is your cameraman. We find him, then there is a good chance that he'll lead us to Cowling, if that is indeed who is blackmailing you."

"Ms. Lambert, your work has caused me tremendous pain," said Brian. "I called you in a moment of anger and hurt. However, I need to do what is best for Richmond Nuclear. I also think that I failed to appreciate both your talent and your professionalism." In a few minutes, he would be addressing the employees of Richmond Nuclear at their Quarterly Employee Meeting, but it was time to take Cowling down.

❦ ❦ ❦

John Anderson just shook his head in disgust. Once, years ago as a power station mechanic, he had been a member of the IBEW, too. It was the most common union among employees at electrical generating facilities. Now, as a supervisor of a crew of nuclear mechanics, the IBEW was a big pain in his side.

"Clyde, I'm not telling you again, damn it," said Anderson, feeling his blood pressure begin to rise. "Get out of that damn crane. I've got a job needs you down in the turbine basement."

"Batman, I'm telling you that you can go fuck yourself," said Clyde, his adrenalin kicking in full force. "I've been TA'd to run this fucking crane. That is what I'm being paid to do. Not no other goddamn fucking piece of work. Go get your damn copy of the IBEW contract and read it. And find yourself some goddamned Valium or something, will you?"

John "Batman" Anderson grabbed his hardhat from his head and flung it down across the gravel. Walking with a heavy stride, he gave the hardhat a brisk kick with his steel-toed boondockers that he'd worn while he was a chief on a nuclear submarine.

"Go Batman, get the hell out of here and leave me the fuck alone," yelled Clyde after him. Clyde settled back into the torn cushion of his seat. Glancing up, his eyes followed the magnificent steel structure of his machine. True, he conceded only to himself, he had not made a single lift yet today. Most likely, according to the Jefferson Davis Nuclear Power Station's plan of the day, he would not have any lifts to make. It was, however, the principle of the thing that mattered.

Clyde Andrews was temporarily assigned as a crane operator because the company did not want the expense of bringing in a contractor or hiring a full time crane operator. So, damn it, while he was TA'd to operate the crane, he would do nothing else. That was how the contract between Richmond Nuclear and the union read. Since he was the only Power Station Mechanic who was qualified to operate one of the large boom cranes, they really could not replace him with someone else that they could persuade to bend the rules. Besides, anyone in the shop even thinking about bending a rule when it came to his cranes, knew that in the blink of an eye he would file a grievance on them.

"Orton," the private investigator answered his phone. He sat patiently in his Volvo in a pull-off a quarter of a mile down the road from Les Lambert's home in rural Hanover County.

"Bud, this is Cowling. Are you making any progress on locating Ms. Lambert?"

"I always make progress," said Orton, pausing to light up his eighth cigarette for the morning. "I'm near her brother's house. I spotted the Nissan 300ZX parked behind a shed. She's been here. I'm going to find out if this is where she's staying."

"Why?" asked Cowling.

"Why?" Bud sounded thoroughly puzzled. "Because you said you want to talk to her, find out what she knows. What the hell is going on?"

"The shit's hitting the fan is what's going on," snapped Cowling. "You can stop looking for her. She's found us. Matkins' has hired her to investigate possible wrong doing by me. I just got off the phone with her five minutes ago. Damn it, she's sitting in Brian Matkins' office right now. She'll be in my office tomorrow."

"Do you have to talk to her?" asked Bud.

"There are federal laws that prohibit withholding information from an NRC official or a Quality Assurance official of a nuclear facility," said Cowling. "Matkins has imposed a special QA Audit on Richmond Nuclear and has hired her in the capacity as a QA consultant. He's stretching it, but with what she has I think it best to play my hand with some care."

"That's an impressive tack. But back up a second," said Orton. "Exactly what is it that she has?"

"A picture of a man who rides a Harley," said Cowling. "And footage of him on the job."

"The world would be a friendlier place without people like her," said Orton.

"Well, if anything has to happen to her, let's hope that it does so before noon," said Cowling.

"Why noon?" asked Bud.

"Because that's when her duties officially start," said Cowling. "She's over at Richmond Nuclear as we speak. It's a federal offense to threaten or cause bodily harm to anyone performing a regulatory function at a nuclear facility."

"So if something happens to her before noon, it wouldn't bring the FBI in?" asked Bud.

"You are so very, very astute, my good friend," said Cowling.

❦ ❦ ❦

Brian Matkins stood at his office window watching Rachel as she traversed the parking lot, walking towards the late model black Celica that he had watched her drive up in. He had spent most of his morning taking whatever phone calls were necessary and then just staring out the window. That was exactly what he was doing when she had pulled into the parking lot in time for the previously scheduled appointment. He had anticipated that she would show up despite telling her not too. Vaguely he had recognized her from the plane and that, coupled with the time of her arrival, left no doubts that it was she. He had called Travis and asked him to give Ms. Lambert the heave-ho.

That she had enticed him with the lure of the photographs, the first good clues towards finding Tanya's killer, had not been his only reason for changing his mind and hiring her. Her passion for pursuing the case impressed him. Also, to his chagrin, she certainly had done an exemplary job for her last client, his wife. Travis had again protested when Brian sent her back to him to take care of the paperwork of hiring her services for Richmond Nuclear. Making her part of a Quality Assurance audit on the company gave her substantial power in gathering information within the corporate infrastructure. She would need it if the trail led, as he believed it would, back to Cowling. Meanwhile he had done his best to address three hundred employees, trying to arouse some enthusiasm for the pending budget cuts and layoffs.

Brian barely noticed as a red Honda Civic meandered along slowly, one row of cars over, parallel with Rachel's path as she walked towards the Celica. Though it struck him as odd, he did not at first find it significant that the driver of the red Honda was staying far enough back to keep out of Rachel's field of vision. At least not until he saw the man near the exit of the parking lot climbing out of a gray, older model Pontiac, slamming its door and hastily throwing a cigarette to the ground. The man then just stood there, looking as though he were waiting for a ride, wearing a black trench coat. Something about the man's mannerism and the trench coat made him think of the two students at Columbine who cold bloodedly gunned down their fellow students. They had used such coats to conceal their weapons. It was then that the alarm coursed through him. Though he wanted to dismiss it as a ridiculous fabrication of his mind, the image of Tanya haunted him. If he failed to do something immediately, Rachel Lambert could be dead in just a matter of minutes.

Call the police; that was certainly his first natural inclination. Immediately, however, he considered the odds of reaching the police and having them respond in time to do anything but begin a murder investigation. His hand went to his coat pocket, pulling out the business card that she had left him when they met on Friday. Quickly, taking a deep breath to calm his trembling hands, he began dialing her cell phone number on his own. He was still dialing as he burst out of his office.

"Call security and then the police," Brian shouted at a very startled Mrs. Hendrickson, who was on the phone. "There is a man in the parking lot with a gun."

Brian continued out the door and into the corridor. His phone to his ear, he sprinted down the hall, bypassing the elevator and escalator; using the stairs instead. They would be faster since they came down closer to the front door. A woman's Franklin Planner went sailing out of her hand and over the stair rail as Brian clipped her elbow. Later, he would track the woman down and make his apologies; but damn, why didn't Rachel answer her phone?

As Brian hit the last flight of stairs, Rachel's phone mail picked up. Knowing nothing else he could do, Brian shouted into the phone, his breathing crisp and rapid from his charge down the stairs.

"Rachel, this is Matkins. There's a man standing at the parking lot exit, a red Honda to your right. It's a setup." And then he clicked the phone off, continuing his charge into the lobby.

Below him, at the security desk, one of the security officers, Bruce Jackson, was slamming the phone down. From his vantage point on the stairs, Brian could see him bend down to reach the weapons locker below the desk. The Senior V.P. wondered why, with violence in the work place being the number one killer of employees and terrorism never below a Yellow, his company hired a security force and made them keep their weapons locked up. During the aftermath of the September 11 attacks, they had carried side arms. With the methodical destruction of al Qaeda, however, security had returned to its normal routine.

"Mr. Matkins, please stay inside," shouted Bruce. Brian ignored him, continuing his sprint out the door and onto the sidewalk leading to the parking lot. He was thankful that it was Bruce behind him. Bruce had once been with Richmond P.D. While there, he had shot and killed an armed carjacker who had shot at him after first killing the young woman who owned the car.

Subsequently, Bruce gave up his badge upon finding out that he had ended the life of a sixteen year old. Now, three years later, the Security Officer said that he had finally come to terms with the fact that he had done what he had to do. Brian just hoped that he had really come to terms with it and would not hesitate if deadly force were necessary now.

Harding had obviously forgotten to give Ms. Lambert the required lecture on driver safety, thought Brian, as he watched the Celica go racing across the parking lot. Did she not know how year-end bonuses could be affected by driver preventable accidents? He shook his head at the thought of his ill-timed humor. Behind him, he could hear Bruce gaining on him, hollering at him.

"It's a professional hit. Gunman at the light pole and in the red car," screamed Brian into Bruce's ear as the Officer caught up to him. Even at that moment, both men could see the Honda as it suddenly accelerated to cut the Toyota off, its obvious mission to force Rachel to a sudden and unexpected stop, making her a sitting duck.

❧ ❧ ❧

Rachel's keys were in her hand. Without intending to do so, she had left her cell phone in the car. As she unlocked the car door, she could hear it ringing. By the time she managed to get the door open, however, the phone had switched over to her voice mail.

Glancing at her watch, Rachel saw that it was nearly twelve o'clock. Les had asked her to meet him for lunch so that she could tell him how her meeting with Matkins went. He seemed to have little doubt that Matkins would change his mind and bring her onto the case. If she was going to make it for lunch on time, she was going to have to hustle big time.

Rachel wasted no time. Her sleek, rented black Toyota Celica had already reversed from its parking space and was screaming towards the exit at an impatient speed.

Rachel had not only left her cell phone off, but had left it sitting in the car on the passenger seat. Normally she would have had it in her purse so that she could have checked messages on her way to the car. As she raced out of the parking lot, determined to not be late for her meeting with her brother, she punched in the number for her messages.

"First message," said an electronically generated voice. "Rachel, Les here. It's ten fifteen. Thought I'd check to see if your meeting at Richmond Nuclear is finished. If it is, then I guess Matkins can't be too forgiving, huh.

Call and let me know how it's going. See you at lunch."

"Second message," said the same voice, at the same time as a red Honda Civic accelerated forward, its driver obviously in a tremendous rush and cutting her off. "Rachel, this is Matkins. There's a man standing at the parking lot exit, a red Honda to your right. It looks like a setup!"

Rachel was processing Brian's recorded message as she reacted to the Honda. Immediately, she released the brake pedal, stomping the accelerator. What had seconds before been a mere pedestrian observed out of the corner of her eye clearly became a man pulling a weapon with a silencer fastened to its muzzle from beneath his coat. Had she heard the message of warning a mere second later, she likely would have become an unknowing and stationary target. Now, however, she was accelerating towards the gunman. A dull thud, felt as much as heard, accompanied the Celica striking the man. Desperately, Rachel tried to steer around the utility pole in front of her as she reached for her weapon in the holster between the seat and the console. There was a second thud as she slid sideways into the pole.

Instinct made her duck below the dash. The sound of breaking glass and a silenced firearm popping off several rounds filled the air. Frantically, Rachel reached across the console for the 9 mm that had slid from her hand when she hit the pole. At the same time, she was frantically trying to unfasten her seat belt.

Brian Matkins heeded none of the Security Officer's warnings to get down. Horrified, he saw the driver in the Honda fire several shots into Rachel's car. Bruce dropped to one knee and fired several shots into the Honda. There was the sound of more breaking glass, barely audible over the ringing in his ears caused by the Officer's gunfire. Whether anyone in the Honda was hit or not, Brian could not tell. Neither could he tell if there was anyone besides the driver in it. The Honda suddenly lurched out of the parking lot and sped off towards Broad Street.

Suddenly the man that Rachel had hit with her car was getting up off the ground. Though obviously in pain, he seemed determined to get to the window of the Celica. In his hand was some type of weapon that looked like a machine gun to Brian.

"Freeze and drop your weapon!" yelled Bruce. "Freeze, goddamnit!" Like a scene in a nightmare, Brian saw the gunman turn his weapon towards them. In short, rapid succession, four loud bangs once again sounded at Brian's side. He watched as the gunman staggered back as the first two rounds caught him in the chest. The next two rounds went into his face and forehead.

Suddenly the door of the Toyota swung open, Rachel emerging with the 9 mm in her hand. "Drop it lady," screamed Bruce. "Drop it right the fuck now!" Brian was petrified as he realized how pumped up on adrenaline the Security Officer was. For a split second, he was certain that Bruce would begin firing again.

Rachel clicked the safety back on, held the weapon out and away, and sat it on the roof of the Celica. Hands held clear, she backed away from the car. She could see Matkins' touching the Security Officer on the arm, saying something to him. The officer then lowered his weapon.

As the afternoon began to wane away, Ray kept his eye upon the clock. At four twenty-five, he picked up his lunchbox and went through the portal radiation monitors. He was out in the parking lot, waiting for Laura beside her car when she exited the Security Building.

"Alright, Laura, suddenly you act as though I don't even exist," accused Ray, not in the least careful to keep his voice down. "Tell me what's going on." Around him, he noticed that those who could, steered well clear of them. Those parked nearby, quickly got in their cars and drove off.

"Damn it, Ray, I just need to be left alone," Laura's eyes went suddenly from a cold, dull brown, to being fiery black coals. "I have some tough decisions to make."

"Decisions, Laura? Is it something that I've done?" Ray pleaded for an answer. He remembered how concerned she had been the other night about him being married. Perhaps he had blown it when he had talked of leaving Donna for her. There were, he knew, women who deliberately had affairs with married men so that they would not have to worry about making commitments. Perhaps Laura was doing precisely that. On the other hand, he grimaced; perhaps he had forced her into a guilt trip.

"Yes, Ray, it was something you did," Laura's words were a whispered scream. "I think that you've put a baby inside of me! And now I have to decide how I want to deal with it." She wanted to pound her fists against his chest and demand him to tell her how she should arrange day care as she circled the globe striking targets in Jihad. Did he know what it was like to be nailed into a shipping crate, and then placed out into the street for a mad crowd to stone? Had he ever watched his mother have her brains blown out of her head by his Uncle? How could she tell him that he had given her something more wonderful than she had words to describe, but it was a curse at the same time?

Ray was stunned. It had been the furthest possibility from his mind. He had just assumed that Laura was on the pill. She never seemed to be concerned with any type of protection.

"Isn't it a matter that we need to decide together? Are you completely sure that you're pregnant?" asked Ray, his voice wavering like dry grass in the wind.

"Ray, my period should have started Friday night," Laura's voice suddenly softened, her eyes no longer fiery coals, but a soft, caring brown. "I didn't think I was able to conceive. Now I'm wrestling with how it has to be handled. I know how you feel about never having had children. For me, however, it's not something I've wanted. But, damn it, Ray, I love you and to have your child would mean a lot to me. Right now, though, I've got to have some time to myself, without you near me. I've got to decide whether or not I'm willing to have this child."

"My, God, Laura," whispered Ray. So much was suddenly spiraling through his mind. Such things as how he could lose his job over all this. After all, he was a supervisor, she a contractor whom he supervised. Most of all, though, he thought of whether or not he should give her the space that she seemed to insist upon. Or, should he try to get near her and convince her that having his child would be the most fruitful endeavor that she would ever experience; for both of them?

"Ray, I'm sorry that I've been such a bitch the last few days," said Laura. She pushed the car door closed and moved next to Ray's side, sliding her arms around him. Touching her lips to his, she smiled, drawing her face away a few inches. "It has just meant a lot to me to see how much you care. Give me some time. I should have come and talked to you. I asked Evans for a couple days off. I told him that my mother was getting worse and I'd take unpaid leave. Let's talk when I get back. Thursday, when I get back and have my head together."

Ray stood silent, watching as Laura drove from the parking lot. Now he could only pray to God that she would decide to have his child.

Chapter Twenty-eight
Tuesday, December 8

"Cisco," said Ray into his phone, answering it on the third ring. He stared at the steaming cup of coffee in front of him. It was his third, and it had done nothing to cut through the fog that enveloped him this morning.

"Ray," said Jack Evans, the Superintendent of Security, his voice unusually business like. "Step on over to my office."

"Yeah, be right there," said Ray, less than enthusiastic. He knew what his boss wanted to talk to him about; he could hear it in his voice. Ellen, Jack's wife, was Donna's closest friend, the first person his wife was sure to call when he packed and left her last night.

Ray stopped in the open doorway of Jack's office, rapping lightly on the door to announce his arrival. Jack was back on the phone discussing manning tables for the outage that was now getting into full swing. He was not discussing manning tables for security, but rather several hundred contractors who were even now swarming into the station. Each outage, they were hired to help with the overhaul of the reactor plant and turbine-generator for the unit being refueled.

Outages were livid nightmares for security. Officers were normally required to work six 12-hour days, for five straight weeks. Even then, the security staff would find themselves overworked and undermanned. Yet, they were expected to perform without error. A constant stream of contract workers would be entering and exiting the plant all day and all night. At the end of it all, however, there was always the overtime check to look forward to, providing a new car or a needed addition to a home. However, there would be no overtime check this outage. Security would be expected to make it all work without pulling any overtime. That meant that the hourly paid security officers would work their forty-hour week, requiring the salaried Security Shift Supervisors to make up the slack. There were going to be some long days ahead for Security Supervisors like himself, who would be expected to work the hours with no compensation.

Outages used to last a couple of months, sometimes longer. Back then the pace was less hectic; things seemed to be under control. That was true not only for Security, but for Maintenance and Operations as well. However, in order to increase capacity factors, the company had aggressively shortened its refueling outages. Shortening the outages was first accomplished by increasing the intensity of the work load, better focus on planning, and performing specific training prior to the outage for the more complex tasks. When the company first took the approach of shortening the outages, the workers had been skeptical; but success easily won them over. The new approach really worked. It was more grueling, but it was clearly the way to go.

Unfortunately, the success that won them over went to someone's head at the top of the food chain. The shorter, very successful outages suddenly led to the attitude among the major stockholders; why not even shorter ones? Prudent methods of shortening outages gave way to putting off work that would normally have been done, and increasing demands on personnel while demanding even greater error free performance. Shorter outages paralleled cuts in department manning, and early retirement packages that resulted in the loss of valuable experience and perspective. It resulted in what Ray heard a Maintenance Coordinator once refer to as "company memory loss".

During the last refueling, a big flap had occurred during the removal of the reactor head from the vessel. Chet Burton, Jefferson Davis' Refueling Coordinator for years, had taken early retirement. His replacement, a pinch hitter from corporate, was an engineer with no experience in the power station. The replacement had overlooked a step in the refueling procedure that required the reactor cavity rail removed in order for the reactor head to clear the cavity. Ray remembered how heads had practically rolled over the fact that the massive steel structure had to be set back down onto the reactor, unfortunately bending several control rod assemblies, while workers removed the railing.

Refueling outages now, thought Ray, resembled performances more akin to a three-ring circus. Maybe rumors of a sellout were true, he chuckled as he stood listening to Jack argue with someone at Corporate over the phone. Perhaps Barnum and Bailey were buying the company.

"The reason that you can't just tell these contractors the rules and expect them to follow them, is because the rules are foreign to them," said Jack with exasperation. "No, that's the problem. We're getting contractors in here to work that don't have any nuclear experience whatsoever. That's what's making our job so difficult. Health Physics had the same problem last outage."

"Because, goddamnit, experienced contractors are starting to avoid our refueling outages," Jack said, his face getting redder as the conversation continued. "Why? It's real damn simple why! We have the shortest fucking outages in the nation right now. All the experienced contractors flock to the nuclear units that still have longer outages. They make more money and don't have to move so often."

"I hear you," said Jack slamming the phone down. "Fucking, god damned idiots," he hissed.

"Jeez, Jack. Not like you to take the Lord's name in vain," said Ray, trying to lighten the moment. "What's happening?"

"Harding won't change his mind about the Security overtime guidelines for the outage. I still want to see us work six, twelve hour days this outage," said Jack, shaking his head. "He says we have to manage with normal shift rotation. Any and all overtime will have to be approved by him personally."

"This will be fun," said Ray. "What makes Harding able to decide what we need in order to do our job?"

"He has a BS degree in nuclear engineering and a Master's in accounting," came Jack's sarcastic answer. "Obviously that enables him to sit in his ivory tower and analytically determine any potential impact that this will have in relation to our vulnerability to a security related event."

"He certainly has qualifications that would set any terrorist quivering," said Ray with a shake of his head.

"Ray, close the door and have a seat," said Jack, obviously finished with brow beating his management. "I know this is personal, well actually, only part of it is," he said, studying Ray and thumping his pencil against his desk. "Ellen talked to Donna last night. Says that you packed your stuff and left."

"Things haven't been working for a long time," said Ray, shrugging his shoulders as if to show his reluctance to discuss the issue.

"So Donna told Ellen," agreed Jack. "Donna told her that Laura called you at home one night last week. She said you made it sound work related. But, when you left, Donna did a star sixty-nine. Laura had called you from her home."

"Hey, I know that our wives are best friends," said Ray, his temper flaring as he spoke. "But this is my personal business. I don't want to discuss it."

"Ray," said Jack, coming upright in his chair. "When you went running out of here, chasing after Laura McClish like a jilted school child yesterday evening, it reflected right negatively on this department. Ralston made it my business during the morning meeting!"

"All, jeez, Jack," said Ray. "Do we really have to have this discussion? Just let me get on with my job. You see a problem with my performance, then we talk."

"You know better than that, Ray," said Jack, shaking his head. "We're security. Performance problems don't show up as low production or work not getting done. Where we're concerned, performance problems show up as breaches in protection of a nuclear core and the people working here. You of all people know better. As an ex-Seal, you have to admit, poor performance sometimes isn't noted until a buddy gets killed or a mission botched.

"Listen to me, Ray," continued Jack. "You've let you're self get side tracked by Laura. Regardless of Ellen and Donna being friends, if you and Laura can have a future together, I'll come to your wedding if you have one. I'll make the toast to your happiness. Laura asked off a couple of days. As soon as she gets back, I'm letting her go."

"Whoa!" Ray came to his feet. "Jack, you can't be serious. She's done nothing to deserve this. Fire me, not her. Get rid of her and I'll be out the damned door!"

As far as Ray was concerned, there was nothing more to say. He knew that Jack wouldn't back down. Neither could he. Ray thought of the new life that was growing in Laura's womb. It was as precious to him as Laura herself. In order to show his solidarity with her, he would find himself a new job. The moment Jack Evans put her out the main gate, he would follow. Damn, though, it was going to be tough; affording a place for him and Laura and making mortgage payments on the house for Donna.

Ray spent his day brooding. It was a miserable day for him and all he came in contact with. The only bright moment came at one thirty when his phone rang. It was a very welcome, yet unexpected surprise.

"Ray, it's me," came Laura's voice over the phone. "How's it going?"

"Laura!" said Ray, setting his mug of stale coffee down. "You just don't know how good it sounds to hear your voice."

"That goes for me, too, Ray," Laura said softly. "I'm really missing you here. Being away from you is making me miserable."

"Being here with me was making you miserable," laughed Ray. They both laughed. The small talk carried on for a few minutes. Ray relished the sound of Laura's voice. When it sounded as though she was winding down, Ray decided to fill her in.

"Laura," said Ray. "I left Donna last night."

"Ray, no," gasped Laura. There was silence for a moment. "Oh, Ray, I didn't want you to do that. Are you okay, where are you staying?"

"Actually I feel alright about leaving," said Ray. "Though I have to say, Pete Burns couch is nothing to write home about. It was going to happen someday. Life for us was nothing more than two loyal friends sticking together. It's the other shit that's bothering me."

"Ray?" Laura's voice was laced with concern. "What is it? Has something else happened?"

"Jack Evans' wife and Donna are good friends," said Ray. "He's figured out about us. I kind of blew it when I went chasing after you yesterday. He's going to let you go when you get back."

"Oh, Ray, my God, no!" said Laura. "Ray, women can be so vicious. Donna getting Ellen to force Jack to do this."

"I've already told him that the moment you go, so do I," said Ray.

"Well, wait a minute, Ray," said Laura, her voice taking on that of an older sister. "If I'm out of a job, eating would be nice. Not to mention it looks like I have something of yours that is going to need the best of care. You know, medical benefits."

"Yeah," said Ray, suddenly feeling as though nothing could bring down the cloud on which he floated. "Swallow my pride, uh? You're right. It just doesn't seem appropriate, though, to stay here since it was me that's getting you fired."

"You did what you did because you love me," said Laura, her voice tender. "If I hadn't acted the way that I did, then you wouldn't have had to chase me down in the parking lot. Hey, got a call coming in, might be my mother's doctor. Got to go. Love you, Ray." There was a click and the line went dead.

Chapter Twenty-nine
Wednesday, December 9

Rachel saw her black Toyota Celica pull up in front of her apartment. Actually, it was the second one, the other not fairing well after hitting the pole. The rental company had refused to rent her another vehicle so Richmond Nuclear had rented one for her. Brian had seemed elated that Cowling would be furious at not only being investigated by her, but paying for her transportation and wages to do so. She zipped her leather jacket and waited until there was a rap at the door.

"Morning, sis," said Les. He gave her only a sweeping glance as he focused warily on nearby parked cars and windows that overlooked their path to the still running Celica. "Your car's ready. How was your first night back at home?"

"Peaceful, once they let me go," said Rachel. "God, I can't believe what a waste yesterday was. Between being questioned by the police about that shooting and the one at the airport, and all the paperwork involved with wrecking a leased car, I didn't hit a lick on this case. Hopefully, today will be better."

"You know, if you weren't my sister, they'd have held you for the shooting at the airport," said Les. "I spent almost as much time as you at Sheriff's office convincing the Commonwealth's Attorney not to book you."

"Yeah, I owe you big time on that one," said Rachel. "Thanks." Together, they walked at a brisk pace towards the vehicle, both casting relentless gazes about them. Against Les' wishes, she had decided that it was time to reclaim her apartment. However, she did agree to placate him on the issue of the car. He drove it home with him to make sure that no one tampered with it. Now that the police knew she was involved with the airport shooting, she could have her 300ZX taken somewhere for repairs. Of course, that would have to wait until the folks at the state crime lab finished with it. They had hauled it to the lab yesterday.

Her brother did not bother with his seat belt. The moment he entered the car, he was jamming gears and pulling away from the area much like a teenager headed to pick up his first date. Rachel had politely protested his taking a leave of absence in order to accompany her during the investigation, but the fact was, she really appreciated it. How would it work, she wondered, to hang out a shingle with both their names on it? It was something they had joked about in the past.

Les never let up on the way to the Energy International Venture Building. His timing was impeccable when it came to missing red lights. Only once during the entire ride, did the Celica actually come to a full and complete stop.

"May I help you?" asked the guard, as Les guided the Celica into the Venture Building's basement parking area.

"Les Lambert and Rachel Lambert," said Les, displaying his Sheriff's Deputy badge. She flashed hers from where she sat on the passenger side. She was counting on the guard scrutinizing the badge closest to him and assuming that she, too, was law enforcement. "Mr. Cowling is expecting us at ten thirty."

"Sorry pal, only Exec parking in the basement," said the guard. "You'll have to use the lot on the other side of Cary Street."

"Can't do that," said Les, scooting the car on into the basement parking area.

"What if they tow us?" asked Rachel.

"That's what cabs and expense accounts are for," grinned Les, swinging the Celica into a space labeled "V.P.–Finance" which was on the very end, next to the wall. It would have been difficult to park something larger like a Lincoln in the space as close to the wall as it was and the pillar that stood right before the parking space. The V.P.–Finance must have been on the bottom of the totem poll to have been assigned this spot. Several other empty spaces, each of which was a V.P. or president, were available. Les backed part way out of the space at an angle to the pillar. "We've got an appointment with the CEO, so they'll be a bit apprehensive about making waves. And if they do, they'll play hell getting a tow truck hitched to us here like this."

They entered the building and found the elevator. Les pressed the button for the twentieth floor. "I'll wait outside in his secretary's office. If I can, I'll take a look to see if there is an appointment book. If I'm not there when you come out, I'll be back at the car."

"Just don't get us arrested. Well, here we are," said Rachel, as the elevator came to a gentle stop. "The Penthouse of Energy International." The elevator had opened up at one end of a corridor, carpeted in plush red velvet. Three doorways came off the corridor, with no mistaking the one that led into Roger Cowling's office. It was located at the end; large, oaken double doors, standing open, allowing anyone getting off the elevator to view the elegance of the outer office.

Rachel felt as though she were entering an exclusive art gallery. Richly done oil paintings, each given the proper attention of lighting, hung upon the walls. Polished chandeliers of brass lit the middle area of the outer office, supplemented by lamps attached to the walls.

"Always wondered why my electric bill was so high," whispered Les.

"Good morning," said the secretary as they entered. The desk that this woman sat behind, Rachel noted, would have provoked envy in the CEO of any prominent corporation. It was bigger than the dinning table that had seated her, her four brothers and their parents when she was growing up. Its lacquered walnut finish and delicate contours inlaid with gold added a majestic touch to an already breath taking arrangement. "May I ask your business?" she asked coldly.

"Ms. Lambert and Mr. Lambert of Lambert Investigations," said Rachel, noting the displeasure with which Cowling's secretary was looking at her brother.

"I see," said the secretary, her look of disapproval not at all diminishing. "Mr. Lambert, you weren't intending to accompany Ms. Lambert into Mr. Cowling's office, were you? He has only agreed to see Ms. Lambert."

"I'm assisting her in this investigation," said Les, sounding irritated.

"I'm afraid that will not be possible. Mr. Cowling," said the secretary, picking up the receiver and pressing a button on her phone. She would offer no further explanation of why Les would not be able to sit in on the meeting. "Your ten thirty appointment has arrived." There was a few seconds pause. "Yes, sir."

"Mr. Cowling is ready to see you. Hopefully I don't need to tell you that his time is extremely valuable and not to be wasted."

Rachel turned to the woman and flashed a smile. "No, you needn't bother telling me at all," she said.

The doors leading from the outer office to Roger Cowling's personal office were identical double doors to those coming in off the corridor from the elevator. The secretary opened the door and announced her, "Mr. Cowling, Ms. Lambert."

"Thank you, Edna," said Cowling, rising from his seat. He reached out and accepted the hand that Rachel extended to him. "Ms. Lambert, glad that you could make it. I'm rather impressed at your fortitude and persistence, given what occurred yesterday. I'm glad that you escaped unharmed."

"Thank you," said Rachel. Roger Cowling was a tall, strongly built man with thinning silver hair. His eyes were intelligent, and she could tell that he was using them to examine every detail about her. Not an examination in the typical male sense, but rather looking for any chink in her armor that might exist, or any weapon of which he should be wary.

Cowling waited until she sat down and then returned to his own chair behind his desk. "Ms. Lambert, I normally have Edna bring me a pot of tea this time of morning, and a little something sweet and fattening, just so my doctor has something to concern himself with. Realizing, of course, that your visit is both official and adversarial, I would ask you the favor of not considering an invitation to join me as patronage. I simply prefer to avoid the awkward position of partaking in front of you," he said, his manner charming, his eyes warm.

"With milk in it?" asked Rachel with a smile. Right away, she could see that this was going to be an interesting game.

"Oh, my, Ms. Lambert," Cowling raised his brow. "My mother was English. Grew up in South Hampton, England. Were I to drink my tea in any other manner than that, I dare say she would roll over in her grave and keep me up at nights." He pressed a button on his speakerphone. "Edna, tea for two, please."

"I don't detect a British accent," said Rachel, though he did speak with a certain precise diction. If Edna was making tea, that would be perfect. It would create for Les the best possible opportunity to get a look at the appointment calendar. She just hoped that he did not steal it and land them both in jail.

"My father was an American Air Force Colonel, stationed at Lakenheath Air Force Base when he met my mother," said Cowling. "I was born in the states. Between my father's Texas drawl and my mothers English accent, I guess I just came out somewhere in between, language wise."

"Is the rug from Iran?" asked Rachel. It was splendid; definitely, the most beautiful rug she had ever seen. Her grandparents had had numerous Persian rugs, but none that came close to the one gracing Roger Cowling's office. It even appeared to be inlaid with gold. She was not sure if it was Persian or Turkish.

For a moment, Cowling was silent, with a far away look in his eyes. Rachel felt much like a boxer who has accidentally landed a blow illegally below the belt. A full, somewhat awkward, minute passed before he answered. Intuitively, she knew that she had hit upon something sensitive.

"Persian. It's Persian," Cowling finally said. His words were void of the fluid resonance that only moments ago had impressed her. He spoke like someone awakening from a dream. "Handmade in Nian, a small town in the province of Isfahan that's very famous for its intricate designs and fine knotting. I spent considerable time in Iran. Regretfully I had to leave there in late '79 because of the revolution. It was a gift from a very dear friend that I was forced to leave behind. I worked in the oil business before getting involved in the electric industry. Terrible, terrible shame what happened there."

Cowling had surprised Rachel with his surprising show of anguish. There was a story here, one that was painful for Cowling. The subject of the rug had caused him to show a chink in his armor. She doubted, however, that it had any bearing on the murder of Tanya Madison or the blackmail of Brian Matkins.

"Do you have questions as to why I'm here?" asked Rachel, realizing that Cowling could probably pass her allotted half hour with charm and finesse, never touching on the business at hand. A part of her, though, would like to have listened to a lot more about his experience in Iran. Not only did his strange reaction to her question about the rug intrigue her, but both men that had died in the two attacks on her appeared Mid-Eastern. Could there be a connection to his past in Iran?

"Not really," said Cowling, leaning back in his chair. "Brian Matkins is desperate to undermine the efforts to shape Energy International for the new era of electrical generation deregulation. To that effect, he has hired a private investigator to conduct an audit to determine if Energy International is involved in business practices that could have a negative impact on nuclear safety and electrical generating reliability. Please don't take this personally, but why doesn't he use a team of auditors that he already has at his disposal and who know something about the nuclear industry? I find it a very distasteful move on his part that will do nothing but fuel the rumors that the news media enjoy spreading. It hurts us when what is needed is open dialogue and cooperation."

Rachel smiled at Cowling; a sweet warm smile. He clearly had a strategy for derailing her interview with him. "Perhaps there are other elements involved that his auditors are not qualified to address." She paused for a second, searching for a reaction. "Are you presently involved, in any manner, in the sale of Richmond Nuclear?" she asked.

"Yes," said Cowling. There was a knock at the door. "Come on in, Edna." The door opened, with Edna slipping in and setting a try down upon a small table. "She always has the kettle boiling at this time," he offered as explanation of the tea's quick arrival.

"To whom are you selling Richmond Nuclear?" asked Rachel, taken back by his open admission to the sale of Richmond Nuclear.

"To a company who currently operates multiple nuclear generating units," said Cowling, moving from his seat to pour the tea. "Only select members of Energy International's Board of Directors is privy to the identity of the company at this moment and the fact that a sell has been proposed. To tell those members opposed, would have resulted in leaks to the public that could have a potential adverse impact on the purchaser's stock. Part of the negotiated agreement was to keep the sale out of the media until Energy International's Board and the purchaser's Board ratified the deal. That will occur this Friday."

"Are you assured of a vote that will allow you to sell the company?" asked Rachel.

"We wouldn't be voting if I had any doubts as to the outcome," replied Cowling, breaking into a wry smile.

"But it's not an absolute certainty that the vote will go your way," said Rachel, her statement as much a question as an observation.

"When you run a large corporation, Ms. Lambert," said Cowling, picking up one of the small cakes that had come in with the tea. "It becomes akin to a game of chess. To survive you have to utilize winning strategies. I do that. You also have to have a thorough understanding of your opponent's strategy. Only when you have reasonable assurance that your strategy is superior to his do you engage him."

"What is your purpose in selling Richmond Nuclear?" Rachel asked. She had come close to asking if his reasonable assurance included blackmail. That, however, would have sounded more like an accusation than a question.

"To use the proceeds for further investment," laughed Cowlings. "It's important to realize that I am a business man. I make it a matter of principle to never grow sentimental to any part of my holdings. At any time, I am prepared to cash them in on more profitable ventures."

"Have you any knowledge of a woman named Tanya Madison?" asked Rachel. It was time, she decided, to change the game to truth or consequences.

Cowling finished chewing his bite of cake. "Not to the best of my recollection," he said, his smooth demeanor not wavering. "These little cakes are called almond slices. Made in Scotland. Extremely delicious."

"Mr. Cowling, I was CIA during Iran-Contra," said Rachel, picking up one of the cakes and taking a bite, her eyes locked with Cowling's. There was that same earlier anguish in his eyes, an almost pained expression at the mention of her being involved in Iran-Contra. It was fleeting. He was aware that she had noted his earlier letting down of his guard. She swallowed the bite of almond slice. "Please be understanding if I show serious reservation to any answer which begins with 'To the best of my recollection'. And you're right; these almond slices are delicious."

Rachel liked the direction in which the game was now moving. Cowling might be able to run circles around her when it came to negotiating business, but on the other hand, her training and experience gave her the edge in separating truth from fiction. Cowling had given limited elaboration along with his answers to every question except this last one. The moment a person has something to hide, they either over explain or divert from the question. He had diverted and then covered his ass against giving false information by prefacing it with the tarnished phrase 'To the best of my recollection'. Being interrogated was definitely not his forte. There was no doubt in her mind that he knew who Tanya Madison was.

"I'm glad that you like them," said Cowling, maintaining his smile. Inside, however, he was not smiling. He was dealing with a professional and she knew he was blackmailing Matkins. How much did she know? Did she know that Madison was dead? If the Atlanta police were not aware of the murder, then perhaps she was not. However, were she aware of it, there was a distinct danger of her tying him to the murder. That had to be avoided at all costs.

"I understand, that should any board member become unable to vote on a matter, and should a vote result in a tie, it is the Senior Vice President of Richmond Nuclear who casts the tie breaking vote," said Rachel. "Is that a correct understanding?"

"Yes," said Cowling. "Although, I have no expectation that Brian Matkins will be called upon to vote. All of Energy International's board members seem reasonably healthy at the moment."

There he goes again, thought Rachel. He elaborates on a question that is safe to answer honestly. "Have you made any attempt by nefarious means, or have you hired anyone to make any attempt to influence Matkins' vote, should it be needed?"

"I know that all the bad publicity that Energy International and Richmond Nuclear has received in the news makes it seem that I don't respect Matkins' ability as the Senior V.P.," said Cowling. "Actually, I admire the man. He is the best in the business at what he does. Unfortunately, he is a man who has developed a loyalty to his people. It occludes his ability to make the most advantageous business decisions. Matkins business strategy fits the pre-deregulation era, not the present.

"His loyalties are confused. He works for Energy International, not the people in the power station. The fight that has ensued has been over the need to increase quarterly profits to receive the highest possible price for Richmond Nuclear. Of course, he's unaware for the moment that we're selling his company. Fact of the matter is, like any other employee, he is obligated to do as he is told by his employer, me. He doesn't honor that obligation with quite the required enthusiasm that I need. Surely, even you realize that if you're selling your home, you need to make sure it looks its best. Fresh paint, even if it's the cheapest brand. Perhaps Matkins can't understand that type of philosophy."

"Thanks for not answering that question," said Rachel as she moved forwards in her chair, her eyes leveled against Cowling's. "You spent a lot of time in Iran. Twice, someone's tried to kill me. Both times, they appear to be middle-eastern. I learned long ago to trust my instincts. I don't know where things tie together, but if there's a potential threat to your nuclear station, you had better make sure that it takes precedence over any business deal. Do you understand that, Mr. Cowling?"

"Ms. Lambert…" Cowling was stunned by the impact of what she said and at a loss for words. Bud had briefed him on Abdul's ties with Al Qaeda. He had always known deep inside that if Abdul were alive, he would someday demand retribution for Cowling's betrayal. Rachel Lambert's suggestion, however, of a possible attack on Jefferson Davis was too horrible to accept. He was not a man to panic under the most extreme circumstances. He had not, in fact, felt panic and fear since that terrible day in Tehran in 1979. Her words had brought back the smell of the office, the chanting in the streets, the sneer on Sayed's face and the choking fear that the little girl would again cry out. "There is nothing but coincidence involved. You say that you're ex-CIA. Perhaps you have enemies. It's most unfortunate that an attack on you occurred on our property." He could feel his own voice tremble as he spoke.

"Mr. Cowling, thank you for your limited cooperation and the tea," said Rachel as she stood to her feet. He had evaded giving solid answers to the questions about Madison and influencing Matkins. However, she had visibly unnerved him when she spoke of the possibility of a Mid East connection. That, in turn, unnerved her. In total, the interview had given her very little to work with.

"I really must suggest, that Brian Matkins is wasting time, effort and money if he thinks that I'm engaging in some type of corporate blackmail," said Cowling, who also stood. He attempted to sound confident and authoritative, but could hear the hollowness in his own voice. What if Abdul was planning an attack on Jefferson Davis? Since the September 11 attacks, nuclear stations had bolstered their defenses but nothing had ever materialized. He had taken advantage of the ensuing complacency to cut costs by reducing security forces. The vote to sale was very close. All he wanted to do was get rid of the power station before anything happened. "A letter is going out immediately to all Energy International Board of Directors concerning the pending vote on the sale of the company. You've not discovered anything that affects the operation of Richmond Nuclear's reactors. Obviously, the sale will have to meet with the approval of both the NRC and the State Corporation Commission. And believe me, I wouldn't sell if I wasn't certain that I could garner such approval."

Les was still in the secretary's office when she left Cowling's. Not until they were on the elevator, leaving the penthouse suite of Energy International's CEO did she inquire as to his success. "Any luck?" she asked.

Reaching down into his coat pocket, Les pulled out a miniature camera. "Piece of cake," he said. "That spot of tea was perfect."

"Yes," Cowling spoke into the speakerphone. The line to his secretary's desk was lit.

"Sir, do you want to dictate that letter to me now?" asked Edna.

"Yes," said Cowling. "Come on in." A few seconds later, there was a sharp rap of knuckles on his door, and then it opened. Edna was a woman in her early fifties. She had been Roger Cowling's personal secretary since he had first come to Richmond Nuclear as one of the company's leading financial advisors. As he ascended to be the company's president and then branch out with Energy International, he had kept her with him.

"Okay, sir," said Edna. "I'm ready."

"Dear Board Members," started Cowling. "There will be a special vote taken at our scheduled December 11th Board of Directors, Energy International meeting. Following the mandates of our corporate charter, constitution, and by-laws, this letter serves as your required twenty-four hour notice of a vote that will pertain to the sell of a major holding, that being Richmond Nuclear. Be advised that since this is not a special called meeting, it does not require a quorum to be present for the vote to occur. Board members may vote by proxy.

"In the event that the Board does approve the sale of Richmond Nuclear, a second vote will be taken. This second vote will be to proceed with a long-term land lease in Mexico and the construction of six, 500-megawatt nuclear generating units. I'll provide necessary details at the meeting. Yours Sincerely, Roger Cowling."

"Alright," said Edna, not blinking an eye at the letter's content. "Let me read it back to you."

Cowling sat silent, listening as Edna read it back. When she was finished, he nodded and said, "Send it in the morning."

"We customarily send a copy of the letter to the Senior V.P.s Nuclear and Fossil," said Edna as she got up to leave.

"That is a courtesy only," said Cowling. "Only a requirement if a board member is legally ruled mentally or medically unable to vote. Or, is dead. No, don't send him the letter. He will find out all that he needs to know."

Once the door was shut and he was alone, Cowling stared down at the rug. He was both disturbed and puzzled. The shadow of Abdul and the possibility that Jefferson Davis was his target disturbed him. The fact that it could be Abdul who had murdered Tanya Madison and was interfering with his blackmail of Matkins puzzled him. How would Abdul have knowledge of it? And if not Abdul, who else?

Chapter Thirty
Wednesday Evening, December 9

Jack Evans felt his pager vibrate while he was finishing up supper. Agitated, he pulled it out to check for the message. "1234" were the numbers displayed. That was the code for a general call in for an emergency at the power station.

"Looks like something's going on at the plant," Jack told Ellen. Rising quickly, he went to the phone. Immediately, as he started dialing, he realized that the line was dead. "Ellen when's the last time you used the phone?" he asked, the frustration clearly apparent in his voice.

"Right before you got home from work," she said. "I was talking to Donna. You know, Ray really has some nerve. He talked her into letting him…"

"Ellen, did you pay the phone bill?" asked Jack, not caring about what Donna and Ray were or were not doing. Ellen was always forgetting to pay bills. Twice they had had their phone disconnected and once the electricity. "My pager just went off and I need to call in. The damn phone is dead. Just like it was a couple of months ago when you forgot to pay the bill."

"Oh, no," said Ellen, coming into the living room where Jack stood fussing. "I really hope that I didn't forget to pay it again. It costs so much to have them reconnect. Let me go check the bill drawer."

"I don't have time for that," said Jack, his level of frustration rising. "I'll use my cell phone on the way in." With that, he stormed from the house.

Out in the garage, Jack went to his car and found his company cell phone. He now left it out here since the incident with his daughter. She had gotten it one afternoon and had made several calls to her friends. Nothing serious, but Richmond Nuclear was fanatical about appropriate use of its property. Some bean counter had determined that the calls had not been work related and Jack had received a verbal reprimand. As he powered up the phone, there was a beep and then NO SIGNAL flashed across the screen.

"Just great," muttered Jack. Carefully he dialed the numbers, but once he hit transmit nothing happened. "Cheap bastards," said Jack. The company had its mobile service with some company that he had never heard of. Any time he traveled he could count on his phone being useless. It was, however, unusual to not have service in the area.

Jack started the car up and pulled out of the garage. Since he could not call, he would go ahead and drive to the plant. With all that was going on, it was likely that he would have ended up there anyway. The door opener raised the door and then closed it again as he pulled away. Preferring the quiet rural life of Caroline County to that of living in Richmond or Ashland, Jack had a sizeable piece of land within seven miles of the power station. It was large enough for Ellen to keep her horses on.

The driveway was about a quarter of a mile long. As he pulled out onto the blacktop of the country lane, Jack heard and felt a sudden thud as though he had hit something with his left front tire. He was a hundred feet down the road when he realized that he was now listening to the thump, thump, thump, of a flat tire.

"Damn it to hell!" Jack roared. What else could go wrong? Pulling over, he located his flashlight and then got out to see what was going on with the tire. It was, without a doubt, flat. It was also ruined. Without wasting time, he tried the cell phone one more time. It did not even power up to give him the beep and low battery warning. There was nothing to do now but change the tire. He went to the trunk where he removed the spare, the jack, and the tire tool. A couple of flares that he had tossed in the trunk eons ago caught his eye. Folks tended to drive this stretch of road a bit fast. Using the flares would not be such a bad idea.

As he broke loose the first few lug nuts, Jack noticed the approaching headlights of a car coming from the other direction. When he heard the car pull off to the side of the road and stop, he really was not surprised. In a rural community like this, giving a neighbor a hand was the norm rather than the exception.

"Jack?" said a female voice. He immediately recognized Laura's voice. Her being here in his neck of the woods surprised him.

"What are you doing out here?" asked Jack. Though he was somewhat curious why she would be anywhere near here, finding out what was going on at the station was foremost in his mind. "You don't happen to have a cell phone on you by chance, do you?"

"Sorry, I left it at home in the charger," said Laura. "It was pretty much dead."

"Unfortunately, mine too," said Jack. "No signal."

"I needed to talk with you about what's been going on," she said. Her voice shivered with the rest of her in her light jacket and dress. "I tried calling, but I just kept getting a message that said your phone was out of order. Do you have a flat tire?"

"I sure as hell do," said Jack exasperated. "There is also a call-in in progress and I need to get to the plant. Besides, I don't think that you stopping by my house unannounced would be such a good idea." If she had made it to his house, once Ellen found out whom she was, the smelly stuff would have hit the fan.

"Oh, dear," she said, shivering even harder. "I didn't think about that. Here let me hold your flashlight while you work. We can talk tomorrow."

Jack gratefully handed over his hefty, long handled maglite to her, one like law enforcement officers use. Not only did he need to get to the station, but also the cold was starting to numb his fingers. Quickly he began to work, faster now that Laura was holding the light. As bad an idea as it had been for her to think that she could just drop in on him at home to discuss what was happening at work, he was glad for her assistance. Suddenly the light disappeared. Before he could say anything, he felt the bone crunching impact of the battery-weighted barrel of the flashlight as it came crashing down on the top of his head.

Fatima watched as Jack sunk immediately onto the road's cold surface. Her blow had been vicious, coming down precisely on the top of his skull, the weakest point. She could hear and feel the bone fracture beneath the impact. There was the sound of her car door opening and closing as someone got out and walked over to her. Together, without speaking a word, the two of them picked Jack up and leaned him against the hood of his car. Jamal held him to keep him from sliding to the ground. Wasting no time, she then went back to her car, driving it a short distance down the road where she turned around.

By the time Fatima got even with Jack Evans' car, she was doing approximately eighty-five miles per hour. It was at that point that Jamal gave Jack's unconscious form a brutal push into her path.

Ray had managed to get Donna to let him take the computer. After all, she did not even know where the on - off switch for it was. Though he knew that this was hurting her, and God how he hated that, she was coping with it in surprising form. When he had arrived to pickup the computer, she appeared to be stone sober. That puzzled him. Hell, maybe the marriage was more of a drain for her than it was for him. It was rather disconcerting to think that he had perhaps been responsible for her drinking.

Now, at least, he could amuse himself playing solitaire on the computer, shaking aside the thoughts of Donna. Certainly, he had no regrets about leaving. What he could not get out of his mind was Laura being pregnant. Perhaps he was just being overly imaginative, but she had sounded very up beat about it. Looking at the clock, he realized that she should be getting back from her mothers in just three more hours. Smiling, he thought of the bottle of Spumante that he had chilling. Most likely she would merely take a few sips of it, but he would handle the rest. He was awoken from his thoughts by the ringing of the phone.

Pushing away from the computer, he answered the phone, hoping that it was not Laura calling to say that she was stuck at the airport or something. There was a lot of snow up in New York.

"Hello," said Ray. Immediately, he could tell from the background noise that the call was coming from work.

"Ray, Pete," came the voice of the B shift supervisor. Ray could hear that troubled tone in Pete's voice.

"What's up?" asked Ray. His first thought was that perhaps another potential act of sabotage had occurred.

"Got some really bad news," said Pete. "Ellen Evans just called here from the MCV emergency room, Ray. Hysterical. Jack's been in a real bad accident. He was found along the road that runs past their place. Looks like he had a flat tire and somebody didn't see him."

"Oh, God, Pete," Ray could not speak for a moment. Sure, he and Jack had had words concerning Laura. However, he and Jack had been together for one hell of a long time. "How bad is it?" he asked, assuming from the way Pete had said "accident" that Jack was still alive.

"Bad," said Pete. "Medics on the scene didn't think that he'd make it to the hospital. Ellen said that Donna's already at Jack's house to stay with the kids. Thought maybe you'd want to go on to MCV. Med Flight flew him in there."

"Yeah, I'm going to head out the door right now," said Ray.

"Ray," said Pete, a hesitancy in his voice.

"Yeah?" asked Ray, anxious to get moving.

"The reactor trips, Danny Miller, the shooting in the parking lot at corporate," Pete ran them off, each one sending an uneven chill down Ray's spine. "Now Jack. Never seen this much shit all randomly happen at one time. I think we'd best be watching our backs."

"Hate to say it," said Ray. "But I'm afraid that I'm going to have to agree with you." The same warning bells were going off in his head. However, there really was not anything concrete. At least nothing that would justify heightening security at the station.

Laura would be home in a couple of hours. Ray called her number, leaving a message on her voice mail explaining what had happen and where he was. Then he was gone.

Henrico Police Officer Tom Lowman was just finishing up with his paper work. As soon as the MCV emergency room staff finished taking this drunk off his hands, he was through for the day. He was on overtime and the city did not like that. The officer paused for a moment. Even in the hospital, he could feel the vibration from the churning air of the Med Flight helicopter flying overhead. The noise and vibration told him that it was approaching for its final. Moments before, a trauma team had gone down the hall to prepare for the patient that was being flown in. This one must be really good, he thought. Not good in that someone was hurt, but an adrenalin rush type of good in that the patient's injuries would pose a challenge to the trauma team that would work to save his life.

It was about three minutes later that a team of physicians and nurses, accompanied by two Virginia state police paramedics in blue jumpsuits, came rushing down the hallway. They minced no words as they ordered bystanders to get out of the way.

Tom never grew bored of watching the trauma team when they were working a good one. From what he could see, this was a good one. The patient appeared to be a male. Two bags of saline were hanging with IVs going into each arm, MAST trousers were in place and one of the paramedics was telling the Docs that they had deflated a tension pneumothorax just before the helicopter set down on the pad.

Once, he himself had been a paramedic with Hanover County Fire and Rescue. It had been while he was working at Jefferson Davis Power Nuclear Power Station as a Security Officer. After having worked there a couple of years, he had left to take a lower paying job with the Hanover County Sheriff's Department. A year ago, he had come to work for Henrico P.D.

Though Richmond Nuclear Security paid better, it was monotonous, boring work. Tom preferred the opportunities that real law enforcement offered him.

As police officers generally are, the ER staff at the Medical College of Virginia Hospital treated Tom very well. Some of the nurses, and even a couple of the attending physicians even remembered him as a paramedic. Therefore, when Officer Tom Lowman slipped into the trauma bay, no one on the staff objected or ordered him out. As one of the Med Flight paramedics laid the hospital's copy of the call sheet on the counter, Tom was watching. Realizing that all of the members of the trauma team were too busy to stop and look at it, and careful to stay out of their way, he reached over and grabbed it.

Tom looked over the call sheet, while at the same time, also keeping track of the various procedures that were taking place on the patient. On the patient's right side, a male nurse was attempting to insert a third, large bore I.V by doing a sub-clavian cut down. The patient was very hypothermic which made I.V. access difficult. On Tom's side of the patient, an intern was inserting a tube into the patient's abdominal cavity to check for internal hemorrhaging. Once the abdominal tube was in place, a steady flow of blood came forth. There was internal bleeding, lots of it. A resident was at the patient's head assessing the intubation that the paramedics had done.

"Not good," said one of the Med Flight paramedics who noticed Tom looking at the call sheet.

"How did it happen?" asked Tom, noticing that according to the call sheet, the man's blood pressure had been 60/30 when the rescue squad had turned the patient over to the Med Flight paramedics. Both femurs, pelvis, left arm in too many places to count, and multiple ribs appeared to have been fractured.

"Changing a flat tire on a dark stretch of road in Caroline County," said one of the medics. "Whoever hit him was flying like a bat out of hell. Wasn't even any skid marks. Poor guy had even put flares down."

"Hit and run?" asked Tom, shaking his head as one of the medics nodded. "Doesn't appear to be any major head trauma, though. That's real fortunate for him."

"Not sure," said the other medic. "He took the impact with his body. It threw him well off the road. Might be some head trauma, though, considering his level of consciousness. Pupils were almost non-reactive."

It was at this point that the patient's name, recorded on the call sheet caught his attention. The only reason Tom saw it was the fact that he was looking for the patient's age which would have a lot to do with his chances for survival. Jack Evans, Caroline County. Immediately the information clicked.

"Well, I'll be go to hell," said Tom, realizing as he said it that he was generating looks of curiosity from the two paramedics and a couple of the ER staff. "I used to work for this guy. He's the Superintendent of Security at Jefferson Davis Nuclear Power Station."

"They had a shooting in the parking lot of their corporate headquarters Monday, didn't they?" asked one of the Med Flight medics.

"Yeah, they did," said Tom, keeping to himself the fact that the case was being handled very carefully. Already the local news stations were voicing doubts about the validity of the incident being a simple car jacking. Police Department investigators knew that the victim of the crime was a private investigator looking into the problems between Richmond Nuclear and its parent company, Energy International. Tom knew that she was also the sister of Les Lambert, one of the deputies that he had worked with while a Hanover deputy himself.

"I heard that it had all the earmarks of a professional hit," said one of the Med Flight medics. That grabbed Tom's attention right away, considering the fact that Med Flight was part of the Virginia State Police whose own investigators were working on the case with Henrico P.D. Most of the paramedics were State Police Officers themselves. "Don't see many carjackings where they use silencers and Tech-9's. They've sent the dead man's prints to the FBI. It'll be interesting to see what comes of it. I know that the car he was driving was stolen."

"Well, looks like that if this fellow lives, he will certainly have you guys to thank," said Tom, placing the call sheet back on the counter. "I guess I'd better get back to work. Hope your night stays quiet."

"You, too," said one of them. "Stay safe."

Tom found a phone out of the hearing of others and called information. "Hanover County, Lesley Lambert, please." He hoped the number of his old friend was listed. For many deputies, that was not the case. Somewhere at home, he had the number. However, he wanted to make this call right now. A human voice said "Thank you," and then the automated voice read off the number. The number was listed after all. Immediately he dialed it.

"Hello," answered a female voice.

"Is Les there," asked Tom. "This is Tom Lowman. I used to work with him. This is Sandy, right?" He crossed his fingers, hoping that Les had not gotten divorced and was with someone else whom he would have just ticked off.

"Yeah, Tom. I remember you," she said. "How you been?"

"I'm doing great," said Tom. "I came across some information that I thought Les might be interested in." It did not surprise him to learn that Les was at his sister's place. Sandy gave him the number.

❧ ❧ ❧

"Les Lambert?" asked Tom.

"Yes?" said Les, pausing a moment. "I recognize the voice… Lowman. Tom Lowman?"

"Hey, you're pretty damned good," said Tom. "Maybe you ought to try for a job in a real law enforcement agency. You know, one like Henrico P.D."

"Man, I heard you got lost and fell off the end of the earth," said Les. "What's going on? You're not working the shooting my sister was involved in, are you?"

"Like which one? No, I don't normally come on until four in the afternoon," said Tom. "Investigators have taken it over and from the sounds of it, the State boys may be taking it from them. She doing all right?"

"Yeah she's fine," said Les. "Doing better than a couple of the others that were involved. Heard anything interesting on your end?"

"Actually, its been kind of hushed," said Tom. "They've sent the prints of both John Does to the FBI crime lab. Most are of the opinion that it had the look of a professional hit. The car that the shooter at Richmond Nuclear was driving was stolen. But I've got something else that you and your sister might find interesting."

"Go ahead," said Les.

"I'm at MCV. I had to bring in a drunk that wasn't looking too healthy. Anyway, Med Flight brought in the Superintendent of Security from Jefferson Davis Nuclear Power Station," said Tom. "It was a hit and run. Looks rather doubtful that he's going to make it. Hopefully he will. I used to work for him. Hell of a nice guy. I don't know what your sister's working, but it's highly suspected that the two stiffs that tried to take her out look pretty middle-eastern. Now the Superintendent of Security at a nuke plant almost gets taken out under suspicious circumstances."

Les finished getting what he could out of Tom and thanked him for the information. Two years ago, he would have chalked it all up to coincidence. However, this was the post September 11 era. Americans were targets and nuclear power stations appeared to be the holy grail of the many terrorist entities that had united. That coupled with his sister's take from her interview with Cowling made for some steep concern. He saw Rachel through the door of the kitchen, heating up some frozen pizza. "Want to take a ride over to MCV with me?" Les asked her.

"What's going on?" asked Rachel. She was exhausted and tonight seemed like her first real opportunity to kick back and relax. "Who was on the phone?" She had assumed that it must have been Sandy.

"Another day, another dead body; or at least a respectable attempt at it," said Les. "Could have been an accident, but sure has some interesting possibilities. The Superintendent of Security for Richmond Nuclear's Jefferson Davis Nuclear Power Station was a victim of a near fatal hit and run this evening. He's in surgery at the Medical College of Virginia right now."

"You know, when I started out, it was simple surveillance to catch a cheating husband," said Rachel. "To me that correlates to a five hundred piece jigsaw puzzle. Then there was the blackmail and the attacks on me. That makes it a fifteen hundred piece. Now this on top of what I got during my interview with Roger Cowling. What do think? A two thousand piece puzzle?"

When Ray Cisco arrived at MCV Hospital, his first priority was finding a place for Ellen to stay and to try to get her to eat something. He knew that this was going to be a long haul for her. Though she refused to leave the hospital for the night, he knew that she would need a place to eventually crash once Jack was out of surgery. Donna, he assured Ellen, would stay with the children for as long as was needed.

Ray racked his brains for an answer. Why would someone want Jack Evans dead? Though an accident could not be ruled out, Ellen had told him about Jack's pager going off, the problem with the phone. It all smacked of a setup. Then he thought of Danny Miller, added to that was the shooting at corporate headquarters. The problem was, was any of it connected? If it was, what did he need to do about it?

There was only on thing that he could do, at least the only prudent course of action. Ray assured Ellen that he would be right back. Making his way outside the ER, he removed his cell phone from the clip on his belt. He found an out of the way place to make his call. If the wrong person overheard this conversation, it would likely end up on CNN. From his wallet he pulled a card, it contained several phone numbers of the power station's management team. The one that he dialed was for Lloyd Ralston, the Station Manager.

"Yeah," came a sleepy voice from the other end of the line.

"Lloyd?" asked Ray, making certain he had the right person on the other end of the line before he began babbling away about a possible terrorist attack on a nuclear power station.

"Yeah, who's this?" demanded Ralston. He had shaken the sleep away and found his normal, unpleasant self.

"Ray Cisco. I'm here at MCV Hospital," said Ray. "Jack Evans is in here. Victim of a hit and run while changing a tire alongside the road. He's in real serious condition..." Ray found himself cut off.

"Oh, damn," said Ralston, his gruff voice softening. "I hate like hell to hear that. How are Ellen and the kids doing?"

"Ellen is having a rough time of it, naturally," said Ray. "My wife is staying with the kids."

"Well," said Ralston. "Let me know if I can help. Guess this puts you back in the hot seat of being superintendent until we get Jack back."

"And that's the other reason for calling," said Ray. "The circumstances of Jack's accident are real suspicious. Like I say, it was a hit and run. Ellen said his pager went off and he left to go to the plant. His flat tire occurred on the way there. We also have Danny Miller's murder, he was one of the technicians who maintained the computer systems for us, and then there was the shooting at corporate. I want to beef up security at the plant. I'll have to put people on overtime."

"I think you're over reacting," said Ralston after a significant pause. "Miller was a fucking pervert. He shouldn't even have had access to the damn security systems. The shooting at corporate was an attempted car jacking that didn't have a thing to do with Richmond Nuclear. Hell, Jack might have been sneaking out of the house to see a damn woman and met up with her husband. You guys in security have a reputation for that, you know.

"No, we're not going to go push panic buttons and get everyone talking about terrorists attacking the power station, Cisco. There's an outage going on. I need my people focused on that. Thanks for letting me know about Jack. Let me know if anything changes with him."

There was a click, and then the silence of the dead connection. Ralston's had not been a totally unexpected response. Right now, everyone was so damn overly sensitive about doing anything that involved overtime or any other type of expense. The loss of the World Trade Center and the other incidents that followed now seemed to be ancient history that no one thought about anymore. The Al Qaeda network had fallen apart far faster and easier than anyone could have anticipated. Everyone thought the world was a safe and friendly place. However, Ray knew better. The fragments of Al Qaeda had attached and integrated into other terrorist groups, in some cases uniting those groups. The threat was still alive and well, like a rattler lying silent in the brush.

Ray dialed the number for the plant's Security Shift Supervisor's office. It rang a couple of times. Pete Burns answered.

"Pete, it's me, Ray"

"Hey, how's it going with Jack?" asked Pete.

"They've just moved him from the ER up to surgery," said Ray. "Lots of internal bleeding. They're not making any promises. You know how the docs don't like to get your hopes up."

"Ellen doing alright?" asked Pete.

"As well as can be expected," said Ray. "Hey, reason I called. I just tried to talk Ralston into letting us beef up station security. It's a no go."

"Hey, like that's a big surprise," said Pete. "I've heard several Officers make mention their suspicions when they heard about Jack. We've all agreed that we just need to be on our toes. This damn outage is already running the shift ragged. Sure wish those National Guard units were still positioned around the plant."

"Those units didn't add much to security," said Ray. "They were only a deterrent against aircraft coming in. Highly unlikely that a group of hijackers will find a Boeing 767 with passengers who'll let them have the plane. Any well-planned attack is going to come unseen. Only personnel who know the plant and how to defend it are going to make a difference."

"Yeah, but it just felt good to see them out there," said Pete. "You going to be able to relieve me in the morning? I don't mind working a few hours over to cover for you."

"I'll be a little late, probably," said Ray. "We'll talk more then."

"Stupid son of a bitches," hissed Pete. "Wanting to save the cost of overtime in comparison with what even a failed attempt on the station would cost them. Everyone said that September 11th would change us forever. It was just a couple of years ago and already it's business as usual. Profit over security."

"Well, Pete ole boy," said Ray. "I guess if we'd gone to college and had taken Accounting 101, we could understand how something like that just isn't possible."

"Alright," said Pete. "Take care of Ellen. Let us know what's going on with Jack."

"Will do," said Ray, hanging up the phone.

⚜ ⚜ ⚜

"Forgot to ask you if you were carrying a weapon," said Rachel. Her purse was open, her fingers curling around her weapon within the confines of her purse as Les parked the car. Her bad feeling about things had gotten worse with the news about the Superintendent of Security at the nuclear station. She was making sure that it was in her purse and easy to grab.

"You kidding?" asked Les. "I don't even cross over into Richmond city limits without Kevlar and a semi-automatic when I take Sandy out to dinner."

"Good point. We shouldn't have to worry about whoever's tried to get rid of me," said Rachel. "With their track record so far, I know they wouldn't want to risk tangling with the locals."

The night air was brisk and cold. Against the streetlight, she could see that there was light snow falling. Soon, they were entering MCV Hospital through the ER entrance.

"Nurse," said Les. One of the nurses at the nurses' station glanced up from a report she was reading. "Les Lambert, Hanover County Sheriff's Department," he said holding up his badge. I'm trying to get some information on a possible hit and run. Patient's name is Jack Evans. Can you give us any information on him, or at least tell us where his wife is? Her name is Ellen."

"Sorry, they've moved him up to surgery," said the nurse. She was matter of fact, yet still polite. "I can tell you that you're not going to be able to talk to Mr. Evans anytime soon. His wife, I believe, is still in the ER waiting room. Go out into the main hall and take a left. By the way, I thought he was hit in Caroline County."

"Yeah, he was," said Les. "But there's some possible link that has us interested. Does Caroline County have anyone here?"

"Haven't seen anyone," said the nurse.

"Thanks," said Les.

"What in blazes are you doing?" asked Rachel.

"Hey, that power station is in my jurisdiction," said Les. "I have every right to ask questions. They've had one murder and possibly a second one

273

attempted. And I damn sure don't like this Middle East connection."

"Wait a minute," Rachel grabbed his arm. "I didn't know someone out at the power station was murdered. Give."

"Some computer type," said Les. "To tell you the truth, I just now remembered it. Everyone we talked to thought he was your basic loner, somewhat perverted type. He certainly didn't manage to draw a lot of sympathy even by getting himself killed. However, he was the wizard who maintains the Jefferson Davis Nuclear Power Station's security alarm systems."

"Just remember," said Rachel, shaking her head at still another bizarre development. "There's no blackmail until my client wants to report it. This could just be an accident. And you said the computer guy was a pervert."

"What blackmail you talking about?" asked Les, attempting to reassure her that he knew how it had to be played.

"Thank you," said Rachel. Perverted or not, finding out about the murder of the person responsible for taking care of Jefferson Davis Nuclear Power Station's security system managed to ratchet her anxiety level up another notch.

As they walked into the ER waiting room, Rachel and Les saw that it was crowded to beyond capacity. Though about three quarters of those in the ER were unlikely prospects for being Ellen Evans, there were enough other possibilities to make it very challenging.

Suddenly Les touched her arm lightly, he nodded towards a man and a woman sitting together against the far wall. Rachel liked Les' style. He had a knack for picking up on things. The only reason she would never want him as a partner, was the fact that he was too valuable a source of information and favors as a law enforcement officer.

Visible on the man's gray jacket, above his left breast, was the symbol of an atom. As they moved closer, the words, 'Richmond Nuclear' was readable. Above the right breast, stitched in red was 'Security Department, Ray Cisco'.

"Mrs. Evans?" asked Les, as he and Rachel stood before the pair.

"Yes?" asked Ellen, as she looked up, staring in apprehension at them. Rachel realized that Mrs. Evans probably thought them to be with the hospital, perhaps delivering word about her husband's condition.

"My name is Les Lambert, Hanover County Sheriff's Office, this is Rachel Lambert," said Les, returning the cold look of scrutiny that he was receiving from the man in the jacket. "We were wondering if it might be possible to find somewhere more private and ask you a few questions about what happened tonight. I realize that it's a very difficult time for you. However, it's always important to collect the facts while they're still fresh in people's minds."

"It didn't take place in Hanover," said Ray. "How do you fit in?"

"Les is my brother and he's assisting me on an investigation," said Rachel. Ray Cisco was easy to read. What she read in him was that if you wanted him to cooperate, you had to play it straight with him. "I'm working for your Senior V.P., Brian Matkins."

Lambert. Ray recognized the name. She was the person that someone had tried to kill in Richmond Nuclear's corporate parking lot. He played connect the dots in his mind, attempting to come up with a picture that showed Lambert knowing about Jack's accident and how that could be connected to the attack on her yesterday. Nothing was connecting, however. When an off-duty sheriff's deputy working a hit and run outside of his jurisdiction was tossed into the equation, it became even more confusing. One thing that did equate, though, was that it reinforced his feeling that the power station was in some type of serious jeopardy.

"I'm Ray Cisco," said Ray, going into his guard dog mode. He placed a hand on Ellen's arm to let her know he would handle things. "I'm a Security Shift Supervisor at Jefferson Davis Nuclear Power Station. I'm acting as Superintendent until Jack gets out of here and is ready to go back to work." He let his words about Jack getting out of here and getting back to work sink in for Ellen's benefit. It was important to keep her thinking positive. Then, to make sure that Rachel Lambert knew that he was on top of things, he added, "Ms. Lambert, I'm glad you were able to escape unscathed from your unfortunate experience yesterday. Seems like there's a lot of bad karma going around."

"You might say that," said Rachel. She immediately realized that Ray Cisco was a man who was used to taking control of any situation that he was in. Nuclear security officers were not the run of the mill night watchmen that most industrial security forces consist of. They were well trained; constantly drilled and pretty well paid for what was most of the time a very boring job. Ray, however, seemed even a step above that. He was definitely ex-military and possessed the demeanor of the men who had performed special operations for the CIA when she had been an officer in the CIA.

"There's a room down the hall that the hospital sometimes uses to talk to patient's families," said Les. "If no one's using it, I can get us in."

Les worked out the details and then led the way to a room used by clergy and social workers for counseling family members who have just lost a loved one. Nearby was a small nook of vending machines.

"Don't know about anyone else," said Rachel, "but I really need a cup of coffee. Anyone else want anything?"

"Coke," said Les.

"I'll go with you," said Ray. "See what they've got. Ellen, cream and sugar?" Ellen nodded. She stayed with Les while Rachel and Ray left for the vending machines.

"So, Ms. Lambert," said Ray when they were out of earshot. "What happened in that parking lot was a hell of a lot more than a car jacking," said Ray. "What the hell's going on? And how did you find out about Jack?"

"Just call me Rachel. My brother found out about Evans through happen stance," said Rachel. "To be quite honest, it seems like a hell of a long shot that what happened to Jack Evans has anything to do with what I'm working on. But like you said, seems like a lot of bad karma when it comes to folks associated with Richmond Nuclear."

"What I hear you telling me is that something's going on and that there could be a threat to the security of my station," said Ray.

"That isn't the nature of this investigation," Rachel replied. "I'm looking into the possibility that Energy International isn't conducting business in…let's just say a business like manner. However, I seem to keep stumbling into unfriendly strangers that appear to be from the Middle East." She thought about mentioning his CEO's connections with Iran. However, without more to go on, that did not seem appropriate.

"Well, I can tell you a few things about Energy International's business strategy," said Ray. "Security operations don't bring in revenue and they've forced some stiff cutbacks in security. It's only been a few years since the 9-1-1 attacks and already it's profit versus security. Al Qaeda may be ripped to shreds, but there are plenty of crazies out there forming into new groups, learning from the failures of those that we've destroyed. Bush's war on terrorism will not be over for a very long time. Just so that you know, I'm also aware of your adventure at the airport. You're an impressive woman. I was a SEAL. I know what it takes to come out on top when you're taken by surprise."

Ray's knowledge of her involvement in the airport shooting caught her off-guard. The Commonwealth Attorney's office was keeping the story under wraps for the time being. Ray obviously had good contacts. Her CIA training instinctively urged her to find a way to deny it. Commonsense, however, said that doing so would be sure folly and useless.

"There's nothing about my investigation linked to terrorist activity," said Rachel. "Both attacks were out of the blue." She was silent for a moment, and then she answered the logical question that they both had. "It's almost as if someone thinks that I know something, something that I'm not aware of. It's not making any sense to me. To be honest, it's really starting to piss me off. And the fact that Richmond Nuclear is decreasing security scares the hell out of me."

"Yeah," said Ray. "I know what you mean. I find myself in a really bad mood when people shoot at me." Whoever Rachel Lambert was, she impressed him. This woman had been in two major shootouts back to back and she was not lying low or ducking out and her assailants were taking up space at the county morgue. Whoever was after her might just be unlucky enough to catch up to her. He also had the feeling that she knew more about a connection between what was happening and a possible terrorist threat.

"Now's not the best time to talk," Ray continued. "I need to be thinking about Ellen. I've told my people at the plant to stay on their toes. No one will let me do more. Do you know how to get to the plant?"

"Am I invited for a tour?" asked Rachel.

"I think that would be appropriate," said Ray. "Do you know anything about the murder of one of our technicians out at the plant, Danny Miller?"

"That and nothing more," she said.

"Danny was odd, a computer nerd to the millionth degree," said Ray. "Most people thought of him as a real pervert. Anyway, he was found shot to death in a sleazy motel. Autopsy showed that he was probably in the middle of having sex."

"Male or female?" asked Rachel. She laughed as Ray nearly gagged on his coffee.

"With a woman," said Ray. "Guess one does have to ask that question now a days, huh?"

Cisco was funny. Despite the moment, she managed to grin. "What concerns you the most about his murder?" asked Rachel.

"The fact that he maintained our Central Alarm System," said Ray. "The guy knew it inside and out."

"If he worked in the nuclear station, didn't he have to have an extensive security background check, take an examination for mental stability?" asked Rachel.

"Security wise, he's clean," said Ray. "No jail time, no links to terrorist groups and the like. He came to work for the company before they started giving the MMPI, the psychiatric examine. Ain't no way in hell that he'd have passed it."

"That's comforting," said Rachel. "Once this is over, I think I'm selling my place and moving a few counties over from you guys."

Rachel wondered if Ray took her expressed lack of confidence in his nuclear power plant serious. Hopefully, he had not. People with sexual preferences outside of the world's perceived norm held responsibility in all walks of life. They were generally no more a threat than someone who flew straight; whatever the definition of that was these days. Sure, they presented certain vulnerabilities; but no more than anyone who was vulnerable to becoming obsessed with sex, money, ego or political motivation and who made that conscious decision to misuse societies trust in them. There were no boundaries.

They had left the door to the room just slightly ajar. Rachel pushed it open with her shoulder and Ray followed her in. Les got up, shut the door and then took his seat again across from Ellen.

"Mrs. Evans, we certainly know that this is neither an easy nor a convenient time for you to talk," said Les. While his sister and Ray had been out of the room, Les had made small talk, knowing that trying to ask questions in Ray's absence would simply have undermined the security officer's willingness to work with them. Such small, seemingly unimportant conversation, however, was normally of value in a police interview. It allowed both parties to feel each other out and, in most cases, to converse comfortably when it was time to get down to business. "However, anything that you know could prove to be very significant if what happened to your husband wasn't an accident. He's the head of security at a nuclear facility. We're here to see if there is some type of threat to the Jefferson Davis Nuclear Power Station."

Ellen hesitated, glanced at Ray, and then slowly nodded. Ray squeezed her hand and nodded as well. Les continued.

"I'd like for you to tell me what you know of Jack's day," said Les. "Anything he said, how he acted, what time he left for work, phone calls to and from him. Whether anyone called him at home. In other words, tell us anything that you know about Jack's day. Even if it's merely speculation on your part and seems to hold no importance at all."

"He went to work his regular time and came home two hours late. But he'd told me to expect that," said Ellen, choking back her tears in an act of fortitude. "We talked once at lunch on the phone."

"We just started a refueling outage," interjected Ray. "That's the reason for him being late. I was there with him."

"How long did you talk?" asked Les, giving Ray a nod of acknowledgement. His voice was soft and gentle. He had Ellen's confidence completely. "What did you talk about?"

Les' eyes never wavered, never gave a clue that he noted with significance the quick exchange of looks between Ellen and Ray. It had not even been a full-fledged glance that they had exchanged; however, it was enough. He could tell that Ellen was unsure whether to discuss the phone call and it obviously had something to do with Ray.

"It was only a few minutes during his lunch hour," said Ellen. "We talked about personal stuff. Nothing that could possibly have any bearing on what happened tonight."

"Okay," said Les, his voice floating like a feather. He was not getting the whole story, but there was nothing to be done about that at the moment. "We don't need to go into anything personal. How about when he got home, Ellen?"

"He came home late, like I said," said Ellen. "He didn't seem at all concerned about anything. Just as we finished eating, his pager went off, it had that code that says there is an emergency at the power plant. When he tried to use the phone, it wasn't working. He got upset and asked me if I had forgotten to pay the phone bill. That had happened once, recently."

Ray suddenly stiffened and turned towards Ellen. He was on the verge of interrupting, but Ellen kept talking.

"When was the last time that you absolutely know that the phone was working?" asked Les. He maintained his focus on Ellen despite the distraction from Ray.

"I talked to Donna, Ray's wife," said Ellen. Again, there was that tell tale hesitation. "I called her about ten of four to see how she was doing? We talked until about five of five. And I checked. The bill was paid on time." Almost as if to see if she had answered satisfactorily, she glanced nervously at Ray, much too openly to try and hide. "I'm not...sure..."

"That's alright, Ellen," said Ray, his hand lightly on Ellen's. "Ellen has avoided mentioning that I left Donna a couple of days ago. They are very good friends. Until this happened, it was preoccupying her a lot. If I'm not mistaken, it's most likely what Ellen and Jack talked about at lunch. But,

Ellen, you never said anything about Ray's pager giving the emergency message." He turned towards Les and Rachel. "There wasn't anything going on at the plant. I'll call and check to see if there's anything I can find out about the page. It would have had to have been generated from within the plant for Jack to recognize it as a valid emergency page." He locked eyes with Rachel. There was something putting his plant, his people, in danger. Somehow, Rachel Lambert was a part of it.

Rachel answered Ray's stare with her own. As if reading his mind, she knew that he saw too many pieces coming together that pointed to a real threat to the Jefferson Davis Nuclear Power Plant. Could it, however, be something totally different? Could Jack Evans possibly have been the victim of a love triangle? Ray and Ellen did not look like potential lovers. Ray was fit and extremely handsome. Ellen was perhaps forty pounds overweight and would not have been overly attractive at her best. However, Ray could have sent the mysterious page that had wrought this personal tragedy. The murdered technician responsible for maintaining Jefferson Davis Nuclear Power Station's security system could have known something that got him killed. Certainly, Ray was a person capable of killing.

There were many possibilities and combinations of possibilities. Illicit love gone astray, however, would not have figured into the attempts on her life or the blackmail of Brian Matkins. Nothing, however, said that one was connected to the other. The prudent prospective was to treat this as a threat to the station.

"Thanks," said Les, noting the interaction between his sister and the security officer. He nodded at Ellen to continue.

Tears began to stream in force now. "Next thing I knew, he was driving off," said Ellen. There was a sniffle, and then she broke into a sob as she continued to speak. "I didn't know about the accident until I heard the sirens and saw the flashing lights half an hour later at the end of the driveway. There's nothing else to tell you."

"I think it would be prudent to heighten security at the plant," said Les, glancing at Ray. One had to be careful at assuming a threat. The general public had been from Threat Level Yellow to Orange and back so many times that they no longer concerned themselves with it. Even law enforcement, at least at his level, no longer put much stock into it. The situation, though, certainly justified an increased measure of vigilance and security.

"I already spoke to the plant manager and asked for increased staffing," said Ray. "It meant overtime and I was told no. But the security force is aware that stuff has been happening. They're top notch folks and their on their toes."

"I'm going to file a report," said Les. "I should at least make my department aware that there is a heightened risk based on the circumstances. That will be routed up to the FBI and sent to Homeland Security for evaluation. It'll take a couple of days, though."

"Do what you can," said Ray. "In the meantime, my folks will make sure that the plant is as secure as we can make it."

"Do you track the pages that go out from the station," asked Rachel.

"Yeah," said Ray. "We do. Let's call the plant and see what we can find out.

Les stayed with Ellen while Ray and Rachel stepped into the hall. Ray called Pete Burns at the station. "Pete, an emergency page went out from the station this evening. Jack was headed to the station when he was hit. Check CAS and see what time the page went out. I want a list of everyone that was in the Central Alarm Station when the page would have been sent."

" Ray," said Pete. "Not a damn thing in CAS to document that a page went out."

"Has to be," said Ray. "We capture all emergency pages for NRC documentation."

Ray waited several minutes until Pete returned with an answer.

"Sorry, boss," said Pete. "There's nothing there."

"All right," said Ray and hung up the phone. "Nothing. Perhaps there really was no emergency page. Maybe Jack had something cooking on the side after all. Who knows?"

"Well, doesn't give us much to go to the FBI or Homeland Security with," said Rachel. "And it doesn't give you any leverage with your management for increasing security."

"Still…there's something going on," said Ray. "Something's not right in Dodge and Wyatt Earp can't figure it out."

Chapter Thirty-one
Thursday, December 10

Brian awoke, his hand searching the bed beside him. Brenda was not there. He grimaced and swung his feet over the side of the bed. The house was empty, not a sound. Quickly he got himself dressed and out of the house. For a few moments, he stared at the light covering of snow that lay on the ground.

It really was not the best weather for driving to work in the green Jaguar parked in his garage. Brenda, however, had taken the Nissan Pathfinder, thus giving him no choice. Starting the Jaguar's engine, Brian let it run for a few minutes before he pushed the button on his key ring to open the garage door. Then he eased out onto the lightly snow covered driveway.

Before pulling onto the street, Brian picked up his cell phone and dialed a number. He let it ring as he continued on his way. After four rings, came the sound of it being picked up on the other end.

"Hello," came the pensive voice of his wife. There was the sound in the background of his two daughters Stephanie and Arlene arguing over bathroom first rights.

"Good morning, almost sounds like home there in the background," said Brian with an effort at levity. "Everything okay?"

"Fine, I guess," said Brenda. "You want to talk to the girls? I'm going to take them to Tyson's Corner for the day to do Christmas shopping."

"I really hadn't expected them to be up so early," said Brian. "Actually, there's something that I need to talk to you about."

"Not us," snapped his wife. "If it has anything to do with apologies or wanting forgiveness, I just don't want to hear it."

"Mom, is that Dad?" he heard Arlene asking.

"I understand," said Brian. Her words hurt him. "Something else. That investigator that you had following me. Rachel Lambert?"

"Yeah?" asked his wife.

"Well, there is something that she didn't tell you about Atlanta," said Brian. He heard Brenda suck her breath in. "I'm being blackmailed. I think by

Cowling. Lambert kind of stumbled in the middle of it while she was following me. It's turned real ugly. Someone has tried twice to kill her."

"Jesus Christ, Brian," said his wife, her voice pensive. "Just what have you got us all into?"

"Just listen to me, okay?" Brian snapped back at her. "Keep the girls with you at all times. Don't let them out of your sight."

"Give him the damn company, Brian," Brenda's tone had changed entirely, she was pleading now. He could tell that she was scared; and she did not scare easily. "When it gets bad enough that you have to worry about something happening to your family, then it's not worth it."

"I'm taking precautions, that's all," said Brian. "I just found out that Cowling is calling a vote to sell Richmond Nuclear. One way or the other, by the end of tomorrow, it'll be over. Then we can get back to ... oh hell, I don't know. Just keep an eye out."

"Brian, this is scaring me. I don't like looking over my shoulder," said Brenda, the sound of each sniffle as she began to cry, reached his ear. "It's not going to return to normal, Brian. We're not coming back. I've decided to file for divorce. I told mother last night. You've played out of the nest too many times. I always worried about you bringing home some damned disease. Never did I consider that you'd put us all in danger. Your daughters as well as me."

"Tell you what, as soon as this mess is sorted out," said Brian, "I'll come on up. We'll have a nice leisurely vacation and spend Christmas with your mother."

"Brian, it's over," said Brenda coldly.

"No," said Brian, his tone patient. "When this is over, it'll be a new beginning for us. I might be looking for a new job, but I don't really care. What I want is to get us back on track. I'm the one with the problem. You know that, I know that. At least think about it. Even if you won't give us another chance, wait till after the New Year. Be fair to the kids; hell be fair to your mother, for God's sake."

"Brian..." Brenda paused. "I don't feel like talking now. Don't let anything happen to yourself. Goodbye."

"Babe, I do love you and it's the truth..." said Brian, realizing that she had hung up on him.

"I've got to go to the bathroom," said nine-year-old Arlene Matkins for the third time.

"Okay," said Brenda, who had heard her the first two times, but had not answered. The conversation with Brian earlier kept replaying itself inside of her head.

The Christmas shopping crowd in the mall was atrocious. It was a battle, especially right now, at lunchtime, to get through the throng of people in the food pavilion. Finally, she saw the sign for the restrooms.

"I'm going to get us some cheese burgers, fries, and cokes," said Brenda, smiling. "How does that sound?"

"Not very good if I don't get to the bathroom fast," said Arlene.

"Stephanie," said Brenda to her twelve year old. "Go in with her while I get the food. Straight in and straight out." She would get the food right next to where the restrooms were located. It was a long line, but at least it would allow her to keep an eye on the girls going in and out.

Brenda watched the two girls enter the restroom, and then she got in line. The line moved quicker than she had anticipated. With a tray piled with food, she found a table near the restrooms. Sipping a cup of coffee, she waited for them to come out. From her vantage point, she could not miss them. Her eyes had never left the entrance and exit of the restrooms for more than a few seconds at a time.

At fifteen minutes into the wait, Brenda knew that they should be out any moment. Then, at twenty minutes, she began to grow impatient and began developing a sense of foreboding. Twenty-five minutes into the wait was too long. Arlene had not looked ill. She hated to get up and just leave the food sitting here. She would give them five more minutes.

Thirty minutes! That was it. This was ridiculous. Though there was still the worry caused by her husband's warning, Brenda knew that it would be impossible for someone to have taken them. She would have seen. As she rose from her seat, the phone in her purse began to ring. At first, she thought of ignoring it. More worried really, than angry, she wanted to find out what was wrong with Arlene. Few people had this number, however. No one would call her on this phone unless there was some urgency; she reached into her purse and answered it. Perhaps it was Brian again.

"Hello," said Brenda, in a tone less than friendly, but short of actually being rude.

"Brenda Matkins, your daughters are not in the restroom," said a voice. The speech was slurred, or slowed, or something. It immediately made her think of the kidnappings in movies where the caller disguises their voice using some high tech device.

"Your daughters are with us," continued the disguised voice. "Do not call the police. Only your husband can get the girls back. But he must do as he is told, when we tell him. We will keep your daughters safe. In a couple of days, if your husband cooperates, you will have them back. There is no money involved, just cooperation. If you contact the police then there will be no further contact from us." Then there was the chilling click, one that signaled that the caller had hung up.

Brenda put the phone back into her bag. Taking a couple of deep breaths, she walked as calmly as she could into the ladies restroom. It only took a couple of minutes for her to validate the caller's claim.

Ray had called Rachel at around four in the morning. Jack Evans had pulled through his first surgery. He was, as the doctor explained it, temporarily stabilized, but still in critical condition. He would need a second surgery immediately so the doctors could place a bolt in his head to relieve pressure from the swelling of a head injury that they had found during an MRI. Jack Evans would not be waking up this morning to tell what had happened.

It had been two-thirty in the morning when she had dropped Les off at his house. He had argued the matter, wanting to drop her off and keep the Celica with him. If she parked it at the apartment, he contended, it would be a simple matter for someone to rig it with an explosive device. Rachel had simply countered that she was not going to be without wheels. End of discussion. Now, she was on her way back to MCV to see how Ellen Evans was doing and to see if there was anything new known about what happened.

"Hello," she said, picking up the phone out of her purse.

"Ms. Lambert?" asked a somewhat disheveled, high-pitched voice. It threw her for a moment, but then she recognized it as Brian Matkins.

"Mr. Matkins? Are you alright?" asked Rachel. The panic in his voice alarmed her. Matkins did not appear the type to come unraveled easily.

"Ms. Lambert, I am at my office," said Brian. His breathing was rapid, irregular. Rachel could tell that he was over the edge, a man who felt himself drowning but could do nothing to save himself. "I don't feel safe talking on the phone."

"I'm on my way," said Rachel, clicking off. Immediately she dialed the stored number of Les' home.

"Hello," said Les.

"Need you to head over to Richmond Nuclear's Corporate Center," said Rachel. "Brian Matkins just called me and told me that he needed to see me right away. Said he couldn't talk on the phone. I think something's happened."

"Damn," said Les. He was tired. "I've got the film developed of Cowling's appointment book. Let me get the list of names that we want him to look at. Meet you there."

Richmond Nuclear's Corporate Center was a good thirty-minute drive from her place. Twenty-one minutes later, however, Rachel was pulling into Harding's parking space near the entrance of the Richmond Nuclear headquarters. Harding's parking space was the closest empty space next to the building's front door. There had seemed a serious sense of urgency in Brian's need to see her. Surely, his good friend would not mind.

"Good morning, Ms. Lambert," said the Security Officer as she flashed her I.D. Everyone going through the front door had to display their I.D. If an employee entered through one of the electronically locked side doors, they used a smart card and a biometric device that read their index finger. "Go on ahead."

Rachel smiled and nodded, and then stepped towards the escalator. This morning, it was not fast enough for her. She ran up it rather than taking the time to ride. At the fourth floor, she quickly made her way to Matkins' office. This time there was no Mrs. Hendrickson. Instead, Brian's office door was open; he was leaning back in his chair, appearing to be deep in thought.

"Brian, you all right?" asked Rachel. Quickly she assessed the answer to that question as a definite no as she saw his tear reddened eyes.

"Rachel, they have my two daughters," said Brian, his voice quiet, subdued.

The chill that ran down her spine was icy. "Brian, who has your daughters?" asked Rachel, pushing his office door shut.

"Whoever is doing this to me," said Brian. "I can only guess that it has to be Cowling."

"But if he already has a tape of you and Tanya Madison, why risk the type of intense investigation that kidnapping your daughters could result in?" asked Rachel. "It makes no sense whatsoever. He should have concluded yesterday that he's a number one suspect in the blackmail. The FBI will nail him before the day is out if he's the guilty party."

"Like all kidnapping movies, my wife was given the standard line about not calling the police," said Brian sarcastically. "They told her that they're not interested in money. Only my cooperation. Just a couple of days, they said. I found out that he's getting ready to make his move to sell the company."

"I just can't believe that he'd go to this extreme," said Rachel. "Damn, if it doesn't almost seem like there are two different groups out there fighting over your cooperation." Two different parties had definitely searched her apartment; one rigging a hand grenade to kill her, the other disarming it.

"Roger Cowling is not a man who is used to losing," said Brian. "My wife has left me. I guess he figures that nullifies his ability to use the tape to achieve his purpose."

Rachel was pondering the latest event as her cell phone rang. "Hello," she said. "Go to the security desk. I'll have Brian call down."

"Who's that?" demanded Brian. His voice was heavily laced with suspicion.

"My brother," said Rachel. "He's helping me with my investigation. He's the other half of the team." Best, she decided, not to let him know that Les was a Deputy Sheriff. "His name is Les Lambert. Please let him come up. This is getting too damn big for just me. You've got enough going on here to swamp several law enforcement agencies."

Brian sat stock still for a moment. She could see his hesitation in picking up the phone, as though something was weighing heavily on his mind and he wanted to tell her about it because she was the only one he could trust. He was a man about to come clean with something. All along, she had felt he was holding back on something she needed to know. Somehow, there was a feeling that it was not going to be an insubstantial piece of this very complex puzzle.

"Brian," she said. "If Les and I don't have all the facts, then we can't make well informed decisions. Your two daughters are at stake now. We can't afford a shot in the dark. What are you holding back? I think you know something that is going to allow us to start making some sense of all this."

"Oh, God!" said Brian leaning back in his chair as he looked up at the ceiling. "When I got that blackmail message, the one that you heard. I was in Tanya's apartment."

There was a pause. Rachel nodded. "I know, I followed you there. Go on." Damn it to hell, she knew exactly what he was going to tell her. If it were not for the fact that he had two little girls now in the hands of whomever, she would walk out the door and tell him to dig himself out of this hole.

"Tanya Madison was there," he said, looking at her through helpless eyes. "She was dead. Her guts were all over the floor, blood everywhere. It was the knife...when we were making love earlier, I was using the knife as ... well you know, sort of a stimulus. A game. Actually, it was her idea." Brian was shaking all over and his voice was weak and soppy.

"Matkins, you are a god damned ass. Do you know that?" she practically hissed the words at him. "How in the hell can I work for you when you lie to me. I am not the fucking enemy! Whoever murdered Madison and has your children is the enemy. Why lie to me? Pick up that phone and have them bring my brother up. Now, damn it. Do it right now!"

Les was at the door of the Senior V.P.'s office within minutes, escorted by a Security Officer since Brian had ordered him brought without doing the normal security routine. Rachel was trying to breathe deep, to get some semblance of self-control back. She could not remember the last time she was this angry.

"Les, yesterday afternoon Brian's two daughters were kidnapped from the mall at Tyson's Corner," said Rachel, waiting until the Security Officer was gone and the door shut. "And he's just now come up with a minor part of this story that he has up to now left out."

"Which is?" asked Les with some trepidation as he took a seat.

"The fact that he has seen Tanya Madison's body," said Rachel. "She was brutally stabbed to death. Gutted."

"Shit," said Les quietly. "It's time to bring in the FBI. Do you realize that you are a key witness to a murder? One that you failed to report. And you've crossed state lines. You could cause Rachel to lose her license."

"No!" shouted Brian. He did not attempt to keep his voice low. "They have my daughters. They said no police!"

"That's the first thing a kidnapper always tells you," said Les. He spoke softly, sounding like a parent trying to explain why brushing your teeth after a candy bar is important. "Of course the kidnapper doesn't want you to bring in the FBI, because they're your most effective tool in getting your children back unharmed and putting the kidnappers in jail. Even though we are working for you, we still have to report the murder. It's all tied together."

"No," said Brian, shaking his head. "If it is Cowlings, and I believe that it is, he'll play it just like it was told to my wife. I want my kids back safe, that's our first priority. Second priority is nailing Cowlings. Do what you have to do about Tanya's murder. But I don't want a word to the police about the kidnapping."

"So, what have they asked for?" asked Les. "Have they made any demands?"

"I haven't talked to them," said Brian. "So far, there has only been the one call to my wife. She was told that we would have them back in a couple of days if I just did what I was told."

"Brian, we know that someone set you up to be blackmailed," said Les. "Now that in itself would be enough to get your cooperation. But, not only are you blackmailed for having illicit sex, but there is the potential for framing you for murder. Now someone has kidnapped your children. Sounds like a damn chess game. My bet is that you're a piece on Cowling's chessboard. Someone else is exerting pressure on you to put Cowling in check, and now Cowling is fighting back by kidnapping your kids. Or vice versa."

"You said that you would have voted not to sell Richmond Nuclear, correct?" Rachel asked Brian. He nodded.

"If something happens to a Board member of Energy International," said Rachel to her brother, "then Brian has a vote on the sell of the company."

"Cowling counters by getting a tape of Brian with Ms. Madison," said Les.

"Somebody wants Brian to vote against the sell, so they kill Madison and set him up to take the rap if he doesn't cooperate," said Rachel.

"Who stands to gain by the sell of Richmond Nuclear falling through?" asked Les, looking at Brian.

"With all that has happened with my daughters, I almost forgot," said Brian. "One of the Board members of Energy International who opposes Cowling on just about all issues, faxed me this." Brian showed them a copy of Cowling's letter outlining the vote on the sell of the company and then the land lease and construction of nuclear units in Mexico.

"Another company?" asked Rachel.

"So it would appear," said Brian. "Deregulation of electrical power and legislation allowing its freewheeling does open up the cheap labor and relaxed nuclear regulatory climate in Mexico."

"It's as simple as the nose on my face," said Les. "Someone wants to see Energy International fail so that they can take over with building power stations in Mexico. I bet that Cowling is as much in the dark as we are. Is it really worth fighting over?"

"Potentially it's a gold mine. A mother lode," said Brian. "Others, even myself, have given the idea some thought. Look at what happened in California with the blackouts and brownouts."

"It's a very simple matter, for the moment," said Rachel. "Vote just like the kidnappers tell you to. Protect your children. I'm not into trade law, but someone is breaking the hell out of them. Once you have your daughters back, we go to the FBI."

"Then basically I guess you're finished?" asked Brian. "I mean there really is nothing else to investigate is there?"

"This is a list of people that appear on Cowling's appointment calendar," said Les. "Are you aware that the person responsible for maintaining your nuclear station's security computers was murdered a week ago Wednesday? And that the Superintendent of Security at the station was the victim of a suspicious hit and run, one that might turn out to be attempted murder. Or murder if he dies."

"Just in passing," said Brian. "I haven't given the operation of the stations my full focus. Certainly that's been obvious to you."

"And understandable," said Rachel. "But is there any reason why this Mexico endeavor would warrant someone undermining security at the power station?"

"No," said Brian. "I really can't see it being connected at all. Though, an overt act of sabotage would likely sink any proposed sale."

Rachel and her brother exchanged looks of concern. Before either could speak, there was a small chirping sound as one of the lines on Matkins' phone lit up. "Travis," said Brian answering it. "I've got Ms. Lambert in here right now. It's gone from bad to worse. Brenda called me a little while ago. Someone has kidnapped Stephanie and Arlene … thanks, buddy. I appreciate your support. I'll talk to you in a little while."

"You need to be real careful about the information that you share," said Les.

"That's the V.P. of Administration and Security," said Brian. "He and I went to Virginia Tech together. Travis is someone that I can trust with my life."

When Rachel and Les left, they rode the elevator down. She shook her head. "How long can we hold off reporting what he told us about Madison?" she asked.

"I think we need to wait until Monday," said Les. "Under the circumstances, it's justified. If Atlanta sends investigators here to interview him before we get his kids released, it'll look to the kidnappers like he's called in law enforcement. This whole thing is blowing up so big that when the FBI does get involved they'll need a microscope to even notice us."

"Les," asked Rachel. "Do they even make a million piece jigsaw puzzle? I feel like we're in one."

⋐⋐⋐

"Resources For Tomorrow, this is Gina. How may I help you?" she answered. Gina had nearly dropped the entire manuscript in the floor; so rare was it that the phone rang. For five days a week she sat in this tiny office waiting for this one phone to ring. It would do so several times a week, always the same caller, always asking for Mr. Henry J. Thomas. In between those sparse phone calls, she read manuscripts from the slush pile of a publishing company. It was added pocket change.

"I'm sorry, sir, Mr. Thomas is in a meeting," said Gina. Long ago, when she had first started this job, her instructions were to never ask the caller for a name or a number. For three thousand dollars a month, paid to answer this one phone, to take a message for this one caller, she could handle that. Especially considering that the three grand was paid to her in cash.

"Just tell him that I need him to call me," said the voice on the other end of the phone. "Tell him that the matter is urgent and that he should call me just as quickly as he can."

"Yes, sir," said Gina. "I'll have someone take the message to the conference room right this minute."

There was no goodbye or thanks from the caller, just the click of the caller disconnecting. Immediately, Gina dialed the number that she had memorized. Henry J. Thomas, or whoever he really was, had explicitly warned her against writing it down or storing it to memory on her phone. Of course, the office had been outfitted with the simplest of phones, one that did not have a memory. She was sure that the reason for the very simple phone was to remove any temptation of storing Mr. Thomas' phone number. The reason certainly was not money. Three thousand dollars a month for her to do what a normal answering service could do for a hundred a month proved that. Drug smuggling or money laundering was what it was; or maybe it could be guns. Gina did not know and was certain that finding out would not be healthy.

Gina had found the job by answering an ad in the classifieds. Henry J. Thomas, who spoke with a strong accent, had hired her over the phone, told her where to show up, where the office key was hidden and how she would be paid. As long as she never had to lay eyes on Mr. Henry J. Thomas, she was certain that she would be safe. And as long as there was a brown paper bag in the bottom right desk drawer containing three thousand in twenty dollar bills every month, she would continue showing up for work.

Gina passed the message on as she had promised. It would be hours, most likely even days before the phone rang once again. Gina went back to the manuscript. In her hands, she held some poor sap's hope of being a romance writer. She could only hope this author still had the day job.

Al-Hamdani walked briskly beside Abdul, the cream-colored cell phone in his hand. Snow had blanketed the entire northeastern corner of the nation. Traffic right now in New York City was at a standstill. That, however, was not justification for suffering through the day on an empty stomach. Moreover, not just any food would do when it was time for Abdul to eat. Today it would be Adeeb's Beirut Palace. There was no better chef in all of New York City than Adeeb. Thankfully, it was not far to walk.

The wind was howling, blowing the newly fallen snow into his face. Certainly not the time and place to answer the phone, thought Abdul. A quick glance to his left told him that there was a light on in the bookstore. Taking a step that direction, he gave the door a push; it opened. Clicking the phone on, he stepped inside.

"Yes?" Abdul answered the phone, his voice sounding crisp, professional; not at all like a man who had just stepped in from the blowing snow and frigid temperatures.

"You need to call. The message is that it is urgent," were Gina's words that came over the ether to reach Abdul's ear.

"Anything else?" asked Abdul.

"No, sir," said Gina.

"Thank you," said Abdul.

"I have a racquetball game over at the club," Frank Baker told his secretary. "I'll be back in the office at three forty-five for the O'Connell appointment.

"Yes, sir," said Darlene, receptionist for the Baker, Anderson & Baker law firm. She watched as the senior partner of the firm made his way out the door. If he was playing racquetball, she hoped that he remembered to carry his nitro-glycerin tablets with him. It had only been three months ago that paramedics had carried him out of General Circuit Court with crushing chest pains.

Frank Baker did not go out to the firm's private parking lot. Instead, he walked down to the street and around the corner where no one could see him from any of his firm's office windows. He placed one hand over his mouth to warm the air that he sucked into his lungs so that they would not spasm. A cigarette would have felt good, but Laura had told him she did not like the smell of the smoke. Not to mention what his doctor had to say about it.

Laura was parked in front of Haggerty's Furniture store on Clay Street. Frank walked quickly, anxious to get out of the cold. As he tapped on the passenger side window, he heard the sound of the power door locks releasing. Opening the door, he climbed in.

"You really look cold," said Laura. "I could have picked you up at the front door of your office. I'll do that next time."

"I'll be fine," said Frank, catching the first glimpse of her thighs. Her short black skirt had ridden up high, exposing a great deal of her long, slender legs. He liked the fact that she had not chosen to drape her legs in hose. It was certainly skimpy for such weather, but it warmed him. Immediately he would have spent a million dollars to be twenty, or hell, even just ten years younger than he was right now. Yeah, he thought, even ten years ago he could have played hard with what Laura had to offer.

Laura pulled away from the curb. Steering with one hand, she fumbled with a pack of gum trying to unwrap it. Suddenly it dropped from her fingers, landing somewhere on the floor in front of her seat. "Ohhh!" she said. "Frank, you able to reach that for me?"

"Sure," said Frank, somewhat surprised at his good fortune. Perhaps this had something to do with Christmas being only eleven days away, he thought wily to himself. Unbuckling his seat belt, he leaned over the gearshift. The gum had somehow bounced all the way to the far side, near her left foot. "I'm going to have to lean over you a bit to reach it, I'm afraid."

"Please, I'm not the kind to yell harassment," she laughed. "You don't have to worry!"

For the first time in longer than Frank cared to remember, there was an arousal as he placed his head over the top of her bare thighs. He stretched his arm out for the gum, his cheek resting lightly on the soft, tan skin of her leg. Though he could actually have grasped the gum at that moment, he did not; feeling as though he had somewhat received an invitation to entertain himself. Almost so lightly, that she might not even feel it, he brushed his lips against her thigh. The sudden heat shot through him like a jolt from a defibrillator, stiffening his arousal. With the slightest turn of his head, he found himself staring up at nirvana.

"Shit!" Laura exclaimed.

Frank at first thought that Laura had not taken well to his peeking. Suddenly he realized that her foot was going hard to the brake pedal. In an apparent move to keep him from harm, he felt her right hand grasping his head keeping him from flying forward with the deceleration.

Unable to raise his head, he was aware of her swerving to the left and then stomping the accelerator. Suddenly he found himself with his head beneath her skirt and his face practically in the mound of dark hair that showed through her white lace panties. He was so close that if he had stuck his tongue out he could have licked her. He could smell her, delicious and musty. Her hand left his head. As he raised himself up, handing her the gum, he actually felt twenty years younger; and it had not even cost the million dollars.

"Frank, I don't know if I should send you to find my gum anymore," said Laura. "I think you enjoyed it just a little too much down there!"

"Well, it was a very tedious task," said Frank, suddenly aware that he was growing tight against his trousers to the point of showing. He had not been what he could call truly horny for a long time. "I'm just glad that I was up to performing to your expectations." He grinned at his own play on words. Though her sunglasses hid her eyes, he saw her return the grin.

"Oh, God, I'm not believing myself," said Laura shaking her head as though she had just thought of the most outlandish idea.

"What?" asked Frank, feeling a sudden desperation to take this moment further.

"What I was just thinking," she said.

"What were you just thinking?" asked Frank. "I'm your attorney. I'll keep it confidential, promise."

"About finding out just how much you're up to performing," said Laura.

Frank found his breath momentarily choked off. His hand went to her thigh with a gentle stroke, feeling the warmth, the firmness. He thought immediately of the saying 'back in the saddle again'. Then her hand came to rest upon his. Up ahead was the Richmond Courts Inn and she was slowing down; then turning in. Her hand slid across to rest on his hardening member.

"I'm not believing that we're doing this," said Laura, removing her sunglasses. She bore into him with dark, haunting eyes. "Yes? No?"

"I'll get us a room," said Frank, drawing a deep breath. It was a nice place, but not so nice as to have conference rooms or a restaurant. That was convenient; the only way he would bump into someone he knew was if they were here for the same nefarious reason as he.

Frank Baker's hands were trembling as he pulled two twenties from his wallet and signed for the room. He could feel his knees shake. But he was not swayed in the least from what he was about to do. There was a time, he remembered, that he would go through this routine several times a week. Key in hand he returned to the car.

"Room 214," he said as he slid into the seat. "Park right over there and we'll be right next to the steps."

Laura pulled over into the parking space. Smiling at each other, they got out and made their way up the stairs. Frank laced his arm around Laura's tiny waist, drinking in the scent of her fragrance. At the room, he unlocked the door and showed her through.

"Not bad," said Laura, dropping her purse beside the bed. She turned around, allowing Frank to slip the fur parka from off her shoulders. As he moved to take her coat to the closet, she reached around, grabbing his tie, sidling up to him. With her other hand, she firmly grasped his manhood. She pulled him close and kissed him. Then she began to work his belt loose.

A loud moan escaped Frank's lips as Laura worked her soft hands along the smooth skin of his hardness, freeing it of his trousers. Then as though he were a child, unable to dress or undress himself, her hands went to his suit coat, his tie, and then the buttons of his shirt.

Laura pressed Frank down onto the bed, where she pulled his pants and shoes away. Then, her eyes holding him captive, Laura stepped back. With a provocative, sensual rhythm, she removed her clothing, move by sensuous move, until she stood before Frank wearing only her stunning beauty.

"Frank, I think you said something about being up to performing the task," said Laura, swinging herself around him and onto the bed. "Can you finish what you started?"

Spreading her legs she guided his head down to her mound of dark hair, her lips moist and inviting. There was the slight scent of her perfume, her heat racing up his nostrils. Delicate at first, his tongue explored her. From there, both his passion and fervor grew. Frank could feel her long arms, reaching to work her fingers along his neck. He continued with his efforts to please her; driven to greater urgency by euphonious moans that she uttered.

Once, then twice, Frank felt his heart skip. Something made him want to grab her hands, push them away from his neck where her soft fingers continued what had become an irritating massage. The moment was just too powerful, too wonderful, however, for him to tell her to stop. If his heart was going to fail him, then perhaps this was how he would prefer it to happen.

"Frank, I want you inside of me," Laura groaned. "Oh, please do it, now."

Frank did not hesitate. Immediately he placed himself over her, felt her hands guiding him into her. Again she pressed her fingers into the side of his neck. He plunged himself deep into the hot fire of her canal; and did so repeatedly. He wanted to tell her to leave his neck alone, but was afraid that it would detract from the moment. Instead, he concentrated on pleasing her. Suddenly, all was a blur, her lovely face fading from his sight. His strength vanished as he suddenly felt a crushing pressure in his chest.

He tried to tell her about the nitroglycerin tablets in his jacket pocket. Whether his words were audible or not, he was unsure. At once, he felt Laura flip him over onto his back. Of that, he was glad. Frank did not want to be lying on her, perhaps die right on top of her. Die he would, however, if he did not get help very fast. Why was she still rubbing his neck? Could she not see his distress? Then her lips were pressing hard against his. He could not get enough air through his nose. Why was she kissing him when it was obvious that he was in trouble? There were those skips again. They kept coming...

Laura checked for a pulse. There was none. "Just in case you were wondering Frank," she said with a laugh, "they call it a carotid message. If you do it long enough, it brings the heart to a complete stand still. But then, by now you've figured that out."

❧ ❧ ❧

"Yes," said Cowling. He leaned back in his chair. If he could only manage to make it through tomorrow it would all work as planned. Was Abdul moving against him? If so, how much did he know? It could be another company. Though it was unlikely that another company would use murder so freely.

"Sir, it's Frank Baker," said Edna.

"Tell him we'll meet and vote tomorrow," said Cowling. "I don't have the patience for him at the moment."

"Frank Baker the third," said Edna. "He sounds very upset."

Suddenly a chill permeated Cowling's office. "Put him through."

"Young Frank, how are you doing?" asked Cowling. In an instant Cowling's body stiffened, his knuckles white from where he grasped the phone. When he finished with the son of his long time friend and fellow Board member on Energy International's Board of Directors, he pushed the button to ring Edna's phone.

"Yes, Mr. Cowling?" she said.

"Please send a letter announcing the vote to Brian Matkins," said Cowling, his voice tight as he forced each word out separately. "Have a messenger hand deliver it to him. It seems to have become required."

Young Frank had said his father had suffered an apparent heart attack in a most embarrassing circumstance in a hotel room. Evidently the woman involved and been scared and had left without even calling 9-1-1. No one knew who she was. Cowling knew that heart attacks could be made to happen. Somehow he was sure that this one had not happened all on its own.

❧ ❧ ❧

The gun bothered Stephanie. It totally fascinated Arlene. Brian's oldest daughter still did not fully understand why it was that their parents could not call them. No matter how nice the FBI agent was, the entire matter was unsettling.

Kathy, the FBI agent, had called this a safe house. The terminology was lost on Stephanie, but one thing was for sure, it was a house fully loaded. For starters, it was absolutely plush. One of the televisions in their bedroom took up nearly the entire wall. Then there was a smaller TV set, providing a thirty-two inch viewing screen. They could use it either for games or to watch something else if she and her sister could not agree on watching the same thing.

They had chosen pizza for supper. Arlene had asked for plain cheese from Pizza Hut. Stephanie had argued that they should get a fully loaded from Dominoes, saying that Arlene could pick the extras off and then it would be plain cheese. Kathy had quickly intervened and told them to not argue. She sent out to both places. They both got what they wanted, except for talking to their parents. "No phone calls," the FBI agent said. Stephanie could tell that she meant it.

Kathy had come up to them in the restroom, identifying herself as a security manager. The women's restroom at the mall had been crowded and noisy and Kathy did not seem to hesitate talking to them in front of all the other people. That somehow had made her story that their mother had collapsed and was on her way to the hospital in an ambulance more believable. Neither girl had wondered how Kathy had recognized them so easily. So that they could get out of the mall quicker, Kathy had taken them out through a service door that emptied directly into the parking lot behind the mall. There, a van was waiting for them.

Quickly ushered into the van, Kathy smiled to calm their worried nerves, and then she shattered them. Her smile had disappeared and her tone became serious. "Listen real carefully, Arlene, Stephanie. My name is Kathy Brown. I'm an FBI agent." Producing a small, black leather wallet, she showed them a badge. Stephanie, suspicious, had scrutinized it. Sure enough, it had big letters, FBI, and looked real enough.

"As you girls know, something has happened, and your mother has brought you here for protection. Have both of you heard about the shooting where your father works?" Both girls nodded in a serious manner. Kathy continued. "The FBI believes that you two girls were going to be kidnapped by Islamic terrorists who want to use you as hostages to get inside of your father's nuclear power plant. They want to blow it up like they did the World Trade Centers. We have your parents' permission to keep you safe until we capture all of the terrorists. It may take a few days."

When Stephanie had asked about why they could not talk to their parents on the phone, Kathy had explained that the terrorists were extremely sophisticated and well armed. It was highly possible that they would be able to trace any phone calls between the girls and their parents, thus undermining the plan to keep them safe. Somehow, though, Stephanie just did not buy it. They had pay per view hooked up to the big T.V. The movie would start in five minutes. She had seen it before and had not particularly liked it, but now she had a sudden urge to watch it again. Going to the refrigerator, she took out a cream soda and settled down for a second viewing of Mel Gibson in "Ransom".

Chapter Thirty-two
Friday, December 11
Jefferson Davis Nuclear Power Station

"Ray Cisco," said Ralston. "If you don't feel like you can do the job, then I'll get the next man in line to take over for you."

"Security comes under the V.P. of Administration," said a defiant Ray. "You don't have the authority to replace me."

"Perhaps," said the annoyed Station Manager. "But I've damn sure got enough clout to call Travis Harding up and tell him that I want you replaced. Care to test me on it?"

"Look, Lloyd, I'm only concerned about the safety of this plant and ultimately the people that work here and the public that lives near it," said Ray. For a moment, there had been an urge to buck the Station Manager. Then he remembered how much he would need a job and good medical benefits for the life that was growing within Laura's belly. "For what it could save us, extra security officers will be cheap."

"Ray," said Ralston, suddenly softening his words. "I know that what happened to Jack has got you guys in Security on edge. Hell, that's the nature of your work. But when there was a threat of terrorists during the Gulf War the State Department issued warnings. We've had warning after warning blown up our ass since September 11th. Al Qaeda has been dismantled; we've made the necessary security upgrades. No one has said jack shit about a possible attack. Come on, Ray. Work with me. You're the best man for the job. I really want you running our security operation while Jack is gone. Hopefully he'll come back in a couple of months and take it off your hands. If he doesn't, then I hope you take the job permanently." Ralston started to turn away, then suddenly seemed as if he needed to get something off his chest.

"I'm going to level with you, Ray," said the Station Manager. "I actually discussed beefing up security with Harding the morning after Jack was hit. After I rolled over and tried to go back to sleep, I decided it wasn't my place to second-guess you. Harding said absolutely not. But I'm Station Manager, I could buck him if I so chose. But with all the damn bad publicity we've had from corporate infighting, I've decided not to. Just keep it under your hat, Ray. You're the best man for this job. And if something does go down, God forbid, I want you calling the shots. I'll take responsibility for my decision."

Ray nodded, and then turned and left. There really was nothing else to do; except to make sure that everyone was performing up to their absolute best. As he walked past Laura's desk, she looked up and smiled. He smiled back, glancing down at her belly and thinking of the wondrous life that was forming inside. For a few brief seconds Ray forgot about the Station Manager's decision. Though it would be a good while longer before she showed, looking at where he had planted his seed made him feel as though he was sitting on top of the world.

"You feeling alright?" he asked, bending over to whisper his question. "You looked pretty ill when you got up this morning."

"I'm feeling okay, now," she said. "You're the one that looks stressed out. What happened?"

"I asked for more security," said Ray. "They won't give it to me."

"You really think someone would try to get in here and blow up the plant or something?" asked Laura, her voice low.

"Not really, I guess," said Ray. "It's just that what happened to Danny Miller and then Jack has me bothered."

"Is there any evidence that Jack was deliberately set up?" asked Laura, her dark eyes searching Ray's.

"Only the bogus message on his pager," said Ray. "The police have said it could have been a ploy to get out of the house to go see a woman that coincided with a drunk driver and a flat tire. They never found the pager to verify whether it had been activated."

"Jack would never step out on his wife would he?" asked Laura.

"Ah, hell, He had something going a few years back," said Ray. "Shit, aren't I a fine one to talk? Ellen found out about it, though. Jack swore he'd never do it again. I think that I'd have known about it. But you never know."

"Can't teach an old dog new tricks," said Laura with a sad shake of her head. "I hope that he wasn't seeing someone, though. And I sure hope that it was an accident."

Ray went back to his office. Just as quick as Laura had improved his disposition, it turned sour again out of her presence. Something was not right. If Jack was having an affair Ray would have known about it. He took Rachel

Lambert's business card out of his wallet and dialed the number.

"Hello," said Rachel. Her voice sounded groggy, as though she was just waking up.

"This is Ray Cisco at the Jefferson Davis Nuclear Power Station," said Ray. "Do you have a moment?"

"Sure. What's up?" asked Rachel.

"I offered you a tour," said Ray. "Feel like taking it today?"

"Why not," said Rachel. "You have to promise that no one will shoot at me. Seems to happen to me a lot."

"I promise," said Ray. At least he hoped that no one would be doing any shooting here today. It seemed like a good idea to show Lambert around. He might also find out if she knew more than she had told him earlier. His impression was that she knew more than she was telling. Certainly, she did not down play his concern about the power station's safety.

"Give me an hour," said Rachel. "How do I get in to see you?"

"Just show up," said Ray. "There's visitor parking not to far from the security building. No one gets to park close anymore. You'll see a visitor's entrance. Everything's well marked. Let Laura out front know you're here to see me and I'll get you in. I'll authorize you to carry your firearm."

❦ ❦ ❦

Clyde swung the boom around in expert fashion as he lined the crane up to make the first official lift of the Unit I refueling outage. It was the first time for seventeen years that a Jefferson Davis Nuclear Power Station Mechanic had operated one of the big cranes during a refueling outage. It was a job, prior to the major cutbacks, that was considered best left to the unionized, construction heavy equipment operators. That he was the only man in Richmond Nuclear who was qualified, and damn good, at operating the large piece of equipment was certainly Clyde's good fortune.

Dropping the large hook down slowly to the first thick, concrete missile shield that protected the reactor containment building opening, Clyde had to keep his eyes on several things at one time. First and foremost, he had to keep his eyes on the signalman. Unfortunately, the rest of the crew that he was working with did not possess the same expertise at crane operation and rigging. That was especially evident when it came to the signalmen. The plural usage of that term was the problem. Only one person, preferably someone who knew what they were doing, was supposed to signal the crane

301

operator. At the moment, at least four different mechanics were waving their hands, pointing with multiple fingers and clenching fists that represented the traditional 'stop' signal. Therefore, that was what he did. He stopped all movement of the crane.

Now other mechanics, six to be exact, were making extraneous hand signals and yelling. Of course, he could not hear a thing that they said over the sound of the diesel engine located behind his cab. Within seconds, John Anderson 'Batman' approached the cab. He was not walking towards where Clyde now sat with his feet propped up inside the crane, nor did he run, he was stomping. Clyde could not be more pleased as he watched the foreman's angry glare grow closer. First Batman had to climb down the ladder from the Equipment Hatch platform, where the missile shields and Personnel Escape Trunk were located. Then he would have to walk about twenty yards to where the crane sat. Forty seconds, given the exceptional burst of energy that Batman was displaying in his fit of anger, and then there would be a war. Batman would come in charging with a verbal barrage. Clyde waited. He would have the foreman stepping all over his metaphorical land mines.

"What the fuck is wrong with you?" yelled Batman. He panted from climbing down the ladder and was flushed with anger. "Those god damned missile shields gotta be off in three fucking hours. Just what the hell do you think you're doing?"

"Operating this crane like it's meant to be operated," said Clyde, his feet still propped up. "I don't think you've ever taken the time to get qualified or find out the requirements for operating a crane. If you had a fucking clue as to how it works, you'd know that one, one fucking person gives the crane operator signals. You dumb asshole, you've got four damn guys up there pointing this way and that, trying to tell me which way to go. It ain't safe. You're the only one not trying to signal me, and that's only because you've got you're thumb stuck up your ass."

"I'm sick and tired of your shit," muttered Batman. He turned and headed back towards the platform. "I'm really fucking tired of your god damned shit."

Rachel moved about slowly at first. Looking at her watch, she shook her head. Eight forty-five; she certainly had not meant to sleep this late. Rolling out of bed, she was already dressed in sweats. She picked up the 9 mm Beretta and padded quietly to her bedroom door. There, she disarmed the personnel alarms that she had connected to it. Taking a deep breath, she yanked the door open; nothing. Stepping into the other rooms one by one, Rachel was able to satisfy herself that no one beside herself was in the apartment.

Heating up an English muffin in the toaster oven and chasing it down with a glass of smooth, cold milk, Rachel finished dressing. She would have liked to have brought her brother along on her trip to the power station, but Les had to go back on duty due to a couple of other deputies being out with the flu.

Ten minutes later, Rachel gave the Celica a good going over, satisfying herself that no one had tampered with it. Then she headed into the Hanover countryside. On route 301, she saw the signs that directed her to the Jefferson Davis Nuclear Power Station access road. The power station was located in the midst of rich farmland and woods. She had skied on its man made lake and had seen the plant in the distance. This, however, would be her first time visiting the site other than her brief meeting with Matkins at its outlying visitor's center.

Turning onto the access road, she came up behind a lumbering flatbed truck carrying long, horizontal cylinders. Drawing closer, she saw that the cylinders were labeled 'Liquid Nitrogen'.

"Thank goodness," she muttered to herself as she breathed a sigh of relief. "The last thing I want to do is to follow a truck fully loaded with explosive hydrogen into a nuclear power station."

Unfortunately, she could find no place to pass the truck. Having no other choice, she followed it to the guard post where the truck pulled over into a lane marked 'Shipments Only'. Rachel drove on up to the post where a Security Officer stepped out and signaled her to stop. A separate security officer was stopping the truck. Both were armed with pistol and M-16. Behind them, in a sand-bagged shelter was another security officer, similarly armed and whose sole purpose was to provide cover for the 'just in case' situation. She was sure the M-16s and extra guard were a post-September 11th addition.

"Rachel Lambert," she said reaching into her purse for her I.D. She flashed both her P.I. badge and her driver's license at the guard.

"Okay," said the Officer, nodding his acceptance of her I.D. "We were told to expect you. Just keep on going straight. The Security Building is the one with the flags in front of it. There is visitor's parking there. Here's your parking pass." He handed her the pass to put on her dash.

"Thanks," she said. "Do I need to tell you if I'm carrying a firearm?"

"Just getting ready to ask you," said the Security Officer. "Mr. Cisco said that we're to consider you law enforcement. That means that you won't be required to check your side arm in. However, I do have to ask you to check in any other weapons." He gave her a grin. "You know, assault rifles, hand held missile launcher. The serious stuff."

"Left the serious stuff back at the office," said Rachel, returning the grin. "I've got a 9 mm Beretta in my purse."

"That's fine. I like a lady with class," said the Officer. "Go on inside. Cisco's waiting for you."

Rachel followed a well-paved road that took her closer and closer to the large domed structures. Those, she knew from looking at the exhibits at the visitor's center, housed the nuclear reactors. Two layers of chain fence, topped with razor wire, surrounded the entire compound. As she neared the facility, large concrete barriers rerouted traffic away from the protected area's main gate. Vehicles wishing to enter the compound, she realized, were stopped considerable distance from the plant so that they could be searched. Only once security had thoroughly searched them for explosives and cleared them to enter the plant, did they then allow them to proceed. It was all actually very impressive, resembling the military's Threat Condition Delta that was imposed during times of extreme danger to ensure safety of its bases. The liquid nitrogen truck that she had been stuck behind was pulling into the sally port where security would search it.

A security officer saw the visitor's pass displayed on her dash and directed Rachel past the search area and into a parking lot nearly two blocks from the entrance to the station. Her vehicle was not searched, but nor was it allowed close enough to the power station to cause damage had it been packed with high explosives. She easily found an empty visitor's spot and parked. About thirty feet away, security officers were preparing to search the liquid nitrogen truck before letting it into the power station.

A security officer directed the truck's driver to get out of the vehicle and to a waiting area. The driver at first caught Rachel's attention because of his dark complexion. He could have been Hispanic or Arabic. Some would have called her interest in him racial profiling. She called it staying alive. After all, men with dark complexions had twice tried to kill her recently.

"Buenos días, Señora," said the driver of the truck as he saw her looking their way.

A sense of embarrassment swept over Rachel. "Buenos días," she replied. "Como estas?"

"Muy bien," answered the driver. "Y tu?"

"Muy bien," said Rachel. She smiled and then headed for the station entrance.

Some distance from where Rachel parked was a door with a large sign above it that read 'Visitors'. She made her way towards it, becoming more and more aware of the massive concrete domes that towered over her on the other side of the fence. She also became more aware of the long line of workers lined up at the visitors' entrance. That line did not appear to be moving quickly. However, as she reached the entrance, she saw that the visitors' entrance had a sign directing temporary employees to enter through the left-hand door and visitors to enter through the right. Rachel breathed a sigh of relief at not having to file in behind 15 smoking and joking hardhats. Several of them whistled as she walked by and a couple more made lewd comments, all of which she ignored.

Stepping through the door, Rachel focused on getting her bearings. A woman sat at a desk in the corner. She appeared to be processing temporary badges, probably for the hardhats waiting in line. This must be Laura who Ray had referred to.

"Good morning," said Rachel, stepping up to the desk. "I'm Rachel Lambert. I have an appointment to meet with Ray Cisco in Security."

Fatima had been aware of the woman entering through the visitor entrance and approaching her desk. However, she had not bothered to glance up from her work. When she heard Rachel identify herself, it was as if someone had kicked her in the stomach. With a quick look at the visitor's schedule, she saw the private investigator's name. Ray must have come out and penciled it in earlier while she was in the ladies room.

Rachel saw the woman's startled look. "Sorry," she said. "I didn't mean to sneak up on you." She said it as a joke to break the ice. However, even as she said it, she felt a sense of alarm. She could not figure out where it was coming from. Automatically, Rachel took in everything about the woman. Her nametag identified her as Laura McClish; obviously the woman Ray had told her who would be out front. She had a deep olive complexion, dark eyes and jet-black hair; all of which gave her extraordinary beauty. Laura certainly appeared Mediterranean; and definitely something familiar about her. Rachel searched her memory, trying to figure out where she could have met or seen her. Glancing down at the table, she saw that Ms. McClish was making a temporary badge for Jose Herrera.

Fatima had been so preoccupied this morning that she had not bothered to check the list of scheduled visitors. The moment was at hand, and the visitor's list was not at all significant in the grand scheme. Rachel Lambert's unexpected appearance, however, proved her to be in error in that respect. Could this be mere coincidence, or did she know more than Fatima and Abdul had thought?

"I'll need to see your badge," said Fatima. She smiled pleasantly at the private investigator that should have been dead days ago.

"Of course," said Rachel. "How did you know I'm law enforcement?" Most likely, Ray had told her. However, if so, then why the look of total surprise, almost shock when she had arrived?

Fatima cursed her own stupidity, but also reacted well to cover her blunder. "It says on the schedule beside your name that you're an investigator. You're not carrying a weapon are you?" Already, she had moved her hand so that the sleeve of her jacket covered the list. "This won't take but a moment." Fatima grabbed one of the blank passes, wrote Rachel's name on it and handed it to her. Each pass had a unique number so that if necessary, security could historically review visitors that had been inside the power station. Fatima was supposed to write that number beside Rachel's name. However, that would mean moving here hand and giving Rachel the chance to see that 'private investigator' had not been written beside her name.

"I have a firearm in my purse," said Rachel. "Perhaps it's noted on the schedule as well." It was obvious that McClish had moved her arm to cover Rachel's name on the schedule. She watched to see if McClish moved her arm to check.

"Okay," said Laura, pretending not to hear Lambert's comment about the schedule. There had never been a situation in all her operations that she had been so close to panic. Lambert knew something was amiss about her. It would only take so long before she realized that she was the woman Lambert had nearly ran over in Atlanta. Once that occurred, the operation would be blown if it had not yet started. She signaled for one of the Officers located behind the bulletproof glass to open the sliding door. "Go through the sliding door and the security officer there will assist you in getting into the station," she said.

"Good morning, Ms. Lambert," said a female security officer, gleaming Rachel's name from the badge that she wore. She spoke with a strong Hispanic accent. Her name tag identified her as Joella Mandoza. She nodded towards the moving conveyor belt by which she stood. "If you'll just place your purse right here, we'll send it through the x-ray. Then, we'll have you step through a detector that checks for metal and weapons. You'll need to take off anything metallic like a watch or portable phone."

"Certainly," said Rachel. She found it difficult to concentrate as she racked her brain trying to place McClish. Thus, she was thankful someone who was patient and good at giving instructions was processing her through. For the first time since all of this had begun, she realized how little she had slept. She was near exhaustion and that kept her mind from processing information at its best. A worker in front of her lay what appeared to be a box of parts on the moving conveyor belt. Following the officer's instructions, Rachel laid her purse on the device just as he had done.

The worker stepped into a gate like structure where he gazed upwards at the equivalent of a traffic light. As soon as he stepped into the gate, he paused. There was the ding of a bell and then a green light appeared. The worker then walked through the metal detector, and picked up his bag of parts. His next stop was a device where he stuck in a smart card and placed his right eye in front of a retina scanner.

Rachel's purse passed through the x-ray machine. She was about to follow the plant worker when suddenly a flurry of activity caught her attention as two armed security officers entered the area. A low, buzzing tone was emanating from the x-ray machine.

Fatima immediately realized what was happening when the red light atop the x-ray machine began flashing. Immediately she went to the door and tapped on it, attempting to get the officer inside to open it. Yet one more thing going wrong. She had been so rattled and focused on keeping Ms. Lambert from seeing the list that she had forgotten to pass on the information about her carrying a weapon. Finally, the door opened. "Joella, I'm sorry, she's Ray Cisco's special guest. I think he's authorized her to carry a weapon, but we need to call him and make sure. I'm sorry," said Fatima.

"I need to see her badge and get Ray to tell me its okay," said Joella. Softly enough that only Rachel, standing close by could hear, "que tonta." Once McClish had left, she turned to Rachel, "Sorry about that. If she wasn't so busy stealing another woman's husband, maybe she could do her job right."

Laura went back to her desk. She could tell by Joella's tone that she was annoyed. The annoying spic acted as if she had God in her hip pocket. She had spent yesterday and most of this morning so far, listening to the officer tell how she was going straight to Hell for seducing Ray and breaking up his marriage. Joella obviously saw it as her duty to convert any poor soul who had not found the one true path to righteousness that she alone seemed to own.

"Ray's already been called," said another officer from a second bulletproofed window. "He'll be here in a moment."

Ray appeared in less than a minute on the other side of the turn-style that separated the protected area of the plant from where they conducted the searches. "I've already verified her credentials," said Ray as he stood with his arms folded. "She's cleared to bring her side arm into the protected area."

"Here you go, ma'am," said Joella.

"Thanks," said Rachel as she slung the strap of her purse over her shoulder. Then she turned to Joella and in a low voice that only Joella could hear, "si, es verdad. Ella es muy tonta." The officer seemed to flush for a second, but then grinned.

"Good morning, Ms. Lambert," said Ray. "Send her through. I'm her escort."

There was a buzzing sound at the turn-style. Realizing that it had been unlocked for her entry into the nuclear power station's protected area, Rachel quickly pushed through it.

❖ ❖ ❖

"Langley is easier to get into," said Rachel, forcing a grin. "I mean that as a compliment." She hoped she did not appear flustered. The incident with her weapon and Laura both had her feeling off balance. Should she say something to Ray about Laura McClish's strange behavior? Something told her it would not be the best move. Ray had mentioned earlier that he had left his wife and Joella had made the comment about McClish stealing another woman's husband. It would be best to get a better feel for the situation before sounding an alarm.

"We do our best," said Ray, taking Rachel's extended hand for a brief, polite handshake. "I take it that you've never been inside of a nuclear power station before."

"No, I haven't," said Rachel. "Are the nuclear reactors in those big concrete domes?"

"Yes they are," said Ray. "They're called the Reactor Containment buildings. The walls are four and one half feet thick with seven layers of high tensile strength reinforcing rod. They are completely sealed on the inside with a steel liner."

"Not easy to blow up, huh?" she whispered the question as they made their way down the hall to his office.

"Actually, even if someone managed to blow a hole in the side of a reactor containment building, there isn't necessarily a threat to the general public," said Ray. "You would also have to have a lot of other things go seriously wrong at the same time. The reactor is located below ground level; so punching a hole in the containment building still wouldn't give anyone a good shot at it. The containment buildings are built to withstand a 747 crashing into them. You hear a lot of talk about terrorists going after a nuclear power station, and the so called experts all talk about how vulnerable we are, but it's a bunch of bull. This place is not an easy target."

"Yet, you seem so concerned that not enough is being done to keep the plant safe," said Rachel.

"We're not an easy target, but they seem intent on having a nuclear station as some kind of trophy," said Ray. "The most invincible army has vulnerabilities. If and when something happens, I want a very large winning margin. The half-life of the material in those reactors is 50,000 years. No matter how safe I think this place is, I don't plan to take chances."

They entered Ray's office. From his window, there was an excellent view of the area around the power station's various buildings. A number of citations and awards, various training certificates and pictures related to the power station hung on his office walls. Notably absent were pictures of his wife or any children. On his desk was a blue coffee mug, bearing the Trident of the Navy SEALs. Beside it, was a styrofoam cup, smudged with the same color of lipstick that Laura McClish was wearing. Her ability to put pieces of the million piece jigsaw puzzle together were hindered by Ray's conversation.

"Back to your question of am I afraid of someone blowing them up," he said, waving to where the two Reactor Containment Buildings could be seen from his window. "I was a Navy SEAL. Let me loose in here with the right stuff and the ability to get into vital areas and, yeah, I could bring the place down. But, the trick is getting inside with the right stuff and getting into our vital areas.

"Our function is to prevent such entry. Make sure that no one has unimpeded access to get explosives or firearms into the power station. Giving Murphy's law the benefit of the doubt, if they do manage to get past us, they absolutely wouldn't have the mobility within the plant to do anything which would actually endanger the public. The Department of Defense, analysts for the Nuclear Regulatory Commission and experts from the CIA's Science and Technology group have told us that a terrorist would have to have almost free rein, high explosives and plenty of time on their hands in order to damage the nuclear core and endanger the public."

"But do you really have the resources to prevent that mobility?" asked Rachel. "From what I've heard you say, from what I've learned from other sources, that ability may have been compromised by the cutbacks in security."

"Stretching it very thin is what Corporate has done," said Ray, sitting back in his chair and crossing his legs. "But...still I think we could respond."

"Thinking you can respond isn't the same as saying you're confident that you can respond," said Rachel. It was a perfect picture. Put a beautiful woman in a low key, yet strategic position within the Security Department, someone significant will fall for her. Get the technician that maintains the security system to rig it, get rid of him. Keep the significant someone in a significant position by eliminating other significant individuals. Those were some major pieces of this puzzle and it certainly seemed that they fit just where she had put them.

Would Ray buy it? Not a chance. Not yet, anyway. She had to come up with some concrete evidence first. To say anything at this point would alienate her from the best ally she had. And there were a couple of pieces of the puzzle that did not fit. Islamic terrorist groups used women for very low-level operations, such as suicide bombing missions. It would be very out of profile for them to center a complex and critical operation such as attacking a nuclear power station around a woman. The amount of security screening done for McClish to hold a security position would be massive. It would be nearly impossible for someone with terrorist ties to survive such scrutiny.

Rachel decided that she would check with some contacts from her CIA days that were working for Homeland Security. It would be interesting to see if they had any information on females being used by Islamic terror groups. She could paint the picture for them as she was seeing it; it might correlate to something they were aware of. Or, they might not see it as she did. It was always good to get someone else's perspective. Rarely was a situation at the critical point where there was not time to get the facts right before taking action. Ray was talking again, she tuned in to what he was saying.

"Can't argue with you. There are the shootings you were involved in, Miller's bizarre murder and what happened to Jack. Since you've never been here before, you wouldn't be able to tell that there are four hundred and forty-one extra people running around here at the moment. Some of them are on the night shift. We are in what we call a refueling outage. Unit 1 reactor and its systems are shut down so that we can replace the nuclear fuel in it and perform maintenance. Both reactor units came down unexpectedly by means that we never really verified. Management convinced the NRC that it was a maintenance problem, but I know for a fact that was never proven."

"Was that before or after the technician's murder," asked Rachel. He had created an opening. Certainly, he would never believe anything she would tell him about McClish, but what if she could get him to put the pieces of the puzzled together for himself.

Rachel cast a studious glance back out of Ray's window, giving him a moment to consider her question. She had not known about the unexplained reactor shutdowns. That was simply one more piece of the puzzle. The big truck with the nitrogen cylinders was being allowed in, driven by one of the Latinos. She was somewhat surprised that they had been able to get through security so fast.

"Christ," said Ray. "I never gave it a thought." He picked up the phone and dialed the number for the Maintenance Superintendent. "Jed, who do we have that's taking care of CAS now? Okay, here's what I want him to do. I want him to check the system from his end. I want to find out if there is any chance that Danny Miller could have rigged the system to allow someone to access vital areas and cause those reactor trips. And Jed, I don't want what he's doing to get out. If I go home tonight and see us on CNN... Okay, thanks."

"If he did," said Rachel, "then there has to be a reason. The reactor shutdowns didn't cause any damage did they?"

Ray shook his head. "No," he said. "But if he was able to do that, it means he may have provided a means to get unauthorized individuals either into the station or into vital areas. With the outage going on and all these extra people, it would be perfect cover."

"They told me it would take at the minimum an hour to see if Miller tampered with the system," said Ray. "Damn it, I should secure all access until I find out."

"Why don't you?" asked Rachel.

"Management would have a cow and probably my job," said Ray. He could feel his frustration growing. If Laura was not pregnant with his child and he did not desperately need this job, he would have risked management's wrath. However, all his life he had done the right thing. It was the reason Donna was the way she was; it was the reason he had never taken his children to Disney World. No, he would wait it out until he had something solid. An hour or so was not unreasonable.

"Even if Miller rigged the system," said Ray. "It's impossible for whoever gained access to get weapons or explosives inside. You experienced how we do things when they checked your purse out front. We're like that with everything that comes in here. For instance, that truck out there." He indicated the truck carrying the liquid nitrogen. "My people go over it with a fine tooth comb before it gets inside. Its driver is required to pass a security background check and then is issued a smart card with a template of his iris on it. We give him a temporary security badge every time he makes a delivery and require him to pass a comparison of his retina to the one on the smart card. Still, we constantly ask ourselves, what if. And with what's been going on, my people are being even more alert. I've had several complaints today because my officers have performed a higher number of random frisks of people entering the station."

"You said you use a smart card with the individual's iris template on it," said Rachel. "What's to keep someone from creating a card and putting their own iris on it?"

"That can't be done," said Ray. "Each card has a serial number that's in our access control database. Those cards are safeguarded and inventoried. Also, it takes special software that only we have to put the iris on the card and then read it."

"Would Danny Miller have had access to the cards and to the software?" asked Rachel.

Ray nodded. "We do inventories with independent verification of the results. Let me find out if we've done one since Danny's murder." He picked up the phone. "Laura, this is Ray. Check for me and see when the last time we inventoried our access control card stock. I need to know immediately. Thanks." Then he hung up the phone. "Three days ago. No discrepancies."

Rachel felt a sense of frustration as she realized that Ray was asking Laura McClish for the information. "How well do you know the woman who processed me in here? Laura."

"Quite well," said Ray, caught off-guard by the question.

"Well enough to risk the safety of this power station?" asked Rachel, watching his face to see what kind of reaction her comment elicited. She was taking a chance.

Ray could feel the incriminating flush that reddened his face. "Yeah," said Ray. "I know her well enough to tell you that she's a trustworthy member of our security team. Just a young woman making ends meet; like most of us. Anyone working in security has the equivalent of a Secret security clearance."

"Ray, you're involved with her," said Rachel. This was not going to go over well, but if there was a card or cards missing, McClish was not the one to trust on whether or not an inventory had been performed since Miller's murder.

"That's no one's business but hers and mine," snapped Ray. There was a silence as he and Rachel stared at each other. "I applaud your wonderful powers of deduction Ms. Sherlock Holmes, but she's not relevant to any of this."

Rachel was shocked at Ray's sudden anger. He also looked startled at her question. It made her think of a phrase 'like a deer caught in the headlights.' Then it hit her, the startled look on the face of the woman whom she had almost ran over in Atlanta. "Wednesday, December the 2nd, Laura McClish wasn't here. She gave you a reason why she had to be out of town."

Ray's anger was flaring and he was battling to maintain control. Rachel Lambert had seemed the only ally he had, but was suddenly attacking the woman he loved. "Bull shit," he hissed. He glanced down at his calendar. December 2nd, Laura had gone to New York to be with her sick mother. "How does Atlanta fit into this?" he asked. He had spent enough time in the Mid East to realize that Laura's features were distinctly Mediterranean. Besides, Rachel had said too much that made sense for him to discount her. He wanted to discount her, but he had not survived Special Ops by acting on emotion.

It was all or nothing. Fifty thousand years of uninhabitable Virginia soil seemed reason enough to violate client confidentiality.

"Whatever's going on is at more than one level," said Rachel. "You're Senior VP is being blackmailed. He was having an affair in Atlanta and the woman was murdered. Whoever did it has it setup so that it'll look like he did it if they produce a tape they made. I don't know how that fits in with a possible attack on this facility, but it's all tied together. I was following Matkins, hired by his wife because she wanted evidence of his cheating. Whoever set him up thinks I saw something. That's why they've tried twice to kill me. Yesterday, Matkins' daughters were kidnapped. Do you see how serious this is?"

"How about that tour I promised?" asked a visibly shaken Ray. "I just need to walk and clear my head." Taking a hardhat and a pair of safety glasses from a desk drawer, Ray handed them to Rachel. When he came back, he would discreetly have someone else verify the inventory had been done when Laura said it was. There was room for doubt now. Laura had not obtained her position through normal channels. Instead, Travis Harding had created her position and given her the job with the mere stroke of a pen. He trusted Harding no further than he could throw him. He would also perform verification of Laura's security background check. If Harding had falsified it, he would have his ass. Unfortunately, where did that leave him with Laura and the baby?

"Jesus," whispered Ray, barely loud enough for Rachel to hear. If Laura was somehow mixed up in all this, could she be responsible for what had happened to Jack Evans? After all, the accident had happened after he told her that Jack was going to let her go.

"Ray, are you all right?" asked Rachel. "Put it in perspective. I want you to question, to consider what could be going on. Everything could be just a coincidence. Don't accept it as fact, not yet." She paused, watching Ray. It was likely that he was placing pieces of the puzzle that she was not even aware of. "Would it be all right if I made a quick call?"

"Sure," said Ray. "Use my phone. Dial 9 to get an outside line. I'll wait out in the hall." He welcomed a few moments alone.

"Thanks," said Rachel. She laid the hardhat and glasses on desk and dialed the Hanover Sheriff's Office.

"Hello. Is Les Lambert available please?" she asked. Things were coming together at a rapid pace. However, there was nothing concrete that Ray could use to button up the station and justify maximum security. She had startled Laura McClish earlier, taking her by total surprise. If Laura McClish was a crucial component of an attack on this station, then it did not seem likely that she should be caught off guard so easily. Not unless she was pre-occupied, as in this was the day that their attack would unfold. Suddenly it donned on her that this was the day Cowling would sell Richmond Nuclear. Yes, if an attack were to happen, it would be today. "No? Well, this is his sister. Get in touch with him as quick as you can and tell him to call me on my cell phone. Tell him it's very, very urgent. Thanks."

Chapter Thirty-three
Friday, December 11th
Jefferson Davis Nuclear Power Station

The liquid nitrogen shipment was actually due in two days. It came in on a monthly basis with a purchase order that called for direct delivery. That meant that the shipment did not have to go through the warehouse receipt process. Nicholson Gas Products made the monthly delivery, verifying the amount delivered with one of the Operations Coordinators. Outage related tasks would likely have these coordinators tied up, thus it was unlikely that they would notice that the shipment was on site. Even if they did, there were other uses during an outage for liquid nitrogen, thus, there was little chance that the shipment's arrival would draw attention. Security would normally call the Operations Coordinator when the truck arrived; today they would not.

Fatima processed the driver straight through, explaining to the Shift Security Supervisor on duty that operations had an emergency and was waiting on the shipment. Ray was the normal shift supervisor, but since he was acting as Superintendent, Security Officer Fred Millens was taking on the position as a new responsibility. She explained to Fred that such emergencies happened on a regular basis and that Ray always told her to process workers through if they had IDs. Fatima offered to handle the paper work for Mr. Herrera. That consisted of taking his shipping manifest, logging it in and contacting the Operations Coordinator. Fred was bogged down with the long line of temporary workers, each one that had to be authorized in. He signed Mr. Herrera's authorization and thanked Fatima for her assistance. She had been helping out in this manner ever since Fred took over for Ray. Thus, there was nothing out of the ordinary to draw alarm.

The only one alarmed was Fatima. Rachel had seen her in Atlanta. Though it appeared that Rachel had not immediately realized that it had been her, there had been a spark of recognition. Ali, alias Jose Herrera, stood in front of her desk. She logged in his shipping manifest, picked up the phone and pretended to call Operations. The whole time, her hands trembled just so slightly.

"How are you today?" asked Ali in his much practiced Hispanic accent.

"I'm not feeling well today," said Fatima. "But I'll make it through the day." It was a pre-arranged code. Fatima's response meant that the operation was in serious jeopardy, perhaps compromised, but to proceed anyway. In Ali's hand was the smart card that she had taken from Danny Miller. She had the temporary badge that was required to go with it, already completed. No further checks were required because non-employees who needed to enter the plant on a regular basis underwent a background check, were vetted and then issued a smart card with their iris scan on it. Their scan was also in the access control system's database. The cards were impossible to forge; the iris on the card had to match the one in the database and, of course, had to match the user's iris when they passed through the scanning device. Danny had found a way to spoof the system. The card Ali held had no Iris template on it. Instead, it had a special code that to the system indicated that a successful iris scan had occurred. The system then unlocked the door, but did not log the individual.

Fatima prayed that the card really did what Danny said it would. There had been no opportunity to test it. If it failed, then the operation would be a total wash and she and Ali would be lucky to escape.

After a few moments of pretending to do paperwork, Fatima glanced through the bulletproof glass door to where Ali was passing through the weapons detectors and getting his iris scanned. There had been a line of people, so his access had not been immediate. The waiting was nerve racking. The light above the scanner began flashing green; Ali was through.

Picking up her telephone, Fatima began dialing a pager number. The plan had been to let Ali first get in place and start hooking up hoses as though this were a normal delivery. However, since she expected Ray to discover who she really was at any moment, there was no time to wait. When she got the beep indicating that she should enter her own number, she entered 666. It seemed an appropriate number to use since they were about to strike a blow to the Great Satan that would leave a more prominent scare in America's landscape than when the World Trade Center fell.

The sliding door was left open to accommodate letting the temporary outage workers through that had been lined up. Fatima heard Ali say, "Como estas?" She glanced up and saw that he was addressing Joella. "Allah be merciful," Fatima whispered to herself.

Ali had been educated in the US at the University of Virginia. His English was as good as or better than her own was. In addition, he had three years of Spanish under his belt and he spoke it well. He had in fact, worked four years in Spain, training the Basque resistance there. Joella was of Mexican decent from southern California. His Spanish would fool most Americans into thinking he was Mexican, but not a Mexican-American.

Fatima heard Joella let loose a burst of verbiage in her native tongue. It came out fast and with a strong accent. To her horror, Ali just stood there, dumbfounded. It was obvious that he had not understood a thing she said.

Fatima leapt from her seat. "Joella," she snapped. "Operations is screaming for that truckload of nitrogen. You can flirt with him on your own time!"

Joella shot her a look meant to kill. Ali mumbled his apologies and appeared grateful for a way out of his predicament. Giving Ali a cover as a Hispanic seemed a good choice. Having an Arab-American driver deliver the load of liquid nitrogen had seemed like a bad idea.

Fatima returned to her desk. She realized that Joella and the security officer behind the bulletproof glass were watching her, but Ali was through security and was getting in his truck. The plan was in motion. Fatima shook her head. In the first World Trade Center bombing, the plot was blown by one of the team going back to get his deposit on the blown up van; one of the September 11 team had nearly exposed their plan by trying to get cheaper training rates by telling the flight school that he did not need to learn how to land. Now, there was Ali, almost taking the cover off of a perfectly planned operation by speaking in Spanish to a security officer of Mexican descent. Perhaps, she thought, there needed to be an IQ requirement for terrorists.

"Hanover to 118," Les heard the dispatcher calling him. He was just about finished with his traffic stop. It was an eighty-three year old lady driving a Cadillac with a brake light out. Les had intended to follow her to her next stop so that he could tell her to get it fixed. He had had no intention of pulling her over for it. He had been able to tell from his car that she was elderly and barely able to see over the steering wheel, so he did not want to do anything to frighten her.

Then she had gone through the stop sign. Straight through it, not even slowing down, let alone stopping. Fortunately, the driver coming towards the intersection had been alert enough to realize what was happening. Les had

had no choice at that point but to flip on his lights and pull her. However, she did not pull over. After following her for about half a mile, he finally realized that she had probably not glanced up at her rearview mirror since she had bought the car, so he gave her the siren. She did not flinch. He stayed behind her for a full mile and a half until he decided that it looked too damned ridiculous to drive thirty miles per hour in pursuit of a white caddie with flashing blue lights and siren.

Dispatch had chuckled over the radio when he described his dilemma. He told them that he was just going to turn off his lights and siren and follow her until she either ran out of gas or stopped somewhere. Finally, she had pulled into the shopping center. There he had given her a choice, be taken into custody for reckless driving and failure to stop for a police officer or tell him who he could have dispatch call to come and take her home. For a few tense moments, Les had thought that she was going to force the issue and he really would have to haul her in. After a few moments of back and forth, she had seen he meant business. Her brother would come for her. Les told her that her car keys would be at the Sheriff's Office. He did not have the heart to tell her that he would also document the situation and try to get the court to remove her driver's license.

"118, go ahead Hanover," said Les, keying his hand held as he walked back to his car.

"Sheriff wants to know if CNN is going to air your thirty mile per hour, light and siren pursuit of a white caddie on Headline news tonight?" asked dispatch. "We think this will beat the low speed pursuit of O.J."

"Wouldn't surprise me," said Les. "By the way I'm bringing her car keys back to the Office."

"10-4," acknowledged dispatch. "Got two messages for you. Deputy Bernhart from Caroline County left a message for you to call him. Said he had some important information regarding the hit and run. Said to call him as soon as you could. Your sister called, too. Said call her on her cell phone. Also said it was urgent."

"10-4," said Les. "I'll be 10-17 to the Office to give you these car keys and make my calls."

Les was surprised to hear anything back from Caroline County regarding Jack Evans' hit and run. They had been very closed minded about the possibility of attempted murder and any connection to the power station. However, they were still hoping for leads to find the party responsible for hitting Evans. The accident had outraged citizens of the county.

The question was which call should he make first? His sister had left the message that calling her was urgent, but he opted to call Caroline County first. Perhaps they had discovered something that he would want to pass on to Rachel. As soon as he got to the office, he made the first call.

"Caroline County Sheriff's Office."

"Good morning," said Les. "This is Deputy Lambert in Hanover County. I have a message to call Deputy Bernhart."

"Right. He's in with Sheriff Wiggins," said the dispatcher. "Let me transfer you."

"This is Sheriff Wiggins," came an answer after a couple of rings. It was a voice coarse from years of smoking. "Bernhart is sitting here. I've got you on the speaker phone. Sounds like you've had an interesting morning. We were listening to the big chase here on the scanner."

"What do you think, shall we put gray flags on our antennas to protest old folks who refuse to quit driving when they can't see or hear?" asked Les, attempting to find the humor in the fact that he had been entertainment for scanner land in several counties.

"Unfortunately, we always come out looking like the bad guys in these situations it seems," Les recognized Bernhart's voice. "Worked an accident last week where two teenagers were killed by someone who should have been taken off the road years ago. It's all in public perception, though."

"Say, it sounds like you have something new on the Evans case," said Les, anxious to find out what they had and to call his sister.

"Sheriff and I are talking right now about where to go with this thing," said Bernhart. "Your instincts were right. I had to go to MCV this morning to take care of some paperwork on the case. The neurologist who's treating Evan's head injury told me something that really changed the perspective.

"The head injury that has Evans in his coma doesn't appear to come from the impact of the car. Just so happens that this neurologist has seen x-rays from a similar skull fracture. One that Richmond P.D. inflicted on a man while breaking up a brawl. It was done with one of the mag-lights like what we carry. There was one sitting beside Evans' car. We're getting it over to the State Crime Lab today. To be real honest, though, we didn't deal with this as though it was anything but a hit and run. The flashlight hasn't been handled in a way to really preserve evidence."

"How is Evans doing," asked Les. He knew that it would take days to get anything back on fingerprints from the flashlight. And, it was unlikely, just as Bernhart hinted, that it would be anything useful.

"Lot better providing his wife doesn't beat him up alongside the head," said Bernhart with a slight chuckle.

"Why's that?" asked Les.

"He's still pretty much out of it, but he keeps saying a name. Sounds like 'Laura'," said Bernhart. "Let us know if you can figure out who she is. She might be someone we need to question. Or perhaps she has a husband that we need to ask a few questions."

Ali crawled back into the truck. He was in a near panic. First, Fatima gives him the code that the operation has likely been compromised. It was anyone's guess as to what that really meant. Any moment now, he expected to see security officers drawing their weapons. He had been vehemently opposed to using a woman. It was not Allah's design for a woman to be a warrior. Somehow, Fatima had slipped. If the mission failed, it would be due to her.

The Officers searching his rig had not questioned the hydraulic jacks in the tool compartment. Nor had they been any the wiser to the fact that the liquid nitrogen cylinders contained something other than liquid nitrogen. A fresh coat of paint on the tanks, after the ends were in place, adequately hid the fact that some serious alterations had taken place.

Ali had come out of the sally port and had taken a left. As much as he hated to, he glanced down at the map. It showed a right. He made the turn that took him between the Radioactive Waste Processing Building and the Reactor Containment Buildings. The Nitrogen Gas Supply System was supposed to be on a concrete slab. There were a lot of concrete slabs with equipment on them. Ali stopped at the first one, then realized that it was merely a diesel driven air compressor. It was the next one down, he realized. He brought the truck up next to it and stopped. Already he could see the others coming towards him. They were supposed to wait until he rigged the hoses so as not to cause suspicion! He glanced up at the guard tower on the fence. As Fatima had told them, it was empty, its person replaced with a camera. Had there been a real person up there with a weapon, it would have caused some concern. Ali thanked Allah for such a kind mercy.

Abdul's plan had been maturing for several years. Nuclear power stations need all levels of extra workers, including those who simply sweep floors and haul hoses from one point to another. Each member of the team had worked at other nuclear stations during the past three years, gaining the familiarity needed for this mission. Many of the experienced refueling outage workers chose to work the longer outages at other plants and that had made it easier to get the members of the team hired on here when the time came. They all were working as common laborers, sweeping floors, carrying hoses and moving pieces of scaffold. Setting up identities and a network of references so that they could pass a background investigation and get unescorted access to the station had been the result of legally immigrating to the US and working mundane jobs for a period of time.

Ali recognized the Spent Fuel Building. It meant parking at an awkward angle to the nitrogen station to aim the back of the truck at it. He made several twists and turns until he was certain that he had it right. Quickly, he got out and begun laying out the metal braid hose that would normally be used to transfer liquid nitrogen from the truck to the station's supply tanks as any on looker would expect to see being done. He was aware that the rest of the team was near the truck. They had arrived too soon. Each was attempting to look busy picking up trash or moving a coil of hose. Their appearance, however, was awkward and would soon draw attention. He hurriedly wrestled the two heavy hydraulic jacks from the tool compartment. These he sat beneath brackets that were welded to the skid on which the horizontally mounted gas cylinders sat. Once they were in place, he crawled back into the cab of the truck.

Chapter Thirty-four
Friday, December 11th
Jefferson Davis Nuclear Power Station

Ray and Rachel walked around the power station. It was not a very informative tour, as Ray was deep in thought and said little. The last stop on their tour brought them into the shadow of the Reactor Containment Buildings. Close up they were mammoth. Rachel glanced just briefly at the truck carrying the liquid nitrogen. Its driver was repositioning it. Somehow, it struck her that the driver was not very familiar with the delivery; he seemed awkward, out of place and unsure of where exactly he was going. However, that likely went with having to make deliveries to a wide variety of liquid nitrogen customers.

"It's all incredibly impressive," said Rachel, attempting conversation. "What's in that green structure between the Reactor Containment Buildings?"

"That is the Spent Fuel Building," said Ray, pointing to it. He needed to snap out of it. So many questions were echoing inside him. Was Laura really pregnant? Had the security system been rigged? Had Laura tried to kill Jack? Somehow, he did not think he would end his day going home and sitting down to watch Sport Center and drinking a cold beer. "During a refueling outage like the one we're currently in with Unit I, we end up replacing approximately one-third of the fuel in the nuclear reactor. For the moment, it's kept in a pool of cooled water which is forty some feet deep."

"Why?" asked Rachel.

"Because when it comes out of the nuclear reactor, the fuel is extremely radioactive and produces an incredible amount of heat," said Ray. "Initially, they unload the entire nuclear core from the reactor and put it in the spent fuel pool. Then they put the fuel that's still good back in along with the new stuff. They only have to replace about one third of the fuel with new every eighteen months. Right now, there are several years of spent fuel stored in the pool."

"How long does the used fuel produce heat?" asked Rachel. "For the fifty thousand years?"

"I don't know for sure," said Ray. "But it produces heat for a very long time. They keep it in the pool for about a couple of years and then put it in what they call dry casks for semi-permanent storage. The Ops Department will start removing fuel from the reactor in just a few days. First, some of the fuel's radioactivity has to be allowed to decay away and the fuel has to cool some more."

"Isn't it dangerous to store the hot fuel in pools of water?" asked Rachel, finding her attention somewhat diverted by the backing and turning of the liquid nitrogen truck. Its backup warning signal made hearing difficult. "What if all the water leaks out?"

"It can't," said Ray. "The sides and bottom of the pool are six feet thick of reinforced concrete. It's completely lined with stainless steel. The worst that can happen is a loss of cooling to remove the heat from the pool. But there are back up systems to handle that, just like there are for everything else around here. Only a precision military attack could destroy the fuel pool."

"How dangerous can used fuel be?" asked Rachel.

"Well, the way I've heard it described," said Ray. "If you were inside that building and they managed to lift one of those fuel assemblies out of the water, you'd be dead before you knew what happened."

"I guess public relations isn't exactly your forte, uh," laughed Rachel.

"I just protect it," said Ray. "There are really so damn many safeguards. I mean if you look at all the years the nuclear industry has been handling nuclear fuel, they have never had a problem with safe storage."

"Sounds like back pedaling to redeem your public relations reputation to me," laughed Rachel again. She wanted to ease the tension.

"I'm hopeless, I'm afraid, when it comes to public relations," laughed Ray. "Damn, I guess you're important." Rachel's phone was ringing.

"Hello," said Rachel, taking it from her purse. "Hey, that's great. I'm standing here with Ray Cisco. Can you believe that I'm standing between two nuclear reactors as we talk? Really, has he said anything else? Actually it does. Hang on a minute." She glanced over at Ray who intuitively realized that she wanted some privacy He walked a short distance from her. "That name, Laura, that Evans is repeating? She works here in Security. I saw her outside of Tanya Madison's apartment building in Atlanta. Get in touch with one of your contacts at the FBI. Have them pull every Laura McClish from DMV. Start with Virginia, but we can't assume she has a Virginia license. See if any of the DMV photos for that name match the photo database that the

FBI has. There's no time for paperwork. Tell them there's a potential plot. Do it, Les. Something inside of me says there isn't much time."

"Ready to head back?" Ray asked coldly. He turned to walk back towards the Security Building. He intuitively knew that Rachel was having someone check up on Laura.

"Sure," said Rachel. "That was my brother, Les. Jack Evans is starting to come out of his coma."

"Really?" said Ray, momentarily forgetting his irritation.

"There is something else, too," said Rachel. Without consciously realizing it, she patted her purse, feeling the bulk of the 9 mm. There was an uncomfortable feeling that the situation was beginning to unfold and that it might gain a momentum difficult to contain. "He keeps repeating a name, over and over. 'Laura'.

"Caroline County Sheriff's Department have ruled the hit and run an attempted homicide," said Rachel. "Jack was hit over the head with his own mag-lite flashlight hard enough to fracture his skull and put him a comma. Most likely, he was then thrown into the path of a car. It makes sense that he was ambushed by someone he knew. Ray, I know that she is the same woman who I almost ran over in Atlanta when I was tailing Matkins. If she was the one who killed Matkins' lover, then she would not have any problem trying to do the same to Evans. The only question is why. How would that really compromise security here?"

There was the sudden burst of activity from Ray's radio. "Officer Lopez to Security One," came the transmission.

"Security One, go ahead," said Ray.

"Security One, we just processed that liquid nitrogen truck and its driver through security," said Joella Lopez. "The driver was passing himself off as Hispanic, but when I started talking to him in real Spanish, he didn't understand a thing I said. Ms. McClish said to get him through Security ASAP because Operations needed the Nitrogen. Everything seemed okay with the truck. Just seems fishy to me."

"Security One to Officer Lopez," replied Ray. "Dispatch someone over to the nitrogen station to stay with the driver until we figure out what's going on." He glanced over at Rachel. "I don't want to get too excited over that. Joella and Laura have sort of a thing going."

"Yeah, even I could see that there was a lot of love there when they processed me through," said Rachel.

Ray shook his head. Joella's concern was worthy. What if the truck contained hydrogen or some other explosive element instead of liquid nitrogen? It was damned close to the Spent Fuel Building. On the one hand, there was a strong urge to secure the station, evacuate people from that area. On the other hand, Ralston would hand him his head for declaring an emergency because the truck driver did not understand Joella. Maybe the truck driver was Brazilian; it would be easy to mistake him for a Spanish speaking person. Portuguese and Spanish were similar enough to sound like the same language, but dissimilar enough to make communication difficult.

"Let's head back," said Ray. "I want to make sure everything's okay. There's something I didn't tell you inside. Jack Evans was going to terminate Laura's employment because of the relationship she and I were having."

"Let me guess," said Rachel. "Right before Jack's attack, you told her." It was another piece of the puzzle that fit snuggly into place.

"I think we better get back," said Ray, increasing his pace. He was not sure how to really handle this. Did he really have proof that Laura was behind any of this? There well could be rational explanations.

"Maintenance One to Security One," came another radio transmission. It was Jed Turner. Ray hoped that this was going to be good news.

"Security One. Go ahead Maintenance One," replied Ray.

"Security One, we've completed that check you requested," said Jed. "Your concern was valid. There was a backdoor…"

"Not over the radio," Ray shot back. Damn it, he did not need the wrong ears hearing this.

"Security One, this is priority," Jed Turner shot back. "The back door has been used approximately fifteen minutes ago. Can't tell who it was, but someone has entered the protected area using a card programmed specifically for that purpose. It was the same card used during the reactor trips."

Ray was frozen to the ground on which he stood. He knew that his face gave everything away. "Security One to Security Supervisor," Ray spat into the mike that was clipped to his shirt. He started moving towards the Security Building at a very brisk walk, paying no attention at all to whether Rachel was following or not.

"Security Supervisor, go ahead Security One," came the response of the Security Officer in charge of the shift. "I heard Maintenance One's report."

Hell, thought Ray, perhaps he really did not need this job anymore anyway as he considered what he was about to do. In just five seconds he would be history as far as Richmond Nuclear was concerned; regardless of whether he was right or wrong. "Go to Security Alert. I repeat, go to Security

Alert status. Dispatch a team to that nitrogen truck and take the driver into custody. Seal the station. I want weapons out of the holsters. Issue automatic weapons and get me shooters in all towers. Do you copy?"

"Understand, go to Security Alert status," came the terse repeat back of the Security Shift Supervisor. There was the sound of commands over the radio as Ray's commands were directed to the appropriate parties.

Ray was essentially shutting down the outage. The order to have his men draw their weapons was not part of any security response plan. Instead, it was strictly a sixth sense, like when a soldier for no explained reason, throws himself to the ground a split second before an unseen enemy opens up on him. Ray's 10 mm was in his hand. "Officer Lopez," said Ray. "Escort Ms. McClish to my office and stay with her."

"Security One, acknowledge that Ms. McClish is to be taken to your office and maintained under surveillance," responded Joella.

By the end of the day, best-case scenario winning out, Ray Cisco would no longer have a job and Laura McClish would turnout to be innocent but hating his guts. The worst-case scenario would be that people would die, people that he knew and liked. And he would be responsible.

It was Dick Trane's turn at being the assigned Shift Supervisor for both reactor units. The Shift Supervisor's office was situated in the Technical Support Center. At least six supervisors, from various departments, were standing in line at his door. They all wanted him to authorize work that needed to be performed.

"Tech Support Center. This is Trane," he said, continuing to skim over a maintenance request before signing it. When he heard the words of the Security Shift Supervisor he bristled. "Okay, I'm declaring an Alert," he simply responded. He stood and walked to the door where the supervisors were lined up. "Everybody out, now."

Trane shut his door and went back to his desk and dialed the Control Room. On the second ring, the Unit II Shift Supervisor answered.

"This is Trane. Security has declared an Alert. Sound the alarm and issue instructions for all personnel to report to their work area for accountability. By my order, commence a Unit II reactor shutdown." Trane listened to the verbatim repeat back of his instructions. Within moments, he heard the alarm sounding. Ralston might not like it, but reactor safety was his responsibility until someone relieved him. Shutting down Unit II was not required, but something in Cisco's voice had alarmed him. On top of the shooting at corporate, Miller's murder and what had happened to Jack Evans, Trane was going to make the plant as safe as he could. Now he reached for the red phone. It would put him into immediate contact with the Nuclear Regulatory Headquarters. He hesitated a second. Once he made this call, Jefferson Davis Nuclear Power Station would be on CNN.

Brian Matkins picked up the phone.

"Matkins," he said. Maybe it was Brenda with news about the girls.

"Matkins, I know that you're getting ready to leave for the Board of Director's meeting to vote on the sell of your company," said an electronically disguised voice. "We have your daughters. If you want them back, then vote to sell. If you vote otherwise, and we do know that there is someone else trying to persuade you to do so, then you shall not get your daughters back."

"Who is this?" demanded Brian. "Where are my daughters? How do I know that you have them?" That he was receiving this call was not a surprise. It was bound to come before he cast his vote. What did surprise him, however, was the voice. The voice that he was now listening to was entirely different from the caller in Tanya's apartment. He had expected it to be the same person.

"Matkins, listen very carefully," said the voice. "I'm going to patch you through and let you speak to your oldest daughter. She believes that the FBI is protecting her. For her sake, don't make her think otherwise." There was a sound that Brian assumed was the phone call being transferred.

"Hello, Daddy," came the voice of his oldest daughter Stephanie. She sounded happy, definitely excited at being able to talk to him.

"Sweetheart," Brian paused, took a deep breath. "How are you? Are they treating you okay?"

"Yes," said Stephanie. "They tell me that they are FBI agents. I don't believe them. I think they're kidnappers."

"No," said Brian. "They are the FBI. Real soon, you and Arlene will be back home. How is Arlene?" It seemed awful to lie to her, but to say otherwise would have truly frightened her and perhaps made their plight worse.

"She's fine," said Stephanie. "Well, the FBI woman says that I have to say goodbye now so that the call can't be traced. Bye."

Brian breathed a little easier knowing that his daughters truly were all right. Providing he did as they told him, there was a good chance they would be released unharmed. Nevertheless, he was perplexed. What was it that the caller said, that someone else was going to try to persuade him to do otherwise? However, there had been no such contact. It was as though whoever had set him up to frame him for Tanya's murder was no longer interested in him. He felt like a pawn in damn game of chess. Of course, how he had been told to vote was evidence that Cowling was the player in control. It would take a hell of a chess master to beat the CEO of Energy International. Now he wondered why he had ever tried. Obviously, Cowling had placed the other player in check, as well. Appeared to be game over.

Fatima already had her purse in hand when she heard Ray's order come in over the radio that she had in her purse. She had gotten one of the spares from Danny several weeks ago and had kept it out of sight just for this day. She had started preparing her exit the moment Joella radioed Ray about Ali. In a moment, Joella would be coming for her. This was probably great satisfaction for the Officer who wanted to see her soul suffer eternal damnation. However, Joella would find out faster than her whose soul was damned.

"Laura, where you going?" asked Joella, coming through the sliding door. "The station is going to Alert status. You need to go with me to Ray's office."

"I have a sick Aunt," said Laura as she continued to go towards the door. "She's very ill. Ray knows that I'm leaving." She was almost at the door when she felt the firm grasp upon her arm.

"Look, maybe you lie in the same bed as my boss, but he just told me to take you to his office," said Joella. "You're coming with me even if I have to put cuffs on..."

When Fatima turned to face Joella, she looked her square in the eyes. Joella never saw the scissors that came from the pocket of her jacket. Her eyes were still locked with Fatima's as she slumped to the floor, the scissors imbedded beneath her left breast, slanting upwards to puncture her heart.

Fatima's only worry was that the attack had been uncovered before it had begun. She should have heard the explosions already.

❧ ❧ ❧

The last missile shield was off. Three hours behind schedule, they now had the Personnel Escape Trunk hooked to the crane and ready to move. Clyde had had at least three good, first class confrontations throughout the morning with Batman. The next one was soon to arrive. It was eleven fifty. Batman was about to have everyone break for lunch. "Uh, uh," said Clyde to himself. Once they hooked his crane to the load, he had to stay in the crane. Batman was going to have to pay him time and a half through lunch; and that while Clyde sat in the crane eating his lunch. He wondered why supervision did not bother reading the damn contract book. Of course the reason why, was that most of the mechanics simply did what they were told, regardless of whether it was in the contract or not. Everybody was scared stiff of the much talked about layoffs.

"I'll be god damned, go to hell," muttered Clyde. He had been watching the truck's erratic back and forth maneuvering and wondering where the hell his company had gotten him from. Now, he saw that the dark-skinned man with the liquid nitrogen truck was hooking up his own hoses! That was required to be done by a station mechanic. Well maybe he would stop right now, go over there, and write the bastard up. Clyde was one of the mechanics that normally hooked their hoses up for them. He knew the way it was supposed to work. Then he realized that he could not leave the crane; he had a load on the hook. If he left the crane, Batman might be smart enough to realize that he could write Clyde for a significant safety violation.

"Now what the fuck is that dumb ass doing?" Clyde asked out loud to only himself and the crane. The hoses were hooked up to the station connections but not to the connections on the truck. Now the driver was back in the truck. Clyde watched as driver shifted the truck around with the cab facing the Radioactive Waste Processing Building and the ass end of the truck facing between the Reactor Containment buildings. The driver got back out and put what looked like jacks under the back of the truck. Then he got back in the truck. Several contract laborers were gathered near the truck, trying to act busy. All dark complexions; maybe it was some kind of family reunion, he mused.

The truck driver was back out and using the hydraulic jacks to raise the back end of the skid. Now why the hell would he do that? The contract laborers had quit acting like they were working and had begun helping him. They were looking over at the fuel building, jacking a little more, and now everyone was getting back. Clyde knew that he had no legitimate excuse for stopping work to watch this farce or whatever the hell it was, but this was just too bizarre to ignore. What the hell were these guys doing? He saw security coming around the corner. That was probably a good thing; find out what these folks were up to.

It all went downhill after the Security Officer approached the truck. Three of the laborers jumped him and took him to the ground. Safety violation or not, Clyde was shifting out of his seat to go to the officer's aid. Though he could not hear the announcement, Clyde could hear the station alarm sounding. Something was up and it was not good. Just as he stepped outside of the cab, there was an audible pop and puff of white smoke, barely visible. The whole end of the array of gas cylinders suddenly fell to the ground. Damn if that did not look just like plastic explosive going off! He had used the stuff in the Marines when he was in Recon. And then he saw something that made him come as close to pissing his pants as anything in his forty-eight years of living. Inside three of the gas cylinders, he could see the warheads of missiles. He did not know what type, but goddamn and go to hell, those were fucking missiles! And they were aimed right at the Spent Fuel Building! That was what the damn hydraulic jacks were for, a crude aiming system. At this distance, they could not miss.

Clyde jumped back into his seat. The personnel escape trunk had not yet been brought clear of the platform. When he started raising it as fast as the hook would travel and raising the boom at the same time, his co-workers scattered. Several, hit by the two and a half ton steel escape trunk, were knocked to the floor of the platform. Batman was one of them. As he swung the crane around, the escape trunk knocked the railing down. Clyde paid no attention. He swung his load on around, the escape trunk's momentum swaying the crane precariously. For one butt hole puckering moment, Clyde thought the crane was going to topple over onto the Waste Building. With an expert touch of the controls, he brought the boom up far enough to keep that from happening.

From other cylinders on the truck, the laborers were drawing weapons and backpacks. It looked like they had AK-47's from where he sat. Some of the laborers were running towards the Unit I Reactor Containment platform, carrying their weapons and satchels. Two were exchanging gunfire with a couple of security officers. One Officer went down. The first Officer that they had jumped was on the ground, not moving. The driver was at the space between the cylinders and the cab of the truck, most likely arming and preparing to fire the missiles. Clyde had the load over the truck. It was time to lower the boom, quite literally, on terrorism. Two and a half tons of steel came crashing down on the truck, the missiles and the driver.

"Cisco!" screamed the Station Manager, walking towards Ray. "What is going on?"

"I'm declaring a Security Alert," said Ray, going into the Central Alarm Station. He was cutting through there to get to the lobby where Laura sat. "I've damn good reason to believe that we are going to be…shit!" Suddenly there was the sound of small arms fire, some of it automatic. Then there was a shudder, and the roar of an explosion, both men barely stayed on their feet as the blast shattered office windows. The security officers responding to the truck only had 10 mm handguns. They were no match for automatic weapons. It would take several minutes for the automatic weapons to be issued and those carrying them to get into position to do some good. The radio was immediately alive with unintelligible transmissions. Something about fire and explosion in the east yard, someone else had an officer down, and yet more garbled radio traffic about armed intruders. For the moment, at least, Ray knew that there was no use attempting to break in on the mostly unintelligible flood of communications. Instead, he sprinted out the door.

It certainly was not going down as they had planned. When Fatima heard the explosion, she knew that Objective One had not been achieved. If the three Hellfire missiles had cut through the concrete, releasing the water from around the highly radioactive nuclear fuel, it would have caused three separate explosions; not the one massive explosion that rocked the station. There was nothing nuclear about the cloud of black smoke that was now rising high above the domes of the Reactor Containment Buildings. Nevertheless, there was still one more objective left. Rajani would hopefully have retrieved the explosives from the truck and gotten the rest of the team in place before the explosion. They would all die. First, she prayed, they would glorify Allah.

"You, freeze!" came the deep-throated command from behind her. She had not once looked behind her after leaving the Security Building. Looking over one's shoulder and running was equivalent to a confession. How many holdup men, leaving a store or bank, could escape unidentified by merely walking or driving away in a normal manner? Thus, as always, she had simply walked from the scene of her operation.

Fatima turned her head to face Ray Cisco whose coarse command she calmly ignored. Continuing to unlock her car door, she watched him; acting as though what she was doing was perfectly normal.

"Laura, or whoever the hell you are, now freeze, damn it!" yelled Ray. He stood crouched, his weapon held in the classic two-handed shooter's pose. How could she act so calm about ramming a pair of scissors through Joella's heart? Especially someone that she had worked with for months. Either she would freeze or he would kill her.

Turning straight towards the man who had been her lover, Fatima made it unmistakably apparent that she had no weapon in her hand. Her handbag hung from her shoulder. With her eyes locked with his, she put a hand over her belly and then lowered her eyes. Then she looked back up at him. The gun in his hand shook, and then his eyes betrayed him. With no further hesitation, Fatima slid behind the wheel of her car. As calmly as though she was leaving work to go home for the evening, she put the car in gear and began to back out.

Ray held his weapon steady. There was no way he was going to kill a woman who might be carrying a child. That it might be his own, made it doubly impossible. He had to stop her, however. At this range, her tires were an easy target and would prevent her escape. Suddenly the car stopped. Ray tensed as he instinctively realized what was coming next. Well, perhaps it was best this way. Still, out of a lifetime of training, he shifted his aim back to Laura.

This was the last thing in the world Fatima wanted to do. She had never loved a man before Ray. However, she could not allow him to live. There was more than just her life at stake. Investigators would take Ray's intimate knowledge of her and connect it to other pieces of the puzzle. Eventually, Abdul's cell would be identified and eventually eliminated. The cell's distant association with al Qaeda had spared it the destruction that the US and its allies had inflicted on most of the al Qaeda organization. Bin Laden and the rest of the al Qaeda leadership had not anticipated America's brutal and unrelenting response to September 11. They thought Americans would never do more than launch air strikes and fire cruise missiles from a distance.

Shortly after the World Trade Center attack, she had heard someone comment, "What is Bin Laden thinking? Doesn't he know that we have an unstable Texan in the White House?"

No one could have anticipated that George W. Bush could have performed even more brilliantly than his father did.

Fatima pressed the brake pedal and yanked the gun from beneath the seat. In mere seconds, she sighted the barrel on Ray's heart. Ray had hesitation written all over him. As a supervisor, she knew he did not wear Kevlar. Fatima attempted to squeeze the trigger. For an instant, her resolve to kill Ray failed. It was suddenly fogged by memories of that day in the streets of Tehran, of her being splattered by her mother's blood and Abdul standing over her, his gun in his hand. It was Ray's baby she was carrying.

Ray saw his death coming. Now, at least, he knew the truth about Laura, what she really was. His weapon was aimed, but his finger was frozen on the trigger. The pistol retort did not even make him flinch. There was no pain; not even the dull thud of the bullet's impact as it slammed into him. Then he realized why. Laura had not fired, but instead shifted back into the driver's seat just a split second before her back window had exploded from a bullet that must have missed her by mere fractions of an inch.

Ray turned to see Rachel emerge from the shadows of a large Dodge Ram pickup. Laura had obviously been as oblivious to her presence as he had. There was the sound of squealing tires and the roar of Laura's engine as she attempted her escape. Rachel had her weapon up and was preparing to take another shot to finish the moment.

"No!" screamed Ray, leaping towards Rachel and knocking her weapon down. It discharged into the side of someone's Ford Mustang.

"You fucking idiot! Goddamn you! Touching fucking way of saying good-bye she has," said Rachel. Her eyes scolded Ray. She was incensed beyond belief.

"She's carrying my child," moaned Ray. "You can't kill her."

"Fucking shit," cursed Rachel. "She was going to kill you! Not to mention the bitch and her friends are trying to nuke the East Coast. Get your head out of your ass, Ray. They need you back inside. I'll take care of this."

Ray said nothing. There was the sound of intense small arms fire coming from the Protected Area of the power plant. He watched as Rachel sprinted to the visitor's area where her car was parked. If she caught up with Laura, one of them would certainly die. He could not think about that.

Rachel did not pay any attention to see if Ray was going to try to stop her or go back into the station where he belonged. The woman that Ray knew as Laura, and loved, had left a trail of bloody bodies from here to Atlanta. Undoubtedly, she had done likewise elsewhere. Rachel had to end that trail right now. She sprinted to her car.

The security guards at the gate would hopefully stop McClish. That would make this a short chase. As she reached the gate, Rachel saw that it was not going to be that easy. One Security Officer lay beside the guard shack, its walls sprayed red with his blood. Another lay at the edge of the road, apparently hit by Laura's car.

The third guard had his M-16 pointed at Rachel, ordering her to stop. She already had her badge in her hand, holding it out the window. She eased up close enough where he could see it. He waved her on. She pushed the accelerator, pressing it all the way to the floor. It was time for Laura to get a taste of her own medicine and she was going to give it to her.

Fatima saw the 300ZX in her rearview mirror. Slowing down at the guard shack had been a mistake. She should have taken her chances and sped on through. It was unlikely that the Officer would have fired at her and if he had, her speeding car would have been a difficult target. Slowing and firing three rounds into him had given Rachel Lambert the opportunity to catch up to her.

Fatima never entered into an operation without a route of escape prepared. She knew there would be a strong law enforcement response to the attack on the power station. That response would be both well planned and well executed. Because she worked in the Security Department, she knew precisely what the response plan was. Roads into the power station would immediately be sealed off. However, the word 'immediately' was relative. It would take county and state units at least twenty minutes, likely considerably more, to seal off all escape routes. They would first begin with the major routes. Thus, Fatima's escape plan involved using the narrow, country roads that led off the main highways. She had driven them often so as to learn them.

For not the first time, Rachel cursed her stick shift. She would have given the world to be driving an automatic. Laura had turned off onto a country road and the curvy, narrow stretch of road with dips and crater size potholes required almost constant shifting of gears. Even though she had managed to speed dial 911, she had dropped her cell phone while shifting down for a steep hill. Her phone was on the floor by her feet. The race to keep up with Laura required all of her focus. There was no opportunity to go groping for it. The good news was that manually shifting gears gave her more power coming out of the sharp curves and was the reason she had caught up with Laura.

The other good news was that the Firebird's center of gravity was not as good as the ZX's. Rachel had both the power and handling to stay on Laura's tail. Then she thought of something else and took her eyes off the road to quickly glance down at her fuel gage. "Fuck! You idiot!" she cursed herself. She was under a quarter a tank of gas. The only way to win this was stop Laura.

They were topping a hill. Below them was scenic pastureland. A barbed wire fence kept cattle inside, where they grazed near a shimmering pond. At the bottom of the hill was a sharp curve. This would be her best shot at taking Laura off the road. It was, however, fraught with risk and it was going to hurt like hell. "Look at the bright side," she quipped to herself. "Once you're done here, you can buy an automatic if you're still alive."

If Rachel missed this chance, she might not have another one. She had never had her airbag serviced; hopefully, that would not be her undoing. She mused at the fact that never once in an action movie, had someone tried to run another car off the road only to get clobbered by their own airbag.

Rachel increased her speed. Laura was slowing just enough to make the hairpin turn that awaited them both. Rachel would not be able to negotiate the turn. Then again, she did not intend to. Just as Laura went into the turn, her tires hugging the loose gravel of the road in a precarious manner, Rachel jammed the accelerator to the floor. The front end of her car caught the left front of Laura's Firebird. Then there was a loud *POP!* and Rachel felt the force of her airbag protecting her from her steering column. Then there was darkness, gnashing of teeth and bright flashes of light.

As Ray walked through the door of the Security Building, he was already busy on the radio, assessing the situation. He made his way to where the truck still burned. The chaos on the radio had now died away. Discipline and training were helping the security officers to organize. Communications on the radio became meaningful.

"Tower 1 to Security One."

Ray keyed his mike, "Go ahead Tower 1, this is Security One."

"This is Officer Ford. You've got six armed intruders," came Tower 1's report. Four guard towers, one on each corner of the double chain link fence, surrounded the Protected Area. Unfortunately, no one was manning them when the attack occurred. Cameras had replaced each tower's armed guard. Oddly enough, none of the cameras had shot any of the bad guys. But they had saved the company money, bottom line, right? Moreover, he would certainly say as much when someone from CNN stuck a camera and mike in his face when this was all over. "They have entered Unit I Reactor Containment Building through where the Personnel Escape Trunk was removed. They had this one planned out, Security One."

"Understood," answered Ray. "Tower 1, can you give me some idea of what happened?"

"The truck loaded with liquid nitrogen exploded when the crane dropped the Personnel Escape Trunk on it," said Tower 1. "Jennings and I responded. We were under fire from automatic weapons before we knew it. I think there were five or six of us trying to use the radios at the same time. I climbed up here to get a better field of fire. Jennings went down." There was a slight pause. "He didn't make it. Took several rounds right in the face."

"Understood," acknowledged Ray showing no emotion over the loss of a man. He would get very drunk when all of this was over. He had lost men before and it was not an easy thing. This time would be the worst because he was largely responsible for what happened. However, the lives of the rest of his men and the integrity of a nuclear reactor core rested on decisions that he would now make. He had to put his emotions and guilt aside.

"Security One to all Officers. Anyone got further info?" Ray listened, his face long as he received several reports of security officers and other plant personnel either dead or in need of medical attention. He remembered the chaos of that night in Iran when the rescue mission had turned sour. The same cold chill and disappointment was upon him now. His team had not delivered the blow, they had received it.

"Brown to Security One."

"Go ahead," said Ray. He briefly thought of Rachel pursuing Laura. What would the outcome be? Would anyone understand why he had not killed her while he had the chance?

"Four of them grabbed back packs from the truck," said Brown. "Looks like they could have a considerable amount of plastic in there with them if that's what they've got. I got the mechanic who was operating the crane here with me. He's hurt pretty bad. Says that it looked to him like they blew the ends of the cylinders off using plastic. He's ex-Marine recon, and he's seen plastic used. Says that there were three missiles on the truck, all aimed at the fuel building. He did a hell of job on them with that crane. Saved our ass in a big way. Hope he pulls through."

"Did they take any casualties?" asked Ray. There was a long silence. Ray shook his head in anger. "Damn it, did anyone shoot at these bad guys?"

"Tower One to Security One. It went down with military precision, Ray. If one of us had been up in the tower, we could have had a chance to hurt them. By the time I got up here, they were up the platform and inside. They had us beat badly on firepower and they knew how to use it. The crane operator took out the bad guy on the truck. That was their only casualty."

"Understood," said Ray. "That's alright, the company saved money when they put cameras up there."

"Fuck the company," came an unidentified transmission.

"Alright guys," said Ray. "Best thing we can do right now is to make sure we keep what we have intact. I'm going to the Technical Support Center. We have two priorities, getting the wounded to safety and preventing these guys from causing a radioactive release."

"Security Supervisor Burns to Security One."

Ray keyed the mike as though he were getting ready to talk to an angel. Overweight and out of shape, still there was no one in the department that he wanted covering his flank more than Burns. "Go ahead, Pete."

"I'm coming through Security, right now," said Pete Burns. "If you want to stage at the Technical Support Center and start worrying about the problem inside of containment, I'll work with the duty Security Shift Supervisor to get the wounded into Unit I alley way. We can let the First Aid Team stage there. I'll figure out how to get the wounded out of the station safely. We've also got one dead, one wounded at the main check point."

"10-4," said Ray. Laura had made it through the main check point, bringing more death and destruction. He had spared her life to save his child. That was insane. Joella had children and most certainly some of the Officers that he had already lost had them. He had failed out in the parking lot, in a very big way. "We've got Ford in Tower One that can cover the Equipment Hatch. He's Sniper qualified. Get one of the .308's with a scope up to him. We need at least three men in the Auxiliary Building in case they try to come out through the Personnel Hatch." Ray didn't think it likely, however, that the bad guys intended to come out of containment. They had gone to a hell of a lot of trouble to get inside. "As soon as our people report in and local law enforcement arrive, put them together and start protecting the vital areas. I don't think we have enough manpower to do it at the moment."

"That's affirmative," replied Burns. "I'll get the vital areas manned as quickly as possible."

"Security One to all stations, I'm switching to Operations Department Frequency." Ray switched over. "Security One to Operations Shift Supervisor."

"Cisco, this is Ralston," came the angry voice of the Station Manager. "Listen, we don't have a damn Security Officer at all guarding the Technical Support Center. What is going on?"

"We have five wounded out here, and four confirmed dead. Six of those are my men. There are six armed intruders who have entered Unit I Reactor Containment through the opening in the Equipment Hatch. We need off-site medical and law enforcement assistance. I'm on my way to your location now."

"This is crazy," said an Officer manning the security alarm panel. "We don't have anywhere near enough officers to cover all of our contingencies."

"You're wrong," said Ray. "We have plenty of men. Just ask the fucking asshole sitting at corporate. Harding took his goddamned engineering degree and figured it down to a gnat's ass exactly how many men we need for a combat situation. We just fucked up, that's all. None of us were supposed to get shot in the attack."

Ralston was right. The Technical Support Center, with most of the station's key personnel gathered there, was a vulnerable target. A hit there would hurt bad, real bad right now. He needed to get there ASAP and secure it."

Ray double-timed along the Turbine Building mezzanine until he came to a narrow passage that broke off to his left. A sign hung over the door, 'Technical Support Center'. When he entered, everyone was staring at the pistol he brandished in his hand. Ray holstered his weapon.

"Have you sent people inside of containment, yet?" demanded Ralston, rolling an unlit cigar from one side of his mouth to the other. Even in the overly air conditioned room with all of its computers and communication equipment, the Station Manager was perspiring heavily.

Ray put his hand up. "No and I won't until I'm prepared to. What have we got coming in the form of off-site assistance?" he asked.

"Well, now that we have finally convinced Hanover County Sheriff's Department that this isn't a drill or a prank, we should be getting law enforcement on scene in the next few minutes," broke in Bob Livingston, the Operations Superintendent. "They're sending us everything they have in terms of law enforcement. They are also notifying the State Police. A procedure is in place for the Governor to activate the National Guard, but that will take a while. Hanover is staging their rescue units until we tell them how many we need and that we have a secure staging area for them. We also have eighteen First Aid Team members up in the Operations Support Center. They keep asking for permission to respond."

Ray keyed his mike, "Security One to Burns."

"Go ahead Security One," came Burns' voice back over the radio.

"We're going to have the First Aid Team muster down in Unit I alleyway. Make sure there's someone there to keep them out of the field of fire."

"Wait a minute," said Dick Fuhrman. He was the station's Quality Assurance Manager. "You can't just make a decision like that and broadcast it out. We all have to consider it as a Management Team. That way, the Emergency Station Manager listens to the input of each team member…"

"Can it, Dick," said Ralston loudly. "We don't have a reactor trip. We're in the middle of a fucking war. What we need is to put our heads together and decide what it is that they plan do inside of Containment."

"Well, for starters, we have officers that saw them carrying backpacks in," said Ray. "They probably have about two hundred pounds or more of plastic explosive, worst case."

"What can they do with two hundred pounds?" asked Livingston. His voice was calm, analytical.

"One hell of a lot," said Ray. "Four backpacks of plastic in the hands of the right maniac can probably destroy the core."

"We simply can't allow that to happen," said Livingston. "We've got to get people in to stop them, regardless of the hazard. Give me a gun and I'll go with you. I'm serious."

"Bob, you're right, but you're not John Wayne and you're not going anywhere," said Ralston. "First priority is to protect our electrical supplies to be able to do flood the core if they do something. Do you have men down at Emergency Switch Gear?"

"No," said Ray. "I had six Officers taken out during the attack. Everyone that I have is being used to contain the terrorists that are in Containment. We have to wait until we get law enforcement and supplemental security personnel on site. It's up to the NRC to call in for regular military support. Best tell them we need it."

"Well, you're the soldier here," said Livingston. "We would be foolish to tell you where and how to use your men. But, here is the deal. There are ninety tons of highly activated uranium inside that reactor. We all know that those men are in there for the sole reason to cause a catastrophe. Personally, I wouldn't expend my manpower to keep these guys in Containment. I'd rather that they get the hell out."

Ray nodded. "Security One to Burns," he said, keying his mike. "Lighten up on containing the subjects. It is deemed advisable to bolster protection of the vital areas over containing them. Right now, they're where we least want them."

"Technical Support Center, Livingston," said the Superintendent of Operations, answering his phone. Immediately he raised his hand, flagging the others in the office to silence. "Alright. Keep an eye on the Reactor Vessel Level Indication System. Fuhrman, take a look at the Power Station Parameter Data System monitor. What are the loop stop valves doing?"

Fuhrman stepped out of the office to look at one, of several monitors that showed the operating status of major pumps and valves that could have an effect on nuclear safety. "They all show open," he reported.

"Unit I Shift Supervisor just informed me that in the Control Room, the Loop Stop Valves indicate a loss of power," said Livingston. "The Data System responds only to actual valve position indication."

"These bastards are scary," said Ralston. "They know how this damn plant works. I bet they're shutting those valves by hand and they've terminated electrical power to them so that we can't reopen them."

"Reactor core temperature is rising," said Fuhrman, still looking at the Data System monitor. "The valves don't show intermediate position, just open or closed. My guess is that the valves are nearly closed."

"That's exactly what they are doing," said Ralston.

"Commence with a Safety Injection and cool the core by feed and bleed would be my suggestion," said Livingston to Ralston.

"It's all that we can do," said Calvin Hayes, Superintendent of Engineering.

"The Control Room informs me that they have entered Abnormal Procedure 29," said Livingston. "That is feed and bleed. It's already in progress."

"That's right, it would lead us into that because core temperature is probably hotter than pressurizer temperature," said Hayes. "They're going to have to really watch the pressure-temperature relationship or else they'll end up forming a steam void inside the reactor. That would take care of the terrorists' work for them."

"Have we shut off all the lights in Containment?" asked Ray.

"Pass the word to the Control Room to do that," said Ralston with a nod.

"Count on them to have the ability to monitor all of your radio transmissions as well," said Ray.

"Cisco, what do you know about these people?" asked Ralston.

"One of the contractors working in Security, Laura McClish, helped set this up," said Ray. "You have to assume that they have every imaginable capability. They know how we operate."

"McClish," said Ralston, casting a fierce glance at Ray. "McClish the dish, the one you've been shacked up with." Ralston shook his head.

"Enough guys," said Livingston. "How long do we have before they can set their explosives? Any idea? Give me worst case."

"Depends on what they plan on doing," said Ray. "If it's something simple, then twenty minutes easily," said Ray. "But I think that even as knowledgeable as they are, it will take them time to get to whatever part of the system is their target. Even our own mechanics that have been here for years have a hard time locating the right piece of equipment to work on."

"Average Reactor Coolant System temperature is two hundred and thirty degrees right now, said Hayes. "That'll make rigging any charges directly to the system difficult."

"Let me tell you what I would do if I was them," said Mike Gunther. Everyone turned to the door to the source of the West Virginia accent. Gunther was the Training Supervisor for the Operations Department. "First, you're going to have more than any twenty damn minutes no matter what they decide to hit. It's going to take them a while to finish up with closing those loop stop valves by hand. That's a hell of a job right there. Remember, there are only six of them. Some of them have to stand guard in case we have people going in after them.

"If I knew the system as well as these guys apparently do, I'd just shoot off that damn padlock on the hatch to the keyway beneath the reactor, plant the plastic, and boom, everything drains out through the bottom where the flux thimble tubes go into the reactor vessel. Then I'd climb down onto the reactor vessel head and blow off the vent lines. Or hell, maybe rig charges around the

Control Rod Drive Housings. That would give us a massive supercriticality if they did it right."

"Mike, thank you oh so fucking much for your enlightenment," said Ralston, looking uneasily at the others. "Somebody make sure he never gets laid off."

"Two very devastating scenarios," said Livingston. "Especially the Control Rod Drive Housings. Hard to imagine that they could do that."

"With the Personnel Escape Trunk gone," said Fuhrman, sounding like a Sunday morning evangelist preaching the wailing and gnashing of teeth. "We have a wide-open release path."

"Interesting that you should mention that, Dick," said Livingston dryly. "Just which one of us did you think didn't realize that the four and a half foot hole that these guys used to get into containment wasn't a release path? If you have a big hole, stuff will get out. We understand that."

Ray listened to Livingston and Fuhrman. The entire power station knew how each liked to antagonize the other. However, their conversation served to help him realize the gravity of the situation. "We really have no choice, do we? We have to make an assault immediately to prevent them from setting up their charges. Tell me how much time we've got before an assault will be too late," said Ray.

"With things as they stand now," said Mike Gunther. "Waiting an hour would make me real nervous about the local real estate market."

"Anyone have anything to add to that?" asked Ray. No one spoke up. "Then that settles it. I'm putting a team together and going in."

"You mean with our own security officers?" asked Ralston, shaking his head. "Seems like something that Special Forces or a Navy Seal team, hell a Delta Force would be needed for."

"Just the amount of time that it would take to get a military unit on site would be too late," said Ray. The phone on the Shift Supervisor's desk was ringing again.

"Burns to Security One."

"This is Security One, go ahead," said Ray, keying his mike.

"Okay, from what we can see they have unbolted the Equipment Hatch. It's hanging loose on its hoist," came Pete Burns' message.

"Understood," replied Ray. "Keep us informed." He turned to the others. "As soon as they create their destruction of the reactor's core, they'll most likely detonate a charge to drop the Equipment Hatch onto the floor. They don't appear happy with a mere four and a half foot hole."

"They drop the equipment hatch, then we'll have a fourteen and a half foot hole," said Livingston. "That's Matkins on the phone. I think we should tell him that Cisco is right. We can't wait. We need to go in there."

Ralston switched on the speakerphone and sat the receiver down. "Brian, I've got my Security Superintendent here, Ray Cisco. Both he and Livingston think that we need to send a security force in. They are shutting the loop stop valves and unbolting the equipment hatch. They also have enough explosives to expose the core."

"The government has a special unit for doing that," said Brian Matkins over the speaker. "We can't be sending our own people into a hazardous situation like this."

There was an awkward silence.

"Mr. Matkins, this is Ray Cisco," he found himself needing to fill the vacuum. "This isn't business as usual out here. This Security Force is trained and expected to do this if required. From where we stand, it is required. I've dealt with this caliber of terrorist as a Navy SEAL. I'm going in with them. If nothing is done, we will always regret how we balanced the scales on this matter. There is too much at stake."

Again there was silence. This time, it was Mike Gunther's West Virginia accent that filled void. "Mr. Matkins, you can sit there in Richmond and worry about how bad getting some of us out here shot, maybe even killed will look on your five year plan, but some of us have lived around here all our lives. Sitting here on our ass is wrong."

"No," said Matkins. "It isn't our place. We will wait for a properly trained counter-terrorist unit."

"To my knowledge, the NRC hasn't even requested military assistance yet," said Ray. It'll take at least a couple of hours to bring in a counter-terrorist unit. Not to mention that to get a military unit requires Joint Chief of Staff approval. God only knows how many hours that will take. FBI counter-terrorism people are not trained for what's going on here and neither is the National Guard. My people are trained for it. They also know the layout of the containment building. We don't have a choice. I'm no nuclear expert, but this sounds like a Chernobyl in the making if we do nothing."

"No," said Matkins with finality. "It is absolutely out of the question."

Lloyd Ralston suddenly did something that he had not done for all the years that Richmond Nuclear facilities had been declared smoke free. He lit the cigar that he had been rolling back and forth in his mouth. Several in the room looked at him in surprise.

"Lloyd, you can't do that in here," said Dick Fuhrman. He was a man who would never learn.

"Do what?" asked Brian Matkins over the speakerphone.

"Tell you to pack sand," said Ralston, blowing a long trail of smoke across the cubicle. "As Emergency Station Manager, the responsibility of the nuclear core's safety and the safety of these people belong to me. I agree with Cisco and Doctor Doom from West Virginia. We have to weigh the balance. I'm sending a team in."

"Absolutely not," came the stern reply from Matkins. "As of this moment I am removing you from your position as Emergency Station Manager and Station Manager."

"I'm sorry, Mr. Matkins," said Dick Fuhrman quickly. "Procedurally, you have to be on site to replace a member of the Emergency Response Team. In fact, you would have to relieve Ralston yourself."

"All right, Fuhrman," said Livingston reaching over and giving him a slap across the back.

"Brian, I'll keep you informed," with that, Ralston hung up on the VP.

"I know it's not really my place to be part of how you go about doing this, but can I interject a couple of things?" asked Gunther.

"I really can't imagine trying to tell you not to," said Livingston. "Talk."

"Well, for starters, why not slow them bastards down in Containment?" asked Gunther. "We can buy ourselves some time and better plan the assault. Let's manually initiate Quench Spray. Thirty-eight degree water pouring in on them in monsoon fashion should definitely slow them down. They're already in the dark."

Livingston held up one hand and, with a nod from Ralston, picked up the phone. "Trane, this is Livingston. Initiate Quench Spray. Yeah, we're going to slow them down." There was a pause. "Okay." Livingston sat the phone down. "Quench Spray has been manually initiated."

"What exactly is it that you're doing?" asked Ray.

"When they design the plant," said Gunther. "They have to be able to contain any type of accident that's even conceivably possible. Well, if you get into an accident where the Reactor Containment Building becomes pressurized because of the reactor's four hundred and eighty degree cooling water being released from a ruptured pipe and turning into steam, there is the ability to spray cold water into containment from up in the dome area. It condenses the steam and depressurizes the containment building. That's Quench Spray."

"Mike, any idea as to how you'd get an assault team inside covertly?" asked Ray. Once this was all over, he was going to recommend that Mike Gunther be locked in a safe. Together, his knowledge and imagination were a threat to humanity.

"Piece of cake," said Mike. "Get whoever you're bringing in and meet me down at the Weld Shop. Bring me a 10 mm and the shortest barreled shotgun you got. We'll go in through the Containment Ventilation System duct piping. There's going to be a hell of a lot of noise in there with Quench Spray going. I don't think they'll hear us. Plus, where we're going in will be away from where they should have any interest. I think we can take 'em by surprise and shoot when we see the whites of their eyes!"

Livingston glanced over at Ralston and whispered, "Did we hire him before the company started administering that mental stability test?"

"I just don't think they bother if you're from West Virginia," said Ralston, letting go a long trail of cigar smoke.

"Isha akubar,' said Fatima as her Firebird was knocked from the road and went airborne. If it was Allah's will that she die, then there was nothing she could do. Eventually, she would die while carrying out a mission. It was a good probability that it would be this one. They had screwed up by not taking out Rachel Lambert.

Lambert's car had come straight through the hairpin turn and had clipped Fatima, knocking her right off the road. Now she was descending right on top of the barbed wire fence. All she could do was hold her breath. When the car came down, it was right on top of a metal fence post. The post came up through the floor on the driver's side, up between Fatima's legs and narrowly missing her face. Even so, the car was still moving. The fence post banged against Fatima's face and chest repeatedly until the car came to a standstill. It took several moments for Fatima to get her faculties back. She knew that she was hurt, but not sure how bad. Also, she did not know where Lambert was and if she was hurt. At any moment, the private investigator could show up beside her car and it would be all over.

Realizing the danger that she was in, Fatima reached to the passenger seat for her weapon. It was not there. Looking around, she saw it on the floor near the brake pedal. She reached for it, but the post would not allow her to grasp it. Where was Frank Baker when you needed him, she thought?

She needed to free herself from this post. As she reached to move it, she saw that it was covered in blood. It had several short pieces of barbed wire dangling from it at chest level. Glancing down, she realized that it had sliced her chest badly. As she fought to free herself, the barbs cut into her hands and arms.

Rachel was not sure if she had been unconscious or not. She simply came to the realization that she was hanging upside down in her car and that her face and chest hurt badly. Vaguely she remembered hitting Laura's car, sliding out of control and then flipping over. And, by the way, she realized that the airbag had deployed and that was why her face and chest hurt. At least she hoped that that was the reason.

Suddenly, something else occurred to Rachel. She could smell gasoline. Panic swept through her. The most horrible way to die would be to burn to death. Immediately she began jerking at the seatbelt latch. It would not release. In her purse, she carried a small penknife. Frantically, she looked about for her purse, but when she found it, it was out of reach. Again, she jerked wildly at the latch. Then, she realized that she was pulling at it from the wrong direction. Hanging upside down had a way disorienting a person. She stopped, took a deep breath and calmly unfastened her seatbelt. However, when she did, she was so focused on getting free that she forgot entirely that she was hanging upside down. She landed on her head.

Rachel paid no attention to the cut to her head that she received from the overhead light when she landed on it. Immediately, she attempted to open her car door. However, it would not budge. Without hesitation, she kicked out the side window. Grabbing the door handle to help pull herself through, she felt the latch pop and the door swing open. Regardless, she was free of her car. Her panic at the thought of a fiery death subsided. Besides, she had nearly been out of gas, so if her car had blown up, how big of an explosion would it have been? That was a stupid thing to be thinking about, she decided. More importantly, where was Laura McClish?

The Firebird sat up right, about 30 feet from where her ZX had landed on its top. With a sense of dismay, Rachel saw that the Firebird displayed no roll over damage and nor was the windshield displaying the typical starring that occurs when an occupant goes head first into it. So why was Laura still in her car?

Rachel debated crawling back into her car and looking for her Beretta or rushing over to the Firebird before Laura could react. If she rushed the car, Laura might be armed, making a for a short fight. Glancing at her car, she realized that both the windshield and passenger side windows had been broken out in the rollover. She had kicked out the driver's side. Her gun was probably anywhere but in her car. There was only one real option. She started moving towards the Firebird. She wanted to run, but her legs would not cooperate.

Travis Harding walked out of the Emergency Response Facility, leaving Brian Matkins to muddle through on his own for a short while. Brian's psyche was close to disintegrating. Travis' legs shook with the adrenaline that coursed through his body. Travis had told a badly beleaguered Brian that he would return to take over the Corporate Emergency Response Facility. First, however, he needed to go back up stairs to his office where he would not be overheard on the phone. Never before had he seen a man like Brian Matkins break down and cry; actually sob like a child. It had to be tough, his children's whereabouts unknown, in the hands of a kidnapper; his wife telling him that their marriage was over; and knowing that Tanya Madison had been murdered because of him. Now this, a deadly terrorist attack on the power station.

Travis did not wait for the elevator. Instead, he ran up the escalator, such was his excitement. Once in his office, he dialed the number that he had committed to memory. He did not want anything written down on paper that might fall into the wrong hands. After all, he was breaking some pretty serious laws. Impatiently he waited for the familiar voice of Henry Thomas' secretary. This was news that Henry Thomas needed to hear immediately. It kept ringing. Never before had it taken his secretary this long to pick up. Perhaps they were all sitting in front of a TV, watching as events unfolded on CNN.

"We're sorry, the number that you have dialed is no longer in service."

Travis clicked off and immediately, but very carefully, dialed again. "We're sorry, the num…"

How could an entire company suddenly not have a working number? He tried information. The number had been taken out of service earlier that morning. The first news bulletins about the siege at Jefferson Davis Nuclear

Power Station were just now hitting the networks. It would be only moments before news crews arrived at the Richmond Nuclear Corporate Headquarters. Matkins would not be able to make any comment; it would be up to him. He headed back to the Corporate Emergency Response Facility; Travis was puzzled, and very, very worried. The attack would certainly ensure that the sale of Richmond Nuclear would not go through and Henry Thomas would be able to purchase the land in Mexico. Suddenly, however, Travis was not quite sure where that left him.

Gina had shown up at Resources For Tomorrow only to find the phone had been physically removed. A hand-written note said, "Your services are no longer required." There was also a thousand in cash in an envelope where the phone used to be. She left the note and stuck the cash in her purse.

Roger Cowling looked at the faces of those seated around him in Energy International's Boardroom. By now, they should have already voted to sell Richmond Nuclear to California's Energy Commission. After that, was to have been a second vote, one to use the money from the sale to build three 1,000-megawatt nuclear generating units in Mexico. In the U.S., the reactors would take fifteen years to build and only maybe get permission to operate. In Mexico they could be built and on line in four years. In the US, the proceeds from the sale would have been barely enough to build one generating unit whereas in Mexico it would build three. With deregulation of the electrical industry and the free-wheeling of electrical power across the United States, this enormously inexpensive source of electricity would have been the equivalent of the mother lode during the California gold rush. Its concept was what had made Cowling such a fan of NAFTA.

Instead of voting, however, the Board of Directors of Energy International was watching the breaking story on Headline News, a terrorist attack on Richmond Nuclear's Jefferson Davis Nuclear Power Station. The door to the Boardroom opened. Edna slipped in and whispered into Cowling's ear, "The Governor of California is on line one."

Cowling said nothing. He picked up the receiver. "Cowling," he said and then listened. "Thank you for your concern." He hung up the phone. "Ladies and gentlemen as though you may not have guessed, the Governor of California has ordered the state's Energy Commission to stand down on the purchase Richmond Nuclear." With that said, Cowling stood, looked as though he were about to say something, but left the room instead.

Though he was not shaking with rage, he was shaking. Shaking with stunned disbelief at his fate, and that of Energy International. Both were ruined. He had lost his shirt a number of times, always bouncing back to claim ultimate victory. Not this time, however. He knew in his heart that he was face down in the dirt with a bullet through the heart. Slowly, he made his way back to his office. There, he made a phone call.

"Bud," said Cowling. "I'm certain that you've seen the news. No, no, I know dislodging terrorists from nuclear power plants is not one of your areas of expertise. There is no longer any purpose in holding on to our insurance policy. I'd like for you to personally return the assets. Make sure that no harm comes to anyone. Goodbye, Bud."

Chapter Thirty-five
Friday, December 11th

Laura had dislodged herself from the Firebird before Rachel could get to her. The fact that Laura was not aiming her weapon at Rachel and pulling the trigger meant that Laura did not have hers either. They were on even ground. It was at that moment that Rachel saw the metal fence post sticking through the floorboard of the Firebird. Damn, just a few more inches and Laura McClish would have had the post right up her cunt. That would have been fitting. As it was, she could see that Laura was badly cut and battered. Perhaps this was not going to be so difficult. The real question was what was she going to do with Laura. She had no gun, no handcuffs, nothing. Kill her with her bare hands? That did not seem out of the question.

Laura was so out of it, she had not yet noticed Rachel coming towards her. If she could get the jump on her, Rachel decided that she would use a chokehold until Laura was unconscious. Then, she could find something with which to tie her up. She had taken only a few steps when suddenly, she felt searing pain in both her ankles and found herself going headlong into the tall pasture. Breaking her fall with her hands, she could not stop herself from screaming out at the pain as the barbwire cut into her. Laura's car had dragged an entire section of the fence into the pasture. It was strewn all through the tall grass around her and Laura.

Carefully, Rachel got to her feet. Only ten feet away now, Laura was looking at her and then looking back inside of her car. Undoubtedly, she was looking for her weapon. She had to reach Laura before she could find it. The barbwire fence was impossible to navigate in the tall grass, but Rachel moved through it, feeling it slicing into her legs as she went. At least she was staying on her feet and closing the distance.

Fatima felt faint. She had already lost a lot of blood and was still bleeding heavily. Her senses felt dull. Almost too late, she had seen Rachel Lambert moving towards her. The only thing saving her was the barbwire that lay hidden in the tall grass like a minefield.

Fatima turned back to her car, frantically looking for her gun. Certainly, it was there, but there was no luxury of time to search for it. Obviously, Lambert did not have her weapon either. If she had, Fatima had no doubt that she would now be with Allah. There was a farmhouse not far away. With Lambert trapped in the barbwire, there was a chance that she could get there. Perhaps she could take whoever was there by surprise and steal a vehicle.

Rachel heaved a sigh of relief. Laura had not found her gun. However, neither was Laura trapped in a maze of barbwire and had started making her way for the farmhouse at the top of the hill. No way was she going to let her get away.

Brenda Matkins was sitting in the kitchen in her mother's Alexandria home when her cell phone rang. They were watching the horrifying events at her husband's nuclear power plant unfold. All that the news agencies really knew was that six terrorists were inside the Reactor Containment Building of one of the reactors that was shut down. The Governor of Virginia had just ordered an evacuation of residents within a ten-mile radius. He had order National Guard units mobilized. Furthermore, the President of the United States had ordered all commercial flights grounded and ordered air patrols for not only Jefferson Davis Nuclear Power Plant, but for every nuclear facility in the US.

When the phone rang, her hand had already been on it, preparing to call Brian. For all of his own self-undoing, she realized how much she loved him. She also realized how difficult it had to be, dealing with the terrorist ordeal and knowing that their own daughters were perhaps in the hands of such men. Thinking that it might perhaps be him calling her, she answered on the first ring.

"Hello," she said anxiously. Brenda's mother stared, her eyes questioning whether this would be more bad news.

"Mrs. Matkins," it was that same voice, the one cleverly disguised by some gadgetry. "Go immediately to Tyson's Corner. You will find your daughters eating ice cream." Click. Brenda was unable to move the phone from her ear. She just stared back at her mother in shocked disbelief. She was too scared to believe that this could be true.

Brian had pulled himself together. He was more ashamed than anything else. Ralston had done the right thing by telling him to pack sand. He was glad that the cigar chewing Station Manager had the balls to deal with the situation the way it needed to be dealt with. For fear of a leak to the news agencies, and the potential for the terrorists inside the Reactor Containment Building to somehow find out, no one at the Corporate Emergency Response Facility beside himself was aware of what the security forces at the power station were going to attempt. He envisioned horrific casualties as they fought to gain access to the formidable fortress that the containment building posed.

"Goddamn you, Cowling," Brian muttered. He was thinking of all the budget cuts that he had forced Richmond Nuclear to make. Many of those cuts had been in security. Men and women in his security force were paying for those cuts with their lives. Then again, how could he curse Cowling without cursing himself. His daughters were paying for his transgressions. They were now in danger because of his infidelity with Tanya. Certainly, Tanya was dead because of him. Perhaps he and Cowling were not so different; they simply had greed for different things.

Rajani knew of the systems used to reduce pressure in the Reactor Containment Building during a high-energy pipe break. He had a degree in Mechanical Engineering. He had worked as an engineer in several nuclear power plants in the US. It had not occurred to him, however, that the operations staff would think to use it against them. Neither would he have guessed how effective it was. The cold spray chilled he and his team to the bone. It also created a deafening roar. They could not hear each other talk. Though that mattered much; as they were all shaking and chattering so badly that they could say very little. Their eyes stung and they could taste the boron and the sodium hydroxide that the water contained. It made the metal surface of the reactor vessel treacherously slick.

Though slowed and hampered by the onslaught of frigid water, Rajani and his men were determined. Their brothers had shocked the world with the fallen World Trade Center. This would strike an even more seriously mortal blow to the Great Satan. Though the death toll involved in melting down the nuclear reactor's ninety tons of uranium fuel would be minimal, perhaps none at all, the effect of scarred, unusable Virginia countryside would shock millions for many years to come. Richmond, Williamsburg and many other cities and towns would be uninhabitable for a very long time.

Rajani had trained each member of the team about nuclear power plants. They all knew what they were looking for and more or less where it was located. The first item had been the Reactor Coolant System isolation valves. By terminating electrical power to the valves and then closing them by hand, they had stopped the plant's operators from feeding water to the reactor and cooling the fuel down.

Shutting the valves, however, had taken longer than he had expected. In the hot containment building, it had overheated them and made them sweat profusely. The cold containment spray had been a physical shock to their overheated bodies. There was also the nuclear radiation. Though they were prepared to sacrifice their lives in the name of Allah, the knowledge that they were being constantly subjected to nuclear radiation was unnerving.

Fortunately, and to Rajani's surprise, it was only after they had found and closed the valves that the lights had been shut off. He would have thought that operations would have shut off the lights immediately. For that, they had brought in powerful flashlights. Later had come the deluge from Quench Spray. They continued. At least the spray cooled the hot metal of the reactor vessel; that at least lessened his concern about the C-4 becoming unstable and exploding while they were putting it in place around the Control Rod Drive Mechanisms.

It had not taken tremendous effort to obtain the outside diameter of the Control Rod Drive Mechanism housings. This had allowed them to make hollow collars, filled with plastic explosive, which he and his mean would place around the steel cylinders that protruded out of the top of the reactor. There were fifty of them. To save time and still achieve the same effect, they would rig only thirty of the housings with the collars, all on the inside periphery. Each collar was fitted with electrical terminals and a firing mechanism.

Rajani did not know how much radiation he and his men would absorb as they did the job. It really did not matter, he attempted to convince himself. They would die fighting the infidels. This was the Jihad. They would all be martyrs and would be blessed in their deaths. Already, deep within the belly of the reactor, the fuel was heating up from shutting the valves.

Pressure was building up inside of the reactor as the fuel got hotter. Operators would be feeding cooling water through the Safety Injection lines to the reactor. However, when the plastic explosive detonated, the pressure would send the housings into the air like missiles, allowing the control rods to be ejected out of the reactor's core as well. The result would be two fold. Loss of the control rods would allow the fuel to react and increase reactivity, perhaps even bringing the reactor to supercriticality. Water needed for cooling would be lost. A reactor meltdown would quickly begin. The fuel's reactivity would actually be enhanced by the infidel's somewhat successful attempts at cooling it. And then they would blow the fourteen and a half-foot Equipment Hatch off of the monorail holding it up. There would be no controlling or containing the melting fuel. The disaster would pollute the entire eastern seaboard.

❖ ❖ ❖

"Dispatch to any available unit," came the voice of the sheriff's department dispatcher. Les expected it to be an update to the situation at the power station. However, she would not have been broadcasting to any available unit. "I have a report of a two car 10-50 on Route 612. The caller said it looked pretty bad and that one of the cars could be that Firebird we put the all points out on."

Les was just coming up to the 612 intersection. He started to pick up his mike and let dispatch know that he would respond to the 10-50. Then he thought better of it. Rachel was at the power station. He did not know what he could do to make sure that she was all right, but he sure as hell was going to show up there and try to find out.

"108 to 118," one of the other deputies was answering dispatch.

"Go ahead, 108," said dispatch.

"I'm already arriving at the power station," said 108. "I saw a silver 300ZX turning onto 612 at a high rate of speed. Looked like your sister's, Les. I didn't see the Firebird, though."

"10-4, 108," said Les. He was all ready locking his brakes and going into a power turn in the middle of the road.

"108 to dispatch, 108 to dispatch," this time 108's voice was shrill and tense. "I've got a man down. Looks like he's been shot. There's two men down. It's the main check point at the power station."

Les did not bother to tell dispatch that he was diverting to 612. It was both hands on the wheel as he accelerated to a hundred and fifteen miles an hour and then went into a slide as he braked for the turn onto 612. Route 612 was windy and narrow, but Les drove it as if it was the Indy speedway.

Fatima fought to stay on her feet. Rachel Lambert had finally cleared the barbwire infested grass and was quickly gaining on her. There was no escape. It was best that she turn and fight while she could still stand. Fatima glanced about for something that she could turn into a weapon, something that would give her a fighting chance in her weakened condition. Her eye caught upon something that would do very well.

Rachel was through the barbed wire. Though she felt dizzy and disoriented, she was gaining on Laura. Her CIA operative training had taught her how to kill a person with her bare hands. Never had she thought there would be a day to use that knowledge. Right now, however, she wanted nothing more than to put that training to good use. Laura was bleeding badly and appeared to be weakening fast. This would be over with soon.

That indeed seemed to be the case as Rachel saw Laura falter and then swoon, hitting the ground with a thud, just yards ahead of her. Maybe she was not going to need that training after all. There was no need to take chances, however. Rachel launched herself on top of Fatima.

The dirty green paint of the somewhat bent and rusted metal fence post made it difficult to see lying in the grassy pasture. It had likely at some point been damaged and replaced, and then discarded where it lay. Perhaps Fatima had only seen it because she was desperate. Perhaps it had been the will of Allah. Either way, she prayed that she had enough strength to put it to good use.

In her peripheral vision, Fatima saw Rachel loom large over her, ready to pounce on what appeared to be her beaten and defenseless form. Fatima, however, was not defenseless. She was weak and badly battered, but she knew how to survive and she knew better that this Lambert woman how to kill. She had fallen on top of the post. As Lambert dove on top of her, Fatima rolled over with the post in her hands. She thrust it into her attacker's abdomen, aiming for just below the breastbone. It did not matter that her thrust was weak; Rachel Lambert's own body weight would provide the force necessary. Though her thrust was off center, just to the left. Its effect, however, was sufficient. Rachel's full weight drove the post into the ground. There was a moan as the air was forced from her lungs.

Rachel realized only too late that she had been setup. The pain was excruciating. She could not breath as she knelt only a foot or so from Laura.

Darkness immediately began to descend upon her. She struggled to stay on her knees even as her world went black.

Mike wore the 10 mm in a holster. One of the other security officers held onto the shotgun for him. Bringing a civilian along and allowing him to carry weapons was not something Ray was anxious to do. However, he needed Mike's expertise and it would not have been fair to expect him to go into Containment unarmed. Besides, he had a high level of confidence that if called upon to use them, he could do so confidently.

Ray followed him into the Containment Ventilation System duct pipe. Just like in the movies, thought Ray, you always get in by climbing through the buildings ventilation system. The Reactor Containment Building had a ventilation system designed to pull air out and send it through charcoal filters to purify it before releasing it to the atmosphere. A second set of air ducts brought air into the Reactor Containment Building. The system could move approximately 430,000 cubic feet of air per minute through ducts that were three feet in diameter. Since the air was moved at a high flow rate but not at a high pressure, the ducts were made from metal about an eighth of an inch thick, compared to over an inch thick for some of the other piping systems which passed through the containment walls. These ducts penetrated into containment one floor above the basement from the Rod Drive Room.

They had entered the vent duct through a cover that they unbolted in the Rod Drive Room. In Containment, however, there was no such cover and if there were, it would have been bolted on from outside the pipe. The only way was to cut a hole. Mike was in the pipe, on his belly and doing that now. Ray lay in the pipe just behind him. Two welders had helped him get the Acetylene rig to the Rod Drive Room and then set it up. The hole that he was cutting would be large enough for one man to easily roll at a downward angle from the pipe and onto the steel grating.

The torch made very little noise as it burnt through the metal. That, however, was of little concern as Ray listened to the deafening roar of water that pounded the outside wall of the duct pipe in which he lay. He was convinced that they could have been using jackhammers and still not been heard. Mike began moving forward in the pipe as he made the final cut with the torch. In just a few more moments, Ray, and the nine men with him, would be inside.

Ray knew that he would later laugh about how it really went down. Mike's technical expertise with the acetylene torch did not put him on quite the same level as that of the power station's welders. As he finished the third side of the cut, the piece that he was lying on folded downward, dumping Mike onto the containment grating like a can of Coke rolling out of a soda machine. The drenching down pour from Quench Spray extinguished the cutting torch immediately.

Ray slid forward and then rolled out of the pipe on top of Mike, his weapon at the ready. He did his best to push Mike and his hoses out of the way as the rest of the security force surged forward through the pipe to make their entry. Within moments, the team was in. It reminded Ray of his nights in the jungles of Vietnam and Laos during the monsoons. Only this time, it was a jungle of steel. There was no mud, just the sharp biting taste of the boric acid and sodium hydroxide in the pouring water.

"All right, muster up," ordered Ray, speaking through his head set. His eyes constantly scanned through the dark wet that veiled the Reactor Containment Building's interior. One by one, he heard each of his team give a name and number. All were inside and the communications gear was functioning. It was a good start at least.

"Gunther, you okay?" asked Ray, realizing that two or three of the team had stepped on him during the entry.

"Yeah," replied Mike over his communications gear. "Feeling a bit like a welcome mat. Welcome to Reactor Containment, guys."

"Good job getting us in, Mike," said one of the team.

"We'll remember to wipe our feet first next time," said another.

"All right, Gunther," said Ray. "You're the point man. Let's check out that hatch which could take them into the keyway area beneath the reactor. Jacobson, you got the rear."

"Jacobson, taking the rear," responded the Officer.

Single file, the team moved up the first flight of stairs following Mike Gunther. Ray was thankful that the Superintendent of Operations had suggested that they wear rain gear and sweaters. This was as cold and nasty as it could get. He just hoped that the lights did not unexpectedly come on and the flow of water stop with them all dressed in bright yellow rain suits.

Ray and his men communicated with the headsets that Richmond Nuclear had purchased for just such an occasion as this. Richmond Nuclear's Security Department was trained in hostage rescue and dislodging terrorists from critical areas of the power station. In terms of their training, they were far better prepared than the law enforcement agencies that were now arriving on site. Though their combat skills were not quite on par with a SEAL team, their specialized knowledge of the station combined with their training made them the best choice for this mission.

Ray had let Pete Burns coordinate with a State Police Captain on the best use of law enforcement Officers to help secure the station. That gave him more men to work with here. The nine men, not including Gunther, which he had picked for this mission were men who had served in Vietnam, the Gulf War, or one of several small military engagements.

"Gunther to team, hanging a left at the top of the stairs," said the Training Supervisor.

"Roger," said Cisco. They were at the top of the first flight of stairs. The plan was to check the Residual Heat Removal System area for bad guys and to verify whether the hatch to the keyway area beneath the reactor had been disturbed.

"Cisco, you see him down there?" asked Mike Gunther. They had reached the stairs that would lead down to the hatch. "They don't look like they're enjoying this."

"Yeah, there are three of them," said Ray. He studied the three images. It was amazing the clarity that he could get using the infrared vision goggles. There were three men huddled together against a structure looking like they were trying to keep themselves warm with each other's body heat.

"Hurd, Wallace and Bradley. Let's go down and check it out," said Ray. Descending the ladder first, his men covering him, he looked around and called down the next man. And then came the third. Carefully, they made their way over to the three men.

"Jacobson," said Ray. "Let me know if they move or act as if they see us."

"I've got my eye and a whole lot more on them," replied Jacobson.

"Shit…" came a voice over Ray's headset. Then came the sound of a weapon discharging. It was a muffled, eerie sound in the confines of containment and the deluge of water.

"Oh, fuck… Jesus, I'm hit!" came the cry of one of the men beside Ray.

"They're up! They're getting up!" came Jacobson's warning.

Ray could see them. There was no sign of any weapon. "Hold your fire! Hold your fire!" ordered Ray hoping that he was in time to prevent a tragedy. It was why he had brought war veterans. Hopefully, they could remember how to hold back the adrenaline in a moment like this. "Where did the shot come from?"

"Shit, this is Wallace," said one of the men Ray had brought down onto the Residual Heat Removal Platform with him. "I fell. My weapon went off. How bad you hurt, Larry?"

Looking back at the three figures that stood huddled together, Ray could tell that they had heard the gun shot. It was obvious they were not the bad guys. He went directly over to them, so close that he could have stuck his arm out and touched one of them. "Thompson, I guess you're the medic. Come down and have a look at Wallace," he said. "Watch out. It's slick down here."

After studying the three men, Ray realized who they were. They were three of the mechanics that had been involved with removing the Personnel Escape Trunk. One of them was a Mechanic Foreman, John Anderson. They had obviously retreated into containment when they saw the terrorists coming up the platform towards them.

"This is Ray Cisco, Security," yelled Ray. "Stay put." There was no sign that they had heard him. "They're mechanics. I saw them on the Equipment Hatch Platform right before the attack. I'm standing here yelling at them from two feet off. They can't hear me. Thompson, what's it look like with Bradley?"

"I can't see jack shit," said Thompson. "I can feel an entrance and an exit, but I can't tell whether I've got the bleeding stopped or not. It's impossible to work in this. He's going to be getting shocky real fast in this wet cold muck."

"Stay with him," said Ray. "Mike, what do you think? Bad guys don't seem to be interested in the flux thimbles."

"No," said Mike Gunther. "Can I make a suggestion?"

"Roger, that," said Cisco.

"Take Thompson, leave Bradley with me," said Gunther. "I'll figure out a way to get those mechanics to help me get him out of here."

"Roger," said Cisco. "Once you have them out, stay inside so that if we need you we don't have to wait on you."

"Roger," said Gunther.

❧ ❧ ❧

Les brought his patrol car to a screeching halt just in time to see his sister lunge onto the fence post. He saw the way that she went down and knew that she was not going to get back up. He scrambled from his car, drawing his weapon.

The tall, dark-haired woman was slowly getting up. He had run the name

359

Laura McClish in DMV's database. It had produced a photo. Her DMV photo had triggered a hit in Homeland Security's imagery database. She was Fatima Hazdiz, an assassin known to have worked with a number of terrorist groups, including Hamas and al Qaeda. Her intent was obvious. She still had the post in her hand and she was going finish off his sister with it. It was much too far for accuracy with his pistol, but there were no other options and no time to think about it. He sighted in her upper torso and fired three rounds.

Fatima had lost too much blood. She had managed to hurt Lambert, but when she stood up, her world began to disappear. She staggered backwards just as she heard the gunfire. The bullets whined as they passed within inches of her head.

Les began making his way through the maze of barbed wire the moment Fatima went down. It was slow going as he made his way to Rachel. She lay on the ground unconsciousness. He glanced over at the woman who had tried to kill his sister. Blood covered her chest. He did not know how many of his rounds had hit her, but it appeared at least one had caught her in the chest. She was not going anywhere.

"Dispatch, this is 118," said Les. "Get me two ambulances out here to 612, stat. I'm going to need an extra officer, too. They'll need to accompany a suspect to the hospital."

"10-4," came the terse reply.

Picking Rachel up in his arms, Les made his way across the field to his patrol car, making a wide swath around the strewn barbwire fence that the cars had knocked down. It took a while. When he reached the road, he laid her on the grass beside his car and raised her feet up.

Rachel was very pale. He realized that she was in shock. He opened her blouse and looked at her abdomen. It was badly bruised and swollen. Les was no medic, but he was certain that she was bleeding internally. He went to his trunk, pulled out a portable oxygen caddy and a mask. It was at least something. He should have gone back to check on Fatima, but he could not bring himself to leave his sister's side.

When the ambulances arrived, the medics carefully placed Rachel on the stretcher and into the ambulance. "Where's our patient?" asked one of the medics from the second ambulance.

"Out in the field," said Les, pointing towards the hill. "She took at least one round in the chest."

"Better have a look at her," said the medic. "If we can get her to the hospital alive, I'm sure someone might want to ask her a few questions."

"I'll go with you," said Les. "This lady has a bit of a lethal history, though I think I may have put an end to it. We need to circle around. There's barbwire there in the grass."

"Where's she at?" asked the medic as they reach the bottom of the hill.

"She was right there," said Les. He was staring straight ahead at the spot where she had lay bleeding from the wounds to her chest. Fatima was not there, though there were stains of blood on the grass.

"Well, there's blood, but no body," said the medic.

Rajani had heard something. In the dome shaped structure of the Reactor Containment Building, sound was a tricky variable. It had sounded like a muffled gunshot but he could not be sure. Best not to worry about it, he decided. They had to concentrate on getting the charges put in place. Fatima had told them that the security force was very capable. Most likely they had found a way inside that was not guarded.

It was going very slow, much slower than expected. Already he had lost one man to the hazardous footing on top of the reactor vessel. The chemically laced water that fell like a monsoon formed a slick coating on the reactor's steel surface, turning it into something akin to an ice skating rink. Rabulla had silently disappeared. Rajani was certain that his friend had slipped and gone over the side. His gear was where he should have been. Neither he nor Amar had bothered to climb down to see if Rabulla was alive or dead. In this ungodly noise, he could be lying on the Reactor Cavity floor, screaming at the top of his lungs and not be heard. They would all die in the end. What was important was to finish rigging the charges. If a security force had managed to gain access into the containment then they would be sitting ducks down in the cavity atop the reactor.

There were so many of the housings yet to be prepared. Suddenly there was the same noise again. Small arms fire, definitely. It lasted less than fifteen seconds and was gone. They were under attack. Rajani went to Amar, guided to him by the powerful light that Amar was using to wire the charges. Finding his friend's head with his hand, he cupped his hands around Amar's ear and yelled, "They are coming. Connect what we have ready. We must do it now."

More gunfire. Though its sound was muffled in the roar of falling water, the staccato rhythm of automatic weapons fire was unmistakable. In his mind,

Rajani knew what was happening. Somehow, a Security force had gotten inside of containment. He had counted on more time and for placing the charges to go faster. The earlier gunfire would have been the lone sentry at the Personnel Hatch leading from containment into the Auxiliary Building. Now, the men who had been guarding the Equipment Hatch were engaging the approaching force. In only moments, forces would be assaulting the Reactor Containment via the platform to the Equipment Hatch.

The gunfire abated. Very soon, he and Amar would be spotted and shot. In his hands, he held the electrical source for the detonator. Amar was feeding him the electrical leads from the charges. Now he needed only to insert the wire ends into the source box. The first one went in. His cold, almost numb fingers fumbled with the second. Out of the thirty Control Rod Drive Housings that they had planned to blow, only thirteen were rigged. Even that, however, was more than the reactor was designed to withstand, considering the fact that they were all adjacent to each other.

"Cisco to team, I see one bad guy," said Ray into his radio. As Ray had expected, there would be a guard at the Personnel Hatch to make certain that no one entered through it. Likely, there would also be charges wired to the hatch. Right now, however, there was no time to attempt to clear them. Neither was there a need to do so. Time was a crucial commodity. Gunther had reiterated his earlier theory that they would be on top of the nuclear reactor. That was Cisco's primary objective.

"I'll take him," said Ray. Raising his M-16, he squeezed off a round into the man's neck.

As soon as the round hit its target the man jerked forward. Ray had to imagine that the man's finger had been on the trigger. Perhaps the shot that wounded Bradley had broadcast the team's presence, increasing the lone sentry's vigilance. At any rate, there was a short burst of fire from the terrorist's weapon as he fell over forwards. Two of the security team, not sure whether the weapons fire was deliberate or reflex, opened up.

"Cease fire, cease fire," commanded Ray. "I'm going to assume that they have anti-personnel devices in place between the hatch and the Reactor Cavity. Let's take the long way around."

The Reactor Containment Building was a cylinder with a dome on top. Between the security team and the reactor cavity was the neutron shield wall.

Between the neutron shield wall and the outside wall of Reactor Containment was a walkway referred to as the annulus. In the dark, drenching deluge, it would be impossible to see if trip wires were running across the annulus on either side of where the Personnel Hatch penetrated the containment wall. Ray knew that if he had been the enemy, he would have wanted to place anti-personnel devices there. It was always his policy to give his enemy credit for being as intelligent as he thought himself to be.

The team would have to walk the annulus all the way to the other side of the Reactor Containment Building to where the equipment hatch was located. There, Ray knew that his team would meet two or three more of the terrorists. It was, however, not of great concern. Any anti-personnel devices that they rigged would have been against a forced entry from the platform. Besides, using the infrared vision goggles, his men could see them, not vice versa.

As Ray and his team neared the Equipment Hatch, he saw that the men guarding it were moving towards the reactor cavity. They were likely concerned that the security team would get past the explosives rigged at the personnel hatch and go through the gap of the neutron shield wall at that point. Regardless of their logic, they did not stand a chance against a team of fine marksmen who had the ability to see in all of this darkness and muck.

"Cisco to team, two bad guys standing at the edge of the reactor cavity," said Ray. "Anyone see anything else?" There were several replies to the negative.

"On my command, we'll take them out," said Ray. "Jacobson, target left. Thompson, target right."

"Target acquired," said Thompson.

"Target acquired," repeated Jacobson.

"Fire," said Ray. There were flashes as the two men fired their weapons. There was no burst of gunfire from either terrorist as they spun around and then fell to the stainless steel cavity floor thirty feet below.

"Hope they enjoy their trip to see Allah," said a voice over the radio.

If he had been given correct numbers at the beginning, three more of the terrorists remained. To be safe, he would assume that there were more. If Gunther was right, they would be on top of the reactor. "Keep your eyes open," said Ray. "Let's move up to the edge of the reactor cavity. Watch your footing. No more accidents."

Carefully the team moved forward to the cavity. The wet stainless steel floor required that they approach the edge with great caution. Down below, Ray could see the two men working on top of the reactor. On the floor below lay another man. From where they stood, Ray could not tell whether the one on the floor was alive or not. If he had fallen off the reactor, onto the hard, stainless steel floor, he would not be much threat.

"Thompson to Cisco, I think the one closest to us has a fucking detonator in his hand!" came the Officer's high-pitched warning.

Without saying a thing, Ray brought his weapon to his shoulder and squeezed off half a dozen rounds. His men, unsure of the situation did the same. The man with the detonator went down, but stayed on top of the reactor. The other man went off the far side of the reactor, joining his friend who was on the floor.

"Enough," said Ray into his mike. He was certain that the one with the detonator had probably taken some thirty rounds.

Rajani had known that he was a dead man from the moment that he had accepted this mission. He did not regret that fact. Nor did he regret failure, because there was no failure. He and his Islamic brothers had performed selflessly. The outcome truly belonged to Allah. Who was he to second-guess Allah if He did not want this nuclear reactor to be blown to bits? After all, perhaps it sorrowed Allah to have his Earth, even this place, home to the infidels, spoiled by a nuclear disaster. Now, as he lay bleeding, he wished for nothing more than Allah to have His Will, whatever that may be. Though bullets had perforated his body, causing his blood to drain out of him in thick streams, he was still alive; at least for a few fleeting moments. The detonator was still in his hands. With his last deliberate act in this life, he squeezed it.

Chapter Thirty-six
Friday, December 11th

"Security One to Technical Support Center," he had switched channels on his communication gear.

"Technical Support Center, go ahead."

"Turn the water off and give me some lights," said Ray. Immediately the flow of water ceased to only trickles of drainage from the spray headers located high above them in the Containment's dome. The deafening roar softened to an echo and disappeared entirely. As the lights came on, Ray and his men began removing the night vision equipment and the communications gear. "Be advised," continued Ray, "that we have secured the reactor.

Rajani went from this life to the next with a glad heart. Both wires had been inserted into the detonator. With his last ebbing flow of life, he had squeezed the trigger, unable to stay alive long enough to know the result. Perhaps that was Allah's way of being kind. The detonator was designed for jungle monsoons and would work even after being immersed in high salinity seawater. However, even with the cooling Quench Spray that pelted them, the surface temperature of the reactor was over 200°F. The detonator had lain in the bottom of the backpack, exposed to the heat, causing the plastic casing to warp. This caused a gap in the internal circuit. Thus, no electric charge was sent to the explosives. The Eastern seaboard of the United States had been saved by fractions of an inch.

The light blinked on his phone. It was Edna again. She had been white as a ghost as CNN news announced that Richmond Nuclear's security force had entered the Reactor Containment Building. Now, it was over. Travis Harding was addressing reporters at Richmond Nuclear's headquarters. His announcement was short and to the point; the reactor was secure.

Roger knew that he should be elated over the news. He was, of course, very glad that Jefferson Davis Nuclear Power Plant had not been destroyed, bringing ecological catastrophe to the entire mid-Atlantic region. There was, however, the question of where this left him. Bankrupt, for sure. "Yes?" he knew that he sounded short, tense.

"Sir, there is a man on the phone who says that he is an old acquaintance of yours. Says you absolutely will want to talk to him," said Edna. "I tried to explain that this was a really bad time, but he said it pertained to what happened at the power plant. And he was so odd, he asked if I had ever noticed the blood stains on your Nain rug. But there aren't."

Cowling's heart skipped several beats. For an instant, he wondered if perhaps he might topple over and die of a massive heart attack. How merciful that would be. He felt suddenly flushed. Beads of sweat began to cover his forehead.

"Yes," said Cowling. "I'll take it." He waited, and then heard the connection made.

"My good friend, Roger. It has been such a very long time," said Abdul.

"So, this was you," acknowledged Cowling.

"Ah, Roger," said Abdul. "Please don't tell me that you thought that I would allow an old debt to go unpaid. You do, of course, remember what I'm talking about, don't you?" quizzed Abdul. "Is it necessary to remind you? Two million dollars that I paid you to safely take my family out of Iran?" There was a pause. "You remain quiet, my friend? Don't you remember how it was? You took my money and built your empire. You took the payment, but left my father, my mother, my sister and her child to suffer for falling prey to your Great Satan. Though they were infidels, they didn't deserve the fate that you left them to. Indeed, there are bloodstains on your lovely rug, Roger. You see them everyday, don't you?"

There was a pause. "I'm certain that my father's rug even now adds decor to your office," said Abdul. "The rug, a priceless antique that he gave you to show his gratitude."

Cowling glanced down at the rug. The brilliant red petals falling from a rose, done in silk, using vegetable dye, suddenly caught his eye. For just an instant, those rose petals looked like drops of blood against bright silk.

"Abdul," Cowling swallowed hard before he asked his question. "What became of them?"

"You infidel," hissed Abdul. "You dare ask? Perhaps I should describe it for you. Even among your own, you are an infidel. Your Holy One is money. I may have failed to release the destruction that I sought, but that is as Allah sees fit. But I have succeeded in separating you from your God, have I not? Praise Allah."

"Why did you go to such lengths to blackmail Matkins and kill Frank Baker?" asked Cowling. "Your attack on the station was enough to ruin me."

"Well, you know how it is with plots," laughed Abdul. "There are those that wanted a nuclear holocaust. Myself, I just wanted the satisfaction of destroying you personnally. If the attack never materialized, I wanted to ensure that you were destroyed. Killing you would have been too impersonal. Taking your wealth was the best way to make you feel my revenge. By the way, kidnapping Matkins' children was brilliant. Had we failed to get into the power station, you might have won. You know how to make the game very interesting."

"Abdul, I was a coward. I let you down," said Cowling without a trace of remorse in his voice. "You were my friend, and I wasn't worthy of your trust. And you are correct, my greed has become my god." He sat the receiver back on the hook.

For the next two hours, Roger Cowling rummaged through his file drawers and worked at his computer. When he was finished, he printed out everything. He then removed his checkbook from his jacket pocket. From it, he wrote two checks. Then he rose from his desk.

"Mr. Cowling," said Edna when he came out of the inner office. "Can I get you something? Sir, are you all right?"

"Here," said Cowling. "I wanted to go ahead and give you your Christmas bonus. I have to fly out of town tonight. Will you post this to Rosetta?"

"But, sir, I haven't made you any flight reservations," said Edna, holding the two envelopes. "Besides, sir, all commercial flights were cancelled because of the terrorist attack."

"It's a private flight," said Cowling. He cast her a comforting smile and turned away. Instead of going to the elevator, he took the stairs. Not down, but up one flight. It brought him to the roof of the Energy International Venture Building.

Abdul had been right. Cowling's god was money. He had sold all but his Energy International stock to invest in the Mexico project. The remaining stock would hardly be worth much after what had happened today. Sure, he could sell his home, slip off into a low profile retirement, and live comfortably. However, Abdul would find him. He had written a check each to Edna and Rosetta, both for forty-eight thousand dollars. That represented the remains of his cash reserve. Rosetta would also find that he left the house to her in his will.

Roger Cowling stepped to the edge of the twenty story high rise's roof. Carefully, he scrutinized the sidewalk below. He had done enough harm to others. He wanted to do no more. It was a clear sidewalk below him. Spreading his arms, he took a flight reserved one night, long ago, in far away Tehran.

—

Chapter Thirty-seven
Friday, December 18
Richmond Nuclear Corporate
Headquarters

"Well, Rachel," Brian looked at her. "I guess you probably want to get paid and forget about this nightmare. I believe that Travis has already cut you a check. We'll also work with your insurance company to make sure that your surgery and hospitalization is covered completely." He was thankful that she was still alive. Rachel had nearly bled to death from a ruptured spleen as a result of Laura McClish thrusting the fence post into her abdomen.

"Brian, if you had leveled with me right from the beginning about Tanya Madison being murdered, it might have prevented the attack," said Rachel. She looked at the nearly full boxes, the personal contents of Brian's office that was packed. "The FBI could have been involved. We might have made the connection between Laura McClish and her accomplices. As it was, we ended up wasting time on Cowling and his petty plot to blackmail you into submission." Speaking of petty, why was she bothering to say all this? "Anyway, thanks for taking care of the medical stuff. Your company wasn't obligated."

"It was petty cash compared to what all of this has cost the company." He paused. "It was hard to think of the blackmail as petty at the time," said Brian. "I was scared that I'd end up as the number one murder suspect. I'm just thankful that the worst didn't happen."

"Ray Cisco and his officers were brave beyond description," said Rachel.

"Yes," said Brian, looking down at his desk. "We seldom realize that we're surrounded by heroes everyday. It simply takes the right moment for it to be seen."

"Hang on a second," said Brian as the phone on his desk rang. He activated the speaker. "Yes, Mrs. Hendrickson?"

"Mr. Matkins, Mr. Harding is in here with a box of his personal items. He wants to know if he might set them inside."

"Certainly," said Brian. "Tell him that I've got the door." Brian hung up and rose from his seat to let Travis in.

"I guess I haven't told you," said Brian. "Travis will be relieving me as Senior Vice President of Richmond Nuclear."

"Good morning," said Travis. He carried a box of files over to Brian's desk; set them down and then propped himself on the edge of the desk.

"Brian, you're going to be missed," said Travis as he placed a hand on his friend's shoulder.

"Your people are excellent," said Rachel. "What Cisco and his men did was beyond heroic."

"You're right, Rachel," said Harding. "We have good people there. All over the company. I'm looking forward to the job of leading them and getting Richmond Nuclear back on its feet."

"Mr. Harding, can I give you a tip that will make your day a whole lot easier?" asked Rachel. She swiveled in her chair towards the eager new Senior VP.

"Why, certainly," said Travis. "Like Brian says, I have my work cut out for me."

"Don't waste your energy carrying any more boxes in here," said Rachel. "But do keep on packing them."

"Ms. Lambert," said Brian, puzzled at her remark. "I'm afraid I don't understand."

Rachel looked towards Les and gave him a brief nod. Then she sat back.

"What my sister is saying," said Les. "Is that I have been working with the FBI and State Police. They should be entering the building even now with an arrest warrant for Mr. Harding. He will be charged as an accomplice with the terrorist attack on the Jefferson Davis Nuclear Power Station and the murder of Tanya Madison and all those that died in the attack. The terrorist attack resulted in a number of deaths. Each one of those are eligible to be tried as capitol murder."

"You see, Brian, what no one has been told during this investigation," said Rachel. "Is that before Roger Cowling took his own life, he left a detailed accounting of everything that he knew concerning the entire incident. He did it to provide us a trail to a man he identified as Abdul Hasdiz. The attack on the power station would have most likely happened somewhere, sometime. Maybe Jefferson Davis Nuclear Power Station, maybe some other station. But the mastermind of this incident chose Richmond Nuclear as his target because he had a score to settle with Cowling from the days when Cowling worked in Iran.

"Cowling felt it his duty to tell everything that he knew, hoping that he might help the FBI catch him. Laura McClish is Abdul's niece, Fatima Hasdiz.

"You and Travis here went to the same university, you've always been close friends. Well, did you know that it was Travis Harding who told Roger Cowling about your relationship with Tanya Madison?"

Brian looked up into the face of his old friend. It took only the briefest glance for him to see that it was true. He said nothing.

"Harding's phone record here at work shows calls to the office of Resources For Tomorrow," said Les. "The FBI has already identified that as the front for Abdul. Harding personally hired Laura McClish. Matter of fact, the paper trail shows that he signed off on a security background check that was never done. He made multiple calls to McClish at the power station. We believe that he helped plan Tanya Madison's death in order to wrest control over you from Cowling. Travis was playing for Cowling and the terrorist both at the same time; he knew he couldn't lose that way."

Harding moved away from the desk and looked out the window. "My god," said Harding, his words filled with fear. "I swear I never knew she was a terrorist. I never dreamed there would be an attack on the power station."

"Abdul set up a false company, lured you into hiring Laura, and then promised you a big fat reward for helping derail Energy International's bid to sell Richmond Nuclear," said Rachel. "Henry J. Thomas, as Abdul called himself, obviously promised you great rewards. Enough that you helped arrange Tanya Madison's murder." Harding was pale and silent.

"You couldn't lose, could you?" asked Brian. "You work for Cowling, and then you work for the company trying to take him down. Whichever one wins, you get the Senior VP slot of the nuclear station in Mexico, right? God, I hope you rot your fucking life away in prison."

Harding turned to the door and walked out. Brian reached for the phone. "Security, this is Matkins. Travis Harding's on his way down stairs. See to it that he does not leave the building. Use physical force if necessary. The FBI has a warrant for his arrest. That's right. No matter what he tells you, detain him."

"So what has become of this Abdul and Ms. McClish, or I guess I should call her Fatima?" asked Brian after he hung up the phone.

Les was silent as he thought of how Fatima had been lying mere feet from him. He had thought her dead or dying. Only later had he learned from Rachel that the blood on Fatima's chest had been from the barbwire, not from the shots he had fired.

"She and Abdul have both vanished like ghosts," said Rachel. "Unfortunately, I'm sure that they will be back to haunt us. Unless, of course, we decide to haunt them first."

Chapter Thirty-eight

"So, where you going to go?" asked Rachel. Ray Cisco's house seemed lonely, depressing.

"I don't know yet," said Ray as he continued to pack his clothes and other belongings. He had to keep it down to the bare essentials; a Harley carried only so much.

"Have you got a job lined up?" asked Rachel.

"That doesn't seem to be a problem," said Ray. He glanced over at the investigator and gave her a sarcastic grin. "This is America. If you fuck something up bad enough, someone will pay you a million dollars to write a book about it. I've got three offers already. For the moment, I'm just going to ride. It's been years since I've done some serious riding. There's nothing like aimless miles to clear the cobwebs that form in your head."

Rachel watched him pack. "Here, pack this with your stuff. When you clear out those cobwebs, you're going to be ready to make this thing right. I've been contracted by Homeland security to track down Abdul and Fatima. When you're ready, I want you to work with me."

Ray gave her a shrug of his shoulders, took the card and placed it in his wallet. There were a few more items to pack. Then he would get out of here. Donna was with her parents. She would come back after he had cleared out. "Why would you want me on your team?" he asked. "You saw how I reacted in the parking lot, even after she killed one of my officers."

"I take what Fatima did to me personal," said Rachel. "I need a team that takes it personal. We all have our demons, Ray. When you're ready, give me a call."

Printed in the United States
19600LVS00007B/37